TIES THAT BOND IN GRETNA GREEN

TIES THAT BOND IN GRETNA GREEN

MIDLIFE RECORDER SERIES
BOOK THREE

LINZI DAY

Published in the United Kingdom in 2023
Midlife Recorder series. Book 3

Copyright © Linzi Day, 2023
The right of Linzi Day to be identified as the author of this work has been asserted by her in accordance with the Copyright, Designs and Patents Act 1988.

ISBN: 9798376517017
All rights reserved. No part of this publication may be reproduced, stored in a retrieval system, or transmitted, in any form, or by any means, electronic, mechanical, photocopying, recording or otherwise, without the prior written permission of the copyright owner.
Requests should be made to: LinziDay.com
First Edition: February 2023

Cover Design: Axe Designs
Book Formatting: ESG

This book is a work of fiction. Names, characters, places and incidents are the product of the author's imagination or have been used fictitiously and are not to be construed as real. Any resemblance to actual persons, living or dead, or to events or places is entirely coincidental.

DEDICATION

For Lynn Ross with much love.
You've been bringing shovels, duct tape, the very best vodka and tons of joy, laughter and support into my life for 45 years.
But how the hell did we get so old without ever managing to become grown ups? 6x

Acknowledgments

This was a strange book to write. I've never been more dependent on trusted friends and beta readers for their assurances that it was OK to break away from the pattern set up in the first two books and return to it for books four and five after a fun sideways meander into Valentine's Day for book 3.

I'd like to thank those of you who have kindly recommended my books to a friend, posted about it online or shown a new author such kindness and support via reviews, comments and humour. And thanks to everyone who shared memes, giggles and things that reminded them of the books. linziday@gmail.com will always find me.

I owe a debt to Wendy MacDonald and Nives Gusetti for their invaluable help with the Naming of Things, their sharp eyes, accurate ears for characters' speech patterns and much more besides. Thanks girls.

My profound gratitude goes to the people who helped with aspects of research, historical queries and randomly weird author questions that had even stumped Google. I'm indebted to them for their expertise, patience and good humour throughout. Several people asked me specifically not to name them. But you really do know who you are and I'm grateful.

Thanks to everyone on my support team, especially Axe for my pretty covers and Krista, my efficient and hilarious editor.

To James, without whom these books wouldn't have happened so smoothly, and I'd have far less hair because he stops me pulling it out in so many ways and the dog wouldn't have been fed or walked as regularly. Tudo. 6264 and counting.

As always, my deep appreciation goes to my FABs – my Freaking Awesome Beta-reading team for all that they do to help make this a much better book for everyone.

For all their encouragement, insights, late night emails, and their unflappable good humour. Not forgetting the actual beta-reading!

This book's team was Beth, Callan, Divya, James, Kara, Lynn, Lisa, Nives, Sam, Sheryl and Wendy.

AUTHOR'S NOTE

I gave away free Bonus Epilogues for the first two books to subscribers to my newsletter. They covered Dola's job offer and HRH's history and then the continuation of L'eon's and Kaiden's story and their bonding and the solution to that little squinting mystery! **You can simply read them online.**

I've tried to include enough information so that anyone who's not read them won't be confused by anything in this book.

But they are **still available and still free of charge** if you'd prefer to read them and catch up before beginning this one.

Get your free bonus epilogues for all the books from linziday.com/newsletter

Don't read the bonus epilogue for *this* book until you've finished it. There are spoilers!

PART ONE
MONDAY

"And the little girl realised that just because things were going to be different, it didn't mean they had to be scary. Different could be fun, and new things could be exciting, and she thanked the Recorder and admitted that perhaps her mother had been right all along."

The Recorder Always Knows Best: Cautionary Tales for Incautious Children by Margarita Encimera

CHAPTER
ONE

Monday, 8th February — Gateway Cottage — Gretna Green, Scotland

It started in the kitchen, like everything else in my new life.

"It's so different in here. Bigger, lighter, more modern and, well … different and—" Fiona Glendinning snapped her mouth shut and looked around in confusion. Her eyebrows couldn't decide whether to shoot up in surprise or compress into a single line.

I'd counted three eyebrow raises and four mono brow frowns, and she'd only been here five minutes.

"That rug is striking." She admired the copper and duck-egg blue area rug in the middle of the large kitchen. "Beautiful blinds," she indicated the new cream blinds with the embroidered duck-egg blue birds flying across them. "But how on earth did you get another window put in so quickly? My mother's been waiting for months for a replacement window in our hallway."

Her eyebrows squinched into a frown. "But it's *all* new. Even the table, that's new too. Well, no, it looks antique, but I mean I've never seen it before? It looks lovely, but how…?" Her voice rose now along with her eyebrows, and her formerly almost imperceptible Scottish lilt became more noticeable.

Dola said, "Thank you, I think it is a significant improvement too. Unlike Elsie, Niki likes change. Welcome back, Fi; I hope your trip went well?"

Fi spun in a circle, her eyes huge and her mouth open. "Wh … Who? Wh ..what?"

Oh crap!

"Over to you, Dola; you two have known each other for years. I think you need to explain this one." I shoved Fi into a chair at the table with a brusque, "Sit down before you fall down, as we say in Manchester."

In her usual low, pleasant, reassuring voice, which no longer sounded the slightest bit electronic, Dola said, "Sorry for the surprise, Fi. I am Dola Neach, what Elsie used to call 'The House.' The entity who has provided you with many of these over the years." A bottle of the Girvan Sovereign and a tall, blue and white latte mug of what looked like … tea appeared on the table in front of Fi. Oh, Gods and Goddesses, was she a tea drinker? It said, *Welcome Home, Fi. Change can be good. Embrace your better future.*

I breathed. Fi breathed.

She picked up her mug of tea but ignored the whisky.

Dola said, "My name is Dola; it means 'toll' in the old tongue." At this Fi nodded. Wow, did she speak Gaelic? "I was the Toll House; then I became the Gateway Cottage. Niki helped me to speak, and now I have a job as the Recorder's Equerry. You and I will be working closely together." Aww, Dola sounded so happy and self-assured about her new role; I felt like a proud mother.

As Fi sipped her tea, she looked as if she might be on the verge of tears. I'd had such high hopes for the real Fi's return to work. I needed her help. She'd worked with my gran for many years. Her expertise and day-to-day knowledge of the Recorder's Office would be invaluable, given we were entering, what everyone told me, was the busiest week of the Gateway's year.

With an edge of hysteria in her voice, Fi said, "But you've only been here a week! How ...?"

Quietly, I said, "No, I've been here two weeks."

Dola said, "No, Fiona, I have been here more than 1400 years but not always in my present form."

Fi laughed helplessly. Well, I'd settle for that. I'd

take laughter over tears any day of the year. "Shall we go over to the Gateway, Fi, and plan this week's bondings?" If I got her onto more familiar ground, her eyebrows and her tense shoulders might relax.

She said almost nothing as we walked to the Gateway. It was another nasty, damp morning. I'd seen an advert the other day: *Visit Scotland. Nine climates. One beautiful country.* In my brief experience of living here, if I disregarded the Gateway and its magical boundary, so far eight of those climates were just variations of damp, wet and miserable, with more shades of grey than even Christian could offer.

As we stepped over the threshold, it started again. "It's all different in here too!" Fi gazed around the vast interior of the Gateway, her eyes wide and her mouth slightly open.

Fiona Glendinning, my gran's assistant, had arrived back after her three-and-a-half-week prize winners' trip to a wedding fair in Las Vegas. So far, every single comment she'd made fitted into a theme of "That's different! Where's that from? Why's this changed?"

Once inside the Gateway, she'd moved on to, "What are those black lines on the floor? When did the desks move and why? Why do we need glass barriers? We never had those before," and somewhat despairingly, "How has it changed in here too?"

I'd tried to let her work through it in her own

time, but I needed to get her logged on to her new computer and collect Autumn before I screamed. I needed to break us out of this loop. "It has. Yes. Some things have changed. Some more things will change soon. Is that a problem, Fi?"

But she surprised me. "Oh no. Not a problem. I'm just confused. Your gran always said the Gateway never changed." She paused. "But then, she didn't seem to know Dola was a person either?"

I bit back the immediate retort that it had been my gran who didn't change and not the Gateway. But I was trying to keep this light and welcoming.

"You were away for almost a month, and a lot has happened. But it *is* lovely to have you back."

I watched Fi closely. Honestly, I was dealing with some stuff myself. Fionn'ghal, the Fae king's youngest daughter, had taken the real Fi's place using a glamour spell to look exactly like her and had pretended to be this woman for my first week in my new role. She'd been part of a plot to prevent me from claiming my birthright as the Recorder. But none of that was the *real* Fi's fault, and I needed to build a relationship with her. She was one of the four key members of my team. We had to work together, and I wanted to make her feel welcome.

"Shall we sit, have a coffee and get us both caught up? I'll need your help with the Valentine's bondings."

Her eyebrows settled in a more normal position. She almost smiled. "Of course, your very first bondings. How exciting! I'd be happy to help in any way I can."

I winced. "Actually, I did my first one on Saturday. It was an emergency."

Fi's eyebrows actually tried to reach down to her nose, so unhappy were they. "An emergency bonding? How on earth could a bonding be an emergency? We have to plan them months ahead."

I breathed carefully. Good old *Good Grief*. *When you're not sure how to cope with anything, take a moment for a long, deep breath. In for four seconds ... Hold... and let it out slowly...*

I let the ritual soothe me.

I reminded myself sternly Fi was a nice woman; my gran had said so. She'd called Dola a person. And her surprise at the changes was understandable. She'd worked here for years, and knowing Gran, nothing would have changed if she could help it. The woman had worn the same style of UGG boots for almost my entire lifetime. Poor Fi must be unsettled. I needed her experience, and I was nervous myself. I'd never had an assistant before, but I couldn't allow my own nerves to mess this up.

Gently, I said, "Well, no, we really don't. Perhaps you just mean that my gran preferred to do it that way?"

"Niki, um, My Lady, um, what should I call you?"

I didn't want to be awkward about this. In fact, avoiding being the same type of employer as my ex-boss Janet was one of my guiding principles. A few weeks ago, I would have said, "For goodness' sake, just call me Niki." But I'd learnt a few things since then, and I was realising why the title was important. So instead, I suggested, "Please call me Niki in private, but in public, of course, it will need to be Recorder or My Lady."

Fi nodded slowly at me. She looked so unhappy, I tapped into my Gift to try to work out what was happening in her head, and if I could help her get through this. I got a wash of mixed concerns: surprise, a small amount of fear and worry, but mostly immense confusion and muddle. Connecting my Gift to her emotions gave me the sensation of her shaking her head constantly as though she couldn't trust her own feelings.

"What's the problem, Fi? I *really* want us to work together happily. I worked for a spiteful, bullying boss for eighteen years, and I truly wouldn't wish that on anyone else. Ever. So, could you talk to me about whatever is bothering you?"

Fi tucked a strand of her glorious hair behind her ear. Long and red, it had natural streaks with several shades from deepest copper to bright strawberry blonde. "I'll put some coffee on, and, yes, let's talk, please, Niki. This is not going how Elsie said it would."

Oh, thank heavens she didn't only drink tea, and now I knew what might be going on.

"Dola, could we have two coffees, please?"

Fi said, "That doesn't work in—" when two coffees arrived on the conference table along with a plate of brownies. She gasped and plopped her butt down on the nearest chair, which currently sported blue leather. *Finn must be on his way in.*

"How on earth did that happen?"

I murmured through our still experimental earbud comms, "Thanks, Dola, that might ease us through it."

I settled at the new conference table with her. "As you keep saying, things have changed. Dola's changed too. In fact, she adores change. Now spill it, please. What did Gran tell you?"

Fifteen minutes later, she'd eaten several brownies, and if she hadn't yet relaxed, at least her eyebrows had stopped their gymnastics. She'd brought me up to speed on all the warnings my gran had given her. I wouldn't know how anything worked when I arrived. It might take me many months to grow into the role, and Fi must be extra supportive of me and carry the load until I got the hang of it.

"She even said you wouldn't remember who Jamie and I were!"

Well, it had all been true, hadn't it? If not for Mabon, it would still be.

But I needed to collect Autumn. Aysha, my best friend and Autumn's mother, was a stickler for punctuality on work days, and Fi looked like she'd had all the surprises she could deal with for her first hour back. So I opted not to explain the whole confusing story to her right now and settled for, "Well, there is a lot to learn, so I'm sure she's right. It might take me years to understand it all. But it's been going OK so far. I was a registrar for almost twenty years—I'm used to marrying people—it's only the correct Gateway procedures for conducting bondings I'll need to get to grips with. I'm hoping you can help me with it."

"You want me to stay on, then?"

"Oh, yes, please." I remembered my gran had said something in the letter she wrote to me the day before her death. I'd check it, but she'd mentioned Fi needed the money. "Perhaps with a pay rise and some additional responsibilities. How about we discuss it at the end of the week when you've processed the changes?"

"I was so worried you wouldn't want me to stay.

With Stuart away now, I need the money. And it's not as though there are a lot of well-paying jobs in the village."

Who was Stuart? Gran hadn't mentioned a husband or partner. "Well, I definitely want you to stay, please. The team is growing, not shrinking. Who's Stuart?"

At that moment, Finn strolled through the green doorway. He was staying in my guest room, and by now he had the timing of his walk from the cottage down perfectly so he finished his bacon sandwich as he arrived. Tilly, my little Bichon Frise, followed him over. Obviously Tilly would be wherever the bacon was.

Finn walked through the new glass barrier as though it wasn't there, and Fi asked, "Should that have happened? I thought you said the glass barriers worked like the iron ones to keep people out of the centre."

"Let me introduce you …"

But Fi had already risen and was bowing. "Prince Finn, lovely to see you."

I saw Finn's well-hidden flinch and made a mental note to fix it. Fi didn't seem to have noticed because Tilly had distracted her. Fi knelt and ruffled her ears, cooing at her. "My mum told me all about you when I was in Las Vegas. I see what she meant now, you gorgeous girl. Aren't you fluffily adorable?"

Tilly lapped up this nonsense and danced on her back legs and clapped her front paws together to let me know she approved of this version of the woman however much she'd appeared to dislike her when Fionn'ghal was impersonating Fi.

I tried again, "Let me introduce you: this is Tilly, and this is one of my new Knight Adjutants, the TEK. He has access anywhere he needs to be, which answers your barrier question. Most importantly, though, he's not Prince Finn in here. So, unless you want him to call you Ms Glendinning, I'd suggest Finn, or TEK if you want to be formal."

Finn gave me a grateful look. One of his current goals was to get away from all the people who addressed him as Prince Finn. But he couldn't get away from Fi—so we would see if this worked.

To Finn, I said, "Fi is having a startling first day back. My gran's advice is proving to be less than accurate. Would you mind helping her get up to speed with the changes?" Finn, always amiable, but a man of few words, nodded.

"*One* of your Knight Adjutants? What's a TEK?"

"It stands for The Electronic Knight. I do the techy stuff, Fi. Have you used your computer yet?"

Fi shook her head.

Finn grinned. "Nice surprise waiting then."

To me, he said, "Got your notes. Saw the changes you want to the news portal. I'll start there?"

"That'd be great." I hoped my look said, *help her settle in and feel useful*. But he went over to his pride and joy, sat down, and in seconds, was in his own world: hands on the keyboard, AirPods in, and deep in conversation with Dola about the changes. So I messaged him while Fi gave me a confused look.

> NIKI:
> Keep an eye on her, please. She's a bit unsettled by the new order.

> FINN:
> OK

Fi asked, "There's more than one Knight Adjutant? I didn't think that was allowed. How did Jamie take it?"

"Have you not seen your mum since you got home?"

"Actually, I haven't—she's away on one of her courses." She consulted her watch. "She'll be back shortly."

"Jamie isn't with us anymore," I said as calmly as I could manage. Fi's eyebrows reached stratospheric heights. "I think you'll find your mum has some gossip for you. I'd be interested to hear what story is circulating locally. Go home early today and let her fill you in. Then I'll tell you what really happened. In the meantime, check out the Recorder's news portal. I think most of the stuff I've changed is on there."

"News portal? That's new too?"

I stopped myself from sighing. "It's only a revamp of the old home page. You know, just something cleaner-looking and more twenty-first century with a lot less animated under-construction GIFs?"

She nodded. "It *was* old-fashioned." Finally, a smile crept onto her face. "I suggested we update it once, and your gran said there was absolutely no need."

"See, now you're getting the idea. Could you make a list of all of your suggestions, the ones that didn't get implemented, and let's discuss what we can do about them?"

Fi smiled now. "OK. In fact, it might still be in my draft emails."

Then I remembered the most important question I needed Fi to answer. "I'm looking for a hairdresser up here. Can you recommend one?"

She surveyed my too-long hair. The style had grown out unevenly. "Of course, there are about six great places. My friend Corby's sister runs one of them. She's a witch with her scissors. She'll fit you in next month, no problem."

There were six hairdressers in this tiny village? What the hell did they all do? "I was thinking this week?"

Fi laughed and shook her head. "Oh, not a chance. It's Valentine's week. The hairdressers around here make most of their money from the brides and bridesmaids, you know. They won't have any open appointments for locals until after Valentine's. That goes on until about the nineteenth in the normal venues to fit everyone in. Then it's half-term. The Scottish school holidays are different, you remember? They have kids, so they'll all be closed that week, so … March."

I sighed, "I'll try Carlisle?" She nodded but looked unconvinced. I moved on. "I'm going to give you an hour to settle in. Then can we go through the bonding requests together later? But first, I need to pick up Autumn."

She nodded hesitantly at me and repeated, "Autumn?"

"My little goddaughter, her mum's a lawyer, and she helped us with a problem in the Pict kingdom last week. In return, I get to play with Autumn for a few days." I checked my watch and realised I was late. Aysha put a lot of store on people being where they said they would, when they said they would. I'd shave some time off in the transport. That'd stop her from bitching at me for upsetting her schedule.

I scooped Tilly under my arm. "Want to go and get Autumn, pretty girl?"

Her frantically wagging tail said it all.

I heard Fi say, "I really was only away for three

weeks—what *kind* of problem in the Pict realm?" as I disappeared.

I landed in Aysha's downstairs bathroom in north Manchester and stuck my head out, calling, "It's only us."

Aysha met me in the hall. "Wow, you're early. Autumn's so excited, I thought she'd never go to sleep last night, and I tried to tire her out at the new indoor play centre."

Tilly wriggled frantically to be put down, and as soon as her paws gained purchase on the wooden floor, she shot up the stairs like a homing missile, and I heard the squealing start. "Tiiiillllllly, you're here!" As an afterthought, Autumn called, "Hi, Auntie Nik."

We walked through to Aysha's large warm family kitchen, and she saw the perfectly wrapped package I was carrying with its seven-pointed star gift tag and took it out of my hand.

Aysha called, "Thanks, Dola, it's arrived," towards her own Echo in the corner of her kitchen as she placed it on the kitchen table.

I settled at the table while Aysha finished applying the minimal makeup she wore to work.

With her flawless, tawny skin, she didn't need more than the basics.

"OK, Shay. Hit me with it. I'm ready for my instructions. What are the current cans and can'ts?" I usually got a comprehensive list if Autumn was staying with me for longer than a quick sleepover. But she surprised me.

"She's on holiday, so just don't do anything I'd go ballistic about. Make sure she eats. You know what she's like when she's excited. Oh, and try to keep the sugar down."

"Dola did some research, and she's with you on this—it's low sugar everything at the cottage now. Mabon's not amused. But you're giving me an awful lot of leeway—you sure?"

"Yes." An interesting expression slid onto and then off her face. What was she hiding here?

I prodded, "You're unusually chilled out today. Why? What do you want?"

"No idea what you mean." Aysha accompanied this statement with her best poker face.

I stared at her. Aysha was the reigning champion of staring contests. Lawyers often were. They must have a class on it before they qualify. But she surprised me again. "No teasing, OK?"

"Oh, I'm definitely not promising that." But it gave me a clue what might be going on. "Did you want me to hang on to her for a few days longer? Do you need a little private time?"

"Oh no, I've still got Thursday and Friday off, and I'm planning to finish early on Wednesday, but I wondered if …" she trailed off.

I waited. She squared her shoulders and lifted her chin. "What are the rules for sassies visiting the other realms? And why *do* they call us 'sassie'?" She wiggled her hips in a sassy fashion and pulled a face that reminded me of Autumn faced with Brussels sprouts on her plate. But her dark eyes were laughing.

"No idea. Well, I know why the sassie, and it's not that kind of sassy." I gestured at her still-wiggling hips. "It has an I and an E at the end. It's short for Sassenach—means 'stranger' or 'foreigner.' It's not just you; it's anyone who isn't from that realm. And I'd have to look the rules up. But I can guess."

"I thought you were the all-powerful Recorder."

"So they tell me—but I'm not all-knowledgeable."

"Well, work on it. It'd build your confidence. But what would your guess be?"

"That it's at the Recorder's discretion; almost everything seems to be. But it isn't always apparent which way I should lean. Why'd you need to know?"

She took a deep breath. "Lewis invited Autumn and me to join him and his two nephews at a winter wonderland sledding, ice skating, skiing thing.

They've had about two feet of snow with more expected tonight, and he said it's always a lot of fun." She gave me a look that conveyed *I dare you to laugh*.

But I didn't want to laugh, and I abandoned my plan for teasing her. Lewis Gunn, the youngest of the three senior Smiths in Aberglas, in the Pictish realm, seemed to be a fun, decent guy. Aysha was long overdue to find someone who understood she was a single mum first, then a responsible co-owner in a solicitor's practice, and, last, if she had any energy left, she could be an outrageous and fun woman.

"No problem. I'll pass you through whenever you want. But first I need to mess with your phone?"

She picked it up from the counter and held it out to me. "Why?"

"Because I might forget on Thursday. Friends don't let friends wander about the realms without a way to get in touch with the all-powerful Recorder." I winked at her.

"Open it, hold it in your left hand and," I waved a hand, "sort of mentally give me permission to upgrade it. But do NOT squeal, or I might blow it up." Autumn had inherited her squealing powers straight from her mother. Aysha did as I asked. I pulled power and gently zapped her phone. It took on the characteristic purple sheen that showed an electronic device had been in contact with the power.

She turned it over in her hand and asked, "So what changed? Apart from the crazy colour, I mean."

"You know how you couldn't call or text Lewis? Like his phone can't connect via mobile just through the lousy wi-fi they sort of have?"

"Yes, it never went through. We've been doing email, which is annoyingly slow," said the queen of let's-get-it-done-yesterday.

"Try him now."

Her thumbs flew, and she put her phone down. After glancing at her watch, she picked up a lipstick. She'd barely finished adding a coat of rich coppery colour to her mouth before her phone buzzed, and she let out a whoop.

I said, "Full disclaimer?"

"OK, what?"

"Dola has now added you to her network so she can track your phone."

In a baffled tone, she said, "But, Niki, we've been on each other's Find My Friends, or whatever they call it now, since they invented it. And aren't I already on Dola's network? I mean, how else does a perfectly timed vanilla latte arrive in the front hall sometimes when I'm running late if it's not through the Alexa-thingy? I asked her about it. She said it was magic. You know me, I don't look a gift coffee in the mouth. Well, I pour it my mouth—oh, you know what I mean!"

Now it was my turn to be surprised. "You do? It does?"

"Yes, and she chats to Autumn. She helped her with her spelling homework last week."

I'd process this later when I could talk to Dola. But I needed to check, "Does it bother you?"

"No, she's lovely. I think she gets bored. It started when she first asked me to explain some legal stuff when she was looking into the paternity problem. We've chatted since then."

I decided not to stick my nose into something that obviously worked for them both and moved on. "I'm coming to get you on Wednesday, right?" I sighed, thinking about my forthcoming week and Fi's attitude so far. "I'll probably be glad to have an excuse to get away for five minutes."

"Why, what happened?"

I filled her in on my multiple "why has everything changed?" conversations with Fi. And several other complaints from the realms that had greeted me this morning. They didn't like things changing, either. Or at least today's correspondents hadn't.

She started laughing.

"What?" I asked.

"Just a stray thought."

"Uh-huh. What?"

"You know how karma is a you-know-what?" She

cast her eyes towards Autumn's room and mouthed "bitch."

"Yes?"

"After you didn't make any changes yourself for almost twenty years, doesn't it strike you as funny that now you're the one trying to force the kingdoms to make some changes?"

"No, weirdly that does not strike me as the least bit funny."

She grinned at me. "You thought Jamie was your enemy, but it might turn out that the kingdom's inertia is a bigger problem to overcome. Oh, speaking of Jamie?"

"What about him?" I sighed inwardly.

"As your solicitor, I had a notification from Fergusson, McPherson and MacDonald—"

"What?" The firm the treacherous Jamie and his father had been partners in told me last week they wouldn't be able to give me any information for "several weeks" when I informed them I wanted the probate of my gran's estate transferred elsewhere. I told Aysha this.

"Possibly my complaint and Jamie's absence, along with their inability to contact his father, have forced their hand. Their official line is the Fergussons had a family emergency, and they'll advise me when there's more information. Have you got any updates?"

"What did you say? And, yeah, Mabon said there's a some sort of sentencing hearing planned for John just before St David's Day, and Jamie's treatment with the Fae is proceeding well."

"I told them we're transferring the probate out to another firm with a more reliable reputation, and if they want to make a fuss, we'll provide evidence of attempted fraud. I said it in lawyer-ese, but they got the message and promised all appropriate co-operation."

Then, using her special mother superpowers, she cocked her head and called, "Autumn, I know you're there. Come down now. Auntie Nik's ready. Don't forget your bag." Turning to me, she added in an undertone, "I'll keep you informed. Also, she's too old now for her ride-on trunk luggage. We're advised those are only for babies!"

We grinned at each other. She handed me a carryall. "Here are her clothes, and she has a brand-new grown-up bag, which currently contains zero clothes but is stuffed with a metric-ton of plush unicorns. She's all yours, Auntie Nik—enjoy."

CHAPTER
TWO

"If I view any more stock photos of hearts or pink fluffy things, I'll scream."

Fi sensibly ignored my outburst and continued to work at her adjoining desk in the Gateway.

Last year on Valentine's Day, I'd discovered my late husband, Nick, had not just been unfaithful to me but had fathered a son with a local woman who worked in his office in Bahrain. He had told me, after fifteen years of marriage, he wasn't ready to raise kids with me until his new business was up and running. So it wasn't surprising I didn't feel at all Hallmark moment-ish about the forthcoming celebration.

But Dola had instructed me that seeing their names on the Recorder's website was the realms' version of the notice of marriage or the banns being read. It would be effective PR to make it appear as attractive as possible. But I was handing the job back to her because I refused to scroll through any more nausea-inducing happy couple graphics.

Then a walking Christmas tree arrived at the green doorway, and a familiar male voice called, "Milady, can I walk through this glass? It's crackling with energy."

Delighted by the excuse to stop looking at romantic graphics, I crossed to the barrier to the Green sector, where, behind a man-sized collection of mobile greenery, I saw a very short brownie with a vaguely familiar shy face. "It's Sage, isn't it?"

"Yes, milady." He tried, and failed, to bow while holding … what was he carrying?

I lowered the barrier for him. "Come on through. Where are you going with all that?"

"Here, milady, it's the binding greenery. Well, some of it."

"Fi, what do we do with this usually?"

Fi looked over from her computer screen, glanced at Sage and bustled towards us. "Sorry, Dola was explaining the new system to me."

"No worries. Can I leave this with you?"

She nodded. "Of course."

Six more brownies, or Hobs, as the kingdoms called them, arrived, also disguised as mobile trees. Bringing up the rear was a female whose name I couldn't quite retrieve. She'd been here before carrying Imbolc food for Juniper, hadn't she?

"Is it Lavender or Rosemary? Or even Thyme perhaps?" I mumbled. Those three looked so alike, I wasn't sure. Then I realised she was crying and rushed over to her.

"Are you OK?" *Ask a stupid question, Niki, why don't you?* She was obviously far from OK. "Hey, come on, sit down. Would you like some water?"

Beautiful green eyes fixed on my face, and shock mixed with longing flashed across her features. Her eyes widened, and she said, "Oh, milady, I couldn't possibly." Her knees wobbled, and she reached out to the back of a nearby chair to steady herself. She looked on the verge of passing out.

I took her arm and shepherded her around to the front of the chair at the new conference table. I watched as three of the chairs changed the colour of their leather to brown. Since I'd realised the power amused itself by changing the colour of the chair leather depending on who would sit on it, I had used it as an early warning system. Two more brownies coming, then.

Gently, I said, "What would you like to drink?" still desperately trying to work out what her name was.

Before she could answer me, a delicate, white china mug of what looked like tea without milk arrived on a tray. A pretty line drawing in green of an herb and the word "Rosemary" adorned the mug. Goddess bless Dola. Accompanying it was a bottle labelled Lindisfarne Mead. I pushed the tray towards the still weeping brownie. "Please help yourself."

She gave me a sideways glance out of her amazingly green eyes. She looked very young, so I smiled gently at her. There must have been something reassuring in my expression because she opened the bottle, shakily poured some of the golden liquid into the tea and carefully re-stoppered it. Holding the small mug in both hands as a toddler might, she sipped it cautiously. Then she took a much deeper draught and let out a long breath.

"I'm so sorry, milady, whatever must you think of me?"

"Did something happen?"

She nodded, and more tears welled up and ran down her smooth cheeks.

"Can I help? Or do anything to help?"

"No, milady." As she shook her head, another tear flew off her face. "You said no."

"I did? What did I say no to?"

"My sister Lavender's binding application."

"I did? Why would I say no?"

She looked startled again and then perhaps a little cross. "I don't know why you said no, milady. They are a wonderful match. Some people don't like to bind Hobs, but after you helped Juniper so much, we thought you must feel differently."

"Why don't people like to bind, I mean bond, Hobs?" Surely we bonded all-comers once we'd established they had a valid soul-bond.

"Sorry, milady, I forget to use the human word. Yes, bond. Recorders have never agreed to do our bondings." She looked down into her tea, and I watched another tear drip into the mug from the end of her nose.

"But why on earth not?"

"I don't know, milady."

"But I haven't told Lavender I wouldn't bond her!" I damn well knew I hadn't sent anything to Lavender. I didn't even know Lavender. Beyond the vaguest recollection of Juniper calling out names last week, and Hobs arriving with boxes of Imbolc food, I couldn't picture anything about Lavender. Except there always seemed to be three of them together, and they looked alike. So what the hell was going on here?

In answer, Rosemary offered me her phone, open to an email her sister had forwarded to her. It appeared to have come from me: *Sender Niki McKnight, the Recorder's Office.*

I got cross.

"Rosemary, please give me your word you won't leave the Gateway until I can find out what's happened? Drink your tea and wait here for me, please?"

She looked baffled but nodded in compliance. "Yes, milady."

As I moved towards the desks, through my earbud, I asked, "Dola, why don't we bind? I mean, why don't we conduct bonding ceremonies for the brownies?"

"I have no idea, Niki. But there have never been any Hob names on the bonding schedules I sent to your gran's computer."

"OK, thanks." Raising my voice a little, I called, "Fi, do you have a moment, please?"

Fi rushed over. Before she could speak, in a low voice, I asked, "Why don't we conduct bonding ceremonies for the Hobs?"

She looked surprised. At least I think she did. Her eyebrows rose, but her eyes also opened wider in confusion. "I don't know. Your gran always sent the requests back as unapproved. I'm refusing the others now. Don't *you* know why?"

"Nope, but I plan to find out. Can you send the bonding application for Lavender Hobs to my phone, please? Apparently I just refused it. Send her a message saying we may have refused it in error and are re-evaluating, and we will get back to her shortly with more details. Please don't refuse any more until I've got to the bottom of this."

"We've two more in the queue, for Rosemary and Thyme Hobs. They're triplets, I think."

Goddess, no wonder the poor girl was crying. She thought her own bonding was next in line to be refused.

I kept my tone calm, "Please don't send anything else out in my name until we've spoken."

"OK." Fi looked puzzled, but I was seething with anger and didn't want to say anything I might regret until I'd calmed down.

I grabbed the Book, opened it and asked, "Why don't Recorders conduct bondings for the Hobs?" It rustled briefly and showed me a page that said,

I have no information on this matter.

Genuine shock surged through me and added to my feeling of powerless anger.

"But I thought you knew everything? Do you know why you don't know? Can you guess? Postulate any kind of theory?"

After a minimal amount of rustling, I was looking at another page.

Perhaps because they don't have their own realm. They have no one to speak for them. Perhaps prejudice. They were once considered pejoratively as vermin. The realms thought of them the same way as humans used to feel about foxes or badgers.

I considered this while I tried to calm myself down. I'd had a very unpleasant run-in with Lis and

Mag Hobs, who were apparently my housekeepers but who never did any actual housekeeping. Lis was as snappy as a fox. So I could see how it might have come about. But all the other Hobs I'd met had been lovely. Juniper was warm, friendly, and a skilled chef. Surely it wouldn't be right to judge an entire race on their Headwoman's personality problems—would it? I considered it. Did Lis have those problems because her people had been treated unfairly?

"Can you give me a quick overview of the Hobs, please?"

Hobs, short for Hobgoblins. However, the goblin part of the name is no longer considered polite in many places. Hob is acceptable, and they often use Hob as their surname.

Other names include

Ùraisg: **the wild variety**

Brùnaidh: **the Scottish Gaelic term**

Broonie: **the colloquial Scottish term**

Bwbach: **the Red Celts name for them**

They frequently have domestic or horticultural talents or affinities and are much in demand as reliable employees.

Their skin is a distinctive golden or pale brown colour.

They possess their own magic, which is not fully understood.

They can be prickly, easily offended, and hold grudges for many generations.

I tapped my earbud and uttered the words I'd never thought I'd say of my own volition:

"Dola, would you contact Lis or Mag Hobs and ask if one of them could meet me in the Gateway at their earliest convenience?"

CHAPTER
THREE

I'd settled at Finn's desk to get up to speed on the bonding requests myself while I waited for him and Autumn to return. Autumn and Finn made me giggle. They'd established their own method of communication last week. Autumn chattered nineteen to the dozen, and Finn was allowed to hold one of her unicorn toys and nod a lot. It seemed to work for them both. She'd talked him into taking her and Tilly to get one of Whirly's sweet bread kurts. They'd left a lasting and happy memory in her brain at the Imbolc ceremony.

Tilly was almost pulling Finn off his feet as they re-entered the Gateway, and the moment he released her lead, she came charging over to me. I picked her up, cuddled her and took a slow breath. What the hell was wrong with me? An email with my name on it had made someone cry. The fact I'd been totally unaware of it had stoked the fire of my anger.

I forced myself to be in the present. Stroking Tilly calmed me, and with Autumn here, I needed to be happy Auntie Nik.

Autumn arrived more slowly, finishing her kurt. She waved the last piece at me. "I saved you some. They call them vampire bread too," she said delightedly.

"They do—it's fun, isn't it?" I took the sweet bread from her and managed what I hoped was a creditable impersonation of a smile.

"Whirly 'membered me from Imbolc." Autumn's smile lit up the Gateway.

"That's nice. If you sit at the table, Dola will send you a drink of water."

Finn handed Tilly's lead over to me. "She's so strong for such a small dog. Does she have her own power?"

"She does, but I think it's mostly empathy and the ability to calm distress. The out-of-all-proportion strength is normal. Bichons have an iron will when they see something they want badly enough."

He laughed. "Going to finish the portal update. Anything else?"

"Yes, could you do me a report on the Hobs and the Gateway?"

He nodded. Finn's summarising talent had

become one of my favourite things about him. He believed no report should be longer than three paragraphs. If it was, people wouldn't read it anyway, so why bother?

I'd joked his middle name was TL;DR. But he said the information he left out was only someone's opinion. If he knew they'd been wrong about other things, why would he trust them on anything important? He believed Too Long; Didn't Read was just a way of saying the writer didn't have the ability to summarise. Accurate data, reduced to the necessary minimum was the goal in Finn's world.

"Hobs. Gateway. Specific info required? Area of search?" Finn waited.

"Sorry, Finn, yes, regarding their bondings and why we apparently don't do those for them."

He nodded, happy now he understood the request, and I added, "Also, can you find me names of candidates to fill the empty slots on the Rainbow Council please? Add yourself for the Picts, L'eon and Kaiden for the Fae, and then we need to fill the others. Dai, or was it Mabon? Someone said Rhiannon would serve for the Red Celts. Don't forget the Hobs too, but not Lis or Mag under any circumstances. I want the younger generation."

His mouth opened, and he was shaking his head.

"What?" I asked.

"Not Rhiannon."

That was unusually assertive for Finn. "OK. Why not?"

He shook his head again. "Ma says she doesn't play well with others. But, erm, the other realms …" I waited. He finally got out, "How?"

I was starting to understand Finn-speak, so I asked, "Do you mean what's the criteria or something else?"

As I'd predicted, he leapt on the idea. "Yes, criteria."

I ticked them off on my fingers aloud, "You should like them because you'll need to work with them. If possible, I want a mix of energy types. I'd like a person with yin energy and a person with yang energy from each realm, if possible. I don't care about gender, but I want different personalities and energies. Know what I mean?"

He was nodding. "Like Caitlin and Juna?" Juna, his other sister, was a gentle soul, quite unlike Caitlin, with her more assertive energy.

"Exactly. They should like technology or at the very least have the opinion that the twenty-first century is a cooler place to live than the fifteenth. Yep, just those three criteria to start us off."

He nodded, looking calmer now he had some guidelines. "OK, when do you need it?"

"Friday would be good. But do ask Mabon about

Rhiannon, will you? I think Dai thought she'd be good."

He looked up at the clock on the wall as though that would tell him what day it was. "Friday this week?" I nodded. He looked horrified.

"Finn, you already know all these people. Who do you design apps with? Or game with? Who's bugged you about bandwidth challenges? Eventually, there will be people neither of us knows on this council. But right now, we're forced to start with the ones we're aware of. I'm not allowing anyone to resign from it until they find two suitable replacement candidates for themselves."

I'd learnt that evil little trick from Janet. "We only have to do this once. Ask Fi for her input—she must know some people too."

He was looking more confident now. "OK. Friday."

As he settled back at his desk, he picked up a prettily-wrapped package with a seven-pointed star and the Pictish triskele on the gift tag. He tapped his earbud. I heard him say, "Dola, is this from you?" After a pause he said, "OK, Caitlin's coming later. She'll give it to Ma." Then, after another pause, he said, "OK, take it myself and install it. Yeah, you're right; Caitlin couldn't."

I wondered what that was all about, but it probably wasn't any of my business.

Right now, I had my goddaughter to amuse. Last week when Aysha helped me to sort out the millennium-old mess in the Pict kingdom, I'd agreed to look after Autumn in return. She'd had a long list of things she wanted to do in Manchester during her half-term, all of them hopelessly impractical given my schedule for this week, so we'd compromised. She'd come to Gretna Green, and we'd see if any of the bonders needed an extra bridesmaid, and perhaps she might see a unicorn.

Now it was time to deliver on my end of the promise, so I called Ad'Rian, the Fae king, and arranged for us to have lunch with him in Fae. I needed to discuss whether we might need a spell for Autumn, so she wouldn't inadvertently say too much about the realms to anyone back in Manchester. And I wanted to show her the unicorn paddocks. It would be adorable to watch.

Ad'Rian said he had no plans today except his book, his slippers and perhaps a small bland lunch. I spluttered with laughter at his quavery grandfather impersonation and told him I'd be there soon. I couldn't wait to see Autumn's face when she met a real unicorn.

CHAPTER
FOUR

It was time to find out why Fi thought she could use my name to announce decisions I hadn't approved. And I needed to work out why a combination of both fury and powerlessness had almost overwhelmed me when Rosemary told me *I'd* said no.

"I will not be like Janet. I am not a bitch," I muttered to myself. Janet began most conversations with an accusation and never gave the accused any chance to explain what had caused a problem.

I grabbed a chair from the conference table so I didn't loom over Fi, another of Janet's unpleasant habits. I settled at the end of Fi's desk, and in as gentle a tone as I could muster, asked, "I wondered why you're sending out emails with my name on them?"

Fi smiled. "We've always done it that way. Everything went out in your gran's name. I changed the Elsie McKnight to Niki McKnight when I started on the emails. Is it a problem?"

"I think it is, yes. Let's change it." Fi grinned at me, and I said, "What?"

"I'm thinking that could be your alternate title. My Lady Let's-Change-It McKnight."

I grinned back at her. Perhaps Aysha had been right when she'd said I hadn't made any changes for twenty years. But now, suddenly, I wanted to change everything. It was probably overdue.

"Fi, do you know how to set up extra email addresses on the server?" She shook her head. "Then swap seats with me for two minutes please."

She gave me a surprised glance as she moved. "You can do it?"

"Yeah, I'd planned a career in computing at uni. Then I took a temporary job at the registration office, got married and ended up staying there for twenty years."

Fi peered over my shoulder as I removed her access from my email and set her up a new one of her own.

"Do you want yours to be Fi or Fiona Glendinning?"

"Fi, please." She still looked calm. She'd simply

been following the procedure Gran had laid down. Well, I'd never had an email from Gran, even after I set up her first account. She could barely manage a text and was much happier with long, rambling, handwritten letters.

This wasn't Fi's fault—we'd start afresh.

"So, best practice, I'd prefer you to only use your own email address. OK?"

"OK, but can I ask why?"

"Sure, I think if you'd had to refuse the Hob bondings in your own name, you might have checked with me first because you knew it would devastate them all."

There was a pause, then she nodded. "I would have, you're right."

"Well, I don't want anyone using my name, so they don't have to think through whether something is a poor decision. There are a ton of out-of-date habits in this Gateway. I want us to review issues as they come up. If Rosemary hadn't been in here crying, I wouldn't have known I'd just unintentionally destroyed three young women's hopes and dreams, would I?"

It dawned on me *that* was why I was angry. One of my goals was to do things intentionally and not by accident—good or bad.

I caught Fi's eye. I would not be like Janet. "Fi,

please never hesitate to discuss things. I like clear communications."

Now she relaxed, gave me what might be the first genuine smile I'd seen from her and said, "Will do." She had a lovely smile. Her wide mouth in her pretty heart-shaped face gave her smile some real power. With any luck, we could work happily together, and I'd see her smile more often.

As I stood up to return her chair, she asked, "Is now a good time to confirm the checks for the couples for tomorrow and Thursday?"

"I'm not sure what this check is or how long it takes?"

"Just a few minutes per couple. That's all your gran took. She said it was the 'make sure nothing went pear-shaped in the meantime' check."

I must have frowned because she continued, "When I first started, there was only the one check. But as your gran got older, she implemented the extra check."

"I'd like to do it a bit differently."

Fi was grinning now. "Why am I not surprised? What would you like to change?"

"Can we bring everyone in tomorrow?"

Fi nodded. "That's a lot in one day—seventy-eight couples in an afternoon?"

"Based on Gran's performance over the last few

years, how many would you say she might have wrong?"

Fi looked both thoughtful and torn. Whoops, was I trampling on her loyalties to my gran? That was not my intention. I rushed to clarify, "I just mean, how many of them will need more than 'Lovely to meet you. Now go away and come back on Sunday for your bonding'?"

She relaxed a little. "Less than a dozen, probably. Your gran left some notes on some couples she was unhappy about. She was aware she wasn't at her best."

"I only hope I do as well as Gran did when I near my own century mark."

"She was incredible for her age." Fi's shoulders lowered into a more normal position. "Probably fewer than ten couples. The rest should be straightforward, as you say, 'Hi. Smile at Ross. Bye. See you Sunday.'"

"Smile at Ross?"

"The photographer. That's why they get so dressed up."

I'd worked with photographers as a registrar, but wasn't tomorrow just an admin thing? "I can see why he'd be here on Sunday, but why's he coming tomorrow?"

Fi gave me a look.

"Oh, Fi, just spit it out please—I have a lot to learn."

"You're a strange mix, Niki. Competent, you make quick decisions, and there's all the new tech, and then there are the simple things you don't get. I'm struggling to work out which will be which."

I grinned. "Yeah, me too. We'll work it out eventually. But back to the point—why do we need a photographer tomorrow?"

Fi looked at me for a beat too long. My Gift suggested she was trying to find a tactful way to say something. I waved my hand in a *just spit it out* gesture.

Fi said, "I'm not sure you understand what an honour it is for people to be bonded in the Gateway. Most citizens in the kingdoms just get married and divorced in whatever their realm thinks is the normal way. You know the Vikings often do it around the autumn equinox in groups in the longhouses; the Red Celts still like druidic ceremonies; the Galicians have their beautiful churches." She waved her hand. "The Gateway is *only* for the soul bonds that last a lifetime or more. Those are rare. They might not seem to be rare when you're working in here. But compare it to the millions of people who aren't bonded in here. Your gran always told me the bonds we do in here are the special ones." She paused and looked at me.

I thought about what she'd said, and she was right. I'd conducted thousands of those ordinary weddings, but I wasn't quite getting how this was different, was I? "So how would you describe the people who do come to us?"

Fi chewed on her lower lip. "Well, the royals want to be sure they're marrying the right people so they can avoid any scandals. Most of the people we bond here are someone important or are connected to someone important. Or they're not important in themselves, but someone important noticed they had a special bond." She stopped and gazed at me inquiringly.

"Sorry, Niki, I feel like I'm womansplaining and lecturing you about things you should know."

I shook my head. "Once you've caught up on the gossip with your mum tonight, I'll explain a lot more. But for now, just assume I have a lot of power, but I don't have the political awareness to go with it—yet—this is helpful."

She tried again. "A Gateway bonding is the equivalent of a wedding at St Paul's or Notre Dame Cathedral or getting married in Vatican City. It's technically possible to marry in those places, but less than one couple in a million actually will. Bondings at the Gateway are extremely rare. They might not feel that way during our busiest bonding week of the year. But they are."

Things were making a bit more sense. But only a bit. Perhaps I should just go with it and hope it got clearer as I went.

"Let's just bring them all in tomorrow. Then, if some aren't a match, or there is a minor problem, we can discuss it privately with them on Thursday. I'd hate to embarrass a couple in front of an audience of all the other realms. At work, I'd have taken them into an enclosed office, but this entire space is open. Caitlin tells me some realms are renowned for their keen hearing."

Fi was nodding along. She looked up to the vaulted ceiling as though searching for a sign, or trying to retrieve some information. She suppressed a laugh and said, "You know, that's just how we did it when I very first started. Your gran used to say, 'Put all the problem kids in one basket. People who find themselves in a glass house can't hurl a half brick at anyone else, can they?' Let me bring the Thursday ones forward. What time shall we start tomorrow?"

"Whenever you think best. You understand the routine." I wanted Fi to realise I was only changing things that didn't work.

We smiled at each other. "Don't feel you have to stay too long today, will you? I expect tomorrow will be a long and perhaps difficult day. And I'm pretty sure your mum will want to see you, send her my regards, won't you? It was lovely to see her last week."

Unwittingly, Mrs Glendinning had provided me with the key to what was really going on when I first arrived here. The least I could do was send her daughter home a bit early.

CHAPTER
FIVE

I strolled past the table towards Autumn and saw the brown chairs had all turned back to green. Weird, I guess the brownies weren't incoming after all. But Rosemary and Autumn appeared to be having a great time. They were lifting tree boughs into an attractive woven herringbone pattern around the walls. Rosemary was using what I guessed was Hob magic, and Autumn was directing the power to help place the greenery. I checked in with the power —it was having fun. It sent bubbles of happiness back to me.

"Do you need a hand, Rosemary?"

She jumped and almost dropped the bough she was lifting. I caught it with power and put it where it had obviously been headed. "Sorry, I didn't mean to creep up on you. I only came to tell you where I'm up to with your bonding requests. How are you feeling now?"

"Better, my lady. I'm very sorry about earlier." A rush of colour flooded her golden cheeks. "I don't know what you must have thought of me. Thyme and Lavender were coming to take me home, but I told them I'm fine."

That might explain the appearing and disappearing brown chairs. I'd monitor the chair colours. It might be useful one day.

"I told them you'd been very kind, and you really are looking into it." She stopped and drew in a long breath before continuing, "Sorry, milady, you asked me to wait at the table. But the greenery will pile up too high if we don't put it in place."

I was no horticulturist, but didn't tree branches die in warm rooms without a water source? I reminded myself my current goal was to add to my knowledge and hopefully weave some wisdom into all the power I'd inherited. So I asked her.

"Oh, yes, that's why I'm here. I'm placing the stay-alive spells. It will look beautiful until we take it down. Lavender will be along in a few days to do the bloom-pretty spell. She's working with Juniper on the bonding food this week, and Thyme will do the smell-nice spell. We all have different gifts."

"I have a lot to learn, Rosemary, but I'm glad to see you looking better. Don't give up hope yet. I'm investigating why the Recorders haven't done Hob bondings in the past. But no one seems to know. Do you have any ideas?"

Her small, vivacious face fell, and she looked down. "I don't think they liked us, milady. That's what Grammy Lis says anyway, although she doesn't …" she bit off whatever she was about to say. Instead, she explained, "Some of our ancestors had fiery tempers and weren't always reliable, but it was a very long time ago."

Grammy Lis? OMG. The triplets were Lis's granddaughters? But they were so nice, although their bonding requests had come in at the last minute, hadn't they? "When did you expect to get an answer?"

"We weren't even going to ask, milady. We knew the Recorder would send it back saying 'not accepted.' They always do. But after milady Elsie died—" she made a gesture in the air and murmured, "—may she reach the Summerlands with joy and without hindrance." Then she continued speaking to me, "And you helped Juniper so much last week, and no Recorder ever did that for a Hob. We got our hopes up and submitted the requests. I'm sorry, milady."

I'd no idea what she was sorry about, but her

Summerlands blessing for my gran reminded me of one I'd previously only heard from Ad'Rian. As far as I knew, only the Fae referred to the afterlife as the Summerlands. I must ask what he could tell me about the Hobs.

"Rosemary, leave this with me. Lavender should have received an email explaining we sent the refusal too soon, and we're still looking into it. I know time is tight, but can you give me a couple of days?"

"Oh yes, milady. Thank you for even considering it properly."

I nodded and reminded myself I'd decided to make gathering more knowledge a new habit. "Rosemary, if I can ask, what do you do," I gestured at the branches, "when you're not making it beautiful in here, I mean?"

A slightly embarrassed expression crossed her face, but then she put her shoulders back. "I work with Juniper sometimes too. Well, we all need money, and she does pay well, but I'd rather work with Crane."

"Crane?" I couldn't picture anyone called Crane.

"Crane is my sister Lavender's partner. It's their bonding you just refused."

Ouch! "I am very sorry about that. I'll—"

But she made a brushing aside gesture and said, "He's only just started his business, and he can't take on staff properly, probably for years. So I just help him out for fun, but I'd rather help people than serve food."

I pictured some kind of gardening business, but I asked anyway, "What type of business does he have?"

"He runs websites. One helps people to import things from the realms. Well, they don't know it's from the realms, but it is. And one for the realms to help them export. He's a smart one. I just help him with customer support."

It constantly amazed me how many people were running inter-realm businesses, and yet the UK I'd grown up in knew nothing about the origins of the goods they bought. I'd met Hugh MacAlpin in the Pict realm last week and heard all about his golf drivers that 'sold for a pretty penny in Caledonia' and now this. I needed to do more to support these people.

"I can see you'd be good at that, and I promise I will get back to you once I can get some information out of someone."

She did the strange combination of a bow and a curtsy I'd seen Juniper do. I needed to find out about that, and the Book was still on my desk. I'd promised myself I would start finding things out—no time like the present before I forgot.

I didn't want to offend anyone within hearing range. The Gateway was busy with Hobs coming and going with tree branches, pots of flowers, boxes of what looked like Juniper's food headed for the Fae realm, and other things I couldn't even identify, so I thought hard at the Book.

Why do the Hobs do the odd curtsy/bow combination?

It rustled a bit. The rustling was just for show. I was pretty sure the Book just created a page on the fly with the answer to whatever I wanted. Perhaps my ancestors had liked the idea that the Book contained the wisdom of the ages and it had to find the right page. Maybe in the days of Google, the Book realised I didn't care how the information came, provided it came quickly. I was still thinking hard, and the Book picked the thought up from my mind when its open page said,

You are correct. There was much mystery and superstition attributed to the Book. I am simply a medium for the power to convey ideas. I am a source of information and historical records. You appear to need less flummery than previous Recorders. Adaption is occurring.

The Book was connected to the power? "Thank you, I appreciate the information, and my other question?"

The Book flicked a single page, and the next one said,

Once upon a time ...

I laughed out loud. Fi and Finn looked over at me, and Tilly poked her head out from under the desk. I waved a dismissive hand at them. "It has a sense of humour. Don't let me distract you, sorry."

The page turned itself, and the next lines wiped the smile right off my face.

A hob was brutally put to death for curtsying to a male royal when they should have bowed. The Hob clans have a different view of gender. They see the core of the person instead of the external façade. In this case, the royal in question took offence. So the Hobs developed a gender-neutral expression of respect to prevent it from ever happening again.

I was so horrified, I just didn't know what to think. Intellectually, I knew history was a brutal place, but this ... just whoa!

I closed the Book with an unhappy feeling in my tummy. I patted the Book to show it I would grow up. I couldn't ask it questions and then not deal with the answers. But I wasn't happy, so I decided to do something that would make me extremely happy.

I retrieved Autumn, who, with a high-pitched, whiny edge to her voice, said, "Can't I stay here instead? I want to help Rosie—this is fun."

But I knew this little one better than she realised. "Of course you can, darling; you're on holiday, so you should be able to do almost whatever you like, don't you think?"

Her little head nodded at me, her face serious. "Thank you, Auntie Nik. I knew you'd unnerstan'."

"Of course, baby, I'll leave you here. I'll only be a couple of hours. Just ask Finn or Dola if you need anything. I'm popping out to have lunch with the King of the Unicorns. I'll see you later. Be good for everyone, please."

I got almost three complete strides away, one further than my mental bet with myself, before she was swinging on my hand to stop me, squealing with excitement. "Unicorns? King? Me come too."

"Is he really the King of the Unicorns, Auntie Nik? I mean, really? Not like a nickname? For reals?"

I'd learnt my lesson about giving Autumn easy answers when she was much younger. My general rule was to give her the highest truth I thought she could understand, so I answered her seriously. "Well, he is the king. And his house is called Alicorn, which is the unicorn's horn. So, for reals, I suppose his title would translate as the King of the House of the Unicorn Horn. But that's a bit long, don't you think?"

She nodded. The squealing had stopped, thank all the Gods and Goddesses.

"He's an important person, baby, so I'm gonna need your finest going visiting, company manners. Do you understand?" I realised I was quoting her Granny Olive, Aysha's fun, fab mother, who said this to her often. Oh well, whatever worked. "The least possible amount of squealing would be great."

"I'll really, really try." She nodded solemnly and looked up at me with her best butter-wouldn't-melt expression. It was as good as I was going to get. I whistled for Tilly and then realised she was right on our heels. As we walked, atop the anvil, I saw another perfectly wrapped package with the seven-pointed star gift tag, but this one also had the Fae's unicorn symbol on it too. I tapped my earbud and asked, "Dola, is this for Ad'Rian?"

"Yes, give it to him please."

"Will do—what is it?"

"It is a gift from me."

I put it in my capacious handbag. "OK, I'll see he gets it." That was different. I was insanely curious about what Dola was sending to Ad'Rian, but it wasn't any of my business, was it? It might be doughnuts; I'd promised him some, hadn't I? But, no, the box was the wrong shape and too heavy.

"Dola, can you phone some hairdressers and see

if you can get me an appointment this week please. I can't look like this on Sunday."

"I will do it now, but Fi was right. Your gran used to note her next appointment on the calendar when she returned from the current one."

As we headed through the Violet gate, I wondered if Ad'Rian could fix my hair magically for me.

CHAPTER
SIX

We passed through the violet doorway into the Fae kingdom, and with a long, reverent "Ooooooooooh," Autumn simply stopped in her tracks. Even Tilly plopped onto her butt, her little black nose in the air. I eased them both out of the path of the gate traffic, and the three of us took it all in.

I remembered my own first visit here. I was probably four or five years old. Unlike Autumn's authorised, accompanied visit, I'd just wandered through the door one day. I recalled standing, then sitting in almost this exact spot for hours, entranced by the strange sky, the odours on the breeze and the iridescent, glittery bubbles until my gran arrived and yanked me back through the door.

I hadn't been here in almost thirty years, since my

gran exiled me from the Gateway. As I wiped away the tears flowing down my cheeks, I suppressed my anger at my gran and the idiotic, ill-advised and cruel decisions she'd made about my life. She wasn't a wicked woman, and I had loved her, but she'd caused me a hell of a lot of pain with her stubborn stupidity and her fear.

I looked around, reacquainting myself with the wonder that was the Fae world. It didn't appear to have changed at all. The gate still opened into a beautiful, lush green glade. The sky still had that strange quality that said *foreign*. With the perfect clear blue sky, and the clouds little white puffs like melted marshmallows, it was gorgeous. I remembered Gran had always said *they have no trouble making a sailor a pair of trousers here.* But searching my memory didn't give me any idea what this phrase meant. Although said in Scotland, it often preceded her disappearing to hang washing on the line. It certainly only ever rained at night in Fae. Maybe that was something to do with it.

Autumn raised a hand to touch a bubble and then giggled as it bounced away from her fingers. "They're sticky; are they bubbles, Auntie Nik?"

"Not exactly. They're seeds. Can you remember why dandelions go from being yellow petals to the fluffy white heads?"

She nodded. "So they can get their seeds spread

further in the wind, and to make dandelion clocks for good children to make wishes on."

Wow, she'd been listening that day. "Well, these are sort of the same. The bubbles are seeds, and people do this." I batted the one closest to me, and it bounced away quickly. "And the seeds can travel further."

"They're prettier than dandelions."

"They are. Baby, I know you could stand here for hours. I did when I was little, but I have to visit Ad'Rian, so let's walk. We can come back again another time."

"Promise?"

I thought about it—could I promise her this? Go with the truth, Niki; it's always best with kids. "As long as your mum agrees."

"Mum would *love* this! Bubbles always make her laugh."

"Then we'll bring her, but for now, we need to move."

We walked, stopping frequently for Autumn to admire the trees with little doors in their trunks. "They're quite small. Are they really fairy houses, Auntie Nik?"

"No, they're for the tourists to photograph. But if we have time, I'll show you where the smallest fairies really live."

"OK, but we're tourists, amen't we? Will you take

a photo of me next to that pretty one for mum? It's like our front door but tiny."

"'Aren't we,' baby, not 'amen't we.' But sure, kneel down." She knelt, holding Tilly's harness to position them both on either side of the tiny, glossy blue door with its brass knocker and handle.

We took several photos in happy tourist fashion, including a selfie of the three of us by a bright green door, which we sent to Aysha with Autumn's message: "Mum, it's too small even for Tilly to go through."

As we walked along the sparkling deep purple, cobbled road, Autumn said, "I'm hot. When will we be there?"

I helped her out of her sweatshirt. It was blissfully warm here and a lovely change from dreary Scotland. "Do you see those turrets over there? That's where we're going."

Autumn's mouth dropped open as she surveyed Ad'Rian's home. "It's Sleeping Beauty's castle from Paris."

Castle Alicorn did look like something from Disneyland, but in grey stone with the royal purple on the roofs and the flags.

"Is the king your friend?"

Don't kids ask the hardest questions? "He was when I was your age, but then I didn't see him for a long, long time. So we're sort of starting a new friendship now I'm grown up. Does that make sense?"

Before she could answer, the man himself arrived on the road in front of us on one of the winged unicorns they called pegacorns. Laughing, he gestured behind him and shouted, "Nik-a-lula, an old friend felt you cross the boundary and insisted on coming to say hello. Want to ride her home?"

From behind Diamant, Ad'Rian's majestic steed, came a curious nose, then a horn and two bright luminescent purple eyes, rapidly followed by the rest of a majestic silvery-white unicorn. She tossed her lilac mane, nickered and trotted towards me. I saw an expression of complete and absolute shock on Autumn's face, her mouth open and her eyes nearly the size of saucers. Our baby unicorn queen had finally met the real thing.

Then I was running to fling my arms around Dusha's neck, whispering apologies for my forced absence and sending her waves of love. She nuzzled my fingers and my hair. As I caressed her horn, I got a clear thought from her that my mane was now too long, but I had grown tall. A crashing wave of love and welcome home broke over me, and I realised I was crying into her neck, but they were happy tears and felt cathartic. Tilly whined against my leg until I picked her up, mounted Dusha, and we were off.

I'd left Autumn behind. Panic mode activated!

Then riding above us, Ad'Rian, with Autumn mounted in front of him on Diamant, waved. Oh, bless the man. Dusha had lots of news and was very forgiving of my absence. Ad'Rian had apparently explained my gran's decision to her. It didn't stop me weeping for the theft of the thirty years I should have had with her loving, supportive, crazy presence in my life. I needed to set up a schedule for this new job that gave me time each week to do the things I wanted to do. I made a mental note to discuss it with Dola.

It was some time before I could bear to leave Dusha, the unicorn I had once stolen out of Ad'Rian's paddock, and who I hadn't seen since my gran exiled me from the Gateway.

But Autumn was hot and thirsty, and I was too. So I left Dusha in the paddock and promised her this time I could visit her regularly. I turned to Autumn. "Sorry, baby, I hadn't seen her for a long time."

"Yes, Uncle Ad'Rian 'splained it all. I rode a flying unicorn!" Her face was glowing with joy, but I was curious.

"Uncle Ad'Rian?"

"He asked me what I called you. Then he said, in that case, I should call him Uncle Ad'Rian."

I felt briefly guilty for abandoning Autumn to

Ad'Rian. Oh well, he was good with small feisty girls. He'd obviously coped just fine.

Tilly had loved riding Dusha. Apart from demanding to be picked up so I didn't leave her behind too, she'd settled on Dusha's back as though she'd done this a thousand times. I remembered all the pictures I'd seen of Bichons in their circus dog days with a ruffle around their neck and riding a horse. I grinned to myself. Tilly wouldn't have liked the collar of shame even with ruffles on.

The two of them were becoming friends. Tilly stood up straight on her back legs to her full height, and Dusha reached her nose down, her relaxed nostrils showing me she was happy, and Tilly licked it—you'd swear they were saying a polite goodbye.

As we walked towards the garden doors of Ad'Rian's study, I was in a daze of happiness, and I was also aware some part of my soul, which had been in shreds since I was evicted from my life, was beginning to knit back together thanks to the much too-short ride on Dusha. I'd better pull myself together. I wasn't a child anymore. I could come back anytime now I was the Recorder, and I had important questions to ask Ad'Rian.

We settled in the room Ad'Rian called his study but I'd thought was a library when I was a child. That was until he showed me his actual library, which was on several floors and had more books in one place than anywhere else I'd ever seen outside of the world's major libraries. I took in his study as an adult, but it didn't seem to have changed any more than his realm had. I recognised the leather chairs, solid desk, low table and endless floor-to-ceiling bookcases.

Ah, it had changed—there were even more books. I spotted what looked like an almost completed, judging by the position of Ad'Rian's bookmark, copy of *Ruling Regally* on the coffee table. I grinned at Ad'Rian as we sipped our fizzy fruit juice. "Breanna found that one helpful."

"It's a gift from Breanna. With a pretty inscription. I am to be invited to the inaugural meeting of a Book Club. What is that, daaarling? Would I enjoy it, do you think?"

"I'm sure you would. It's Breanna's way of setting up a meeting of all the royals without Troels interfering."

"Ah, alright. I shall RSVP and attend the first one. After that, we'll see. I'm terribly lazy, you know. I often agree to do things and then regret it. But I do love books, and this one is most amusing and makes some excellent points."

"I'm going. It will be fun; Juniper is catering it."

At this information, a beatific smile wreathed his face.

"Daaarling, why in the world didn't she just say that? I shall definitely be there."

I smirked. "Is this where I'm supposed to find my manners and introduce Autumn properly? But you met her at my ascension, didn't you?"

"Autumn and I have now established our proper relationship; your debt is discharged, my lady."

"Oh dear, what did I do wrong to become 'my lady'?"

Now he quirked a brow at me. "Nothing at all, daaarling, is that better? But you're here because you need something. Shall we dispose of it first and then enjoy our lunch? Perhaps on the lawn—it's so beautiful today, and you're developing a Caledonian pallor, Niki. Some sun would do your heart good."

I remembered the astonishing mind-to-mind connection I'd had with him and Mabon last week and thought hard at him. *Could we find somewhere fun but safe for Autumn to be for an hour while we talk?*

Ad'Rian leaned over and ruffled Autumn's curls. "Little one, would you like to cool off swimming with a mermaid and then perhaps give Diamant a carrot and some berries before you come and join us for lunch in an hour?"

Give Autumn her due. She didn't squeal, and her

manners were impeccable. But her head nodded at me like a metronome, and she was almost dancing in place on Ad'Rian's priceless rug. "May I, may I, Auntie Nik?"

"If you'd like to, you may."

De'Anna, L'eon's mother, opened the door. Ad'Rian must have invited her telepathically. She greeted me then held out her hand to Autumn, who took it happily and danced off beside her.

"Nicely done, Ad'Rian, my heartfelt thanks. Her mother makes raising her look easy, but I have to work hard to reach her standards."

"Remind me, Niki, who is her mother?"

"Aysha?" He'd seen Aysha at my ascension. Was I missing something?

"Indeed, the attractive mixed-race woman whom you introduced as your best friend. How long have you known her?"

"Since I was nineteen, and she was eighteen—we met at university. Why?"

"And does she have powers of her own?"

"Oh, I see. I don't know honestly. Yes, she reads runes and has amazingly accurate instincts about people. However, if you asked her, she'd deny it and say she is a realistic, logical woman. She can't see the power. But her mother's side come from the Caribbean, where there's a long history of inexplicable powers. Her grandmother definitely had the sight. Again, why?"

"The child bespoke Diamant. She asked him to fly higher and to circle, and he did, which I did not expect. It was very like watching you as a child. With the darker hair and skin, of course, but the heart of that child is much as yours was. She was just as openly fascinated by my purple skin as you were at about the same age."

Tilly grumbled gently at my feet; she obviously thought it was lunchtime. I pulled her up onto my knee to quiet her. As I moved my handbag to make room for Tilly, Ad'Rian's gift fell out of my bag.

"You're probably right, and I'm a bad influence. Tilly and I have known her since she was born."

Ad'Rian grinned at me. "So now we're alone, what may I help you with? And is that for me?"

"Sorry, yes, it is." I handed the gift over. "Dola asked me to give it to you."

"Dola did?!"

"My thoughts exactly. I'm intrigued. Will you open it?"

He opened the prettily wrapped gift and looked baffled as he handed me the contents. I thought, *Dola, you devious little madam. What* are *you up to?*

CHAPTER
SEVEN

An elegant electronic device, almost nothing like an Echo Show, sat on my knee. The screen was fifty percent larger than the original Amazon device that lived in my bedroom. This was a classy piece of kit. Slim and stylish with its brushed aluminium finish, it could have been an expensive modern photo frame, the kind you might gift someone for a significant anniversary.

Ad'Rian echoed my thoughts. "What is it? Do I put artwork or a photograph in it?"

Well, crap. Did I tell him the truth? Dola had essentially just sent him a bug? A bug through which she would hear anything that happened in his study? Or did I just pass it off as a communication device he might find useful? Dola should have warned me so I could have thought this through properly. I was a lousy liar, and the Fae could be walking lie detectors, so it would have to be the truth. Just perhaps not all the truth.

"It's a new design but similar to devices Dola has been repurposing to communicate with people. She uses the one at my friend's home, for example, to speak with Autumn and help her with homework or to send coffee to Aysha when she's having a rushed morning. If we set it up and you say 'Dola,' she can talk to you."

"How intriguing. Could you," he waved his hand in a fix-it gesture, "do it for me, daaaarling? Phones are my technological limit. Isn't it kind of Dola to think of me? You've been a wonderful influence on her, you know. Mabon and I were anxious about her some years ago. It was sad to be inside her, so I avoided your grandmother's cottage."

I smiled at him, and while I was setting it up, I tried very hard to keep my thoughts to myself.

Ad'Rian could read people's surface thoughts easily, and I needed to check with Dola exactly what she planned to do with this before I ratted her out to Ad'Rian. So I kept a memory of Autumn's gleeful face as she knelt by the fairy doors on the top of my mind and tucked all my concerns about what the hell Dola thought she was doing underneath Autumn's cheeky grin and Aysha's delighted response to the photo in our family chat group.

A question about something different but technology-related might distract the king. "Are you still OK about L'eon and Kaiden being on the Rainbow Council? I'd like to start it next month."

"Yes, daaaarling, I'm fine about it, and they tell me they're looking forward to it. But next month? You do not let the grass grow, do you, Nik-a-lula?" I supposed if you were several millennia old, then next month must seem ridiculously speedy. I continued poking my phone to set up the not-Echo.

"Dola, can you really hear me?"

"Ah, Your Majesty, you received my gift? Happy Monday."

"I did. How thoughtful of you. Goddess, is it Monday already? How fabulous to talk to you from my own home."

"You are welcome, Your Majesty. I'm sure the Recorder needs to discuss important matters with you, but I suspected you might need her assistance to install my device."

"You were right. Perhaps we can speak later when Niki and the delightful child have left?"

"If you say 'Dola' when you are ready, I will hear you, sire."

Ad'Rian turned to me with a huge smile on his face. "What a wonderful gift. Thank you for your help. Now I am doubly in your debt. What can I help you with today?"

I decided he was right. He and Dola were in my debt. I would speak to that cunning little entity when I got home. For now, I said, "Before I move on to the main thing, just a quick question: what do you know about the Hobs, or Brownies, or whatever you call them? Actually, what *do* you call them?"

"We call them Brownies. What do you call them?"

"Dola, please send Ad'Rian and me a brownie each." The chocolate would help me relax, and Ad'Rian had a very sweet tooth.

Ad'Rian's eyes opened wide in his normally unexpressive face. "Really, Niki, no thank you. There are hundreds of them about the palace; if you have need of some, I'll summon them for you. There's absolutely *no* call to send for more."

Then a plate of chocolate brownies appeared on the table in front of the device. He usually had quite an immobile face, as though he had decided many years ago not to show his emotions, but now his nose twitched, then his mouth formed a small, surprised O. I offered him the plate. "This is what I call brownies."

He sniffed again, took one, bit into it, and I watched his eyes change from their usual silvery blue-violet to the pure lilac of Fae happiness. "Oh my!"

"There's a problem with the Hobs, which in England we also call Brownies. I didn't realise they were real until last week. These were the only brownies I was familiar with." I waved my chocolatey treat at him.

"Now I've discovered the Hobs are being mistreated by the Recorder's office, and no one can tell me why. I don't know what to do about it yet." I heard my voice rising in annoyance, realised I was ranting, and made myself pause.

"My apologies, I had a lovely young woman sobbing all over me this morning. Sorry, Addie, I'm still cross about it."

"Oh, do tell. Perhaps I can help."

So I did.

At the end of my recitation, he said, "Yes, I see the problem. It's a kind of outdated prejudice, isn't it, really, I suppose? Times change, Niki. And we must all change with them. But there are so many of them, you see, we couldn't give them all full citizenship in Fae even if I wanted to, and they have their own culture, which is different to ours. We give them all the jobs we can."

Ad'Rian's casual admission of something that was starting to feel close to racism startled me. He was a caring man, but when you've lived for several millennia, you develop the ability to call it like it is. But then why wasn't he changing it? One of the things his long life had given him was power and lots of it.

Noticing my expression and perhaps misinterpreting it, he rushed on, "And we pay them very well, truly. They have such talents. But you're aware of that—wasn't it you who encouraged Juniper to launch her business properly? The Imbolc meal at Breanna's was stupendous. She's catering L'eon and Kaiden's wedding feast for us too."

"But where do they come from, Ad'Rian? One of them gave the Summerlands blessing for my gran, and I've only ever heard that before from a Fae. What are they? Are they Fae? And why do they have so many names? And why can't I marry them? I mean bind them; I mean bond them. Oh, for heaven's sake, you know what I mean!"

He laughed.

"I'm not sure even I can identify their origins. They've always been around. Not everyone can even see them, you know. Some people think they're mythical. What does the Book say?"

"Not much, which is why I'm here. What do you mean, not everyone sees them?"

"Just that, Niki. In the same way as some people can't see any of the higher energies and say ridiculous things such as auras aren't real, just because they don't see them. Or like some people are colourblind. Vikings, for example, often refuse to see anything they can't hold in their hands. Which, of course, is how we realised what must have happened with Kaiden when you pointed out his squinting." He took the last bite of his brownie as he concluded, "I should know the Hobs' origins, but I don't."

"OK, I'll keep looking for answers."

He paused to swallow then added, "I should. I'm sure I should, but don't you find until someone asks you an inconvenient question, you're unaware of your own ignorance or prejudice? It doesn't make it right, and I will look into it. I'll need to visit the library, look for myself and probably set one of my librarians a task. It could take some weeks, but I will report back to you."

"It's quite urgent. I must give a decision on three Hob bondings on Thursday."

"Then, Recorder, you must make the choice that feels correct to you."

I nodded. This was my problem then. OK.

"But you said this wasn't the main thing you came for?"

Oh, heavens, I'd completely forgotten the real reason I'd come was to ask about something to protect Autumn. I quickly explained my concerns and the decisions I'd made about what I wouldn't do and asked for any options or ideas he might have.

"I wish to be sure I understand your desires here. You will not use a memory block on Autumn ever?"

"NO!" I paused, breathed and muted my own anger. What happened to me wasn't Ad'Rian's fault. "I can try to understand my gran meant well. But what she did to me was undeniably abuse. It was cruel, and it damaged some parts of my life in ways she could never have imagined. It also kept failing, and I'd have dreams where I woke screaming that they couldn't take it away from me, or that he would come for me. No one knew I believed Mabon would rescue me. They thought I was frightened because someone was chasing me."

I paused and breathed to quell the hysteria that still threatened to overwhelm me when I remembered those horrible, powerless nights when no one understood.

"I went through years of therapy—pointlessly. It destroyed my confidence in myself and messed up my ability to make good decisions. I'd even forgotten Dusha! So, no, I definitely wouldn't *ever* do that to *anyone*."

"But you're also recalling your mother's problems and how her ability to speak about the realms meant people decided she was mentally ill?"

I nodded. He asked, "How old is the child now?"

"She'll be eight in April."

"I'm picking up stray thoughts from you, Niki. You must be most concerned about this. Normally, your shields are impeccable. May I see this family chat that is so on your mind?"

Huh, I'd only been thinking about our family chat group to distract him from my concerns about Dola's new devices. But I opened my phone and handed it to him with the group open. His long, elegant finger scrolled and scrolled. I saw a tiny smile twitch at the corners of his thin lips.

He held the phone out to me. "This photo. Would this be a normal sort of thing?"

I glanced at the screen and grinned. It showed Autumn on her bed in a purple nightie with a silver unicorn on the front. She was trying to find space to sleep amidst about two dozen plush stuffed unicorns varying in size from Sparkle, the finger puppet she kept in her pocket, to one large enough for her to sit astride, which was currently acting as her pillow. The caption from Aysha said, *She's going to need a bigger bed—obvs less unicorns are not an option.*

"That would be completely normal, yes," I confirmed.

"So if, for instance, she went into school, and the teacher asked what she did during half-term—she tells me they make diary entries?" He quirked an eyebrow in query. I nodded.

"So she writes about some fairy doors but says real fairies don't live in them. They're just for the tourists to photograph. Also, she rode on a winged horse that liked carrots and patted one that didn't have wings and preferred to eat fruit. What, I wonder, will her teacher assume?"

I saw where he was going with this. "You're saying that, at her age, teachers only look to make sure children understand the difference between their rich fantasy life and reality? And that perhaps a visit to a petting zoo became far more exciting in Autumn's mind? But she understood the concept of fairy doors as a photo op concept, and that might make her a pretty normal seven-year-old?"

Ad'Rian smiled now. "I believe in using minimum necessary force with magic, like everything else." He feigned a yawn and waved a languid arm. "Because I'm so terribly lazy, you know."

I laughed, and he continued, "Also, because, to borrow that wonderful Caledonian saying, there's no need to use a gavel to release a tree fruit."

I hid my smile. "Do you mean it doesn't take a sledgehammer to crack a nut?"

"Yes, quite. We should revisit this in a year or two, but right now, the child's rich fantasy life will simply have her educators wondering if she may grow up to be a writer."

He was exactly right. Before I remembered the Gateway existed, I'd thought that Autumn's ability to hold long, multi-sided conversations during one of her frequent unicorn tea parties, or even with Tilly, might lead her into a creative field as she grew up. And she understood her boundaries. I said all this, and Ad'Rian stood up. He'd settled it in his mind.

"Don't hesitate to ask me again, Niki, but right now, we don't need to do anything. If or when we might have to act, then let's try the restriction I think would work on her mother first so she can experience it, and we'll have parental consent if we ever need it."

I hugged him, and we strolled outside to find a table set for lunch on his sunny lawn. The beautiful embroidered sunshade over it leant a festive air.

Autumn skipped up the lawn towards us, accompanied by Fionn'ghal. I shot Ad'Rian a startled look. "She told me she'd met my daughter. That was what made me ask about her mother's possible gifts. I hadn't told her who I was at that point. I'd only introduced Diamant."

I remembered Autumn and Fionn'ghal sitting on the floor in my kitchen. Autumn had reached a hand out to Fionn'ghal's face, and they'd felt as if they were sharing energy or communicating without words. I might need to have a conversation with her about how much information she could pick up that way. I was definitely missing something.

CHAPTER
EIGHT

When we returned to the Gateway after lunch, I had a well-fed, sleepy child on my hands. She'd get fractious soon, and I really needed to get some work done with Fi. But if I suggested Autumn go back to the cottage for a nap, she'd tell me she was too old for naps.

It was so easy when she was younger. Once she'd fallen asleep in her buggy, we could throw a party around her, and she wouldn't wake up. Which gave me a crazy idea. After a quick consultation with the power, and with Dola's help, we created a small mattress with a rainbow-striped duvet, and Autumn's own enormous unicorn pillow arrived from her bed at home. They all went under the large conference table.

I casually said, "Oh, look, Autumn, there's a den

under the table. Would you and Tilly like to play in it?"

There was squealing, but I couldn't complain about it. Her behaviour in Fae had been exemplary. Five minutes later, child and dog were cuddled up, both snoring softly. I snapped a photo for Aysha and added the message: *Don't have a fit when you get home. Dola transported her unicorn pillow up here.* She sent back the face-palm emoji.

I would have loved a nap too. Instead, I gave myself a stern talking-to about this being one of the busiest weeks of the year and the importance of checking the plans for the bondings. Dola sent me a very large, very strong black coffee in a mug with the slogan, *Coffee—Because who the hell has the time for sleep?*

I considered the two large desks that had served my gran and Fi for years. The way my team was growing, I'd soon need more desks, chairs, and computers. For now, I asked the power to move the anvil to the middle of the conference table.

The difference between the work environments of my two assistants amused me. Finn had screens everywhere. The large curved monitor, his new laptop and his phone were all in use, and his desk was swamped under a small hillock of printouts and a snowstorm of Post-its. The box, which looked suspiciously like the ones I'd delivered to Aysha and

Ad'Rian earlier, was still there. I must ask Dola about these devices once I'd kept my promise to Fi to get briefed on the bonding plans.

In contrast, Fi's desk was completely clear, apart from a checklist and a pen. I grabbed a chair from the conference table and, smiling at her, asked, "Room for a small one on this end? Any problems?"

"No problems, just queries. We have a sample menu from Juniper. It's *very* different, but when I checked with her, she told me you'd already approved it, but she'd still like you to check it, which confused me."

"I think we've all had enough vol-au-vents and trifle to last us a lifetime, don't you?"

Fi's laugh rang out. It was an attractive laugh, low and melodic. With one eye on her screen, she asked, "These A Peach of a Bond pancakes are new. Don't they sound intriguing?"

"Oh, the wishing pancake things? I don't think they are new. I think Gran just wouldn't have anything she hadn't eaten before. But Finn already knew about them when we had them at Imbolc. My wishes are already coming true, and I think Finn's are too—they seem to deliver, so be careful what you wish for. Tilly's certainly had more chicken than usual."

Fi gave me a confused frown.

"Sorry, Fi, just my strange sense of humour. I gave

Tilly one—she looked like she was wishing for chicken."

She laughed. "My mum is still talking about when she met Tilly. She's trying to talk Dad into getting a dog now she's got time to take care of it." Then, as if realising she'd relaxed, she pulled herself sharply back to the task at hand. "So, did you approve the menu already or not?"

"Not exactly. I told her a chef of her calibre could serve whatever she thought appropriate."

"That makes more sense. She asked if you'd let her know before Wednesday if you want to change anything."

I opened the menu email. "Well, damn, doesn't this look better than Gran's beloved cold meats and salads? What do you think, Finn?"

He didn't even twitch. I tapped my earphone. "Dola, can you switch Finn's earbuds to transparency mode, please? I think he's got noise-cancelling on again."

Finn looked up from his screen, and I repeated, "What do you think of this menu, Finn?"

"It looks good. Never enough berry cheesecakes. People steal them. Hide them in handbags, pockets. Messy. They always run out."

For a placid guy, he sounded unusually aggrieved about it. He'd also spent some of his carefully rationed words bitching about it.

Fi added, "He is right, my lady; people do steal them, and they take them home for family who couldn't get to the ceremonies. They run out about halfway through the bondings. They're magically good, and I think Juniper only does them for bondings and for weddings in the realms."

"Then let's come up with a solution—so everyone gets one."

They both just stared at me.

"People, think, please. We're in charge now! We can change things. It's not written in stone, is it? If they're in such demand, they must be good. How can we keep it fair?"

I looked at the menu. I couldn't see anything that looked even vaguely like it could be a berry cheesecake. Then I started giggling.

"Niki?" Fi had a concerned tone in her voice.

"Sorry. Cheese! Cake!"

She looked confused now and shot a glance at Finn.

I added a broad Bolton accent. I'd lived in the area for enough years to imitate it, "Cheese ... Cake! Together? Cheese and cake? A cake of cheese? Disgusting!"

At this, Fi started grinning too and chimed in, "We're in Peter Kay's garlic bread territory here, aren't we?"

I nodded and said, "Silly memory, when Jamie

was trying to prevent me ever getting a handle on this role, I asked him whose job it was to onboard me, and he looked at me like he had never heard the word before and said, 'On Board? On boarding?' I started thinking about garlic bread and …" I trailed off, laughing as Finn's face made it clear I was making no sense. "Ask Google, there are videos—you might need to be from Manchester for it to be funny. Anyway, what are these cheesecakes actually called?"

Finn had obviously had quite enough nonsense. With all the contempt of a young man who'd never given his heart away, he said, "Love's Young Dream."

"And, Fi, how many people are we expecting throughout the whole day?"

"Well, originally there were seventy-eight couples, but with the Viking gate being sealed … if it still will be by the fourteenth, that would cut it down by seven couples. So, seventy-one couples and their guests."

I gaped at her. "Wow! I was a registrar for decades, and the most I ever married in a single day were about twenty couples, and that was on the tenth October 2010. A lot of men thought it might help them remember their wedding anniversary. How on earth do I get through so many people in one day?"

"We do them in batches. They mostly organise it

themselves, and, of course, they'll often have individual celebrations once they get back to their own realms."

"OK, batches. Makes sense." I pictured my gran surrounded by a crowd and remembered being told to play quietly.

I made a mental note to inspect the couples closely using my Gift, not just for their bond with their partner, but to see if some couples might fit better into one group than another for the actual ceremonies. I didn't know why, but my Gift thought I should shake up some of the nationalism.

Finn's hand headed toward his earbud, to turn noise-cancelling back on. Before he did, I said, "I meant to ask you both, would we normally work the Saturday before the Valentine's bondings? If it's on a weekend, I mean?"

Fi replied, "Not usually, but I've no plans on Saturday if you want to work, Niki."

Finn just nodded.

"I think I would, if you guys don't mind. Perhaps do half a day just to be sure I'm ready for it all? Then we'll take Monday and Tuesday off instead and have a short week to make up." I was determined to be better than Janet, who'd hated it if anyone dared to take a day off in lieu.

They both nodded, and Finn turned his noise-cancelling back on.

Fi looked sheepish. "I think I owe you an apology, my lady... I was slow getting up to speed this morning. But Prin—oops, Finn and Dola have been so kind. You've made a lot of changes in a few weeks, but they all seem to work."

"No apology necessary, Fi, really. It must have been jarring for you, expecting one thing and finding something quite different."

"Honestly, Dola being a person was the most startling thing; why didn't we know that?"

I shrugged. "I've no idea. Some of my ancestors seem to have been a bit close-minded. Gran called Dola 'it' in her letter to me. She told me I should be polite to 'it.' So I don't think she knew, which is crazy but for another day. For now, talk to me about these bondings, please. What do I need to do?"

We spent a pleasant half an hour planning, and I felt tons happier about Fi. She appeared to be good at her job and had cleared half the backlog from her holiday already. Which suggested she was being underutilised. Then tomorrow I needed to check the candidates' bonds, and on Thursday I had to fix any problems. But otherwise, there wasn't much for me to do until Valentine's Day itself, which was odd. Wasn't this supposed to be the busiest week of the year?

I was pondering what I might be missing when

Caitlin stormed through the Violet Fae's gate and stomped towards the centre.

She was one unhappy woman. Her furious face and unnecessarily loud voice made that apparent.

I glanced over at Autumn, who was still asleep, and put a finger to my lips to shush Caitlin. I might as well have tried to turn back the tide.

CHAPTER
NINE

A couple of days ago, I'd invited Caitlin, the heir apparent to the Pict Queendom, to have a week's trial as my second Knight Adjutant. Even though we'd all been in the middle of some dramas at the time, she'd been incandescent with joy at my offer. She was still incandescent, but that certainly wasn't joy on her face now.

We hadn't yet found time to discuss what I hoped the two of us could discover this week. Could we work together for a year or two? In her well-worn leathers in the usual gorgeous shade of Pict blue and with all her Pictish tattoos and many piercings, she looked like the love child of a biker gang leader and a self-righteous Valkyrie as she strode towards me. She did not look like a princess, which was only one of the reasons I liked her so much. She wore black trainers with a distinctive blue swoosh. Oh crap. She'd probably marched all over Fae trying to find me, getting angrier with every step, to judge from her expression.

Her voice became progressively louder as she closed on the centre of the Gateway, completely ignoring my repeated requests for quiet. I swirled the power and wrapped it around her mouth. She stopped dead and gave me an angry scowl accompanied by a glare that was truly scary.

"Caitlin, I apologise. But you aren't listening to me, and I have a child asleep under that table. If you wake her up, I won't get any more work done today. Please shut the hell up."

I saw her breathe in and out several times; her shoulders shifted and lowered, she nodded at me. I recalled the power.

In a furious whisper, she said, "You can't do that ever again."

I was completely in the dark. What had I done? "Do what?"

"Leave the Gateway *alone*. Dola said you went to Fae unprotected. Unaccompanied!" Her voice rose again.

"Caitlin, I'm going to do that anytime I want to, and you need to get used to it. I didn't offer you a trial as my Knight to be a damn bodyguard."

The princess drew back her shoulders and

breathed in. In a more reasonable tone and at a lower volume, she asked, "My lady, can you focus here? You're not taking your security seriously. I could kill you where you stand."

"No, you couldn't."

She glared at me again, disbelief mixed with a large helping of frustration on her face. Then she backed down. "No. OK. In here, I couldn't. But you weren't in *here*. You were in Fae, *unaccompanied.*"

I looked her over. She was angry, but, underneath, I picked up something much closer to fear than anger. I'd learnt from *Good Grief* that sometimes anger is what comes out when we internalise too much fear. I needed to fix this once and for all.

I tucked my hand through her arm and led her towards the Green sector and my cottage. I was trying to give off calming energy, and she began to feel less stiff, so maybe it was working.

Conversationally, I asked, "Did you want to try? To kill me where I stand?"

"Yeah, I do. But I don't want to embarrass you. If we were alone and not surrounded by the Gateway power, yes. I'd like to teach you how vulnerable you are. So you'd stop sneakin' off without me."

I checked. Autumn was still asleep. I sent Dola a quick message asking her to alert me if Autumn woke up, and to the still unhappy Caitlin, I said, "Come on then."

I walked through the green door and towards my cottage. Caitlin stomped alongside me.

"Could you let me know when you feel we're private enough?" I asked.

She pointed to the clearing just before the cottage. "There would be fine, my lady." She'd moved from anger to icy politeness. But then, thawing a little, she said, "The grass looks soft. I don't want to hurt you. I want you to understand it's one thing being all-powerful in the Gateway, but you need to be careful when you're not in there. You need to take me with you."

I stopped at the cleared area that merged into the end of my garden. "What do you want to show me, Caitlin?"

She didn't rush but walked determinedly towards me. I watched her carefully and waited. As she almost reached me, I transported myself behind her and tapped her on the shoulder. "What was it you wanted to show me?"

She spun around, but she recovered quickly and marched off towards the cottage, calling over her shoulder, "Sorry, I thought we'd cleared the Gateway's energy. Can you tell me when we have?"

I followed her. "We are clear of the Gateway."

From her waist, she removed two short, tapered, iron sticks connected with a piece of chain.

"Ooh, I've seen those in movies, cool." She held

just one of the two sticks. What were those things called? I'd seen them in a movie recently. They were Japanese or something, weren't they? Holding one, she swung the other stick in a circle. She looked like Xena, and I grinned.

"I bet the iron-sensitive races hate those. I can't remember their name, though."

Caitlin held on to her temper. But it took all of her impressive self-control as she muttered, "You're not taking this seriously."

"I am, but you're not listening to me." I drew a little power, took the weapon out of her hand and examined it. Oh yeah! She was still mad. As she rushed me to reclaim it, I tangled her feet with the power.

She fell with an audible "Ooomph!" hard onto the grass.

"Oh, my god! I'm so sorry, are you OK?"

I dashed over to check she was only winded. One of her hands clamped around my throat. She retrieved her iron sticks with her other hand. Then I was lying on the grass with her knee in my back, securing my arms. Wow, she was fast.

And cross.

"My lady, this is the point I'm trying to make. You've had no training. I could be that idiot Leif. You're not safe."

"Pretty sure we could charge people to watch this,

you know." I smirked. "I mean it's not mud wrestling but …"

Caitlin focused her confusion on me. "What?"

My face was pressed into the icy grass, but with the one eye, I could see the wire-wrapped handle of her sword peeking out from under her hair. I used the power to pull it out of the back sheath she wore it in. I asked it to poke her in the back, not too hard, with the blunt end.

Her body stiffened. She dropped my wrists in surprise as she looked behind her and saw her own sword floating in the air.

I lifted my face out of the grass. "Do you call that end the hilt or the handle? I asked the power to poke you with the blunt end. It seemed to know what I meant, but it would be nice to be clear on the proper term."

There was a moment where she froze, and then she spluttered, swore and, still laughing, stood up. Eventually, she gasped out, "How can you use the power outside the Gateway? I know I moved you far enough away from it—I felt it get colder. I've been so slagging worried about you and my responsibility to keep you safe, and you can do this?"

"I tried to tell you. But there were always too many people around, and I didn't want everyone to realise it's a thing."

"Hell yeah. We don't want anyone knowing about this."

Now we both laughed helplessly.

When we got our laughter under control, I dusted myself down and headed towards the cottage. I needed coffee.

"KAIT, can I entrust you with something I don't want known outside of five people? You would be the fifth."

"I don't know. And I really do prefer my full name."

I ignored her; now wasn't the time to give her the bad news. "Why don't you know?"

She said, "S'pose it depends who the first four are. I can speak for myself, but can they be trusted? If they're weak or blabbermouths, I don't want you to think *I* can't keep my mouth shut when it's one of the four who's the idiot."

"Fair point. The first is Dola?"

"Oh, yeah, she's cool. I've no idea how anyone could make her speak if she didn't want to."

"Mabon?"

"That man is a vault. At least he's a vault who talks so much nonsense, you never even notice he ignored your question. So yeah."

"HRH?"

"The cat?"

I nodded.

"She speaks?"

"To a select few, but yes. Especially if they offer to feed her. She speaks to Finn."

"She does? OK? If you trust her, then OK."

"Well, she might use the knowledge to set the odds on a bet more accurately, but I don't think she'd wantonly discuss my business if she ever expects to be fed again, so yes. How about Dai?"

"Dai? Prince Dafydd ap Modron, Mabon's heir—that Dai?"

I nodded again.

Something unhappy flitted across her face. "OK, I'm out of my league here, aren't I?"

"I don't think so, no. You asked a sensible question. I answered it because you might know if any of them would betray me, even unintentionally. There may be two more soon—Finn because he's in the cottage so much now, and possibly Ad'Rian if he starts visiting again."

I waited. It was important she understood I wasn't taking this lightly. She was a serious young woman and a future queen, after all.

"Recorder, with allies like those, and the amount of power you have, why the hell did you ask me to be your Knight Adjutant?"

I shivered. "It's cold out here. Come to the cottage and have a drink, or actually, as I'm on stand-in mum duty, I'll have a coffee. You can have a drink if you like, and I'll explain." I grinned at her.

We sat at the kitchen table. Obviously. This was where I discussed all the serious business in my life. Caitlin looked calmer and a lot less stressed. I guessed this from her smile and the fact she'd accepted a beer.

"Before I forget, is your mother OK?"

Caitlin smiled. "She's chilling out nicely, thanks. She told me you're holding a life debt now. Well, she had to. It had to go in the Albidosi debt book and the Book of Strictures. She says you're having dinner with her, and she mentioned Sorcha the other day at breakfast without snarling or weeping, so, yeah, she's getting there."

I smiled. I liked Breanna. She'd been a damn idiot last week, but she'd been under pressures I could barely imagine. "I'm looking forward to her book club. Do you know when she's starting it?"

"She was putting royal seals onto the last of the packages and envelopes this morning, so I think the remaining invitations are ready to go out."

Then her face changed as she realised I was only making conversation while she calmed down. "But seriously, why did you want me as your Knight if you can use the power anywhere?"

"Mostly I want you for misdirection and as an agent of change."

She frowned as she repeated my words, "An agent of change? Sounds right in my forge; we need more change. But who or what am I misdirecting?"

I considered how much to tell her. My Gift had trusted her brother, Finn, even before I'd met him. As a result, last week, I'd offered him the role as one of my Knights and a place to live. But every time I was alone with Caitlin, my Gift told me she was hiding something and kept telling me to ask her what she was hiding. And last week, I'd been far too busy to unearth what it might be.

So I'd offered her a week's trial in the role to give us both the space to see if we could work together. In this supposedly "busiest week of the year," I seemed to have time to spare.

I started slowly. "What message would it give the realms if I said I don't need a conventional Knight Adjutant? Wouldn't they start wondering what I knew that they don't?"

Now she tilted her head to one side and watched me carefully. I opened my Gift.

"Also, I don't need one Knight Adjutant—I need

at least three, possibly only two publicly, but really three."

"Why?"

There. There it was. A sealed box in the middle of Caitlin's aura. I poked it gently. She didn't seem to notice. She just asked, "Why three?"

I wanted to poke harder. The box was blurry and tightly sealed, and she seemed unaware I was digging in a private part of her mind.

Huh?

I pulled back. I needed to work out how far to go with my Gift now it had powered up so much. It hadn't ever been an issue before I ascended because my Gift had been quite limited, and knowing how someone felt by using my Gift, or being able to tell if they were lying, was no different in my mind to skill at reading body language.

But now I was so much more powerful, it felt … wrong. Perhaps the power had given me an important lesson when it refused to update anyone's phone to the Rainbow Network without their consent? Whoops, Caitlin was still talking.

"Why … do you need more than one, my lady? Haven't the Recorders always only had one Knight? Why are you different?"

"Can we take a step sideways for a minute?"

With a small frown, she said, "Sure?"

"You know I'm sort of psychic, right? I mean,

apart from being able to use the Gateway power, I inherited the McKnight women's psychic Gift?"

"I guess. No idea what it really does, but I assume that's how you saved our lives last week? So, what kind of psychic? Like the Fae?"

"Honestly, I'm still learning myself." I'd never had to explain this to anyone since my Gift increased so dramatically. "It's always told me when someone is lying to me. Or sometimes just lying to themselves. But since I truly ascended to the Recordership, it's got a lot more powerful. It's started suggesting things to me."

"Like what?"

"In this case, it keeps saying, 'Ask her what she's hiding.'"

She laughed. "Well, dur, as Finn would say. That could take a while."

"It could?"

"Yes, obvs."

Now I was really confused. "Why? What are you hiding?"

"Niki?" Then she paused. "I can call you Niki in private, right?"

"Of course, Caitlin, sorry, thought we'd settled that last week. But what are you hiding?"

"Thousands of family secrets, I would imagine. I mean, I don't do it consciously. But, shit, I grew up having all the slagging Albidosi confidentiality rules drilled into my head daily. Literally. Daily."

The Picts always made me smirk with their so-frequent use of the word "slagging." It had completely baffled me until Breanna explained it was simply an iron manufacturing word and meant "useless." Now it made me smile and Caitlin asked, "What? What's funny?"

I just shook my head. But I had a strong sense whatever she was hiding was nothing to do with the Pictish royal family's secrets. It was connected to something I needed to know about.

I tried to explain. "But, KAIT," I ignored her wince at what she thought was the shortening of her name—she'd work it out, eventually, "none of that is any of my business. Maybe last week, when the Pict realm was in arbitration with the Recorder, it might have been. But not now. This is something my Gift thinks I should know, and I don't. Do you see?"

She rolled her head on her shoulders and speared me with a look she would use often once she became queen. I recognised it from Breanna. "Can you guarantee to keep anything connected to my family confidential? On the word of the Recorder?"

I considered it. The power thought I needed to know about this, so I phrased my words carefully. "Yes, on my word as the thirteenth Recorder, anything I uncover that's unconnected to me or the Recordership will never leave my lips."

She looked at me carefully for a few moments and then nodded. "So can you dig about for it? Like the Fae do?" She waved a hand around her head.

"Yes, that's what I was doing when I found it, and then I felt guilty because I hadn't asked your consent."

She waved her empty beer bottle with a grin. "I think if we're about to get close, Niki, I might need another one of these. Mud wrestling indeed, I had no idea the Recorder had a sense of humour! You should come out with us one night. We're all going to *Carnaval* this week."

"*Carnaval*? Is it a club or a bar?"

She spluttered with laughter. "No, it's the Galician version of what they call Mardi Gras in your world. The big blow-out before that religious thing of theirs where they can't have sex for forty days or something?" Now she looked confused. "Or maybe they just can't eat meat. I don't know. All their ancient religious rules confuse me." She sighed, "Do not tell my mother I couldn't explain this. I'll look it up. I'm sure I'm supposed to know. Their rules are different to the same church in your world. But, anyway, *Carnaval* is fun, a parade, dancing, special foods and drinks. Come."

I laughed, and Dola exchanged the empty bottle

in her hand for a full one. "That is very creepy, Dola, no offence meant. But thanks. OK. Knock yourself out, my lady." And with that, she relaxed back on her chair and closed her eyes.

I dug in. Yes, now I had her permission, it wasn't blurry. OK, good to know I must be doing this right. A carved wooden box. Antique, hand-crafted with sturdy iron straps around it and a large strong padlock keeping those iron fastenings securely closed sat right in the middle of her aura. Whoa, was I being dumb here? Not so much right in the middle of her aura as in the yellow-green area that probably indicated her solar plexus and heart chakras. I needed to learn more about chakras; the power seemed to use them for … something? Or even several things. I added it to my mental study list and got back to the task in hand.

I gave the box a poke with my Gift, and a violet Alicorn symbol on the top of the box glowed. She'd been to the Fae for healing of whatever this was. I asked my Gift, *did you mean this?* And got back a solid feeling of *yes, that*.

"Can you feel that, Caitlin?"

She opened her eyes. "Wow, you're quicker than the Fae, and no. Feel what?"

I decided discretion was the better part of valour here. If she'd had help from the Royal Fae Healers House to lock an event or an issue up so securely, and if whatever it was connected to her emotions, her confidence and her heart chakra, I didn't care what my Gift thought. This was none of my damn business. I couldn't see how whatever personal difficulty she'd obviously dealt with by sensibly getting Fae healing could have any connection to her ability to be my Knight Adjutant.

"Well, mystery solved, so thank you for allowing me to follow through on my Gift's insistence." I'd need to think about this and why on earth my Gift wanted me to know about it, but I damn well wasn't going to cause her any distress about it.

"I'm done here. If you would like to be the Knight Adjutant In Trust, you need to know what you're getting into. So let's get back to why I need more than one Knight."

She frowned. "Do I need to know what you found?"

I gave her the truth. "I found something that was none of my business and left it untouched. So, no. As my gran would have said, 'least said, soonest mended.'"

She just nodded calmly. "OK, back to the Knighthood, what am I misdirecting people to or away from?"

"The Knight was supposed to help create change, not be a bodyguard. The last few recorders have needed that because my ancestors lost all sense and reason after Agnes was apparently stoned to death."

Caitlin winced. "Nasty way to go."

"Oh, yeah, awful way to go. But as we said last week, it also meant the Recorder's Office achieved very little for five hundred years. It wasn't always this way. And it's not supposed to be like this, so I want to change it."

She swigged her beer and nodded. "I like that about you."

I grinned at her. "If you think about it sideways, three elements instigate most changes. They might be called the power, the might and the thought, or perhaps the plan."

Caitlin's brow was creased, and she squinted. Perhaps I wasn't making sense. I tried again, "A more modern way to say it would be the actions and content, the people and the process." I'd been sent on many courses about how to drive change. Janet didn't like change or courses. So send Niki and then ignore any ideas she brings back. But perhaps now they might come in useful.

She swigged more beer and waved the bottle at me in a *please continue* gesture.

"So if those elements were people, they might be called the change-maker, the warrior and the teacher. I want you to be the teacher."

Her eyebrows shot up, and her jaw slackened. "But… but I'm the warrior."

"Oh, no, that would be Finn and Dola. They work together like they're one person; you must have noticed?"

Complete silence fell. I could almost hear her brain whirring. Eventually, she asked, "Could you define 'teacher' for me? The way you understand it?"

"You know the phrase, 'when you have them by the balls, their hearts and minds will follow'?"

She snorted. "I might have heard that one, yes."

"Well, the type of teacher I'm talking about grabs a person by something that seems unimportant. Then the person notices a world of pain is being caused by the person doing the squeezing. If the squeezer does it carefully, the enemy can give in without admitting why, and no one loses face, and there's no need for bodies to pile up."

"Don't get it. Sorry. If you squeeze someone's balls, they notice a long time before the world of pain arrives!"

"What if you just bend their thumb to its snapping point or their shoulder to dislocating point?"

"Oooh, OK—might be getting it now."

"I think warriors squeeze too hard and too fast. True teachers might look like warriors, but they do it more carefully, and their teaching lasts a long time after the end of the battle."

Her furrowed brow told me I wasn't getting through to her. I tried again, "Have you heard of Alexander the Great, long-dead Macedonian guy?"

She nodded happily. "Greek, sort of? Famous warrior? Took over half the world before he was thirty? That guy?"

"Yes, him. Did you know that after the battles, he moved on with his army to battle some more? But he left behind colonists, and some soldiers, sure. But mostly colonists. Thanks to him, Greek became one of the most widely spoken languages of the time. Greek culture, Greek gods, their rituals, even their food, went with him wherever he went. And stayed behind long after he was dead."

Her face made it clear I wasn't conveying this well. One last try. "Caitlin, sometimes you have to think about what you want to leave behind after the battle. Warriors tend to leave a bloody mess. Teachers clean it up, and the actual change goes forth from there."

Then she crossed her legs, and I caught sight of her trainers again. I pointed at them. "What are those?"

"My sneakers?"

"Mmm hmm. What are they?"

"Nikes?"

"And do you know who Nike was?"

She shook her head. Her expression suggested

she wasn't a woman who cared much about footwear, provided it served its purpose.

"Nike was the Greek goddess of victory. Alexander the Great worshipped her."

"You're just making shit up now! You can't know that! Wasn't this like, three thousand years ago?"

I smiled. "More like two and a half thousand years, and you're right, I can't know it. But I do know he put Nike's image on the reverse side of many of the coins he had designed and minted. So I can assume she was important to him. The myths say she had wings, and that's where that comes from."

I pointed at her shoes and traced the swooshy tick mark in the air. "So, you see, history might say he was a great warrior, but his legacy isn't his battles. All those countries he conquered eventually went back to being what they were, or changed into something else, but the culture, the teachings he took with him—those stayed. We still use a lot of Greek words today. And you're wearing trainers named after his goddess. That's why teachers need to work alongside the warriors. Dola and Finn can win us some wars, but what good stuff do we want to leave behind when we clean up after the war? That's the real question, don't you think?"

We sat in silence before I tapped my Gift, realised what might be confusing her and added, "Think about it, because it's the reason Finn and Dola are the warriors, and you're the teacher. Warriors strategise and are sneaky. Teachers are allowed to be much more straightforward, which probably suits you better."

"How do you know all this slagging stuff? Weren't you some kind of civil servant before you became the Recorder?"

"Yeah. I was—sort of. I read a lot. That helps. Somebody said, *'The supreme art of war is to subdue the enemy without fighting.'*" I looked up as though it would help me remember who. But I had nothing. "It was probably either Sun Tzu or Terry Pratchett. They seem to be stored in the same place in my head. Anyway, my point is, if we leave this to Finn and Dola, they'll help us create the change we need, mostly without the people we care about getting injured. But we need to work out what kind of change we want, and you know the realms far better than I do."

She still looked baffled, but she pressed on, "And what does a teacher do? I mean, what do you want me to do if I'm not to follow you around all the time? 'Cause right now, I'm no teacher!"

"Oh, you can follow me around and look scary in your leathers, just not when I'm only having lunch with an old friend."

"Niki, Autumn is waking up."

"Thanks, Dola. Sorry, Caitlin, we'll have to

continue this later. Why not give some thought to what we need to teach people before, during and after they change? Oh, and stop worrying about my physical safety, please. You can worry about my sanity. I have a seven-year-old to care for." I stood up. "Come on, I need to be there two minutes ago."

I grabbed her arm and transported us to just outside the green door, and we strolled towards the Gateway.

Caitlin said, "Hey, cool, my beer didn't even spill. Oh, slag, when does this stop? Why don't you do it?" And then she threw up, narrowly missing the flower tub by the door.

PART TWO
TUESDAY

"But the Recorder said his father was right. Bullying *is* something only cowards do. Sometimes they pick on people who are different because they're afraid of being judged themselves.

The Recorder suggested the father should give his son more attention to discover what the child was covering up and what he was so frightened of being judged for."

The Recorder Always Knows Best: Cautionary Tales for Incautious Children by Margarita Encimera

CHAPTER
TEN

Tuesday, 9th February—Gateway Cottage—Gretna Green

"There will be someone, Mum. Like Grandma always says … *you gotta have faith.*" Autumn sang the last words over FaceTime to Aysha doing a creditable impersonation of George.

We were enjoying a peaceful start to the day. I half-listened as they made plans for their long weekend in Aberglas with Lewis. Autumn informed Aysha she was going to find someone who wanted an extra bridesmaid this afternoon. So she'd have to be back in the Gateway to be the best bridesmaid ever on Sunday fourteenth.

"Is it likely to happen, Nik?" Aysha raised her voice to get my attention, but she sounded more concerned than cross.

"Honestly, not sure—I was very careful not to promise. I only said if she found someone, she could." She nodded approvingly at me.

Later on, while Tilly slept on my bed and Autumn practised her breaststroke in my stupidly large, new bathtub, the Dola device behind my magical bathroom mirror came to life. It showed me the Gateway with Fi and Finn already at work. The Green sector was stuffed with yet more greenery. Presumably, there were people under all those branches. It was quite the traffic jam. "Niki, can you lower the glass barrier? The Hobs are waiting for access."

I connected with the power and lowered the barriers for all the realms. "Autumn, time to stop swimming in that bath. I need to catch up with Fi and find out when the couples will arrive."

After a healthy breakfast, with a lot of fruit, a nutrient-dense but dusty cereal and far too little bacon, we walked to the Gateway to give Tilly a chance to stretch her legs and empty herself.

"Auntie Nik, how do you know if peoples should get married?"

"They have a glow around them when they're together." I waved my hand around my head. "It's not there if they're apart, but once they're close enough to each other, the glow arrives. It's hard to explain."

"Like you and Tilly then?"

Whoa!? She was aware of those connections already? "What do you mean, baby?"

She turned her serious gaze on me. It told me I was being slow. "Tilly has the rainbow, and when you're cuddling her, you both have it. You and Dusha had it too yesterday."

"Did we?"

She gave me her disgusted look until I said, "Hey, I can't see myself. Can you see your own glow?"

"Oh. Didn't think of that."

I was still processing the idea that she was aware of people's soul bond glows. And thinking that might explain why, even as a grown woman, I'd always loved unicorns. Dusha was a soul animal too? The fae had soul bonds with their unicorns. But as a non-fae, I hadn't known that I could have one.

We walked through the area that used to have overgrown and eye-gouging trees, but it was clear now. Sage and Hedge had been working hard. Those overgrown branches were probably on their way to decorate the walls of the Gateway.

I recalled Ad'Rian's comments yesterday about Autumn's possible talents and asked, "Hey, do you want to play a game today?"

"Yes. What?" She stopped and turned to face me, dancing on the spot with excitement.

"Do you want to be my assistant and check the glows with me?"

"Yes. Is there rules? How do I won? I mean, what do I win?"

"Hmm, let's see. When the couples come in, you wink at me if you spot a glow. If you get twenty of the couples right, there's ice cream for you and Tilly after tea. If you get almost all of them right, I'll buy a unicorn from your wish list. But if you don't win, I get to pick the next bedtime storybook. Deal?"

"For reals?"

I almost sang, "Would I lie to you? I'm asking you, sugar?"

Autumn danced, making the quick updo I'd given her hair bounce like her favourite unicorn's tail, and finished the line off—her mum and I had passed some classic songs into family lore.

She stopped, offering me a high five. "Deal, but if you win and pick the book, can it be *A Wrinkle in Time*?"

"Mum says that's too old for you right now. How about *The Little Prince* or *The Hundred Dresses* instead?"

"But when will I be old enough?"

On this eternal question, we arrived at the green door adorned with its Scottish thistle that led to the

Gateway. As I walked in, Dola's voice crackled in my ear, "Niki, an email arrived from Prince Rollo of the Vikings, King Troels' heir. Do you wish to respond, or should I?"

My stomach immediately tightened. I'd thought the sealed gate would buy me some time free of Viking issues. Obviously, I was wrong.

"I'll take a look before we do anything. I'll be logged on in a minute."

I settled at the end of Fi's desk again and watched Autumn and Tilly chasing about. "Be careful, baby; the floor is slippery sometimes."

Tapping my earbud, I asked, "How did he even get this email through, Dola? Didn't you turn their access off?"

"Not exactly. Remember when Finn and I checked their emails to see if the Vikings were trying to get through to support the Pict dissidents?"

"Yeah."

"We had to allow the emails to send at their end. Then we held them here on the server, awaiting your decision. We left them there because I wanted more information about any other plans they might have."

This worried me. "It feels like a dreadful invasion of privacy. It was one thing when we suspected a crime, but just reading all their emails without any justification feels ... dirty."

Dola had obviously connected the three of us

because Finn's low voice came clearly through my earbud even though I couldn't actually see him behind his screen. He asked, "My lady, have you ever read the agreement the realms sign before they're allowed access to the Rainbow Network?"

"There's an agreement?"

"I wrote it myself." Dola sounded very smug. It baffled me how she could put emotion into an electronic voice. But she did. "Your gran agreed, reluctantly, to requests from the younger royals in almost all the Houses to let them access a network of some kind. You know the kingdoms only have the most basic communications. Elsie asked Fi to organise it. This is not one of Fi's strengths, so I sent her a proposal. She leapt at the chance to pass it off, and I have run it since."

"Did Fi even realise who you were back then?"

There was a pause. It lengthened.

"Dola?"

"I may have suggested I was a telecommunication specialist working for your gran."

I breathed a sigh of relief, "Oh well, that's true—so we're all good."

"We are?"

"Yes, you used your normal email address, I assume?" A mumbled assent came through my ear. "Then it's not your fault if no one ever bothered to find out who you were, is it?"

Finn laughed. "She's right, Dola. I asked who you were the first time you emailed me."

"I've read Rollo's email. It's very polite—what do we think? Options please." The email was cautious and courteous. Everything I'd learned about the Vikings so far had been negative, so the polite, even caring tone was a surprise.

Rollo, the prince and heir apparent of the Viking kingdom, said he understood there had been problems, and they had yet to be resolved. However, he had eight distressed women and eight unhappy men trying to comfort them. Their bonds had been approved, and they were scheduled to be in the Gateway on February fourteenth. He wondered if I could see any way those bondings could go ahead. He realised it would change nothing about the current issue, which would remain to be dealt with.

I felt completely out of my depth. I didn't know or understand the Vikings well enough to be sure if I could take his email at face value. My gran had always forbidden me from entering the Viking realm when I was a child. And she kept them out of the Gateway unless they had appointments, whereas the Red Celts, the Fae and the Scottish had been allowed to come and go pretty much as they wished.

"Any thoughts on the email, Fi?" Then I saw she was still reading it.

Finn got up from his desk and walked over to our

side. "I told you about him last week, Niki. He's not the playboy he wants people to think he is."

I remembered that conversation. Finn had told me Rollo wasn't just handsome Viking warrior eye candy. He had several degrees from excellent universities and had helped Finn and L'eon when the Rainbow Network expanded the service to the realms, which made me wonder…

"Finn, couldn't Rollo have hacked the network after Dola shut the Vikings off? Didn't you say he did advanced computing stuff at Cambridge?"

Fin nodded. "And his Masters at Edinburgh. Yes, he could do it, but he wouldn't."

I'd obviously made some shitty assumptions about Rollo. I was a bit ashamed I'd allowed his half-clothed body and oiled muscles to disconnect my brain the only time I'd met him at my ascension. It also showed with my previously weak psychic Gift I could be fooled just as easily as the next person. I was starting to take my new powers for granted, wasn't I? I thought I'd like to meet Rollo again, now I'd really ascended.

To Finn, I said, "Why not?"

Slowly, as though he was trying to decide how much to say, Finn began, "Cait and I know him better than some of our counterparts in the other realms. L'eon and Dai, they're sooo much older than us."

I hid my smile. L'eon really was much older. He

was Fae and had their crazily slow aging. But I must tell Dai that Finn had lumped him in with a 150-year-old Fae. Finn probably thought if I wasn't the Recorder, I'd be ready for my pension too.

Finn added, "Rollo's older than us too, but he was always kind to me. All Troels' sons are slag-brained and the two older ones are the worst. At events … you know I grew up … mostly without my dad. He grew up without his mum… It …well, sometimes … look, he was always kind," he finished defiantly as though I would argue with him, and that was a lot of words Finn had forced himself to share.

"Isn't Queen Randi his mother, then?"

Fi chimed in, "No, Randi is Troels' fourth wife. Rollo's mum was Troels' older brother's widow."

"He married his brother's widow?" Gods and Goddesses! Every time I thought I'd got a handle on these realms, something else came along to surprise me. "Then why is Rollo the heir? I thought they were pretty traditional about that."

Fi looked as though we had bumped up against yet one more thing she thought I should know but didn't. In a patient voice, she explained, "No, my lady. I think you might be confusing two things. Queen Randi is King Troels' fourth wife and a pleasant woman from a very wealthy family. The first two wives were shield maidens. I think King Troels met his match with them. The third died. I don't have much info about her. No one discusses her. But Inge, the first wife, is an excellent source of gossip, and she runs a thriving export business to Caledonia, so she and I speak often."

I nodded. OK, good to know, but it didn't answer my question, did it?

But Fi wasn't done. "The second part is, although people often refer to Rollo as his son, he's actually Troels' nephew. The eldest brother, Rollo's father, was killed in an accident. Rollo's mum only lived long enough to give birth to him before she followed her husband into death. Elsie always said it was all fishy —apparently there was gossip at the time, and she never trusted Troels. But he became Rollo's guardian and King in Trust."

I was intrigued. Then why was Troels still the king? What age was the Viking majority? Shouldn't Rollo be the king by now? I'd have to catch up on all this soon. But right now, what did I say? My Gift was no help; it wanted to see Rollo. Maybe hearing him would work.

"Do we have a phone number for him?"

Fi produced one. "Would you like me to call him and then transfer it to you, my lady?"

"Sure, thanks, use my phone, will you?" Then Dola could hear both sides of the call, and I might need her insights.

I took a deep breath and thought about the man

my gran had called that little bastard Thor-wannabe, Surfer Dude Viking Boy. He'd had warm eyes, a sexy smile and killer abs; I remembered him vividly. At my ascension, he'd seemed to want to distance himself from the man I'd believed was his father. Let's see what my Gift could tell me about him now it was so much more powerful.

CHAPTER
ELEVEN

HRH appeared, as always, out of nowhere, strolled across the conference table and jumped up onto the anvil. She sneered down at me from her perch.

Fi said, "I'll put you through to the Recorder now."

I waited.

Nothing happened.

I turned around just in time to see Fi give the phone a very femine smile as she added, "Thank you, sire. You're very kind," before handing my phone back to me.

"Niki McKnight, how may I help you today?" I realised I'd reverted on autopilot to the way I'd answered the phone at the registration office for eighteen years.

"You're much more welcoming than your grandmother, my lady. Thank you for reaching out. I appreciate it." I could hear the smile in his voice.

"Am I? Do tell—how did Gran answer the phone?"

He laughed—a warm, friendly sound. "She often said something like 'Recorder's Office. Stop mumbling and speak up now. What do you want? I haven't got all day, you know!'" His mimicry was accurate, he'd even got Gran's Lancashire accent.

I laughed. "That definitely sounds like Gran. So, what can I help you with?"

He sighed. "I would have called to apologise earlier, my lady, but our phones won't make outgoing calls while this ban is on. So I emailed, hoping I might reach you through …back channels." Huh, that sounded like he knew we were monitoring their emails. Well, Finn said he was smart and computer-savvy.

His tone stiffened. "I've made my opinion clear to Leif. He *will* apologise to you himself once his broken jaw can be un-wired and he can speak coherently. However, that may be some weeks as the Fae healers are refusing to aid him."

They were? Ad'Rian must have been cross on my behalf. Without thinking, I said, "I didn't break his jaw, did I?"

"No, no, I did that myself."

"Okaaay?"

Finn had told me Rollo had broken Leif's nose and his cheekbone after his assault on Caitlin and me—but he'd said nothing about his jaw. I decided not to mention it. It just felt rude because Finn obtained that info by hacking their emails.

Rollo had an almost perfectly neutral British accent. Nothing like Leif with his harsh, guttural Scandinavian accent. There was just the slightest twang of something my ear perceived as Northern European, Dutch, German or even Scandinavian, but it was very soft, attractive and almost imperceptible. His English was perfect, probably thanks to his years of studying in the UK.

"My lady, I don't blame you for your actions."

Well, that was big of him.

But he continued, "I would have done worse myself. The current problem is I have eight distressed men and eight weeping women."

My left shoulder pinged. *Ah-ha, the lies begin.*

But then he added, "Well, that's not true, and I shouldn't say it. I have five weeping women and three furious shield-maidens who are currently destroying every practice target on the training grounds. But it's the same emotion, even if the outward expression appears different."

My right shoulder agreed with him.

He wasn't what I'd expected, this man. After all, I'd learned about his uncle and the now more than forty petitions alleging paternity claims against him. When I added in the odious Leif's attitude, I'd assumed Rollo would be cut from the same cloth.

I'd wanted this call so I could use my Gift on him. I needed to ask him something requiring a long-ish answer. "What do you suggest we do to get around the sealed gate?"

He began to talk, and I opened my Gift to its fullest, feeling my behind leave the chair seat slightly. The power was obviously heightening my abilities.

I heard, "I've had a few ideas …"

And then a tsunami wave of emotions crashed over me.

His energy writhed with fury. He was angry with almost everyone, including himself. He was also frustrated in every possible way. With himself, with Troels, with his future kingdom, and sexually. How the hell could a man who looked like he did be sexually frustrated? The picture of him at my ascension flashed into my head again. Half dressed, sexy as hell, with Thor-style crazy blond hair and muscles in all the right places, which might explain my gran's nickname for him. She hadn't avoided all modern movies, no matter what Mabon thought.

Rollo was also desperately sad and lonely. There was a huge hole where his happy vibes should have been. I dragged myself back to the conversation and tamped down my Gift.

The problem with using my Gift on the phone is I often missed what the caller was saying. I tuned back in, in time to hear, "I'm cognisant of the difficulties and could offer assurances on behavioural standards." Cognisant? Behavioural standards? This guy was verifying everything Finn had told me about his education. He was no dumb warrior. So why did he deliberately try to appear that way in public?

Then Autumn sidled up to me and made the sign she wanted to whisper. This had started when she was tiny and wanted to tell me things without her mother hearing. "One moment please," I muted my phone and asked, "What, baby?"

"He needs to come here with the ladies, Auntie Nik." She stood back and looked at me. Her expectant expression showed complete faith I would work out her meaning.

Thor, I mean Rollo, had paused. I tried to gather my confused thoughts and said, "Prince Hrólf, I'm—

"Oh, please don't do that, my lady. Call me Rollo, won't you?"

"OK, Rollo, there's an issue, apart from the Gate. We have seven approved bonds, but you mentioned eight women. Could I pass you back to Fi to check the names, and I'll call you back in fifteen minutes when I've checked some things and considered what you've said?"

"Of course, my lady, thank you for even trying to resolve this for the girls. Well, and their men. To be truthful, the guys are only holding it together because the women aren't. But they're going to lose it soon as well."

I caught Fi's eye. "I'll transfer you to Fi, and I'll get back to you shortly."

To Autumn I said, "Come sit with me, baby. What's bothering you?"

My head was spinning. I needed coffee. Something was very wrong with Autumn, and HRH was watching me very carefully. Did I feed her this morning?

Stroking Autumn's shoulder, which was very tense, I asked, "Your Majesty, did you want breakfast?"

"Thank you, yes. But primarily I am concerned about Rollo."

The penny dropped, she wanted to know if I was going to open the Viking doorway. She must have taken even more bets on when it would be unsealed.

"Autumn, baby, do you want a drink and a snack?"

"No, thank you, I'm not hungry, but can I have a hot chocolate please, and one for Rosie too? She's still sad."

I looked around and saw Rosemary, her head down and her shoulders up around her ears, slowly lifting branches into place.

"Sure, see if you can cheer her up. Let's ask Dola what can she do to help."

I ordered tuna for the cat, hot chocolate for the girls and a coffee for me. "Why does he need to come here with the ladies?"

Autumn looked crestfallen and shook her head. "I don't know."

She was rubbing her tummy. I knew that sensation all too well. Ad'Rian might be right about her talents. "Does it feel as though something bad might happen if he doesn't?"

She nodded so hard, her ponytail swung about crazily. "YESSSS!"

She wrapped her arms around me. "And that something good won't happen unless you let him come. If you say you'll let him come with all the ladies, but specially one 'ticular lady, it'll all be better."

I picked up the two hot chocolates. Dola had excelled herself with edible glitter, a unicorn topper, and a sparkly silver net over the froth and marshmallows. It was a seven-year-old's dream drink. We would hope adult Rosemary was OK with it too.

Firmly, I said, "Don't worry, sweetie; I'll tell him he can come and bring all the ladies. OK now?" She regarded me thoughtfully, rubbed her stomach one last time, and nodded at me.

I took her and the drinks over to Rosemary. "Please don't despair. I am looking into this, I promise. Can Autumn help you?"

She nodded at me, and I handed her a hot chocolate. "Autumn wondered if this might help cheer you up."

Oh dear heavens, she was another squealer. I must have been very bad in a past life to deserve this many squealing women in this lifetime. Tilly bounced over as she always did when anyone squealed—it was her usual clue that Autumn had something fun happening. And I, coward that I am, left them all to it.

As I picked up my own coffee, I noticed no tuna had arrived. I huffed. I'd thought Dola was softening in her attitude when, at the weekend, she'd ordered a seafood pizza and allowed Finn to give it to HRH. I'd obviously been wrong. I sighed.

"Dola, I'm starving. That crunchy, dusty cereal for breakfast didn't fill me at all. May I have scrambled egg and salmon with toast please?"

It arrived; I picked up the toast; I really was still

hungry. Then I pushed the scrambled egg and smoked salmon towards HRH and walked outside for a breath of fresh air so I could speak to Dola without being overheard.

I tapped my earbud. "I have no idea what Rollo said on our call after he said he had some ideas. I was deep into my Gift. Did you, by any chance, record his side of the conversation?"

"Yes, would you like me to replay it for you?"

I was so glad I'd offered her a job. She made my life so much easier. But we really would have to talk about this not feeding HRH nonsense. Her holding a grudge for centuries was excessive.

The wholewheat toast was delicious, the coffee even better, and I listened as she played my own voice back—it always sounded strange. Did I *really* sound like that to other people? Rollo was taking this seriously. He was offering a surety. Was "surety" a Viking legal term? I'd ask the Book.

He was prepared to bring everyone, ensure their participation in whatever was necessary, and remove them again. But, and this part really made me laugh, "Please, my lady, I swear by my blade, Nanok, I will do whatever you wish that is within my own power. But please I beg you just get these couples married, erm, bonded, erm, whatever I should call it so I can get them the hell out of my longhouse. I have eight women and all their female relatives here. My father has the men because the brides' mothers refused to stay with him. I'm in real danger of losing my mind."

It felt like an unusually frank admission, but given what I'd been hearing about Troels' reputation, it wasn't surprising. It sounded like the mothers of the brides had their heads screwed on to me. So what should I do?

Back in the Gateway, I headed straight for Fi, who was talking to Caitlin. I'd noticed my hearing was keener inside the Gateway itself. Was it just the excellent acoustics, or was it something the power did? As I got closer, I caught Fi's comment, "Ye cannae be serious?" Fi normally had a neutral local accent close to what I thought of as standard English, but if something was bringing her Scottish side to the fore, I wanted to know what had upset her. It was only her second day back at work—this couldn't be good. I hustled over.

"Everything OK?"

Fi looked shocked and angry, but she nodded at me. Caitlin said, "Fi was just asking about Leif. I filled her in."

A surge of fury rushed through me. The problems that abusive asshole was still causing me and now

Rollo too. I'd followed Caitlin's suggestion to seal the gate to give the Vikings time to get the facts about Leif. I'd fully expected Troels to send profuse apologies within the day and normal gate passage to resume. But the yellow Viking gate was still sealed a week later, and we'd heard freaking nothing from the Viking king.

Fi said, "I can't picture a Leif, so I've not met him, but, Niki, things like that just don't happen here. I often worked alone in here, and I've always felt safe. It's doesn't seem right at all." She sounded angry and worried. "Caitlin didn't seem to know what caused it or why he was here?"

"Do you know Kaiden?" Her face broke into a smile.

"Oh, yeah, he's lovely and," she fanned herself, "fit. Aren't the hottest men so often gay?"

"Did you know he was the Vikings' candidate for the Knight Adjutancy?"

"No, but my mum told me last night that Jamie disappeared, and no one has seen John either. That was hard enough to believe. But Mum saved the local papers for me—it was all in there."

What the heck had they printed in the local papers? I'd need to fill Fi in on the real events. But not now. There was enough to do today.

"Oh, I've not seen those—I'd love a quick look at them."

Fi nodded at me, made a note on her ever-present checklist, and I refocused on the current problem.

"Well, Kaiden and L'eon were the emergency bonding I mentioned to you yesterday. Kaiden lives in Fae now they're bonded. That's why it was an emergency. Once they were bonded, Ad'Rian could give him Fae citizenship so the Vikings couldn't …" I trailed off.

Caitlin had no such qualms and finished my sentence, "Eliminate their mistakes."

I cringed, but she was only saying what my Gift had shown me last week.

I turned back to Fi. "So the Vikings sent their second candidate, who turned out to be the odious and abusive Leif. After Caitlin had finished with him, he still hadn't learnt to keep his hands off women. He grabbed me by the crotch, and I gave him a shove, which fixed the problem." I paused. "You know Dola will have video footage if you want to see it."

Caitlin was making a circular motion with her hand. "You should watch it, Fi—he looked like a bowling ball—it was hilarious."

Into the air, Caitlin said, "Dola, could you send the footage of Leif to Fi's screen please?" There was no response from Dola, but then Fi's screen lit up as we all watched Leif push himself up behind Caitlin, saw her quick flick of iron beads in his face.

As she locked his arm behind him, Fi glanced at

Caitlin, admiration on her face. "Could you teach me to do that?"

I laughed because I'd thought exactly the same. Then, seeing Fi's hurt face, I said, "No, no. I agree, Fi. I'm laughing because I said exactly the same. Caitlin should run some self-defence classes for us all."

Caitlin looked thoughtful.

Fi smiled and went back to watching the footage as I offered Leif tissues for his bleeding nose, and he clamped his hand first on my boob and then between my legs. Fi frowned and then let out a whoop as Leif turned into a bowling ball and careened down the Yellow sector.

"You don't look that strong, Niki?" Fi was shaking her head.

"I'm really not, but I'd just ascended. I got a power boost, and I wasn't very good at controlling it. I truly did only shove him. But I was screaming obscenities at him in my head. I think the power wasn't happy with him either." From the video, we heard the multiple cracks of Leif's bones as he landed, and Fi winced again.

Caitlin said, "I wonder if we should put that footage up? The other day someone said the Recorder had 'taken against the Vikings for no reason.' Should we show them why?"

I said, "Maybe. Let's talk about it, but perhaps not

this week—it's supposed to be all fluffy pink romantic and happy bondings, this week, isn't it?"

Caitlin nodded. Fi made another note.

Remembering what I'd actually come back in here for, I said to Fi, "So, did you work out why we have seven approved bondings, but Rollo thinks there should be eight?"

She nodded and looked unhappy. "Your gran saw and approved seven couples. The eighth …" She sighed. "How to put this politely?"

I was intrigued. "Politely or otherwise, it's only us. Just say it, Fi."

"The eighth is a princess and her chosen match." She clicked her mouse and scrolled. "I have the original email here from last autumn, if you'd like to see it?"

"Just read me the relevant bit or tell me. I promised Rollo I'd get back to him, and I feel like my fifteen minutes are running out. He was very polite, so I don't want to be unnecessarily rude."

Fi rolled her eyes to the very high ceiling of the gateway, sighed again and then, in a monotone, read, "'The Recorder is a public servant; our match has been approved by the Gods. She will conduct our marriage. There is no authority higher than the Gods.'"

A laugh burst out of me, and Fi looked shocked. "Sorry, Fi, but you've no idea how many entitled women I've married during the years I worked as a registrar. They all think the rules, the law or even the appointment diary don't apply to them. It's a pleasant change to be back on familiar ground instead of all the 'my ladying' and bowing I've had since I arrived here."

Now it was Fi's turn to laugh. "Your gran hated those types. She ignored her and didn't even call her in to confirm the bond."

"Oh, I don't like them either. But I bet I'll like them a lot more as the Recorder than I did when I really was a powerless public servant, with all my calls recorded 'for quality monitoring,' and bound by the rules, the laws and the required politeness."

The more I thought about it, the more I liked the opportunity for eccentricity that this role gave me.

Fi might be a useful source of gossip. "Do you know anything about her?"

She grinned at me and twirled her ever-present pen, "Oh, yes, I do." Her grin had changed to a smirk.

"Spill the tea please."

Caitlin frowned and looked around in confusion. "Tea?"

In perfect unison, Fi and I said, "Gossip," and smirked at each other. "My potential Knight obviously doesn't spend her evenings watching reality TV."

Fi actually grinned conspiratorially at me. We were making progress. "Princess Karina, whom I call Princess Entitled, privately anyway, regularly used the Gateway. She came through to 'go to the gym.'" Fi made air quotes with her fingers. But I wasn't getting it.

"And the problem with that is …?"

"She's a Viking. Their training programs are legendary! Why would she need to go to a Scottish gym?"

"Ah, I see. So where was she really going?"

"To the gym."

I was losing the plot here. I just glared at her and looked at my watch. She took my hint.

"Sorry, Niki. Ross, you know the photographer—we just spoke about him?" I nodded. "Well, his friend, Ben is the trainer in residence for the gym at the posh hotel. The one opposite the Blacksmiths?" She gave me an enquiring look.

I nodded. I'd seen the large, modern hotel when Tilly and I were exploring, a very upmarket place.

She twirled her pen in a circle as though to say *and there you have it*. "She's been visiting him for about two years now. Sometimes for several weeks at a time."

TIES THAT BOND IN GRETNA GREEN

I was confused. "So, is she cheating on this man she's supposed to be marrying?"

But Fi was shaking her head. "No, no, their engagement was only announced a few months ago. The princess was always so happy, she would dance through here. But the last time she came through in December, she was in tears. I got the impression it was an arranged marriage thing. She did tell me she'd just met the future groom, and he was a gutless idiot with no brain, no muscles and no sense of humour."

Every time I thought I'd got a handle on these realms, some simple piece of information would blow it apart. "An arranged marriage in this day and age—seriously?" I supposed I'd better get to the bottom of this.

I thought for a minute. "Would you call Rollo back for me? Tell him we're doing the checks this week and slot them in on Thursday with the other problems. Tell him we'll confirm their matches and schedule them in for Valentine's if all goes well. But we will hold him responsible to deal with any issues. You'd better add my gran didn't approve the bond for Princess Whateverhernameis." I thought about it. "But she can come on Thursday too with all the other problem children; sounds to me as though she'll fit right in."

Fi murmured agreement, and I walked away.

Then a picture of all their mothers and female relatives whom Rollo had mentioned flashed into my mind. I didn't need them all deciding to come too. So I added, "Fi, please confirm I will allow passage *only* for the names on our list and Rollo. Anyone else, especially any random relatives, must apply directly to King Troels for passage through to the Gateway. Let's see how he deals with that."

CHAPTER
TWELVE

Back at the cottage for lunch, I was taking my auntie responsibilities seriously. Aysha had asked me to try to get Autumn to remember to eat. We settled at the kitchen table with club sandwiches, Autumn's request, and a salad—Dola's choice for a healthy meal for a child. Had Dola and Aysha been talking about diet, I wondered? Tilly tucked into her chicken, and I put some tuna out for HRH, in case I forgot to feed her later with all of the bonding checks I had to do.

Feeling as if I was closing the door after the horse had bolted, I should probably have checked this before I agreed, but I'd trusted my gut and Autumn's. I grabbed the Book. "What does it mean when a Viking swears by his blade? Oh, and what would it mean if a Viking prince offered a surety?"

The Book quickly offered a page:

Swearing by a blade, especially a named blade, is a Viking's penultimate oath. Swearing by Odin would be the ultimate.

Vikings rarely offer surety. But the term refers to one who takes responsibility for another's performance or behaviour.

It is an ancient concept that began in the old world. There it referred to a guarantor for a debt. More recently (the last millennium), and in militaristic societies, it commonly means the individual giving surety will take responsibility for the conduct of a third party.

I giggled at the idea that the last thousand years was "more recently," but it confirmed for me these bondings were important to Rollo. I wondered why. Crying women, while annoying, didn't seem enough to offer what sounded like a serious oath. Was there some subtler issue here I was missing? How much power could Rollo really wield, while Troels was stuck somewhere in the philandering sixteenth century?

As though she were reading my mind, Dola chimed in, "Niki, we received four more petitions against Troels. I acknowledged their filing. Petitioners may be passing the word to other possible victims to submit their own petitions. You are gaining a reputation for fixing unfixable problems. News is getting around about the solution to the Pictish predicament."

With Autumn at the table, I didn't want to discuss the fast-growing pile of parental liability arbitration cases filed against Troels, so I said, "Let's get Valentine's Day out of the way, and then I'll work on those petitions. How long do I have left to deal with them?"

I needed to ask Aysha if she thought the women should form a sort of class action, or if I should hear them all separately. It could take me months. How many times would I have to listen to the details of *we bonked; I got pregnant; now he doesn't want to know?* I'd help them if I could, but I was not turning the Recorder's Office into Baby Daddy Central.

"Your ascension reset the timer on all the petitions, so you have until the end of March to send the first ones your decision about whether you will hear them. Once you decide, you can schedule them for later. But there are several other minor petitions you might wish to hear before then."

"OK, let's talk about those later in the week." I hoped she would take the hint I meant after I'd handed Autumn back to her mum.

. . .

My phone buzzed with a text message. I smiled when I saw who it was from.

DAI:

See you later today? I'm best man for Glyn. We're coming in for the bond confirmations. Time for a coffee?

NIKI:

Love to. Want to stay for tea? Autumn is visiting.

DAI:

Yes, please. I look forward to meeting her and seeing you. x

A kiss, hmm. That was confusing, wasn't it? Did he mean it as a kiss, or did he just add X's on autopilot as some people did?

"Is this a good wink, Auntie Nik?"

Startled out of my Dai-induced confusion, I said, "Sorry, baby, I missed it. Do it again."

Autumn promptly closed both her eyes. I tried not to giggle.

"No, you've not quite got it. Are you practising for telling me about the glows?"

Over the next ten minutes, we discovered Autumn couldn't yet wink reliably. "Maybe instead, you could hold something in your right hand if you think they have a bond and put it in your left if they don't?"

With a thoughtful gleam in her eye, she disappeared into her bedroom. I took the opportunity to tell Dola to keep the conversation about work issues child-friendly until after Autumn was asleep or out of the room. Troels' decades of allegedly impregnating any woman who stood still long enough were not child-friendly. But it was my fault, not hers. Most adults censored themselves on auto-pilot when a child was around. I sometimes forgot Dola wasn't most adults.

There was silence. Then my phone pinged with an apology and a message from her saying she would research child-appropriate topics. "You might just chat with Aysha about her guidelines. That would probably please her."

"Thank you, Niki. I will do so when she gets home.

Autumn ran back at full pelt, chased by Tilly and clutching her unicorn finger puppet. "Sparkle can show you, Auntie Nik. Right hand for right and left for no glow, no go. OK?"

I rubbed Sparkle's horn for luck and grinned at her.

When Autumn went to wash her hands and face to remove the salad dressing, Dola said, "Niki, I requested Lis or Mag to meet you in the Gateway as you asked."

"Oh, good. Who's coming and when?"

"They are too busy right now and said they will get back to me."

"Are they still sulking? Did you tell them what I wanted to discuss?"

"No, I simply passed on your message that the Recorder requested them to meet her in the Gateway at their earliest convenience."

"OK, thanks." Lis would be furious when she worked out my request was about her granddaughters, but that wasn't my problem.

Back in the Gateway, Fi had changed into an attractive, professional peach skirt suit. It toned perfectly with copper-coloured suede shoes and a striking twisted copper hair ornament. She looked fresh and elegant and made me feel scruffy.

"Lovely suit. It looks terrific, Fi, particularly wonderful with your glorious hair."

She blushed and mumbled, "Thank you."

"Would you ask the Hob triplets to pop in with their future spouses for a bond check on Thursday, too? I'm still not sure what to do, but we need to know if they have soul bonds. Are we ready to go otherwise? And what do I need to do?"

"Yes, we are. I've arranged for them to come in groups as usual. Finn has put a notification on the Rainbow news portal that the Gateway is closed to other traffic this afternoon, Thursday afternoon, and all day on Sunday for preparations and bondings."

"Is that usual too?"

"Well, no, because of the one-in, one-out rule, we had more control and far less traffic during my lady Elsie's tenure. But since I got back, even in a day and a half, I've seen how much busier it's become. We don't need people trying to push through the middle of nervous brides and grooms." Now she sounded uncertain, but I wasn't sure why. So I said what I did whenever Dola sounded unsure, "Great idea and good thought about putting a notification on the portal."

Her shoulders lowered, and her smile was much less tentative. "All you need to do today is meet the couples individually. Your gran used to do the initial check, then, in this meeting, she'd meet briefly with each couple individually. She …" Fi trailed off.

I waited.

"Of course, Niki, you can do it however you like."

I shook my head. "Nope, I'm happy to be guided, truly."

"Well, your gran used to do the checks at the anvil. She said the proximity and strength—she called it the weight of the iron—kept the damn fool questions to a minimum and let her get finished before hell froze over. When she did it at her desk, it dragged on."

I tried to picture it.

"You know, Fi, she might have a good point. We've got a heck of a lot of people to see, and with Autumn staying, I don't want this dragging on for hours. It's going to be hard enough for me doing it for the first time and with so many couples to get through."

Fi observed, "The Picts and the Scots tend to drag it out a bit more. The iron doesn't bother them."

"I think Caitlin might be my secret weapon for the Picts." I looked at my watch. "She should be back any minute. And she can intimidate the Scots too. How many Scots are there?"

Fi consulted her ever-present checklist. "Just four couples, but actually, they're not Scottish. They're coming in through the Green gate from all over the UK. But they're from the other kingdoms and just work in the UK. Gretna Green has pretty good transport links, airport access, train station, the motorway, you know? Most of them will arrive here. Get checked. Then go through to their home realm until they come back with their families for the bonding on Sunday. And Ross, of course, he'll be here any minute too."

"Ross?" I vaguely remembered the name, but I

felt like I'd heard a lot of unfamiliar names in the last couple of days.

"Ross, the photographer? We spoke about him? Do you not remember him? The three of us were all at school together. His friend runs the gym the Viking Princess Karina visits."

I tried to picture a small boy called Ross with zero success and shook my head.

Fiona prompted, "We called him Red at school, although he isn't anymore."

A picture of a slightly strange kid with bright ginger hair, who had disliked Jamie, popped into my brain. "Oh, now I have him. He was always telling Jamie Fergusson to shut up and stop boasting?"

She laughed. "That's him."

"Why is he coming again?"

"He's the photographer; he became a talented visual artist. Yes, he can be a little temperamental and a bit standoffish, well, with me anyway. They have the contracts for some of the normal weddings in the village. But the realms pay much better, and he says the outfits in here are far more upmarket and far less white." There was something sad in her eyes, but before I could track it down, she finished, "And Finn is livestreaming it to the realms, so that will be fun."

I gaped at her. This time, the importance of what I was about to do truly clicked in my head. My knees wobbled, and I planted my butt in a chair. I'd thought this was the part of the Recorder's role I could do. I had almost twenty years of experience with it, after all. It should have been the easiest bit. But I hadn't fully understood it at all. Photographers, livestreaming and upmarket outfits. I probably didn't want to do this in my jeans and shirt. It wouldn't be appropriate for couples who viewed this as the equivalent of St Paul's or Notre Dame Cathedral, would it? I needed to get changed.

Autumn and Tilly were happily helping Rosemary as I rushed towards the green door.

"Fi, need to get changed. I'll be back in a minute. Call the Hobs about Thursday, please." She was wringing her hands, and her lips were a tight, thin line under their copper lipstick.

As soon as I was out of sight of the doorway, I checked my watch and popped myself over to my bedroom. I stripped off and put on the pearl-grey trouser suit I'd worn for my ascension. I needed to make a trip to my Manchester house and collect more clothes. Perhaps tomorrow when I went down to get Aysha.

To the suit, I added comfortable low-heeled court shoes in dark grey leather with wonderful cushioned insoles that had got me through many a long day in the registrar's office. I wouldn't make the mistake I'd made at my ascension of wearing too-high heels and falling out them of them while Finn was livestreaming. That was not the impression I wanted to give the realms of their brand-new Recorder.

I did a quick but thorough job of my face and hair, making myself look groomed and authoritative. I really needed a new hairstyle. Getting my hair cut shouldn't be the hardest job of this week, should it? I was new up here, so I didn't care who I went to. Surely one of the many damn hairdressers could fit me in?

"Dola, did you have any joy getting me a hair appointment?"

"I am sorry, Niki. I am continuing to call salons further afield in between other tasks. But Fi was correct; everyone is booked up. Their tone is quite mocking when I ask if they have any available appointments this week. One woman said, 'Perhaps you'd like an instant facelift before lunch if you're wishing on a star.' I think that was sarcasm?"

"Oh well, the realms will just have to take me as I am. Who would have thought getting a haircut would be the thing that defeated us? Thank you for trying."

I settled the Recorder's robe on my shoulders, straightened my Recorder's star pendant so it peeped through the keyhole design of the robe, and added the new dangling earrings the Quack Pack had given me with their thanks for helping them sort out their 1000-year-old mess. I admired the matching seven-pointed stars and finished myself off with a deeper shade of lipstick than I'd normally choose. The mirror told me it was as good as it was going to get until I could get an appointment with a new hairdresser.

"Are you OK, Niki?"

"I think so. Fi just enlightened me about how important this is to the prospective couples. I thought it was just a necessary admin day."

"Your gran used to tell her friend Tina there would be less fuss for a royal engagement."

"Yup, I just realised that."

"And, of course, Finn and I are streaming it for the first time, so that might be exciting too."

Could the pressure get any higher? "Fi just told me. Did I approve that?"

"No, is it a problem?"

"Not exactly, but I'd have liked a warning, so I had time to stop looking like a bag lady in a pair of tatty jeans."

I was being childish, and I knew it. The clash between the picture I'd had in my head of a necessary admin day, which I'd thought today would be, and how everyone else seemed to view it was making me shaky.

I've never been a woman who admired expensive designer things—well, I'd never had the money. But the emotions I'd picked up from Fi suggested I hadn't grasped some of the future brides had started getting ready for this afternoon's event—yesterday.

I landed back outside the green door exactly two minutes after I'd left. Time travel was brilliant sometimes. Fi was outside too and on her phone. I heard her say, "Got to go. Hurry him up, will you? She's back, and he should be here already." I watched as she switched her phone to selfie mode and checked her face.

We strolled into the Gateway together. I was doing my best to give the appearance of a woman who had, if not everything else, at least herself under control.

Fi gave me a smile. "I didn't know if you could do the super-speed thing yet. Your gran used to do it when she'd forgotten an event. But not to your standard. That dress is beautiful." She reached out to touch it and then hesitated. I nodded.

"It's so soft, but it's not a dress, is it? More like the coat part of a coat and dress ensemble. I left a message for Lavender, the Hobs triplet, saying I've scheduled them in."

I nodded and wondered who else she'd been calling. It was none of my business, was it? She was a hard-working adult and could take a moment for a personal call if she needed to. She continued to stroke my rainbow robe as we walked, and I explained, "It's called the Recorder's robe. Apparently it's ancient, but it doesn't look it. According to Dola, my gran said it made her feel like a damn parrot, and she wouldn't wear it. But I like it—it reminds me I'm at work."

When we reached the centre, Fi glanced around and seemed to find everything to her liking.

"Are we ready to go?"

Fi nodded, and I saw she held the little purple device that checked my power level. "Hey, what do you call that? I've used it, and Finn has too. He pulled a ton of data off it for me, but we didn't know its name."

"Elsie just called it the power-checker."

"How disappointing. I hoped it had a cool name."

Fi winked at me. "Then why don't you give it a cool name? If you want the truth, I always think of it as the purple peril." I raised an eyebrow, wondering why, and she continued, "Your gran never liked the results. I usually kept a cup of tea and some biscuits on hand for her. For after the temper tantrum, you know?"

I had no idea what she was talking about—but I wanted her to feel part of the team—so I just grinned at her as if I understood. "Shall we get this party started?"

Fi nodded, and I pulled power until it coated me, adding a layer of rainbow light to the Recorder's robe. If it was an important day, I'd better look like I was an important Recorder, hadn't I? Then I coated my left hand in power, ready to wake the anvil. It always looked to me as though I wore one rainbow-coloured boxing glove. But the power didn't feel quite right again.

Fi stumbled backwards, her eyes enormous and her jaw dropping open. She looked from me to the purple peril and back at me.

Finn arrived. "Told you she was strong, Fi. Whoops, careful, my lady; it's 16006 again."

This instability thing had happened after I fully connected with the power and got a huge power boost. The power worked best when the amount I drew showed as a prime number on the purple device. No one knew why, but everyone could feel the difference. Mabon had told me to breathe in and relax. I did that now and felt something shift.

"16007, prime number. All normal now," Finn commented.

Fi was looking at Finn, then at the purple peril, and back to Finn. "This is NORMAL?" I heard the edges of panic in her rising voice, and she'd gone pale.

I grinned at her. "Well, I keep telling you I haven't got everything nailed down yet, Fi. Sometimes it takes a little adjusting, that's all."

Fi opened and closed her mouth several times, breathed in, and finally got out, "Well, I guess, unlike Elsie, you won't be having temper tantrums because the power won't do what you want! I was expecting to see a three-figure number here, Niki. Not a five-figure one. Your gran's lifetime high was around a thousand. She told me she'd hit 1100 once, but I never saw anything that high. Towards the end, she struggled to get above 500! And what are all these colours?" She gestured at me and my left hand.

I'd better take this slowly. I couldn't afford for her to lose her shit now. Carefully, I said, "Fi, I'm sure it's a surprise. But we have plenty of time in the future to get up to speed with each other. Remember, it's only your second day back?"

Her breathing was calmer now. She nodded. "Yes, yes, change can be good." It sounded as though she planned to repeat the mantra to herself until she believed it. "I was just startled. Sorry."

"Did you, by any chance, make a nice cup of tea in case I had a tantrum like Gran?"

Fi nodded sheepishly.

"Excellent, let's put some sugar in it for you then. I think your need is greater."

She giggled now, produced the tea, and swallowed gratefully, dunking a ginger nut into the cup.

"OK, listen, Fi, I need your support today. Because I've no idea how this is supposed to go. I'll need your guidance. The power is stable now, and it will stay stable the whole day. I really have a lot more of it than Gran did. We can chat about it tomorrow if you like, but for now, take a minute and then give me the nod when you're ready to go."

Finn was patting Fi's back, and he appeared to be holding a bar of chocolate. Goddess bless a man with sisters.

Fi took the chocolate, muttered a heartfelt thank you to Finn, sipped her tea and breathed. "Just one thing, Niki. What *is* your high point with the power? Oh, no, two things. Why is it so bright and colourful?"

"I've no idea. I can tell there's a lot more I could draw—but I've not tested it yet. I keep meaning to gather some data properly." Finn was nodding at me like a demented thing. He did love data. "But then one crisis or another has intervened, so I've been too busy."

Fi nodded. She seemed calmer.

"And the power is all the colours of the rainbow."

I asked the power on my left hand if it would split into its component colours, and it obligingly did so. "See?" I showed Fi. "That's why it's called the Rainbow Gateway."

Fi's mouth fell open again.

I continued, "My gran just had a few problems with it. Did you see her power as faint and silvery?" I remembered the very faint silver lines I'd seen on the floor during my first visit to the Gateway instead of the sturdy iron and glass barriers now delineating the sectors. Might it be why the new barriers had disturbed Fi so much yesterday? Damn, I was a lousy boss. I hadn't even understood what she was confused about, had I?

Fi said, "Yes, I had to squint to see it sometimes. I think some things your gran said just made sense. As she would say, the penny finally dropped."

How many times had Gran said that to me when I'd understood something? *Has the penny finally dropped, our Niki?* Oh dear, my throat was closing, and I could feel tears forming behind my eyes. But I couldn't grieve right now. I needed to focus on today's job. I swallowed hard and breathed through my nose as *Good Grief* had recommended.

Fi helped me out. "We're running a few minutes late now, and we have the Picts up first. Where on earth is Ross?"

Finn said, "Caitlin's coming through now. OK to start the streaming? Dola said to check."

I nodded at Finn and walked over to the anvil,

still on the conference table, to ask if it could move itself back to the centre so I could open the gates. But the power was pulling at me. What did it want? I dropped my shields and sensed it was asking for permission. It was showing me something I didn't understand? With wooden flowers? No, that wasn't right.

I was aware we were running late, so I just thought, *sure, whatever. Do what you need to do*. Then I was moved swiftly backwards.

CHAPTER
THIRTEEN

The power stopped pushing me and swirled madly, cyclone-like, around the very centre of the Gateway. It was so dense, it was impossible to see what was happening. Then, as quickly as it had begun, it stopped.

The desks had moved to one side, and the anvil now stood on an impressive-looking piece of obviously custom-created furniture. *Niki, shape up and gather your brain! Of course it's a custom piece! You just watched the power make it.*

"It's so beautiful. What an amazing idea." I sent the power waves of approval and admiration as I moved back towards the desks.

Fi exhaled as if she'd been holding her breath. "Wow! Just wow!"

"My lady, you're gonna want to see this." Finn

thrust the purple peril at me. It showed 99877. "That wasn't you. And I don't think it's right either. I think this device only goes up to 99,999. So it stopped at the highest prime below that." We peered at the device and then at each other in confusion.

I took a moment to admire the new ... what the hell should I call it? Installation? Anvil support? Custom-built display? Bespoke surround?

Words actually failed me.

It was a single large piece of glossy, curved wood with a beautiful grain, perhaps twelve feet wide and narrower from front to back. An indentation in the wood at the back made it kidney-shaped. On the surface in front of the indentation was a small green, rectangular leather mat with a seven-pointed star on it. It might as well have said, *The Recorder stands here.*

The anvil now sat on a raised oval plinth of the same wood, on one side of the new installation. On the other side was a similar, smaller, but also oval plinth in the same fabulous wood. Scattered across the front of the surround was a trailing bouquet of sparkling, glowing rainbow-coloured flowers made of power. It looked as though someone had sculpted the aurora borealis into a tabletop flower display.

I walked into the indentation, reached out to the anvil and only then realised I could barely reach the base of it. I certainly couldn't see the top to touch the correct runes for the individual kingdoms. I connected with the power, suggesting a small step for me to stand on. But I didn't really want that because, sometimes, if I needed a stronger connection to the power, I liked to stand barefoot on the floor. In response to my thought, the plinth supporting the anvil sank down flush to the top of the new furniture as though the feature was an integral part of the new design.

Finn said, "Cool! What's the other pedestal thingy for?"

I'd wondered the same, but I didn't know, so I just shook my head in confusion and asked, "How late are we now, Fi?"

"Only about five minutes, my lady. We'll make it up easily, don't worry."

Finn was shuffling.

"You OK, Finn?"

"Sorry. Supposed to tell you, Ma is planning with the Smiths today. Sends her excuses. Cait and I need to stand in for her. Cait's on her way with our bondmates."

"No worries, send Breanna my regards. Right, are we ready to go?" I got nods from everyone. I placed my left hand, encased in its boxing glove of power, onto the anvil. "Approved prospective bonders for today, I invite you to the Rainbow."

Only four doors swung open. The indigo and the yellow doors remained closed, which was to be expected today, but the Fae's violet door should have opened. The realms would arrive on the pre-agreed schedule, but opening the doors let everyone know it was time, and we were open for business. It had been dizzying at my ascension. It still was.

I pulled my earbuds out of the pocket of my robe and said, "Dola, the Fae doorway didn't open. Can you contact Ad'Rian and ask him if there is a problem?"

Then the anvil rose back up again. Was it my imagination, or was it blacker, glossier and just more polished-looking than usual?

Then a tiny green mat, barely coaster-sized, appeared just to the left of mine as Autumn said, "Sorry, Auntie Nik, are we starting? Rosemary wanted to finish getting the branches up. Don't it look pretty?"

I looked around the walls at all the greenery, and she was right, it was beautiful. It would be like getting married in a fairy bower when the Hobs completed it.

"'*Doesn't* it look pretty,' sweetie, not 'don't it.' But, yes, it's charming. You and Rosemary did a wonderful job, thank you." I rubbed her back and checked my Gift. She was excited and happy but relaxed. All good then.

"Niki?" Dola came through my earbud clearly as always. "Ad'Rian says they thought the bond check was on Thursday. No one is prepared today. I am looking into why it happened, but I think it would be easiest to bring them through early on Thursday afternoon. They will be out of the way before you get started on the problem cases."

I thought about it. Honestly, I'd probably taken on too much, thinking I could do them all today, especially with Autumn here. So I just said, "Thank you, Dola, that would be great. Would you set a reminder for Thursday morning to make sure he remembers? I swear, sometimes Ad'Rian and the Fae simply don't know what day it is."

I heard, "Yes, Niki," in my ear. Then, behind me, a man and woman walked out of the Green sector, and Fi said, "Hello, Ross; hey, Corby."

Ross barely noticed Fi or me as he threw a formal-sounding, "Good afternoon," over his shoulder and strode towards the anvil. Then he came to an abrupt halt by the new installation. He gazed at the floor, shot me a startled look and said, "It's moved! But it never moves. How could you let it move?"

Something about his tone rubbed me up the wrong way. I didn't need difficult people today. I needed a seasoned professional snapper who would hang off a ladder to get the right shot if that was what it took. Fi had suggested that was what this guy was.

I gave him a long, cool look. Tall and slender with

blond hair. Not the red hair of his childhood, but an artfully streaked blond mane. Huh! That must have been what Fi meant when she said he wasn't Red anymore. Had it faded as he aged, or did he dye it to get away from his childhood nickname?

Not trying too hard to keep the sarcasm out of my voice, I said, "Good afternoon to you too, Ross. How lovely to see you again after thirty years. You haven't changed. What's the problem?"

He shook himself and almost found his manners. "Ah, yes, Niki."

I glared at him. It had taken me a few weeks to realise that the very few people who didn't give me my title were challenging my authority, whether they realised it or not. Probably he wasn't; he was just disconcerted by the changes, but I'd start as I meant to go on, and something about him made my neck itch.

I waited, just looking at him.

"Sorry, I mean, my lady, yes. I mean no." His soft, local accent and muddled speech patterns hadn't changed since primary school. But he seemed to be flustered rather than difficult. I backed off a little.

Photographers I could actually manage. Years of dealing with them as a registrar helped me now, and my professional self emerged as I tried again. "Ross, the first batch today, the Picts will be here in one minute. Where do you usually set up?"

He pointed to a spot that was now under the anvil's new surround.

"Oh dear. Well, I'm afraid the anvil gets first call on location, so pick a new spot, and let's get cracking."

He looked around helplessly.

I threw Fi a look that said *come and get this dithering idiot sorted out, will you?*

She arrived, chatting with a slim, vibrant woman who had the red hair that was so common in many of the realms and in this part of Scotland. Hers was a lovely colour. Quite close to Caitlin's gorgeous copper colour. A true, rich auburn, short, spiky and stylish and paired with a lipstick that almost perfectly matched her hair. She had milk-white skin with cute freckles across the bridge of her nose and wore a bright green shirt the same colour as her eyes. She'd completed her outfit with jeans and sturdy-looking stylish boots. She looked comfortable and competent. I envied her the comfort.

She turned a brilliant smile on me, bowed and then held out her hand to shake mine. "My lady, lovely to meet you. I'm Corby. My condolences on your grandmother's passing. Let me get Ross out of your way. He doesn't deal well with change." She glanced around quickly and gave the impression of measuring something with her eyes.

"Isn't this beautiful? Love the flowers. Gorgeous wood."

Ross looked vacantly around, asking, "Flowers?" and then focused on the greenery around the walls before nodding curtly.

Corby pointed at the flowers made of power strewn across the wooden surface of the surround, and he just looked baffled. Her brow furrowed. She caught Fi's eye, and then relaxed when Fi nodded at her.

"Right then, Ross, over here, do you think?" It surprised me to hear Corby didn't have a Scottish accent. Perhaps she just looked like a local? But she could see the power. Curiouser and curiouser.

Maybe I should keep an eye out and see who noticed the flowers and who didn't.

Arriving beside me, Fi said in an undertone, "He hasn't changed, still has the social problems, but he's worked here for years. He's always telling us about the awards he's won, and Corby does everything else. It will be fine."

I smiled as I saw the Picts arriving, led by Caitlin, and said to Autumn, "You ready? The bet is on." Autumn pulled a little power to match mine, grinned up at me, and nodded.

Fi looked down at Autumn's left hand with its own mini boxing glove with startled eyes, which she turned to me. I just nodded, smiled and said, "Are you ready to remind me of the names now, Fi? If I remember correctly, we didn't have any doubts about this batch, did we? Just a quick check, a photo and a rubber stamp approval?"

And it was. The sixteen couples waited patiently in the Blue sector. They all looked chilled and happy. Most of them were in casual clothes, which was not at all what Fi had led me to expect. Their bonds glowed like fireworks when I dipped into my Gift.

Fi brought them over to me one pair at a time. I smiled, tapped my Gift for each couple, saw a wide selection of beautiful glows and giggled at Autumn with her unicorn finger puppet, which hadn't yet moved off her right hand. She was using it to wave at the second-to-last Pict couple. I said the same thing to them I had to all the others, "No problems at all, I look forward to bonding you on Sunday."

The last couple approached. They had a bright perfect bond, and I could see why Gowan's first thought about his future, once he realised his life was safe, was how he wanted to spend that life with this woman.

I gave him a big smile. "Hey, Gowan, you talked yourself out of the doghouse, well done." Smiling at the woman, I said, "You must be Lesley. I heard a lot about how important you are to Gowan last weekend."

The small, cute, dark-haired woman with the

sparkling hazel eyes turned to Gowan and said, "OK. You win. The Queen, the Prince and the Recorder on your side. How in all the slagging hells can I argue with all of them?"

It didn't look to me as though she wanted to argue with anything. It looked to me as though she adored her stupid but well-meaning future husband. Then Lesley caught Caitlin's glare and said, "I beg your pardon, Recorder. He did say you would vouch for him, and, truthfully, I didna believe him."

I looked at the young man I'd last seen coming through the Gateway at the end of a very stressful day. "Did you tell her the whole truth?"

He nodded dumbly at me before he finally got out, "I followed your advice and told her everything, my lady."

My right shoulder said he had. I asked Lesley, "Did you know Recorders are human lie detectors?"

The expression that crossed her face held calculation. "I didn't. How very handy. Did he just tell you the truth?"

I liked her bluntness, and I could see why Breanna valued her work at the Broch. She looked exactly like the kind of woman who might help the queen to drag the Pict kingdom out of the Middle Ages and into the present. "Yes, Lesley, he did. And your queen spoke highly of you too. I'm pretty sure we'll be meeting again, but for now I'm genuinely delighted you two got everything straightened out, and I'll be bonding you on Sunday."

The Picts chilled-out attitude had made it a quick and easy process. It was sped up further by the fact their princess and heir stood to one side of me with a big-ass sword on her back, and their prince was on the other side, holding a mobile phone in one hand, which he pointed at me, and a livestream camera in his other. I glanced at him as Gowan and Lesley headed back to the Blue sector. "All going OK, Finn?"

"All good, we're not livestreaming, my lady. Dola decided on a few minutes delay. She's mixing streams before transmitting it to the kingdoms. That way, they can see you and the couples. We're not including audio at the moment, but we could?"

"You can include audio today, I think. It should all be smooth. But not on Thursday with the problem bonds. I don't think we need to embarrass anyone. There are at least two couples with queries in the Galicians. Tell Dola to be cautious. I'd hate to spoil anyone's day. My gran marked some she particularly wanted to re-check. Fi could give you a heads-up on those."

He just nodded, then added, "Did the report on the Hobs. Nothing startling in it except—" then we both looked over as the Galicians arrived, "—Fill you in later. Not urgent, but it explains a lot."

I surveyed the arriving Galician couples and endured the damn bagpipes as the piper led the couples through their gate. To me, it always sounded like an animal being tortured. My name was McKnight, but my tastes were all formed in Manchester. I wondered if it would be rude to turn on noise-cancelling as I noticed Finn doing. Probably.

I sighed and tapped my earbud. "Dola, can you send Aysha the link to the video stream? She might want to admire her daughter's composure in the face of these bagpipes."

But, checking on Autumn, I saw she wasn't just composed. Her face was alight with delight. Oh well, it takes all tastes.

Fi arrived back, having shepherded the Picts out, and said, "There were two couples your gran wasn't happy about in this Galician batch. She said something funny was going on, but she couldn't understand it. She put a star by them to check them carefully this time."

"Am I running very late now?"

"Oh no, you're about ten minutes early, my lady." I gave her a surprised glance, and she said, "I think Elsie may have become slower than I'd realised over the last few years. You fairly whipped through the Picts."

"Good. That gives me some leeway, but from here, they all look great."

The cat-strangling sounds had stopped. This group was dramatically different to the casual Picts. There was a king's ransom in beautifully cut designer clothes, elegant eye-catching jewellery and accessories with expensive labels glittering in the Orange sector. They had that indefinable air of European elegance that always made me feel scruffy.

Their bonds sparkled too. Only the piper at the front and one older man at the back weren't glowing. The man appeared to be unaccompanied and carried a large basket, which he placed at his feet as I watched. All the couples were giving him a lot of space.

Then my view of the Orange sector was obscured by Ross and Corby, who were moving their equipment. Corby walked over to me. "Sorry, my lady, we couldn't get the anvil into shot along with the couple from that spot." She pointed to where they had been. "The anvil is higher, but the photos including it always sell the best."

"How much too high is it?"

"Oh, please don't concern yourself. We can work around it."

I looked directly into her amazing green eyes.

"Yes, Corby. I'm sure you can. But how much too high is it *exactly*?"

Now panic flared in those eyes. "Only about three inches, my lady; please don't give it a thought. Honestly, it's my problem, not yours, but it changes the composition. On Sunday we'll want to get you, the anvil, the couple and their rings all in shot."

"One minute." I reached out to the power, put my hand gently against the anvil, and tried to send it a picture of the anvil, the couples and my request. It sank about three or four inches.

"Better?"

Corby's mouth dropped open.

"Didn't you know I used to be a registrar? I truly get the importance of great photos, whether it's for a wedding or a bonding."

She rushed back to Ross, and I saw her tapping his shoulder and pointing, and then she mouthed "thank you" to me as the two of them moved back to where they had been before.

"Fi, who's the chap at the back of the Orange sector?"

His energy was odd. He felt nervous or stressed and maybe even a little angry. There were twenty-three couples from the Galician Empire. And everyone looked fine apart from Mr I'm-here-on-my-own-and-I'm-not-happy lurking in the back.

I heard a muffled, "Oh, crap, be right back," as Fi

shot over to the Orange sector and cleared him a path to the front.

She arrived back, still looking slightly flustered. "My lady, may I introduce the Galician Emperor, His Imperial Highness Alphonse of House Asturia?"

"Oh crap" indeed. He was wearing a stylish suit, but he didn't seem particularly royal. He looked more like a politician.

I inclined my head, smiled and said, "Your Majesty, I welcome you to the Rainbow. To what do we owe the honour of your visit?"

He gave me a smooth smile as he handed his basket to Fi. "Various farmers and merchants desired to send the Recorder samples of their wares to express their thanks to you, my lady. And I wished to convey my gratitude in person for the changes you are making for all of us. Rescinding the one-in, one-out rule and updating the Rainbow Network has been a godsend. Once you have settled into your role, we would appreciate discussing trade opportunities."

So not much an emperor as a salesman for his realm—but that was good, wasn't it? He obviously cared about his people. I should play the game. "Ah, sire, the thanks for the Rainbow Network go to my new TEK, the Knight Adjutant for all things technological. I would introduce you, but as you can see, he has his hands full right now."

But to my surprise, Finn looked up from his screen, "Hi, Uncle Alphonse."

Huh! I glanced at Caitlin. She inclined her own head as she said, "Alphonse."

But the emperor was focused on Finn and smiled straight into both cameras. His gleaming white teeth sparkled as he said, "The Galician Empire realm and I are excited to be a part of the progress."

He turned back to me. "I would not want to delay you, my lady. My daughter is here today with her beau for the bond check. And I believe you met my youngest son, Alejandro, when you were testing your Knights."

"I did. A lovely young man. You must be very proud of him." In my experience, that was usually a safe bet, but not this time, it seemed.

"I am, of course, but also sad he could not see the power. It must come from his mother's side. Your gown is glowing with power; I don't know how anyone could miss it. I was sorry to be absent for your ascension. We were holidaying in the winter palace. My wife insists on quality couples time," he gave me an almost shy smile, "so the power summoned my representative in my stead."

"You got the message, though, about the need for two young representatives for the Rainbow Council?"

He looked startled. "Is it urgent?"

"Not urgent, no. I plan to announce them on Sunday and begin next month."

"Next month? I hadn't realised it was happening so quickly. I'll ask … someone." He looked overwhelmed, but then the politician's smile snapped back into place, and he noticed Autumn. "And may I inquire who this delightful young lady is?"

"This is Autumn, my goddaughter, who is spending a short holiday with me, and I think hoping that someone's bridesmaid will drop out so she can be fortuitously on the spot when it happens."

He laughed with genuine amusement, reached out, took her hand and bowed over, not quite kissing the back of it. Autumn giggled as he said, "You have much in common with my own daughter, Natalia; you will meet her shortly. She has had clear goals since she was about your age."

Autumn looked absolutely delighted as the emperor played with her unicorn finger puppet. I tapped my Gift quickly. It was his daughter he was nervous and stressed about. Something wrong there? I thought about how my gran had always kept the Galicians at arm's length and decided to try something different. He was the identical rank as Mabon and Ad'Rian, and I always invited them to the centre, didn't I?

"Your Majesty, would you like to join us in the

centre of the Rainbow while I check the bonds for your subjects?"

He hid his surprise well and said, "I would be delighted, my lady. I've never received the honour of an invitation to the centre, other than for my own bonding."

Well, damn, no wonder I knew nothing about his realm and pitifully little about his people. "I would invite you to stand with me, but I understand it's unpleasant for iron-sensitives. Please stand wherever you are most comfortable."

"Actually, my lady, my mother is Queen Breanna's aunt, so with that bloodline, I am not sensitive to iron. If it wouldn't offend, I will come behind and stay out of everyone's way. Emperors, I have found, should not get underfoot." He gave me another charming smile.

I caught Fi's eye, and she escorted the first couple to the anvil. Everything was fine. The emperor congratulated them, which pleased everyone, even Ross. An emperor in the shot probably sold more photos. I'd worked my way through the first fifteen or sixteen couples; honestly, I was losing count. Autumn's finger puppet stayed on her right hand. The bonds varied with each couple, and certainly some were stronger than others, but they all had valid bonds.

I looked over at the quickly emptying Orange

sector, and the glows were still there. So why did I have an unpleasant feeling growing in my belly?

More perfectly bonded, impeccably dressed and quickly approved couples later, I found out. Fi escorted the penultimate couple over to the anvil, and their glow had disappeared!

Autumn took her puppet off her finger and held it in her hand as if not sure what she was seeing. She saw it too, then—or, rather, didn't.

I caught Finn's eye and put my finger to my lips briefly, hoping he would understand we had a problem incoming and the audio should be off. He obviously did because I heard him speaking in an undertone to Dola. I could have sworn he said, "We may need to go to an advert break, Dola." What on earth? We had commercials? Whose bright idea was that?

CHAPTER
FOURTEEN

I addressed Finn's cameras, "We're taking a short break now, then we'll return with the Red Celt bonding applicants. I hear His Majesty King Mabon and Prince Dafydd are accompanying their subjects today, so we'll be back with them soon."

Huh! Who could have guessed all my hours of watching reality TV would have given me the perfect words to say instead of blurting out *turn that damn thing off right now, Finn*?

Finn looked up from his screen. "OK, my lady. We're clear. Dola's dealing with it. I'd like to film this, anyway. We can decide later if it's transmitted."

"Agreed, but please be damn sure Dola understands she needs my authority before she releases this next bit." Into my earbud, I asked, "Dola, did you hear me? I need your assurance please." I'd noticed the concept of unintended potential embarrassment to humans could be one of Dola's blind spots.

"Yes, Niki. Do not transmit the next part without checking with you."

As the penultimate couple reached the anvil, it was obvious they had no glow, definitely no soul link. My Gift suggested they didn't have any feelings for each other beyond a warm friendship. But that wasn't what had drawn my attention. What was baffling me was the last couple remaining in the Orange sector had no glow either. And yet, five minutes ago, that sector had been glowing with bonds.

I gestured Fi to come to me around the back of the anvil's new mounting. I moved away from the emperor and Autumn and asked, "Is this one of Gran's Galician queries?" She nodded. "And the couple who's still waiting too?" She nodded again.

Leaning in, she whispered, "The last couple still in the Orange sector are Natalia, Emperor Alphonse's daughter, and her beau…" she consulted her ever-present list, "…her beau, Miguel. She made everyone else go first. Her betrothed is this guy's brother."

"And the woman with this guy?"

"Is her best friend."

I moved back to the emperor and dropped into

my Gift as deep as I dared with so many people around.

"Houston, we have a problem," I mumbled to myself.

"I beg your pardon, my lady?" the emperor asked.

I looked and saw the finger puppet had taken up a place on Autumn's left hand. She'd let the power go to put the puppet there. Well, she'd definitely earned tonight's ice cream for her and Tilly.

"My lady?" he repeated. Whoops, I was ignoring an emperor.

"I'm sorry, sire. There's a hitch. These two don't have a bond. Give me a moment, please."

He looked worried. His nervousness rose to the top of his emotions again.

We'd decided we would recall any problem couples on Thursday. So what I was supposed to do now was send them home to come back then.

But the strain the emperor was under was affecting me. I couldn't imagine how it felt to him. Why was this so important to him? I'd built the beginning of a bridge during the approval of his people's bonds. I didn't want to destroy that by putting him through two days of hell waiting to return here.

I checked the Gateway. The Red Celts were arriving. I tapped into my Gift. It had no opinion. I asked the power; it had no opinion either. I was on my own then, and I'd have to just go with what felt right to me.

While I was gazing around, I noticed Rosemary was watching the proceedings with interest. She lifted greenery up to the wall at the end of the sector in preparation for Sunday. Intelligence shone in her eyes as she glanced from the couple left in the Orange sector, to the couple almost at the anvil and then back again with a tiny smile. I must ask her what she saw.

As Fi arrived, I said, "Slight change of plan, Fi. Would you take …" I paused. I'd no idea what their names were.

Seamlessly, Fi said, "May I introduce Sophia and Tomas, my lady?"

I gave her a grateful smile. "Would you take Sophia and Tomas to the conference table, please, and bring the last couple over?"

She didn't allow even a flicker to betray that this hadn't been in the plan. "Of course, my lady."

"Your Majesty, we have a problem. Normally it would be my problem, but I assume she," I pointed at the last couple remaining in the Orange sector, "is your daughter. Natalia, did you say?"

Waves of panic and an odd sense of resignation came off him now as he nodded.

"I'm sorry to tell you they don't have a bond

either. But something isn't right here, and I need to find out what."

He was trying to keep his regal countenance in place, but it kept fraying and being overridden by a father's concern.

I debated with myself. My gran had made the point that kings and queens were ten-a-penny in the realms, but there was only one Recorder. Fi and I had settled on a new procedure. Surely the only fair thing was to apply it to everyone. But I wanted to be seen as fair to all the realms, not just my gran's old favourites. If Mabon felt like this, I wouldn't have just sent him home to spend two days worrying, would I?

The emperor looked as though he wanted to shake me and say, "Just spit it out, Recorder." But I didn't know what the problem was yet, so I couldn't. He'd just have to wait while we all worked it out.

Emperor Alphonse said, "Natalia told me your grandmother informed her she and Miguel must be checked again. But I thought she was just …" he trailed off.

I prompted him, "You thought she was just what, sire?" Was there some more specific problem I didn't know about between the Galicians and my gran? "What exactly was it you thought the former Recorder was doing, sire?"

"No, my lady, not the Recorder. My daughter, I assumed Natalia was…" he trailed off again.

Now I resisted the urge to shake him.

Slowly he said, "It's nada, a nothing. My daughter has some … peculiar beliefs and a … strange faith in the Recorder. She's been that way since she was a child. There was this book she loved…" he trailed off yet again.

I squared my shoulders and turned back to the emperor. "Your Majesty, there is a system. If there's any problem, we are recalling the couples on Thursday when we will have the time to deal with any problems privately."

The emperor's face retained a polite, if taut smile, but through my Gift, I sensed his anxiety was reaching worrying proportions. It made my stomach roil and my chest feel tight. I could hear my own heartbeat in my ears. What was the point of being the boss if I didn't know when to change a plan for everyone's good? Wasn't it one of the things I'd hated most about Janet? She never gave a toss for how unhappy her self-imposed rules made everyone else. I decided to do what was right, but he needed to be more honest with me too.

I continued, "However, I'd hate to see you worry for two more days. Why don't we see if we can resolve it now?"

He gave me a blinding smile with those very white teeth. "I would be grateful if it is possible."

I saw the Red sector was filling up rapidly now and gave him a stern look I knew I'd borrowed from my gran. "But we are holding everyone else up. You could speed things up if you wished, sire. Is there anything you think I should know right now?"

The emperor sounded weary, "Natalia has *always* said there was no spark between her and Miguel. But the boy is a true prince. Life is easier when your life mate understands the pressures. Natalia is a wonderful princess. She does much hard work in our kingdom. Miguel understands the importance of work. His older brother will be king one day. Tomas is the youngest, the playboy prince. He takes nothing seriously. I would not want my realm in his hands. Natalia and Miguel grew up with the same expectations upon them. I've told her the feelings grow once you're married. My own parents' marriage was virtually an arranged one to give us stronger ties between House Albidosi and House Asturia, and it was a happy one."

But my Gift was prickling at me. I checked it and smiled. "And yet you chose your own bride."

He gave me a rueful half-smile. "When you meet my wife, you will understand."

"And does she approve of this match?"

He glanced at Autumn and looked shifty.

"Autumn, would you wait at the conference table please? We're taking a break soon. You can ask Dola if you want anything to eat or drink." She nodded happily and wandered over to the table, chattering away to the unicorn on her finger.

I gave the emperor my gran's stern look again. "I don't mean to be rude, sire, but you've got," I glanced at Fi's back, which was headed towards the Orange sector to bring Natalia and Miguel over to the anvil, "one minute if you want to tell me anything privately before your daughter gets here."

He sighed again. "My wife tells me I'm an idiot. But she says Natalia isn't, so she's leaving it between the two of us to sort out."

I managed to keep the smile off my face, but I looked forward to meeting the empress.

"I shall be guided by the Recorder's expertise in this matter. I have informed Natalia most firmly if the Recorder approved the bond, the marriage must go ahead for the sake of our realm."

I laughed; I couldn't help myself. "Oh, that ship has already sailed, sire." I checked the couple moving over to the centre, nothing. Absolutely nothing. "Natalia and Miguel have absolutely no bond. But what I need to find out is how they faked a bond for so long and then dropped it when their turn came. The only way I know to do that is with a specific Fae spell. It would work until it got close to the anvil or the power. Then the power itself would burn through that type of spell. But it isn't what's happened here. Shall we find out what has?"

We met Fi halfway, and the five of us walked over to the conference table. Tilly came out from under my desk to see what was happening. As we got closer to the table, all four of the young Galicians glowed again. I put my arm straight out to the side in front of Natalia and Miguel.

"Step back a few feet, please." Miguel looked confused. Natalia hid a smile, but they did as I'd asked. The glows died. All the glows died. Oh dear. As my gran often said, "There's a first time for everything." But I thought I could see the solution now—I just wasn't certain.

"Miguel, please take a seat at the table." He looked at Natalia as though for permission. I wrapped power around my left hand and said, "Right now please."

The emperor, his own bemusement obviously growing, said something in his own language. It sounded short-tempered, and Miguel moved immediately to sit at the table. A glow now surrounded the three at the table.

"Sophia, would you join us here?" Now Natalia was watching me closely, intense focus shining out of intelligent eyes.

As Sophia left the table area, the glow died, so the men weren't gay.

I moved us back another few feet. "Sire, please take a seat. The fewer people here, the quicker this will be." It wasn't strictly speaking the truth, but he was getting in my way. He'd been right when he said an emperor underfoot is a pain to everyone.

As Sophia approached, absolutely nothing happened. So the women weren't gay either.

Which only left …

Natalia, with amusement in her voice, said, "You're very good, Recorder. That didn't take you long at all. Your grandmother, my condolences on her passing, couldn't work it out. Although she was aware something was wrong." She was grinning at me like a child now. I ignored her—she hadn't needed to play these games, and I was irritated.

"Thank you, Sophia, please return to the table and send Tomas over here." I watched the table carefully as Sophia approached, and sure enough, she and Miguel lit up like beacons. It was a strong bond they had. I waited. Had Autumn noticed? Yes, the unicorn puppet got moved to her right hand. I winked at her.

As soon as Tomas got closer to us, he and Natalia's glow was almost blinding. Every colour of the rainbow. It looked like a seven-fold bond to me. She was about to get her man. He may not be the senior prince, but she knew the man her heart needed.

We all took seats at the table, and I laid out for the emperor what I believed had caused my gran's confusion and her demand to recheck the bonds. "I'm guessing the four of you went up to my grandmother together?"

They nodded. "And she told two of you to move back, but you didn't move far enough back?" They all nodded again.

"Why?"

Natalia spoke, "Papa was on vacation."

"So what?" Whoops, that sounded rude, but she didn't even notice.

"My father is a stubborn man. If he doesn't see something with his own eyes, then poof, it simply isn't true. I love him very much," she smiled at her father, "but I also know him well. Tomas and I will argue. All couples do sometimes. Every time we have the smallest disagreement, my father would say, 'If you'd married Miguel, this wouldn't be happening now. Natalia, why didn't you marry the so-suitable Miguel as your dear papa wanted?'"

She smiled at her father again and then pulled a comically fierce face. "I would not want to kill my father, but his stubbornness might have driven me to it." The entire table laughed.

"We have a children's book, my lady. The title would translate into English as *The Recorder is Always Right* or perhaps *The Recorder Knows Best*."

I laughed. I couldn't help myself. It was the exact concept the Book kept trying to drum into my head.

"It was my favourite book for several years. It's short stories for bedtime, you know? Various children take their problems to the Recorder. She shows them almost always their parents are right. But occasionally there is a story where the parents are not right, and the Recorder helps the child's parents to understand and fix the problem."

Autumn piped up, "Auntie Niki is always right. Evens if you don't want her to be."

The whole table laughed, and I wished again it was true.

Natalia continued, "I hoped if I brought my father with me, you could show him what you perceive, my lady? I would owe you a great debt, and my father would owe you his life." More laughter.

But I had to be honest. "I'd be happy to. But I've no idea how to do that if he doesn't see the bond glow for himself."

Faces fell around the table. I realised Autumn was trying to get my attention. Bless her, she was almost bouncing in her seat. Quietly, I asked, "You OK, baby?"

She slid off her seat and stood between Fi and me to whisper in my ear. Everyone around the table simply pretended this wasn't happening in that way the best people do when a child needs something.

"Mummy can see more if I hold her hand. He feels like a nice man, the 'mperor. He's sad and worried."

"He is, baby. You're sure mum can see more?"

She nodded so hard, her ponytail flew about wildly. I knew Aysha hadn't been able to see the power, so if Autumn had found a way to show her, perhaps I could help Alphonse and Natalia.

"P'haps you could hold his hand; that's all I do with mum."

And that was exactly what we did.

We split the four of them up, sending them north, south, east and west, and asked Sophia and Miguel to come together while I touched the back of the emperor's hand.

And it didn't work.

He couldn't see a thing and looked at me helplessly.

Then Autumn reached in and took his hand in her tiny one, and he gasped. Eyes wide, he looked around and then back to Sophia and Miguel. Their glow was a nice solid one, sparkling green around their upper torso and shoulders and fading into blue around their heads. I took my hand off the emperor to rub Autumn's back. She was channelling power. I really must get her to show me how to do this.

Then Emperor Alphonse looked at Natalia and Tomas, gestured and said something in Galician that obviously meant "now you two" because they began to walk slowly towards each other. Their bond was blinding!

He must have thought he was prepared for the brightness of the bond after he saw Sophia and Miguel's. But he wasn't. He couldn't have been, because a seven-fold bond glows so much brighter than a normal bond. The couple walked in rainbows as they approached each other. When Tomas reached his hand out to Natalia and gave her an intimate smile, the glow coalesced into one bright, beautiful, rainbow glow surrounding them both.

This time the emperor didn't make a sound. He just sat there with one hand over his open mouth as a single tear rolled down his face.

CHAPTER
FIFTEEN

"That was weird!" I was confused by just how devastated the emperor had felt. After all, no real harm had been done.

Once everything calmed down, we'd accepted Natalia and Sophia's thanks and the emperor's assurances of eternal gratitude. If I ever needed anything from his kingdom, I had only to ask. Alphonse had confided in me privately that he was horrified that his stubbornness and pride might have resulted in his daughter being tied to the wrong man. Especially when that man had a bond with another woman.

After she escorted the Galician party out, Fi came back to me with a worried look on her face. As I spoke, Fi said, "We have another problem." And then, "After you, my lady; what's weird?"

I said, "No, let's get the problem out of the way first."

"OK, the ap Modrons are running late. They asked if they could swap their place in the running order."

"Why's it a problem?"

Fi looked concerned and uncomfortable. "Mabon asked his daughter Rhiannon to email. She said," she glanced at her phone and then continued, "her father apologises, but they need to wash the dragon reek off before they stink up the Gateway. They'll be an hour late."

"OK. So we should do some of the others first? Or eat first?" Now Fi looked confused. "Spit it out, Fi—what am I missing?"

"Nothing, my lady, really, it's just your gran…" Now she paused, still uncomfortable.

"My gran what?" I was losing my patience a little. Fi and I had been working like a well-oiled team. I'd thought it was all going swimmingly. I couldn't imagine what I'd done wrong to make her so stiff and tentative.

"Your gran really didn't like it when people were late."

Oh! Now I knew what was happening. My gran could throw a tantrum to rival a two-year-old while muttering old proverbs under her breath if anyone ran even two minutes late. I laughed. "Are you waiting for me to huff and rant that punctuality is the politeness of kings, and unspecified people would be late for their own bloody funeral?"

Now she grinned at me. "You're a lot more laid-back than she was, you know."

"And you're efficient, Fi. So you've already fixed this. What did you decide to rearrange?"

"I informed the waiting Celts. All but one woman said they'd prefer to wait for their royals. In typical chilled-out Welsh fashion, they've taken themselves off to the pub by the gate at their end. I'll message them when Mabon arrives, if he doesn't call in there himself on his way. You know how relaxed the Reds always are."

I nodded. As my gran had often said, they were all too frequently as relaxed as newts.

"And the woman who didn't want to go?" I had an unpleasant tingle about her, but no real idea of why.

"Got overruled by the majority. Probably just nerves, Niki—we see that quite a bit."

"Yeah, it used to happen a lot in the registrar's office too."

Fi said, "The four couples coming in through the Green sector have arrived. The train was on time for a change. I'm sure they'd like to get to their home kingdoms. What if you did them now? They would have been next, after the Red Celts. Then we could have a meal break. So what was weird?"

"Oh, it's nothing, Fi, just the emperor's emotions were a bit extreme at the idea he might have made a mistake about Natalia. Just struck me as weird."

But Fi was shaking her head. "No, it would have been awful for her. The Galicians' religious beliefs." She paused and glanced around us, then lowered her voice and leaned in. "They don't have divorce, you know."

"How do you mean?"

Fi was realising there were big gaps in my knowledge. "My lady, you're thinking of the Galicians' religion as Catholicism, aren't you?"

I nodded. She was right, I was. "But it's not?"

But she was already shaking her head. "No, their emperor is appointed by God. Then he appoints their Pope. How's your history? Of the Catholic church in about 900AD, I mean."

"I must know a bit." I dug about in the depths of my memory. "There was a schism or something, wasn't there? And then weren't there crusades and stuff …and persecutions and problems and the Spanish Inquisition? No, that was much later, wasn't it?" I trailed off—it turned out my religious history was lousy.

Fi glanced at her watch. "Ask the Book. But for now, just remember when they founded their realm, their church was nothing like the modern Catholic church you might know. The emperor was God's representative on earth. Our world has progressed. Theirs hasn't. If Natalia had married Miguel, that would have been it. He would have become emperor; obviously women can't rule in their realm. And if he didn't love her, because he has a bond with Sophia..." Her face looked genuinely panicky. "Well, just think Henry VIII. At best she might have ended up in a convent ... At worst ...well, I don't *think* they actually behead people there anymore."

My jaw fell open. I'd really missed what actually happened today, hadn't I? No wonder Natalia was prepared to do whatever it took to get her Tomas.

Whoa! That would explain the emperor's tears and guilt then. "OK, I'll learn more as quickly as I can. Thanks, Fi."

She nodded. "Don't worry; it all worked out nicely, didn't it? So, the next four couples and then some food?"

"Now you're speaking my language. I'm hungry. Any queries with those four, or should they be straightforward?"

"Very straightforward."

And they were. I looked at her list and pointed at several names. "Am I right thinking these are Red Celts who've come in through the Green gate because they work in our world?"

She checked where I was pointing and nodded. "They're Welsh, yes."

"Then why don't you ask them if they want to join the party in the pub and come back when their king and prince are present?"

"Will do. Shall I ask the Fae couple if they want to go through to Fae and come back on Thursday with the rest of them too?"

"Yes, sure. I'll do the last Galician couple while you do that. We should have offered them the chance to move to the Orange sector, especially as their emperor was here. I'll know better next time."

Fi was pulling a strange face, and I asked, "What?"

"I must sound like a broken record. But, apart from a little part-time job at the Broch when I was a teenager, Elsie was the *only* boss I ever had. I think I'd got myself into a rut too. And you're *very* different to her." She looked as if she was on the verge of tears. "My lady Elsie always said if people couldn't get themselves to the right place at the right time, they could stay where they'd landed and lump it."

Yep, sounded like Gran. But it wouldn't help anything to criticise her or her methods to Fi. So I passed it off with a casual, "It's probably the registrar in me. I like to see couples happy."

She nodded, and we got on with moving closer to a meal break.

The remaining Galician couple were lovely, and their clear, bright bond was quickly confirmed. Then the woman, Rosalia, asked, "My lady, may I enquire what happened with Natalia's bond?"

"It was confirmed." Her face fell into worried lines until I finished my sentence, "To Tomas."

She actually squealed with delight, dancing on the spot. Her shyer partner gave a small smile and also looked relieved as she hugged him hard. "St Jude be praised. And Sophia?"

"Are you a friend of theirs?"

"Yes, the three of us shared an apartment before I had to move to London for my job. I miss them both so much. We were all so frightened for them."

Shit. Thank goodness I hadn't dropped the ball on those particular bondings.

But I was intrigued about this woman. Why did she have to move away from Galicia? "What is it you do, Rosalia?"

"I create the back-end databases for large retail websites, my lady." Then she repeated, "Sophia?"

"Sophia's bond with Miguel is also confirmed," I answered her on auto-pilot, but I was also wondering why she wasn't able to work from her home realm. Finn might know. I added it to my ever-growing mental list of things to find out.

Rosalia blurted, "But how in the name of the blessed Madonna did you convince her stubborn papa…" She trailed off, blushing and looking embarrassed. "Apologies, my lady. I forgot myself."

"Well, your own bond is delightful. Why don't you go home and get all the news from Natalia and Sophia?" I was smiling now.

"Natalia says the Recorder is always right. It seems she's correct. Thank you, my lady."

As Rosalia strolled towards the orange doorway and home, hand in hand with her love, I smiled. Then I thought about the book the Galicians had mentioned and wondered where it had come from? I'd never heard of it. Wouldn't it be awesome if it was true? I'd freaking love to grow up and become the Recorder Who Knew Best!

The conference table had grown again, and the leather on the chairs had changed. It varied now between Pict blue and the Scottish green.

Dola had sent in an enormous stack of pizzas with a wide variety of toppings. The smell of spices, warm cheese and bliss floated in the air. Everyone was digging in and finding their own favourites. I took a huge bite of a spicy barbecue chicken and sweetcorn slice and felt the soothing warmth of the cheese on the roof of my mouth.

There was an empty blue chair opposite me with Corby. That was the assistant's name, wasn't it? She was on one side of the gap and Ross on the other. The empty chair must have been Fi's, but why was it blue? Did she have Pict blood? I wanted to ask her, but she was nowhere in sight.

Corby saw me looking around and said, "Fi needed to make a phone call, my lady. This table is brilliant; beats standing around trying to eat."

I mouthed "thank you" with my mouth full, then swallowed and asked Autumn if she was tired. She looked at me as though I was insane.

"There's so much energy. It's everywhere." She waved an arm all around, nearly knocking her juice over.

She was right. There was power everywhere, but I was flagging. It was all very well to think it was still only mid-afternoon outside the Gateway, but I felt like I'd worked for twelve hours today and eight of them on my feet. The time dilation thing in here could mess with union rules on working hours. But I'd never felt weary in here as a child, had I? My gran's voice sounded in my mind, saying things like *you've the energy of a long-life battery, child. Are you sure you're not tired?* But I never was.

The power pushed at me again. Wow, it had been assertive today. What did it want now?

It pressed on my chest the way it had when I'd undergone my true ascension. Was it trying to tell me something? Or show me something? I closed my eyes for a moment, lowered my shields, breathed in and smelt that seaside air full of ions scent that was there when I ascended, right before the power suspended me in the middle of the Gateway.

I opened my eyes, but I was still in my chair. So I went back to breathing. In about a minute, I noticed my aching feet, knees and hips—weren't aching anymore. Odd but extremely cool, and I felt much better.

I reached for another piece of pizza while there was still some left, snuck a piece of bacon to Tilly, who was lurking hopefully under the table next to Autumn's feet. I watched as some chicken surreptitiously appeared in front of Tilly's nose from Autumn and grinned.

My phone vibrated in my pocket and, pulling it out, I saw messages from Mabon and from Dai. I took a quick look at Dai's first. It was only a touching base apology for the delay. He assured me they'd be here, and he was looking forward to meeting Autumn. That was sweet and considerate.

Mabon was getting pretty good with his phone. I suspected HRH was about to lose money on the bets she'd taken suggesting he'd destroy it within the month, especially as we'd protected it with every shield known to Dola and me.

> MABON THE MAN:
>
> We're in the pub now; we'll come in when you're ready. Dola says you're eating. A problem there might be here—prepare yourself.

I grinned at the new identifier; surely Dola was having fun with him to make him learn how to change things? I must ask her. But a problem, crap, that didn't sound fun.

Finn said, "I sent the report on the Hobs you asked for. Have you looked at it?"

Swapping to email, I checked Finn's report, which surprised me. I scrolled back to the beginning to check it again. Seriously?

"Is there any proof of this, Finn?"

"Nope. Nothing to prove against either. Wondered if the Book might know."

"I asked it, but maybe not the right questions. Moira, huh?"

I thought about Moira, a former Recorder and my great, great-something-grandmother. I considered what I knew about her. She'd brought in the rule about wearing cloaks to festivals so she would know where to return any drunken idiots. That seemed to be all I knew. Moira had been grandmother to Florrie, whom I knew far more about. She was the one who liked "The Bubbles," had drunk the Recorder's cellar dry of decent champagne, and who time-travelled to fit in her "healthy exercise" bonks with her lover. So, no, I mostly knew about Moira's descendants.

"I'll ask again with this in mind. Thanks, Finn."

He nodded.

I turned to Caitlin on my right. "You OK?"

She looked surprised and, through a mouthful of food, said, "I'm solid. Why?"

"You're doing a brilliant job today. Very discreet, but your menacing expression when the couples try to linger is a work of art."

She laughed. Then she choked and eventually managed to swallow her mouthful of pizza.

"I never thought my menacing looks would be a positive attribute. Ma is always telling me to smile and be nice."

"Don't worry about it, Caitlin. There's no shortage of people who can smile and be nice. A truly effective menacing glare is a rare thing of beauty and a genuine talent."

She grinned at me. "You say the sweetest things."

Across the table, I saw Fi had returned and taken her seat. I barely suppressed my gasp. Fi was still keeping a discreet, but watchful, eye on Ross. But he only had eyes for the food.

Corby was watching Fi as closely as Fi watched Ross. Hadn't my gran said something about them? Looking at the strange glow surrounding the three, I made several mental notes. How had I not noticed that earlier? Had dropping my shields to use the energy boost from the power also boosted my abilities? It wasn't a bond glow exactly, more like a family one, but not quite that either. The Book might help. I'd better look at it properly.

I mumbled, "What was it Gran said in her letter?"

Finn asked, "Pardon?"

I just shook my head at him. "Sorry just thinking aloud."

He grinned back at me.

I should get to know Corby a little; she'd been kind and competent. Her energy was clean and refreshing, unlike Ross's. In fact, without her, I might have thrown Ross out. I had no patience for photographers who thought they were more important than the couples getting married, or bonded, in this case.

I was just working out how I could get to know Corby a little when Finn said, "Hey, Fi, cheesecakes, remember? Your idea."

Fi grinned like a kid with an ice cream. "Oh, yes, brainwave! I stole an awesome idea from the US. Now they really know how to give stuff away fairly. When I was at the wedding expo in Vegas, they had these swag bags or goodie bags—some of them were amazing. Just incredible."

I waited, but she looked like she'd drifted to a happy place. Corby's hand moved under the table. Fi jumped a little and focused back on the room.

"Erm, sorry. So I called Juniper, and she says she can box up the cheesecakes and put them in gift bags. Two in each bag, along with some of the wishing pancakes so all the guests get two each. One for them and one for whoever they want to eat it with. There won't be *any* on the buffet tables. Some of her staff will hand them out as people leave."

"Great solution, Fi, nice job." I couldn't see why mini cheesecakes merited this much fuss. You could buy them at any flipping supermarket, surely? "Why are they worth stealing? I could understand people stealing the wish-granting pancakes." I'd been impressed with those pancakes; they really seemed to grant most of the things I'd wished on them. In fact, watching Autumn slide more chicken under the table, I'd say Tilly's wish for more chicken was still coming true.

Corby spoke up, "They're called Love's Young Dream because, if you eat one with your partner, they remind you of those first heady days when you fell in love. It's a bit like a time travel device in a dessert. But you get to experience your partner's emotions as well as your own. So, if they say it was love at first sight, the cheesecake will verify if it's true, or so I'm told."

Fi and Corby laughed. "They give happy couples quite a high. No good for single girls, like me, but they're a welcome gift or a great bribe. I usually give mine to my grandparents or my sister and her wife. They don't snipe at each other for about a month. It's blissful."

In response to my confused look, she said, "I live with them. Well, I live in the cottage at the bottom of their garden." She stopped as though she'd said too much.

I was still trying to place her accent. "Where's your accent from, Corby?"

"Near Kettering, my lady."

I had no idea where that was. It must have shown on my face.

"Centre of the country. It's just off the M1 south of Nottingham. Corby."

Now I was lost. Fi jumped in, "Corby is a nickname, my lady. It's a small town, where Corby lived before she came back up here."

OK, I was being dense. "Sorry, Corby, I get it. We have a friend who's known as Pointy; her home town is Poynton in Cheshire. But Corby makes an intriguing name. Unusual."

I thought I heard her mumble, "Better than my actual name, that's for sure," and as I was about to query it, Fi glanced at her phone and said, "I think we're heading back to work, everyone. The king is on his way in." Lowering her voice, to me she said, "He says there might be—"

I interrupted her, "I got the same message, thanks." Then, realising I owed Caitlin a heads-up, I re-opened the message and passed my phone to her.

She glanced at it, and with a delighted smile, passed it back to me. "Oh, thank the Goddess, all these well-behaved, well-mannered luurved-up couples were putting me to sleep."

As Fi got up from the table, I said, "Fi, take two minutes with me, would you, please? I need to mention a couple of things before I forget. And Tilly might want to stretch her legs. Let's get some air."

Once we were all outside the green door and Tilly was sniffing around, I said, "Fi, I know my gran didn't look for seven-fold bonds because Mabon told me he hadn't seen one for many years. They're rare—but not that rare. You need to know I can't do the ceremony for a seven-fold along with a bunch of others in a batch the way you said Gran did things. We'd have to do Natalia and Tomas before or after the others. I just wanted to mention it before I forgot."

She was nodding, but with her pen poised on her

ever-present checklist, she said, "Seven-fold? I don't know what that is."

"It'd be much easier to show you rather than try to tell you. I know you see the power, but do you see the normal couples' soul bond?"

She shook her head sadly. I thought about it. "Well, Autumn's here. She might show you a normal bond, and then once I've worked out how she even does it, I'll show you the seven-fold on Sunday. Would you like to see it?"

"Autumn could show me?" She looked like an eager puppy presented with her first bone.

"Yeah, I didn't know she could do it either, but it's what convinced the emperor there was no point fighting Natalia."

"I wondered what I'd missed. I've worked for your gran since I was nineteen. I left school, there was Stuart and then your gran offered me the job, just part-time at first. But later I moved to full-time. So, twenty-two years here and almost eighteen years full-time without ever knowing what was really happening. Could I really see it? Even once would be amazing."

She'd worked for my gran longer than I'd worked for Janet—wow. No wonder these changes were having such an effect on her. I'd make more allowances; she did seem to be excellent at her job.

"When you bring the first couple over, just come

behind the new plinth thingy, next to Autumn. But do me one favour please?"

"Anything."

"Don't squeal."

She looked baffled. I said, "One, it's unprofessional, and two, it hurts my ears. I loathe squealing. Autumn is seven. She has an excuse. You don't."

She looked like she was on the verge of giggling, but she bit down on it and simply said, "Noted."

"Anyway, my point is please allow extra time in the schedule for any seven-folds we get. The sevenfold is a different ceremony with the eternal rings and stuff."

Her brow wrinkled in confusion.

"You know, like Kaiden and L'eon's?"

She shook her head.

"Ask Dola. I think Finn said she had footage of their bonding."

Fi looked over her shoulder, and I could see she was twitching to get back inside, but I wasn't quite done with her. "One more moment please. Is there a problem with you and Ross?"

She flushed a deep pink but then looked unhappy, which confused me. "Is it that obvious? I'm sorry." I didn't know what to ask, so I waited and hoped she'd just enlighten me.

"I had such a crush on him before we left school. We almost ... well, it didn't work out, not after Stuart obviously. But later, people kept saying I just needed to give him some time. But he doesn't even notice I'm alive, and he's so rude. I used to think he was shy, then I wondered if he was gay. He never goes out with anyone, you know, but he's just oblivious. Verity says he'll come around, but she's been saying that for years."

So many names here I didn't know, and yet she was acting as if I should know these people. Stuart? Verity?

I just waited again. She seemed to be one of those people who rushed to fill a silence. And she did. "My mum says he's absolutely wrong for me, and I should notice there are other people in the world. Corby— she's a wonderful person, you know—says I should get on with my own life and stop tiptoeing around him. But I don't know how to do that."

She obviously knew nothing about the strange bond I'd seen. I'd have to work out what it was exactly and maybe tell her about it.

I patted her on the shoulder. "It will come, Fi. Once you see what's really there, you'll be happier. It took me too long with my ex, but I know what you're going through. Just ask yourself what does the person's actual behaviour tell me? Not my fantasy about it, but what do they do for me; how do they treat me when they don't want something from me? Think about how they are outside of a work environment, and is it different? Then trust yourself."

She looked uncomfortable. Oh hell. I had no right to give her advice, did I? I waved my hand at her. "You go in. I need a minute to breathe fresh air. I'm flagging a little."

After she'd left, I thought about the suggestion I'd given her. I should probably take my own advice. I didn't think Ross had any romantic interest in her. Did he have an interest in Corby? Was that why the glow surrounded them all?

I saw similarities between Fi and Ross and Dai and me. It was difficult when you'd known someone since you were a child to be sure what the adult felt. Although Dai had really helped me last week when everyone just assumed I could get myself up to speed about the brownies and Smiths. But that was work, wasn't it?

Hadn't I just told Fi to ignore that and think about how Ross treated her as a person? But Dai had invited me to dinner; that was personal, wasn't it? Maybe it was different, but he hadn't actually arranged the dinner yet, had he? I was muddling myself now. Time to get some work done. It would be easier than this mess of emotions and confusion, wouldn't it?

A cute little ginger cat looked astonished to see me standing by the door and slunk off into the undergrowth. Tilly looked tempted to chase it but instead she shot into the Gateway at top speed. I guessed Dru had arrived. I needed to be back inside soon. But I wanted to check my lipstick, and I needed a moment to ask my Gift why my stomach was so unhappy when everything Gateway-related appeared to be going so smoothly.

CHAPTER
SIXTEEN

As I reached the centre, I saw them. Dai stood with his father at the front of the Red sector. I hadn't seen him since last week, but he'd emailed at the weekend and invited Tilly and me to spend time in his home before the St David's Day festival in the Red Celt realm. I was confused about this guy. I reached out with my Gift, and Mabon felt happy and celebratory, but from Dai I got nothing except slight nervousness.

"Hi, guys." I wrapped my arms around Mabon and breathed him in. His smell always made me happy. His wood smoke, pine and autumn leaves scent soothed something in my heart.

I wasn't sure how to greet Dai, but he had no qualms and gave me a hug. I relaxed into him. He was always so warm. He didn't soothe me as his father did, but he did confuse me. He smelt a little like his father, but with coal instead of wood smoke and a delicious woody undertone I still hadn't identified. There were less smoky autumn leaves in his scent than in Mabon's—usually. I sniffed. He smelt weird. Was that apple? There was a burnt undertone to it, though.

He started laughing. "You were right, Dad."

"Told you. A good nose the girl has."

I pulled away from Dai, looking up at him. I buried my nose in his chest and sniffed again. "Apples and something sweet, maybe honey? And burning? Have you guys been barbecuing?"

He grinned down at me. "The dragons were being flaming little arsonists again, and Dad finished up all the shower gel. I ended up using some expensive-looking imported shampoo of Rhiannon's. Something like Pommes et Miel. I took a photo. I'll need to replace it. My sister has a temper about those things."

"She's a candidate for the Rainbow Council, isn't she? Any ideas on another member from your realm?"

He looked startled—not another one.

"I don't know if she'll do it. I only said she'd be good if she would. There's no hurry, is there?"

I sighed. None of these royals thought there was any hurry. "I'm announcing the names on Sunday, so in five days. I don't know, is that a hurry or not?" I cocked my head to one side and waited.

Nothing.

"The inaugural meeting will be next month. After I get back from your realm." Then I put my frustration with everyone who seemed to think any time in the next decade was unreasonably swift aside.

"I invite House ap Modron to join me in the centre of the Rainbow." The formal invitation now tripped off my tongue. I'd made progress, even if it didn't always seem like it to me. I glanced at Dru, who was sniffing Tilly's nose. The iron barriers didn't bother her in the slightest. "That includes you too, Dru." He bounced into the centre with Tilly.

I glimpsed two burly boyos, as Mabon always called his guards, standing behind them. Surely nothing here needed guards? But my roiling stomach disagreed.

Dai shook his head. "I don't think I need to be there." He was frowning.

I grinned at him. "Sorry, new policy, having the bond mates' royal families in the centre has speeded things up wonderfully. It's cut down on dumb questions and chit-chat, and appears to have significantly increased everyone's happiness."

He looked unconvinced.

"Also Corby tells me it sells more photos. We don't pay them. Apparently they make money from the photos they sell. So anything that helps them do well and helps us too is probably a good thing."

Although I planned to ask Fi if we had an alternative for Ross or if we were stuck with him, and if so, why? His unhappy glowering every time he peered through his camera was bugging me. It was off-putting. He made me feel as if I was doing something wrong. Add in his inflexibility, and I wasn't sure how or why he'd become the "official" photographer.

Especially as Corby was the one who caught the most creative and different shots. She was often on her knees or winking at the couple to make them smile. Ross just stood there like an angry stick figure, immovable behind his tripod. There was just something about him I didn't like. I didn't think it was anything to do with my Gift; he just made me uncomfortable. I didn't like him, and neither did Tilly. I'd promised myself I'd take her preferences into account because she'd proved her instincts for problem people were reliable. I really must find the Book and remind myself what my gran had said about him. I'd meant to do it earlier.

To Mabon, I said, "So far we've had the Pictish prince and pr—" I was about to say "princess." Then I caught Caitlin's eye, recalled her views on being called a princess and changed it, "Heir apparent and the Galician emperor. Now we'll have you two. The anvil and the power are loving it—it creates a celebratory vibe."

Dai was still frowning, but Mabon said, "I'm not standing next to the bluddy pain-making machine of an anvil unless you hold my hand, Niki."

In a formal, stilted tone, Dai said, "As you wish, my lady."

We were back to "my lady," were we? With a snarky smile, I said, "Well, I do wish, thank you, Prince Charming." I heard a snort from Mabon, and Dai looked confused.

Dru and Tilly bounced off together, headed for their usual safe place under one of the desks. I took a quick look at the waiting candidates. They all glowed. So this batch shouldn't be a big deal, whatever my stomach thought. I'd probably just eaten too much pizza.

"What's with the guards?" I asked Dai.

"Da is taking them with him tonight, so they tagged along. One of the bond candidates is a niece, or a cousin of theirs. Is it a problem?"

I shook my head at him, but somehow I didn't quite believe him. I rubbed my left shoulder and thought, *wow, did he just lie to me? And if so, why?*

"Well now, lovely, that is." The anvil's new home held Mabon transfixed.

He stroked the wood and ran his finger around

the energy of the flowers made from rainbow power. They seemed to shiver under his touch, and several glowed red briefly. He turned to me with a big smile and said, "Good taste and a good nose, Nik-a-lula."

I shook my head at him. "Nothing to do with me. It was all the power's own idea."

He drew in a sharp breath through his teeth. "Was it now? Well, well. Interesting it is—isn't it just? And it's made the wood wide enough so it shouldn't give me pins and needles from the iron."

I settled myself in front of my mat and gestured the men to the side of the large plinth between me and Caitlin's chosen spot to the side. Mabon was correct. The wood was wide enough, especially with the anvil's new height, to give him a safe distance from the anvil. I wondered if it was done deliberately. Perhaps the power *was* lonely as I'd wondered. I'd ask the Book.

Mabon leaned behind me and was teasing Autumn about her unicorn finger puppet. I heard her say, "His name is Sparkle." I had a clear view of the back of Dai's neck and jawline. He had a good profile. He didn't move his head, but he winked at me—impressive peripheral vision too.

I nodded at Fi to bring the first couple and leaned down to ask Autumn if she would hold Fi's hand to show her the bond glow.

"I like Fi; she's kind. I don't want her to be unhappy anymore, though."

Fi was walking back with the first couple, so I said, "We'll talk about it later, baby. Are you OK right now? Shout if you get tired." She just giggled.

The first couple arrived in the Red Celt's traditional dress. The woman's red skirt and black blouse-cum-jacket were topped with the traditional ballerina-length apron of the red and green ap Modron tartan. She looked festive and happy as she stood proudly with her shoulders back and her head high. Her man didn't seem to be as thrilled, but the tartan of his kilt matched her apron, and it looked good on him. They made an attractive couple.

Unlike the Welsh in my own world, the Red Celts wore the kilt on many ceremonial occasions. I liked them—they gave the proceedings a festive air. This couple's bond was clear and bright. It circled their heads and upper shoulders in a red and orange glow.

Autumn's puppet stayed on her right hand, and I watched as she reached out with her other hand to hold Fi's. Fi gasped. There may have been a tiny squeak too, but she resolutely bit down on any squealing. She turned enormous wide eyes to me.

I nodded at her, and to the couple said, "No problems here, lovely outfits too, and I look forward to conducting your ceremony on Sunday."

Mabon nodded at the man and said, "See, *bachgen*, told you I did, nothing here to fret about."

As Fi took them back to bring the next couple, I said to Mabon, "You can see the bond glow too?"

"Oh, yes, comes from my mother's divine powers, I expect. But Dai doesn't. Though sometimes smell it, he can."

"Smell a bond, huh?" Interesting. "What does it smell like?"

Dai said, "The bond doesn't smell, but if someone is with the wrong person, it's a faint burning odour. You know if you burn toast, you can go back to the kitchen an hour later, and it's still lingering in the air?"

I nodded.

"Just like that."

"Huh, I could have used you earlier. We had quite the conundrum with Alphonse's daughter."

They both looked fascinated, and as the next couple approached, Dai said, "I'd love to see it. I see the power, so I'm not sure why I don't see the bonds."

I looked at Autumn, who nodded, and I said, "Come around this side, Dai. Autumn might be able help you with that."

The next couple were fine, and I watched as Autumn held Dai's hand. He managed not to make a sound as his eyes opened wide. But as they were being led away, he squatted down to Autumn's eye line and said, "I owe you a debt, Miss Autumn. An incredible gift you just gave me." He must have been genuinely moved, as his Welsh accent had thickened.

Autumn shrugged at him, held her hand out towards his face and paused, as if waiting for permission. I'd seen her do this once before with Fionn'ghal. Dai nodded. I sensed the energy flowing between them. I'd turned to greet the next couple, and then I heard Autumn squeak, not quite a squeal, but I was instantly alert. However, when I looked down, she was giggling and waving Sparkle at Dai. Dai was smiling and winking as he moved back to the other side with his father.

Corby was doing something with what I thought might be a light meter. She swapped her cameras out and then frowned slightly as Ross reached over and took it out of her hand. But she just nodded at him and went back to the bag before returning with a different smaller camera. There was a bond between them, but it wasn't a romantic one. I'd seen something similar once when a friend's mother was terminally ill and her nurse had come in. I'd thought at the time the bond was one of dependency. I'd need to see Corby and Fi without Ross around.

Several happy, beautifully dressed, friendly, bonded couples later, four people approached the anvil. Fi's usually calm, pleasant demeanour looked a little frayed as she came to speak privately with me. Autumn's cute little nose screwed up as she looked at the couples.

In an undertone, Fi said, "They say they're a foursome. There's a note from my lady Elsie saying they wouldn't let her check their bonds properly. I wasn't at work that day." She lowered her voice even further, "But your gran said, the blonde is a bitchy, rude little madam with no damn manners, and she needs taking down a peg or two." Fi huffed, "For once I'd say your gran understated it."

CHAPTER
SEVENTEEN

I surveyed the two couples. A foursome, hey? I'd encountered several variations of this type of relationship as a registrar. In my prior world, the solution was simple and clarified by the laws of the land. People could marry whomever they wished and live their lives however they liked, with as many or as few people as they wanted. But any individual can only be legally married to one person at a time.

I'd done weddings where other partners had stood in the bridesmaid's or best man's role. Those couples had asked me to include all of them in any way I could. There was a surprising amount of leeway for inclusion in the official ceremony, provided everyone was clear the marriage certificate could only have two of the names on it.

But in the Gateway, I didn't have to obey those

laws, as all of the realms considered a Recorder's bonding to be the same as any other formal partnership, whether they called that marriage or thought civil contracts were more normal.

I wasn't sure having all the power was an improvement. Because now I had to decide for myself. I knew three-way bonds were common. I saw them all the time when I walked Tilly. We'd walk past a couple and their dog or a couple and their child, and they'd have a bond glow that encompassed them all. Bonds didn't have to include a sexual component. I saw family bonds all the time. But for the Gateway bondings, I was looking for a romantic bond that would last a lifetime. A few years ago in a Manchester nightclub, I saw a true four-way bond. I tried to remember how I'd worked out they must be a poly group rather than simply two couples having a night out.

I considered the four in front of me. There was a glow surrounding them. But just like the two Galician couples earlier, they stood too close to each other for me to work out who the glows originated from or where they attached to.

I found my Recorder voice and announced, "I'm happy to conduct a four-way bonding. But to do so, I'm required to confirm it *is* a four-way bond and not simply several two-way bonds or a three-way bond with a power spillover."

The shorter of the two women shrank into herself as I spoke. She had dark hair and enormous, wary, deep blue eyes with the blue-white Celtic skin that often went with her colouring. She gave off a gentle unhappy energy. Why was she unhappy? Was one of the men pressuring her? Well, that wouldn't fly in the Gateway. She might have been pregnant, although it wasn't showing yet, and I wasn't sure why I'd even thought it.

But I quickly found out why she looked worried. The second woman was a tall, well-built, well-muscled blonde. She'd been in the middle of the foursome, but now she took a half-stride forward, her face screwed up in a determined expression.

In a firm voice that stopped just short of shouting, her Welsh accent sounding harsh in the air, she said, "It's not your job to judge us, Recorder. It's your job to bond us. Do your job."

I hadn't said a word that could be deemed judgemental, had I? What the hell was her problem?

I gazed at her and sank into my Gift. Oh, yuck!

What an angry, frightened woman. Her aura had a horrid greasy feel. My gran was right, I thought, but I should be polite. Perhaps she was used to people judging her.

"I'm not here to judge you. My job, as you call it, today, is to validate your bond. Please step about ten metres over there." I pointed to my left towards the Viking doorway.

At my request, she stepped back towards the other three and said, "No."

I was in danger of losing my professionalism, but I held on to it—just. "If you won't allow me to validate you have a four-way bond, then I can't put you forward for bonding on Sunday."

She stepped forward, almost a full pace this time. She looked like she wanted to grab me by the throat.

"You will do your job. You don't have a choice." Blondie waved her arm as she said this with such certainty, it startled me. It also amazed me how wrong she could be and apparently not know it. She wore a ring with a huge sparkling stone on her engagement finger.

I looked straight at her. "You are incorrect. Let me explain what activating a four-way bond over the anvil will do to you all. It will bind the four of you together for the rest of your lives. It's not a thing to do lightly or without the proper checks. There is no way back from it, and I won't—"

She interrupted me in a harsh tone, chopping her hand through the air as though to cut me off. The ring sparkled. "I know what it does. Do your bluddy job. That's all we're here for."

"No, it isn't. You're here today for a bond check. That's a check of *all* four of your bonds. You didn't allow my lady Elsie to check them, so you're not approved for bonding on Sunday—yet. If you don't allow me to complete my checks, then you won't be put on the schedule. It really is remarkably simple."

"I know all that."

"Good, then move about ten metres over there, please."

"I don't have to do that."

"That's true, you don't. Your other choice is to go home right now. Unbonded. So …" I pointed towards the Yellow sector.

She swept her gaze around the Gateway as though if she ignored me, I would just give in. But she got no support from anyone, and that bothered me. Not one of her future bond mates stepped to her side.

She sighed in a way that reminded me of the kids who'd done work placement in the registration office. Some of them had been big with the sighing. But this woman looked to be in her thirties—surely that was too old to think a sigh was an answer. Would she roll her eyes next?

I waited. But she didn't move.

To Fi, I said, "Show them back to the Red sector, please. I'll finish these others up. No need to keep them all waiting, and then I'll come over and see if we can sort this out."

Blondie said, "I'm not moving. This is my turn."

She said it for all the world as if she were in a checkout line at a supermarket. I bit down on the bubble of laughter. This was starting to amuse me. I heard muffled sniggers from the Red sector. Time for some education, perhaps?

I looked straight at her and said, "A bond over the anvil is for life. It is unbreakable, and I cannot conduct one that isn't approved by the power. I have no issues with how you all choose to live your lives. I have an issue with good manners. Display some please. Otherwise, you're dangerously close to pissing off a Recorder, and there will be no bonding for you this year or any other."

"I realise it's unbreakable, you stupid woman. I want to see your manager."

The laughter I'd suppressed burst out of me. Oh dear, it felt very unprofessional, but her comment was so bizarre, it caught me by surprise. My manager? Good grief! Did I have a Karen here?

I looked at the other three. "Please accompany your potential bond mate to the end of the line in the Red sector, or I'll put her there myself."

One of the two men, tall, brawny with sandy blond hair, who had an arm protectively around the small, dark-haired woman said, "Good luck with that!" And then he looked horrified. "I'm so sorry, my lady, that came out wrong. But Gwyneth is … stubborn."

Gwyneth, formerly known as Blondie and not Karen—at least in name—gave him a look that could have curdled milk.

This was holding up all the other happy, patient, polite Celts. I linked to the power and wrapped it around Gwyneth, transferred her to the very back of the sector right by the doorway, and deposited her none too gently exactly where I wanted her. I saw wide grins in the Red sector as people moved to give her more space. It didn't seem like she was Ms Popular.

Her three potential bond mates all gawped at me like stunned fish. I waved a hand at the three in front of me. "Shoo. I'll deal with you all last." As I spoke, I realised I had inadvertently chosen the same intonation I might have used if Dru and Tilly were getting under my feet in the kitchen—but it worked. They moved.

Gwyneth was already striding towards the front of the Red sector. I touched the anvil and murmured, "A barrier just for her—she stays in red."

Gwyneth pushed past the two boyos Mabon had brought. One of them grasped her arm, but she broke free. Those boyos were solidly muscled—she must really be strong. Then she crashed into the iron barrier. Strong but dumb, oh dear. Well, she'd have time to calm down while I dealt with the others.

"Well, I've seen it all now," I observed to the air. I

glanced at Mabon, who shook his head, "Told her, I did, to behave herself. Not big on the listening, that one."

With an admiring wink, Dai said, "Remind me never to piss you off in the Gateway, Niki."

I was feeling a tiny bit smug, and his admiration warmed me. But Autumn brought me back to the here and now swiftly when she piped up, "That's a bad word, Dai."

Mabon reached a hand out to pat my shoulder. "Sorry I am, *bach*. She's the problem I messaged you about; a nasty baggage she is."

Autumn was busy sharing Aysha's lecture on the importance of a good vocabulary with Dai. And how, if we had that, we didn't need to use bad words. He gave her a bemused smile.

The remaining Red Celt bonds went smoothly. The last couple were two men with a nice bond. When I said my usual, "No problems here; I look forward to conducting your bonding ceremony on Sunday," the shorter of the two cleared his throat.

"Was there something else, sir?" I must try to remember all these couple's names for Sunday. Perhaps I needed an iPad. I could keep lists on it without giving bonders the impression I was bored and looking at my phone. iPads were professional, weren't they?

The nervous chap was struggling to speak, so I

smiled at him encouragingly. He was small, slim and dapper with a deep green and red silk bowtie featuring the Red Celt's dragon motif. He shot an uncertain glance at Mabon and Dai and a positively terrified one at Caitlin, who was giving him her best glower, and squeaked, "Could we …" He stopped, cleared his throat, and shot an imploring glance at his partner, who reached out and took his hand as he tried again. "My lady, could we have rings like Kaiden's?"

Oh, what had the power started with those damn eternal rings?

"One moment, please." To Fi, I asked, "Their names?"

"Simon and Bryn," she whispered.

How did they even know about L'eon and Kaiden's rings? I took a closer look at the men. They had a solid bond, but it wasn't anywhere close to a seven-fold. How to put this tactfully but succinctly?

"Simon?" The shorter man nodded at me. "Do you understand why Kaiden and L'eon have those rings?"

They both shook their heads, and Simon said, "No, we just saw them on the Recorder's News Portal. They're soooo cool, though!"

"Let me explain." I focused on Finn, who adjusted his camera subtly, and I told myself not to lose my nerve. I should forget this stream was going out to millions of people and speak to this one guy. I needed to set the record straight, or I was going to spend the next sixty years explaining why people couldn't just request the "cool rings."

"I can't choose to give you those rings. They're a gift from the power itself. In recognition of a specific type of bond."

Simon said, "But we're gay too."

"They're nothing to do with being gay or straight. They're nothing to do with anything except the strength of the bond. The power gave those rings because Kaiden and L'eon have what we call a seven-fold bond. Those are rare."

Out of the corner of my eye, I could see Mabon nodding firmly, and I turned to him. He was their king, after all. Perhaps he could help. I gave him one of those looks Ad'Rian often gave him, which seemed to mean, *you should talk now*.

I must have got the look right because Mabon spoke up, "Boys, not seen a seven-fold in half a century. I haven't. A lovely bond you have; it will last your lifetime. In about another…" he squinted his eyes at them, "two or three lifetimes together, you might come back here one day with a seven-fold bond. But not this time, lads. Get tattoo rings instead, eh?"

His partner Bryn patted his shoulder. Simon had received far more information than he'd expected and looked abashed. "I'm sorry, my lady, I didn't understand."

I wanted to make him feel better. He'd done nothing wrong, and unlike his unpleasant countrywoman, he'd been very polite. "There's no reason you should have, and you've given me a terrific idea, so thank you."

He perked up like a freshly watered plant. "I have?"

"Yes, I'm going to put an article and maybe even a quiz on the Gateway news portal to help everyone understand. I owe you my thanks for the idea, and I look forward to conducting your bonding on Sunday."

Now he really cheered up. "Fab idea. I work in social media. I've even made quizzes. I'd be happy to help, erm, if you need any help, I mean."

"Thank you. Fi will take your contact details so we can collaborate on it."

They toddled off hand in hand over to Fi, looking much happier. Surveying the foursome remaining in the Red sector, I wished everyone was as easy to deal with as them.

I turned to Mabon and Dai and said, "Shall we get these four sorted out? Then I'm finished for the day. Are you both coming to eat?"

Dai nodded, smiling at me, and Autumn and Mabon said, "Sorry, *bach*, see you soon, but watching tonight, I am."

I thought he meant something on television, so I asked, "What are you watching, Boney?"

He huffed, "Bluddy dragons' eggs." Then he speared Autumn with his stare as he said, "That is not a bad word, but it is Welsh like me, so you can't use it."

I was sure Aysha wouldn't agree, but before I could get another question in, he continued, "Now what to do with the stroppy *ast*?"

I knew *ast* meant bitch, but it *was* Welsh, so it seemed even Mabon had taken Autumn's lecture on board. I almost giggled.

"Fi, would you move those four to the conference table?" She nodded, and to Caitlin, I added, "I promise to stay right here, but will you be menacing and keep an eye on Fi, please? I don't trust Karen, whoops, Gwyneth."

Caitlin nodded easily, and I saw them both escorting the foursome to the table.

If in doubt—ask for advice. "Do you know any of them?"

Mabon said, "Mostly why I'm here. Two of them I know. Gwyneth, I knew her grandmother, or could be her great-grandmother—who can tell anymore? She was a fishwife." Dai and I both started laughing and then just laughed harder as Mabon spluttered, "No, an actual fishwife, I mean. Worked on the salted herring trade up and down the coast. Used to be big business, it did. Shouty, bossy sort of woman she was."

That summed it up. It obviously ran in the family.

"And Megan *bach* now," his voice softened, and he pointed at the tiny, dark-haired woman who had almost reached the conference table. "Her grandda was a fine friend to me. I've known that child since her birth, and she's been unhappy of late. Used to help me walk Dru and Lassie, she did when Alun neared the end."

"Lassie?"

"Yes, you know, one of those collie dogs. Alun wasn't a man with much imagination in the naming. But a kind heart he had, and a strong back until his last few months."

He looked wistful. One of the problems with a life as long as his must be that you lost a lot of good friends along the way. And then he let loose with his wonderful melodic, infectious laugh. Heads turned around the Gateway.

"Dru kept Lassie alive for years. Thirty-five, that dog was when he died. Alun always said it was the fine Welsh lamb he fed him. Silly bastard. Dru used to lick him all the time. Lassie would start a hill walk with us, hobbling and whimpering with the arthritis pain, and by the end, with Dru cleaning him from nose to tail like a mother would, he'd be frolicking like a puppy. He lasted until the day after Alun's funeral." Now he looked so sad.

I reached a hand out to his arm. "I'm sorry, Boney. How about I'll take the men, and you have a word with the women? Gwyneth might be more circumspect with her king than someone she perceives to be a minor public servant. Let's see what we can do to help Alun's granddaughter, shall we?"

CHAPTER
EIGHTEEN

Mabon pulled on what I always thought of as his mantle of ultimate authority. When I was a child, this body language meant I really wasn't getting any more ice cream. In the short distance between the anvil and the conference table, he changed from being my relaxed friend and advisor to an impatient former god. As he closed on the table, angry red and silver sparks decorated the floor with each step.

Dai dropped back to give his father more space, but Dru and Tilly strolled past us both. Well, Dru strolled; Tilly was running almost full out to keep up with the Scottish deerhound's much longer legs.

The quieter pair of the foursome turned out to be Megan, Alun's granddaughter, and Owen, short, dark-haired and tall, broad and sandy-haired, respectively. They sat close to each other and clearly had a healthy, glowing bond. The slim, unhappy-looking man who stood some distance from everyone, as if he didn't want to be any part of this, introduced himself as Emrys.

I couldn't yet see anything between Gwyneth and Emrys. The lanky, nervous-looking man stood as far away as he could get from her. I suspected Gwyneth knew exactly how the bond check worked and had intended to conceal herself amid the bond the other three shared. But to be certain, I needed to check the men and make sure they had their own bond with each other and not just that Megan had a bond with them. I wanted to be completely certain of every aspect of this. Four people's lifelong happiness was on the line, after all.

"Emrys, step over here, please." He looked uncomfortable, but then Dru circled behind him and gave a soft growl, and the man moved over quickly. As Emrys reached us, the glow around Owen and Megan intensified dramatically, and I mumbled, "Well, those three have a bond. I'm getting there."

I ushered the two men back towards the anvil and out of both women's earshot. Gwyneth half-stood to follow us, but Caitlin dropped one hand onto her shoulder, and she subsided with a glare. Owen moved closer to Emrys and reached out to stroke his back. "The old Recorder told her this would have to happen. She can't just keep bullying everyone. We need to co-operate with this, or she'll just make us all unhappy."

I said, "You two can predict how this will play out, can't you? It's not complicated, but what made you realise it?"

I heard a slight commotion over at the table and, "You're just a lazy baby-making slut, and you're not having them both," carried clearly from the table. A quick glance told me Mabon had it under control. I saw Emrys shudder—was it revulsion or fear? What the hell had been going on here?

"Gentlemen, you know the two of you have a bond too, don't you?"

They both nodded. "And you know Megan has a bond with you both?"

The soft smiles on both their faces said they did.

"And you can predict the likely outcome today?"

They nodded again.

"Then why is little Miss Bossy-Pants here with the three of you?"

Total silence.

"Explain why you haven't sorted this out. Don't force me to use the power to make you speak."

Dai stood a few metres away, apparently looking at his phone, but I saw his real focus was on Autumn. He was checking she was OK in all this anger and chaos. Aww, that was kind.

Autumn stood behind the anvil. She was in her own world, as I'd always been as a child when the power played with me. She was making a figure of eight infinity symbol with her finger and the power. Her puppet was on her right hand—wow, she was accurate. As if she felt my eyes on her, she looked over towards the men and me.

"You still OK, baby? I'm almost done here. If they don't sort this out quickly, they can come back another day, and we'll get you home for some supper." I caught Dai's eye too and mouthed *sorry, I'm almost done*. He just grinned back at me.

Then Autumn looked straight at Owen and Emrys, and with an honesty untainted by any politics or manipulation or even practical considerations, the type only a child can offer, she stated, "The nasty lady is a bully. She wants to hurt the baby and the frightened lady. She wants you for herself, and then she can hurt you both too." Looking straight at me, she added, "She's like bad teddy; he always had to stay away from the unicorns."

Bad Teddy Gate, as Aysha and I had called a strange little drama with one of Autumn's toys, had been a confusing time.

Autumn's verbalisation of what I'd sensed had a profound effect on the men. Owen looked at me and asked, "You realised she's pregnant, my lady?"

I nodded.

They looked at each other for a long moment, and they both nodded. "We don't know who the father is …"

I waited, but no more was forthcoming. "Well, no. How could you?"

Owen said, "It's driven Gwyneth over the top and round the bend, I think. She didn't want children. But we all do. The three of us have been so happy, and the happier we are, the angrier she gets."

"It's all my fault." Biting his lip, Emrys said, "It was just the three of us for four years, and it was perfect. But I was a naïve idiot. Gwyneth arrived one night and just never went home. She was fun at first. But—"

Owen interrupted, "Now she's unbalanced?"

But Emrys was shaking his head. "I don't think she is crazy; I think she's sane and controlling. She frightens me." His face reddened, and he gazed at the floor.

As I walked them back to the table, I said, "I need to check if either of you has a bond with Gwyneth, so you need to stand next to her separately. When you're all together, your bonds with each other outshine everything. I need to see hers with each of you. Do you understand?"

They nodded, but they didn't look happy about it.

As I almost reached the table, Mabon said,

"Recorder, a word, please?" I nodded and walked over to him.

Gwyneth's shriek pierced the quiet around the table. "I won't be ignored. I have a right to be bonded."

Mabon put an arm around me and moved me further from the table saying, "Megan *bach* is very pale. She doesn't look well. Your word is the only law in here, Recorder." He only ever called me Recorder when he wanted me to remember that, in fact, I was in charge and should behave like it and get this finished.

Caitlin stood between me and my view of Gwyneth, but I saw both the men either side of Megan. Their three-way bond was clear, but they hadn't done what I'd asked, so I *still* didn't know their status with Gwyneth. I wanted proof, not just my gut feel.

But Mabon was right, and Megan didn't look good. It was probably best to send them all home until Thursday and sort this mess out then. "You look pale, Megan. Let's get you some water and get you home." I led her over to Dola's magic sideboard. "This is your life too. If you want to speak, now's the time."

She wanted to speak. "Emrys was the one who wanted to bring her home with us. Originally, I mean."

"Well, we all make mistakes."

She looked thoughtful. "What made me angry was when he doubled down on his mistake and wouldn't admit he'd messed up. Whatever she did, he'd make an excuse for her. But you know I've been a bitch too?"

I'd no idea what she was talking about, so I just waited.

"She kept pushing for the bonding. The three of us weren't in a hurry—but she was. She bought herself that ring, called it a promise ring. She kept saying she wanted a commitment. The three of us have one, but I've never felt one with her, and she just didn't seem to understand Recorders don't lie about bonds. I asked Mabon *bamps,* and he said, 'Never do they lie about whether a bond is true.'"

Wow! Mabon had told me this woman was his friend's granddaughter, but she had just called him Grandaddy Mabon. *Bamps* was an affectionate Welsh term for a grandad or an honorary grandad. No wonder he was here keeping an eye on the proceedings, and it explained why he was so angry. I couldn't send them home now. I'd need to finish this.

"So, you planned for my gran to tell Gwyneth the truth instead of any of you?"

She nodded. "It was cowardly of me. But once she knew about the baby, she threw a fit. She told me to terminate it, and when I said no, we all wanted children, she tried to get me to lose it. When we came to see your gran, she wouldn't let any of us step away, so your gran couldn't do the check. I don't know what she thought she would achieve—I really don't."

My Gift suggested what Gwyneth wanted to achieve had something to do with Emrys, so gently I said, "Is she closer to Emrys?"

"She's horrible to Emrys. She treats him like a servant, and he's so gentle, he just lets her." She looked less pale now. Anger had given her splotches of red on her cheeks.

As she looked at her men, her face softened. "She doesn't love them, and she hates me. She just wants the three of us to run around after her. She can be uncanny. Maybe she's psychic. It's like she knows if we talk about her. One time, we'd all decided to ask her to move out. Then she came home with presents for everyone, even a stuffed penguin for the baby with an *I'm sorry* button on it. She'd finally got the test results from the doctor and was sorry if she'd been a bitch, but she'd been so worried about it all. She was more relaxed for a couple of weeks after that. And there never seemed to be a chance to bring it up again."

I nodded. There was a shadow in her eyes, and following my Gift's urging, I asked, "But …?"

Megan looked surprised. "But?"

"What bothered you about it?"

"Oh, it wasn't true. My auntie works for that doctor. She said Gwyneth hadn't been in for months, never mind on that day. But what could I do about it? Accusing her of lying would have just set everything off again. I shouldn't be asking you to tell her what I'm too cowardly to say. But she frightens me, and I can't risk what she might to do my men or my baby. I'm sorry."

"Let's see what we can do about it. Come on, chin up."

Gwyneth stood up as we approached and addressed Mabon. In a wheedling voice, she said, "Your Majesty, I need your help. This incompetent new member of the Recorder's staff is refusing to bond us. Make her do her job. Her boss told us to come back today to be bonded."

I realised Dai was biting his own finger to prevent himself from laughing. Fi stood in front of them with Autumn, and Caitlin had a mile-wide glare as she moved around to Gwyneth's other side.

Mabon looked at her for a long time. "Your grandmother would be ashamed of you, Gwyneth. She was many things but never a liar." He glanced over at Megan and Owen and stepped firmly back. "All yours, Recorder."

I was still playing catch-up in my head. Gwyneth

thought I was some kind of junior Recorder. Maybe I could see how it happened that way if she'd met Gran recently, based on what Gwyneth said, and then come in to see me here today. But Mabon didn't believe her, and neither did I. If someone moved me several hundred metres in the air using Gateway power, I wouldn't assume they were a flunky. And I wouldn't be rude to them or anyone else without cause. And I'd given her no cause. I was calling bullshit on this one. I pulled more power because something was badly wrong here.

I tried factual. "You're labouring under a misapprehension, Gwyneth. The woman you met was my grandmother. She died. I'm now the Recorder. I do not have a boss."

I paused just for a moment to consider how happy those words made me. Gwyneth moved towards me as I continued, "You've been rude to two Recorders; now you're out of options. We don't tolerate abuse around here. Go home and think about whether you wish to send in a written apology to me and my staff for your behaviour today, or if you'd prefer to remain unbonded."

The woman hissed at me. I'd never heard a person hiss before. She sounded like an angry pressure cooker. I felt it coming seconds before it happened. I calculated quickly, caught Caitlin's eye and stepped back, throwing the power I'd pulled behind me as a shield to ensure Autumn couldn't see whatever Gwyneth was about to do, and that she, Fi and Dai would be safe behind a screen of the power. I took a step back as I pulled more power, but I didn't do either quickly enough.

Her hand shot up and across with incredible speed and almost the full weight of her solid, muscled body behind it as she struck me across the face. She was going for a back swing too. Her fake engagement ring would make a mess of my cheek if I didn't stop her. The power rushed towards her as she jerked backward.

The power was the only thing that kept me on my feet. It supported me as I clutched my face, which was as numb as if I'd been to the dentist. Then my vision blurred.

When I could focus again, Gwyneth lay on the floor on her back. Caitlin turned her over and snapped iron handcuffs on her. I assumed they were iron; Gwyneth screamed as if she was in iron shock.

Dai and Mabon were suddenly in front of me. Mabon made sure Caitlin had her secured. And Dai was trying to check on me. My face had started to throb and burn. The worst of the pain was behind my eyes and at the top of my nose, not on my cheek, which was still numb. With cautious fingers, I assessed my nose. I didn't think she'd broken it.

Other than an occasional sporting injury, I'd never

been involved in any kind of physical violence. No one had ever hit me. My own stupidity amazed me, and I definitely owed Caitlin an apology for my arrogance. Well, shit.

Emrys, Megan and Owen were making horrified and apologetic noises. Caitlin had snapped a string of iron beads through the handcuffs and was literally dragging Gwyneth on her face towards the Red sector. I called, "Caitlin." When she stopped, I held up a hand. "Hold one minute please."

Dai caught my eye and simply said, "Niki," in a low, furious tone. Why was he angry with me? And what did it have to do with him? I reached out with my Gift to see what his problem was, but I got a smooth wall. His shields were up.

"I'm fine, or at least I will be. But, damn it, I have a job to do, and I'm going to finish this off properly."

Everyone took a step back, except Megan, who said in a low voice, "My lady, I am so sorry. She did that to me once, and I had a black eye for a week. Can I get you some ice?"

At this, Owen and Emrys both turned on Megan and almost in unison they said, "You said you fell down the stairs!" and then an ice pack appeared, floating in the air in front of me.

I snagged it and said, "Thanks, Dola," just to compound everyone's confusion.

Megan said, "I did fall down the stairs—after she

slapped me across the face so hard she knew I'd fall down them. She hoped I'd lose the baby."

I felt dreadful and dizzy, but now I had a mystery, and I really wanted to solve it. What had the stupid woman been trying so hard to hide that she would hit a Recorder? She must have known the penalty. All the realms made sure their citizens knew there were severe penalties for "interfering with the Recorder about her rightful business." These penalties ranged from imprisonment right up to forfeiting their life. It had freaked me out when I'd first read it. Then Aysha reminded me that the same used to be true of various couriers, messengers, and even the Royal Mail in our own world.

And she was guilty of interfering with the Recorder because, somewhere in the physical contact, my Gift had told me she knew exactly who I was. But she'd thought, because I was new, she could bully me. I had a strong feeling she was up to no good in some other way, but I didn't know why or about what, and I damn well wanted to.

To Megan, Emrys, and Owen, I said, "That woman is about to be barred from the Gateway for life. Before she is, I want to be sure she doesn't have a bond with any of you—don't you?"

Megan nodded so hard, I thought she might give herself whiplash. The men still looked shell-shocked that Gwyneth had hit Megan and they hadn't known about it.

"I need the three of you to stand in a line with at least a ten-metre gap between each of you. Can you do that?"

In less than a minute, they'd found space and were placed exactly as I'd asked. "Caitlin, drag that bully past those three slowly, will you?"

I dropped my shields and tuned as fully into my Gift as I could, observing the show carefully. Caitlin pulled Gwyneth, still on her stomach, slowly along the line, and I absorbed it all. I also admired Caitlin's competence. That was an effective method of restraint if your captive couldn't tolerate iron. As Caitlin passed Emrys, who was the last in the line, I got a flood of information. It wasn't just Megan she'd hit. Emrys had been her punching bag. How on earth had the others not known?

"Emrys, come here, please."

He came over, looking horrified and shaky. "Please don't tell me I have a bond with her?"

"No, you don't, but I need you to make me a solemn promise over the anvil." If this man hadn't felt able to tell his bond mates about Gwyneth's abuse, he'd need some help to encourage him to open up. I couldn't be his therapist, but I might give him a shortcut. I could do this much for him.

I put on my Recorder voice, directed my gaze to

Emrys and my voice to all three of them. "Promises over the anvil are binding. Once you swear, you'll have to tell them. Clear? If you don't, you'll be in pain, which will get worse. Will you do it?"

"What's the promise?"

"You'll tell Megan and Owen all the things that happened with Gwyneth you've kept from them. It's the only way you can heal your relationship with them. Given you all have a true three-way bond, you need to do it."

"How could you know?" He looked dumbfounded. "I can't. I'd be so ashamed. She did twist everything, but I was *such* an idiot."

Caitlin called over, "My lady, may I take this trash out? The screaming is giving me a headache."

Mabon walked over, gave me a hug and said, "The boyos and I will be leaving now, *bach*; Gwyneth I'll see to. Someone from my realm strike a Recorder. I don't, I really don't …" he trailed off, directed a stream of musical but authoritative-sounding Welsh at Dai and walked over to Caitlin.

To Owen and Megan, I said, "Emrys has something he needs to do; excuse us one moment." I marched him over to the anvil and chanted the old spell almost under my breath.

Flesh to the iron
Force to the mind
What e'er you state

Iron will bind.

He swore softly, hissing, as I held his finger to the anvil. I could see Dai squeezing his eyes half shut in sympathy.

I took him back to the other two and shook their hands. "If you contact the Recorder's Office when you're ready, I'm happy to bond you all. But right now, you three need to rebuild the trust Gwyneth broke. Emrys needs to tell you everything. Remember, he swore on the anvil, so the sooner you encourage him to talk and listen properly, the less unpleasant it will be for him."

They thanked me and followed Mabon and his boyos out of the door. I heaved an enormous sigh of relief.

CHAPTER NINETEEN

"How does it feel now?"

Dai and I lingered over our coffee at the kitchen table. Once I'd convinced Dai the painkillers had kicked in, the three of us had enjoyed a fun and relaxed dinner. Dai had informed Autumn he'd known me when I was only a little older than her. He'd shared some fun stories about my antics at her age, including how he'd sneak the red gate open and whisper my name so my gran couldn't hear, but somehow I would always hear him and arrive to play him at backgammon.

"Would it still work, do you think?" It took me a second to work out what he was talking about.

"Didn't we have this conversation last week, Dai? I'm sure it would. Why don't you try it, then we'll know?" I didn't add that thanks to the weird occurrences in the Gateway during the last few weeks, Dola and I had now installed a state-of-the-art surveillance system. He'd been up a mountain and wouldn't know about it all. And this didn't feel the right time to explain all of it. So I just grinned at him.

Once her tummy was full, Autumn had gone willingly to bed. I'd watched, amused, as she rearranged the unicorns into tonight's correct pecking order. She'd insisted on taking the remains of her uneaten tuna pasta to bed with her. "In case I wakes up hungry. It's nice cold."

I'd just laughed. I couldn't see the harm in it. But I was planning a relaxing day where I could just focus on her. She'd been a trooper today. Tomorrow was her turn.

Once I was finally alone with Dai, it surprised me how uncomfortable I was. It was all very well to remember I'd known him as a child, and we'd always had fun together, but that was over thirty years ago, and I didn't know anything about the man he'd become, did I? I should make a start on fixing my missing knowledge—it might settle my nerves.

So I said, "I'm fine, really; the painkillers are working. Your invitation surprised me. I know nothing about the St David's Day festival, and I've not had time to ask the Book yet."

Last week, Dai had invited Tilly and I to spend a few days with him in his home before the big St David's Day festival in the Red Celt realm at the end of February. Today, while I'd checked bonds for dozens of happy couples, I'd thought about it several times. It was a novelty for me to have something personal to look forward to.

"But it pleased you, obviously." He grinned at me.

"Well, yeah, it did. But what makes you say that?"

"You responded about five minutes after I sent it!"

My stomach churned even more. Now I was unsure. Was that a problem? "Well, yes, Dola told me it had arrived, so I read it." His forehead furrowed in a frown. "I'm sorry. Was I supposed to ignore it for some prescribed time? I've not had an invitation from a man in twenty years. I'll have to brush up on the current protocols."

I tried to say this lightly, but I wondered if the trust issues that all the revelations after Nick's death had created were going to be a hurdle to overcome as I tried to move forward? I hoped not, but I was determined not to repeat my past mistakes.

Dai reached over to clasp my cold hand in his very warm one. "No, I was glad you didn't keep me waiting, but I thought you might. Does Dola read all your emails?"

"No, of course not."

"Then I wonder why she would specifically read mine?" There was tension in his voice now. What was I missing?

"Dola is my Equerry now; you know that, so—"

He interrupted me mid-word, "Yes, Da told me, but it doesn't answer my question."

This was exactly the kind of shit Nick used to do. He'd ask some weird question, and my answer, whatever it was, would never be good enough for him. Well, hell.

I breathed in slowly and continued, "—so, of course she reads all the Recorder's email." I gave him a quizzical look. "You sent your email to the Recorder's address, not to my personal email."

His almost silent "oooh" suggested he'd realised the mistake was his. I waited for his apology.

It didn't come.

I let the silence lengthen. I'd finally realised my failure to draw healthy boundaries with Nick in our earliest days was one reason he thought he could walk all over me once I was married to him. I'd made an unbreakable promise to myself that I wouldn't do that again, and not just with men. It wasn't just dumb; it was actually unfair to the other person as well. It was my responsibility to show people who I wanted to be and how I wanted to be treated by anyone who might matter to me.

He'd invited me out to dinner and to stay with him. If I didn't make who I was clear, I couldn't blame him later, could I? Wouldn't I be complicit in allowing him to treat me any way he wanted to?

I didn't know if it would work, but I'd given it a lot of thought, and I was going to try to really be myself with people from now on. All of myself. And I was done with being go-along-to-get-along Niki to fit in and make myself smaller for anyone.

The silence was becoming uncomfortable now. The urge to fill it rose in me. "You didn't tell me why you invited me? Or why you thought I'd make you wait?"

Damn – he still hadn't apologised, had he? I'd spoken too quickly—another bad habit I should break. It made me cross. I wasn't a woman who played games, and it surprised me he thought I might be. But we really didn't know each other as adults, did we? Wasn't that the point of his invitation?

Still holding my hand, he said, "Well, you haven't been single for very long, and I didn't want to rush you. There are some things I must tell you, though. I thought a few days in my home might give us a chance to get to know each other again and to speak privately. And I haven't beaten you at backgammon in thirty years." He gave me his crooked grin.

I'd promised myself a large glass of wine once

Autumn was asleep. Now felt like the perfect time. "Would you like a drink?"

"A beer'd be good, thanks."

Our drinks arrived, and Dai raised his glass. "To new adventures."

That sounded like a distraction. Did I want new adventures? I raised my own and responded, "To deeper understanding and better communications. There. That was almost assertive. So what do you need to tell me in your home?"

But he side-stepped my question again. "You've not had much time for yourself since this role landed on you, have you?"

"Tell me about it. I didn't realise being the boss meant it's hard to give yourself a day off."

"That was another reason I wondered if you'd like to stay at my house. You'd get a few days off and have some time to get reacquainted with our realm before all the official stuff starts." He paused, looked closely at me and continued, "I didn't mean to rush you into anything."

"You didn't. As you said, I was the one who rushed to say yes."

He laughed. "Oh Gods and Goddesses, I'm never going to live that comment down, am I?" He rubbed his hand over his face. "I'd prepared myself to wait patiently for days, then your answer arrived so quickly. I was delighted, OK?"

I nodded. "OK. Sorry. Nick used to say stuff like that, but it was never because he was pleased. Usually, it was his oblique way of saying I should have behaved differently."

In a sincere voice, Dai said, "It's such a shame he's dead."

He'd said something like that when we had a drink together in a pub in Aberglas. I'd waited for my left shoulder to ping to tell me he was lying, and it hadn't. It didn't now. I didn't understand his comment, but I didn't want to talk about Nick now. Thinking about him was bad enough. Anyway, wasn't there some rule about that? Don't talk about your ex to someone new you might be interested in. How the hell would I cope starting afresh with all this stuff in my forties?

I tried again, "So, what did you want to tell me?"

He looked around my lovely kitchen, as though it dissatisfied him and shook his head. "Not right now, Nik; your face looks so sore. When we have more time; and you're not in pain. You're coming to stay. Then would be good, don't you think? We'll have time and privacy for some honesty."

I nodded. Time and privacy sounded scary, but honesty sounded essential, and he was right, I was starting to think about taking more painkillers. Then Tilly came bounding into the kitchen, and I used that as an excuse to change the subject.

. . .

"Hey, Tilly Floppet, did you put Autumn into a nice deep sleep, and are you hoping for a reward?" I pulled one of the little sausage treats she loved out of a cookie jar on the table and held it up for her.

She danced and twirled, and Dai and I moved into what I thought would be safer waters when he said, "The little one is quite a character, but she couldn't keep her eyes open, could she?"

"Nope, a long day for a seven-year-old. But she confided it was the fifth-best day ever as I put her to bed."

"The fifth-best, hey, not a ringing endorsement, is it?" Dai grinned the same quirky grin that had me smitten at eleven years old. My gran had always said he was full of devilment.

"She's a very specific child. She's like her mother in that respect."

"This would be your best friend? I'd like to meet her, but I'm intrigued. What were the four better days, do you know?"

I counted on my fingers. "Number one was riding a unicorn."

Dai's eyes shot open. "Ad'Rian permitted it?"

I shrugged. "Well, he was on it at the time, so yeah."

Now his eyes opened even wider and his

eyebrows rose. "Let me get this straight. Ad'Rian took a sassie child *on Diamant*?"

I didn't like the tone of his question, but I couldn't work out why. But I was just feeling vulnerable tonight, wasn't I? Gwyneth's violence had shocked me. I shouldn't take it out on Dai. So I refused to get offended and just said, "Sure, why wouldn't he?"

"Did he ever take you on Diamant?"

"Well, no." Dai raised his hand and turned it palm up. I pointed at his hand and asked, "What does that mean?"

He looked at his own hand. "Oh, it just means, 'well there you have it then.'"

"So there I have what? Why would you think Ad'Rian wouldn't take Autumn on his pegacorn?"

Dai pulled a face and looked as though he wished he hadn't said anything. In a patient tone, which I found irritating, he said, "A strange sassie child ride on Diamant?"

"Why not?"

"Diamant? His soul-bonded stallion and the royal flying, not unicorn—sorry, I forget what they call those."

"Pegacorns," I repeated flatly. He didn't notice; he was in full flood.

"Diamant, the one no one but Ad'Rian ever rides. You said it yourself—even you've never ridden on him."

I looked at him, still trying to work out what was annoying me about this. I tapped into my Gift quickly. But I just got very little from him again, which was weird. I was wondering about it when he said, "I mean, we all know Ad'Rian adores you. Or so my Da always says. But he didn't take even you on Diamant, did he?"

"No."

He was nodding and smiling again, making the same gesture until I continued, "But that would be because I was riding Dusha."

"Dusha?"

I nodded.

"Who's Dusha?"

"*My* soul-bonded royal unicorn, Diamant's mate. Tilly got on famously with her yesterday. Dusha and I have missed each other. My gran has a lot to answer for, you know."

I drifted into a space where fury at Gran and delight at reconnecting with Dusha warred within me.

Dai drew in a quick breath. His face, when I looked up, held an expression I didn't think I'd ever seen on anyone before. It was made up of parts I recognised, but the entire expression was more than the sum of its elements. It was composed of almost equal parts shock, horror, awe, confusion and fear. He was blinking rapidly.

Oh, Gods and Goddesses, this evening was going so badly. Whatever his expression meant was his own problem. But I needed to know why he thought Autumn shouldn't be on Diamant; it felt important. So I asked him again.

His reply made his train of thought clearer. "Sorry, but what if she goes back to wherever it is she's from and says she rode a unicorn on her holiday?"

I laughed and inwardly sighed in relief. He wasn't being a dick. "Ah, OK. Take your point. In fact, I discussed that very thing with Ad'Rian yesterday." I grabbed my phone and showed him the same photo Ad'Rian had found on our family chat of Autumn in bed surrounded by unicorns, wearing unicorns and generally being the unicorn queen.

"Unicorns are mythical in Manchester. She might as well go back and say she rode a dragon. Seven-year-olds are allowed to live in a fantasy world …" I trailed off as I caught sight of Dai's face. He'd gone pale.

"Are you OK?"

"Don't let her ride a dragon. They're not like unicorns."

"How d'you mean?" He looked really flustered now. I tapped my Gift again, but this time I hit a wall. A nice smooth, keep-the-hell-out wall.

I waited, poking the wall a little. What was he

hiding, and why would he be hiding something about unicorns, or was it something about Ad'Rian from me? Was he even hiding anything? Did he just keep his shields up constantly? Or was it just my imagination? I mean, I'd had no clue Nick was hiding a whole other life, had I? Was I going to think anyone who kept any secrets was a Nick? No. Although my Gift, weakened by my gran's memory block, had been far less trustworthy back then. These days I was starting to rely on the extra information my Gift gave me almost constantly.

Then he pulled himself together and in a light tone asked, "Don't you have to be a virgin to ride a unicorn?"

I laughed again. "Seriously? Do I look like a virgin to you?" I smirked and stuck my tongue out at him.

Now he grinned back at me. "I thought someone said …"

"You have to be a virgin to bond with one or for one to allow you to ride it for the first time. But how do you think the Fae queens ride them? Well, OK, not the current Fae queen, 'cause the unicorns hate her. But previous queens, royal family members and, well, you know …" I trailed off.

He smiled and looked more relaxed now. "I hadn't thought that one through, had I? Isn't it crazy how much misinformation there is between the realms?" He took a swig of his beer.

I thought I was being distracted, but away from what, I couldn't tell. I decided to go along with his preference for a lighter topic. "It is. So, tell me, *can* you ride dragons? I've never heard of that. I'm sure I'd have tried it as a child if I'd known you could. I must ask Mabon why he didn't suggest it."

Dai seemed to be choking with laughter now. Oh no, he actually was choking. I stood up to slap him on the back, but he waved his hand at me to show he was still breathing.

And then, he finished his beer and stood up. "I'm really sorry to eat and run, Niki, but I have to get back. We're short-handed."

"Oh, OK. Yeah, Mabon said you guys were busy. Let me open the barriers for you. I can do it from here now."

And with a brief and uncomfortable hug, he disappeared out of the door, and I was left shaking my head. What the hell had just happened?

PART THREE
WEDNESDAY

"The Recorder explained not all little girls want to go to ballet classes; some want to excel at Glima. And not every small boy wants to be covered in dragon soot all the time. Some want to make beautiful clothes for their sister's abandoned dolls.

She told the parents they needed to see the talented children they really had and stop trying to change them into the children they'd planned to raise before their actual children were even born."

The Recorder Always Knows Best: Cautionary Tales for Incautious Children by Margarita Encimera

CHAPTER
TWENTY

Wednesday, 10th February—Gateway Cottage—Gretna Green.

I woke up at five a.m. sweaty and confused by a dream about a teddy bears' picnic. I could hear the old children's song circling round in my head. The entire right side of my face throbbed agonisingly, and I staggered out of bed half-asleep in desperate need of some painkillers.

"Are you alright?"

"Shush! Sorry, Dola, quietly, please. If Autumn thinks she's missing something, she'll be in here. I'd like to be functioning better and in less pain before she wakes up."

At a much lower volume, Dola said, "The obnoxious cat is prowling around me. She is in the kitchen now."

Blast, I'd forgotten to feed her last night. I'd taken more painkillers and collapsed into bed ten unhappy and confused minutes after Dai left.

I headed into the kitchen, starting my apology in a low voice the moment I crossed the threshold, but HRH interrupted me, "What on earth have you done to yourself, girl? House, provide the Recorder with coffee; she does not look well."

Colour me amazed, but a coffee arrived on the table. My needs appeared to override Dola's refusal to do anything for HRH until she apologised. I offered a general thank you to them both and plopped into a seat. The mug, a nicely shaped white one, was blank. How unusual. Perhaps Dola had surprised herself when she did what HRH asked.

Picking up where I'd left off on my apology, I added, "I really am sorry. I just flaked out once I relaxed after the stress of yesterday." I gingerly fingered my face. Ouch. "And the pain and shock of it all."

"That bruise stretches from your black eye to your jawline. You will not appear powerful in the bonding photos. Why on earth haven't you fixed it?"

"I am fixing it, truly. I've kept ice packs on it. I've taken vitamins, anti-inflammatories and painkillers. It's getting better."

"Well, Recorder, I could agree with you—but then we would both be wrong." She prowled across the tabletop and sniffed at my cheekbone. "I'm enquiring why you have not healed it with the power." She said this with a growl in her voice, as though I was an annoying burr stuck in her fur.

I told her the truth: "I don't know how. I only learnt yesterday I can boost my energy with the power."

"You will make me a promise."

This wouldn't be the first promise I'd made to HRH. Based on my experience, it was better to agree than to waste my time arguing.

"OK."

"Just OK, not demanding every detail? No arguing? By Sekhmet's tail, you must be in severe pain, child."

"The painkillers will kick in soon. I'll be fine."

Her tongue shot out at the speed of a striking snake. I was so startled, I dribbled coffee on the table. "Be still. Do not make me regret this decision."

Where she had licked my face, there was a patch that didn't hurt. It was a bizarre feeling.

"You will give me your solemn word, if I fix this before the child wakes, so she does not worry, you will ask the Book about healing, boosting energy, increasing magic and the many other useful things you could do with the power that you appear to be woefully ill-informed about."

"OK. Thank you." I was gobsmacked that

Autumn being worried would concern her. HRH had always been wholly self-centred unless extremely well-bribed with some variety of fish.

Following her instructions, I held my hair out of the way. "Your conditioner is repulsive and full of chemicals. You should use something with more class. You have the money; spend it." Then I sat with the unbruised side of my face almost flat on the table so she had access to the bruised side. Her tongue felt strange, not rough like a normal cat's tongue, but as though it trailed energy in its wake. Where she'd licked, tingled.

Barely a minute later, the pain had gone. She tapped the back of my head with her paw. I sat up and stretched my jaw. "Wow, thank you. It feels normal."

"You will not embarrass me by looking like a battered wife or a mugging victim instead of the all-powerful Recorder for these events."

Her statement sounded more like an instruction. I wondered why she cared. "What would you like to eat?"

"I'm fine, thank you. I shall wait until breakfast, for which I shall take more smoked salmon with egg please."

I gaped at her. "You're fine?"

"The child gave me her pasta."

I looked her over carefully. I hadn't seen her since

yesterday, but the pattern on her coat was nice and bright; her fur was glossy; she looked slim and elegant. She looked exactly how she had looked since the power shared some Indigo energy with her last week.

Perhaps my silence inspired her to add more details, "She said, and you *will* understand I am quoting and *never* think to use the words again yourself now you're an adult?" I nodded at her, but I was confused.

She said, "'Awww, poor cute kitty-cat. You're so hungry. You can have mine,' and she placed the bowl on the floor of her room and went back to sleep." She twitched her tail toward a bowl. It appeared to be the one Autumn had taken to bed with her but which now sat on the draining board.

"She reminded me of you when you were her age. Such delightful manners she has. I may have encouraged her to sleep a little deeper and more restfully so we could talk. And I may have touched the surface of her thoughts as I did so. She was concerned about you."

I decided I would need far more time than I had right now to process this astonishing blip in HRH's usual curmudgeonly attitude and simply said, "Thank you. What did you want to talk to me about?"

"The Vikings. You are opening their gate for Rollo?"

Ah, that made sense. She thought her betting pool on when I would unseal the yellow doorway was in danger. It wasn't. So I grabbed my laptop and read to her, "This is the current position of Prince Rollo, and now I'm the one who's quoting." I smirked at her. "'Could you see any way those bondings could go ahead? I understand it would change nothing about the current issue, which would remain to be dealt with.' Does it help at all, Your Majesty?"

She was cleaning a paw, and I thought that was her cheerful expression. "It does. You are reliable, thank you, Recorder. I will leave you to your day. One further thing?" She stopped licking the paw and directed her bright green eyes straight at me.

"OK?"

"Whatever Bad Teddy did needs fixing. Swiftly." She twitched her tail and strolled off.

Bad Teddy Gate was the name Aysha and I had given to a peculiar drama when Autumn was almost five. She still believed in Father Christmas, and we'd taken her to see him at a local community centre, famous for hosting a good Christmas pageant. Santa arrived in his sleigh, trailing Christmas songs and good cheer in his wake. The kids got to visit him; cute photographs were taken and made into Christmas cards to delight grandparents.

A local business donated gifts for the children; another gave complimentary selection boxes for all of them. It was a nice community event, and it raised money for local good causes. Autumn's present from Santa, along with most of the other little girls, had been a cute plush teddy with a glowing nightlight heart. Even back then she preferred unicorns, but she'd offered a well-mannered thank you.

Aysha put the bear on her night table. The next morning, the teddy was high on a bookshelf that Aysha didn't realise Autumn could reach. He was facing the wall. She sent me a photo, and we laughed about the fact he'd obviously been a bad teddy. She put him back on the bed. Autumn put him back on the shelf, facing the wall.

Aysha put him on the toy box. Autumn put him inside the toy box, still facing the wall, and buried him in other toys.

It was a bit like an elf on the shelf, but in reverse. At first it was funny. Kids do weird things. But one afternoon when I was there, I caught her putting him into the kitchen waste bin. I'd asked, "Shall I take teddy away?" She'd nodded firmly then said the strangest thing, "But don't take him into your house, Auntie Nik. Put him in a dustbin outside."

Bad Teddy sat in a bag in the boot of my car until I made my next run to a charity shop. And no one thought any more about it until a mother on Aysha's neighbourhood mum's chat group posted a photo of the same type of teddy. Her daughter got one from Santa too, and their new Labrador puppy destroyed it. It had a nanny cam inside it.

The police were notified, sex offender registers were checked, but some weeks of investigation later, nothing could be proved and no one could be charged. However, the police were pretty sure none of the cams had been activated.

But this was several years ago now. So why had it cropped up again? Autumn said Gwyneth was like Bad Teddy. I'd woken up with "Teddy Bears' Picnic" going around my head. and I probably shouldn't ignore a warning from HRH. I just wasn't sure I understood it properly.

"Can I have more coffee please, Dola?"

My mug said, *Your schedule today is empty. Fill it with fun stuff before someone fills it with problems.*

I giggled and took my coffee into the bathroom, thinking about my mug while I drank and surveyed my healed face. In the shower, I decided Dola was right. As I'd thought yesterday, Autumn and I were due a day off—anything Recorder-ish could just take a number and wait until after we'd had some fun.

As I emerged from the shower, I heard, "Niki, Finn and Fi have taken the morning off as you instructed. I redirected the phone line here. I have just taken a call from Princess Natalia of House Asturia."

"They did two days' work in one yesterday; good idea to switch the phones through here, though, Dola, thank you. What did Natalia want? Is there a problem?"

"She wanted Autumn's measurements and permission from her parent or guardian to include her in the royal wedding party."

"That child is a wicked little goal setter!"

"I don't think Autumn is bad?" Dola sounded distressed.

"Sorry, Dola, it's slang. Google it—it means extremely good." I sometimes forgot who I was speaking to. Dola did such an amazing job of appearing to be a person. Well, she was a person, but … my own thoughts tangled me up. The fact that this type of misunderstanding didn't occur more often was surprising.

"I see. Yes, Autumn is clear on her objectives. Would you like me to provide Natalia with her measurements, or do you need to check with Aysha? She is breakfasting now."

"Yes, best to call her, I think." I didn't want to delve into how Dola knew that—not right now, anyway—when I needed to call Aysha. But I suspected it was something to do with the prettily wrapped parcel I'd delivered to Aysha's on Monday, and it jogged my memory, "Dola, remind me to speak with you about the device I installed at Ad'Rian's please."

"OK."

I called Aysha and conveyed the news that her determined daughter had found someone who wanted her as a bridesmaid. And not just anyone but a Galician princess. Aysha was amused but unsurprised and had no objections. I decided to follow HRH's advice.

"Hey, remember Bad Teddy Gate? Has Autumn ever mentioned it since?"

"Nooooo, well, not exactly. Why?"

My Gift tickled me. Aysha was the least evasive person I knew. She was supremely straightforward. If you asked a question, you'd better be prepared to deal with the answer because she was going to give it to you. I loved it. It meant I could never upset her by accident.

"Spill it please, Shay; it might be important. There's a nice pregnant woman whose safety I'm concerned about. Autumn's picked something up too, but I don't know what, and I'd rather ask you than her."

There was silence. I could hear her breathing, so we hadn't been cut off.

"Aysha?"

"You're just doing so well, and I'd hate to put you back there."

Now I was panicking. What could put me back into being the sad, spineless Niki of the last year?

"I'm pretty sure I'm good, but Megan might not be if I don't find out what triggered Autumn to mention Bad Teddy yesterday."

"Is she OK?" Concern laced through her voice.

"Yes, of course she's fine, or I'd have told you. She's still asleep. It was a long day, and she was having too much fun to take a nap, so I'm letting her sleep. I'll get her to call you later if you like. She's good, but I do need info."

I waited.

"OK, if you're sure."

There was a pause.

"I'm sure, Shay—what?"

"Autumn used to say Nick was like Bad Teddy."

Stupidly, I said, "My Nick? Bad Teddy?" I got a "mm-hmm" down the line and was no wiser.

"What did you take that to mean? Why didn't you ever mention it?"

"I saw no reason to—my child is adorable but weird sometimes, and she isn't always right, and you had enough on your plate. I took it to mean Nick was spying on you while he was out of the country. Given I knew you weren't doing anything interesting from his point of view, I didn't bother you with it."

Fury rose in me. When would I stop finding out about all the invasive, horrible, weird stuff Nick had done? Because the moment Aysha said it, my right shoulder told me she was correct. "OK. I'm going to have to think about this, but it might be a clue to the problem here. So thanks. Want to talk to the little madam later?"

"Nope, I'm trying to get finished early, so I'll see her in no time. You guys have fun. Send a photo from wherever you end up though, yeah?"

"Will do, message whenever you're ready, and we'll come and get you."

I told Dola she could send Autumn's measurements to Galicia and asked if she had any idea what had spurred Natalia into offering her this opportunity. Apparently, she'd asked her father at breakfast why he'd given in. He'd confirmed it was Autumn who'd allowed him to see her bond with Tomas. She announced she would send Autumn a thank-you gift, and the emperor told her Autumn was hoping someone might need a bridesmaid.

I smiled to myself. He was a sweet man to have

remembered. Also a clever one because now he had a grateful Recorder on his side, didn't he? Perhaps to help with his trade agreements? Which reminded me, "Dola, did we get a basket of samples from the Galicians?"

"We did. Fi alerted me. I told her she should take the honey cakes to her mother as we are doing low sugar, but the meats, cheeses and pates are in the fridge."

I bit back all the rude words that sprang to my tongue. "We need to have a word about this low sugar, health thing, Dola. I did not sign up for this. Perhaps we have a misunderstanding? It's fine when Autumn is here. It's Aysha's right to have her opinions about her child's diet respected. But let's be super clear. I'm an adult. I have a right to eat sugar whenever I damn well want to.

"At certain times of the month, I don't just want it —I need it. Especially now when those times seem to be less easy to predict than they used to be. And I don't especially like salad with pasta, not in February. In February, I like garlic bread. Don't get carried away, OK? Mrs Glendinning is lovely, and I'm always happy to share, but please bear in mind I am not now, nor do I ever plan to be a low-sugar, vegetable-loving, salads-in-winter person. Aysha is, and she intends Autumn to be one too, at least while she still has control of her diet."

There was silence. Then in a small voice, she asked, "Have I overstepped?"

She'd asked me the same question several times over the last few weeks, but for the first time, I thought she had, so I opted for honesty. "Yeah, you have a bit. I don't need you to police my diet. If anything, stress makes me lose weight, not gain it. I'd quite like to get my curves back. I used to have some before bloody Nick thought I should be super-slim to impress his work colleagues. So break out the brownies once Autumn's gone, OK?"

"I can do that," said a subdued voice. Oh dear, well, it had to be said. Maybe I could have been more tactful, but right now I'd kill for a brownie, or a doughnut or a cookie or — I was probably hormonal. Who the hell knew these days? Peri-menopause indeed, perhaps that idiotic doctor hadn't been wrong. I wondered if the power could fix hormones.

CHAPTER
TWENTY-ONE

Wednesday, 10th February—Gretna Green, Scotland and Carlisle, England

The three of us had a lovely Autumn-centred day doing normal things. The kind we'd shared many times before all this Recorder craziness began. Autumn chattered away to Tilly in the back seat. Scotland gave us a sunny but freezing day with a vibrant blue sky, and in the distance, the Cheviot Hills with their blue-grey splendour and mustard highlights marched along the horizon to our right and then moved behind us as we turned and headed south. This was a beautiful part of the world.

I'd had no idea when I arrived in Gretna Green that the nearest town of any size was over the English border. The squealing began as Autumn's head swivelled back and forth when we crossed the border. I parked the car in a lay-by on the quiet country road. The idea of crossing the border to have lunch and shop in "a whole other country" had fascinated Autumn. She walked from one country to the other between the two signs that respectively said "Welcome to Scotland" and "Welcome to England." Then, indicating the twenty-metre space between the two signs, Autumn stamped her foot on the road and pointed. "So, if there is England," she swivelled around, "and that's Scotland, then where's this, Auntie Nik?" She stamped her little boot on the road again as though to check it was real.

"We'd better look it up, baby—it's sort of nowhere, isn't it?" This amused her, and she stood between the two signs, pointing at them both while I took a photo, which I sent to Aysha with the caption, *Look, Mum, I'm standing on nowhere!*

We set off again, and, monitoring her through my rearview mirror, I asked, "Autumn, what made you remember Bad Teddy yesterday with those people?"

She was unconcerned as she answered, "The nasty lady watches and listens to them when she's out. She wants to know what they're doing all the time."

Sometimes with Autumn, a non-word would spark more information, so I tried, "Mmm-huh?"

But she'd moved on now and was admiring the local black-faced sheep. I asked the other thing I really wanted to know, coming at it obliquely, "Are you excited about being a bridesmaid?"

Five minutes later, we'd established that, yes, excited might be the word.

"So how did you know you could show the emperor the bond glow?"

She was blasé about it. "Mum couldn't see how pretty the power was, and I really, really, wanted her to, 'cause it's beautiful. Then she held my hand and she could. So, when the 'mperor was muddled and unhappy, I really, really wanted him to see how happy those people could be."

So simple then. A powerful, genuine desire to show the person in question. I'd try it myself.

Five minutes further down the road, we saw a lovely park just below Carlisle Castle. "Auntie Nik, look, it's a proper castle."

It was a real almost thousand-year-old castle with walls. The walls pleased Autumn. We did lots of activities designed to work up an appetite for us and so Tilly would be ready to stay in the car for a nap while we went shopping. Autumn played on the swing, and I tapped my earbud and filled Dola in on what Autumn had said about Gwyneth bugging Megan's home and suggested she speak with Mabon about it.

It struck me as creepy as hell—but probably not

illegal. However, laws wouldn't restrain Mabon, and the king might get it checked out.

But Dola surprised me. "I would prefer to alert Rhiannon. Would Mabon know a surveillance device if he saw one? But Rhiannon would; she is excellent with technology. Shall I call her?"

I told her to do whatever she thought best and got on with having fun with a bouncy child and an even bouncier dog.

The blissful normality of it centred me after the craziness of yesterday.

We behaved like tourists, had a cheap and delicious lunch of homemade soup and a cold pork, cranberry and brie pie with excellent hot water pastry in a friendly little café overlooking the castle. While we were waiting for food, I checked my phone. I thought Dai might have messaged to see how I was. He didn't know HRH had healed my face, did he? And he'd shot out of my kitchen as though he were being chased. But there was nothing from him, so after a moment's thought I sent him a message.

Niki: *You left in a bit of a hurry, is everything OK?*

I wasn't giving a man who couldn't communicate any of my energy. As Aysha would say, that's a Hard Pass.

There was no response by the time we'd finished eating. He might have been busy or just out of range, so I put him out of my mind, and the three of us got on with having fun. On our way home, we popped in to a large out-of-town toy store. I paid up, as Autumn had won the bet to get a new unicorn by correctly spotting every match yesterday.

"You can buy from my wish list anytime, Auntie Nik, but what if there's something 'mazing in this shop that isn't on the internet?" When did an actual shop become such a novelty, I wondered?

She found a purple and silver unicorn, which she informed me was different in all respects from every other unicorn she owned! On the way to the checkout, she spotted a small red dragon about the size of my hand and swooped on it with all the enthusiasm of a seven-year-old who knows her aunt is putty in her hands.

I bought them both.

Back at the car, she gave the dragon to Tilly. "Pupsicle, it's a present for you, so you have a dragon friend."

Tilly sat on it, licking it happily the entire way home.

Back in my office, I'd spent some time with the Book while Autumn played with Tilly and worked through my list of questions. I re-read Finn's briefing and tried to validate the origins of "The Recorder won't bond Hobs" and find out why Moira had cared. And I worried because I'd forgotten half the things I'd meant to ask the damn Book. I needed to get better at this job.

The conclusion I'd arrived at after the Book answered a lot of my questions was many things were being done simply because other people had done them and no one knew why anymore. It reminded me of a training the council had sent me on about steering change, or was it driving change? It was some pointlessly macho-titled course anyway, but the content had been useful.

The Book also suggested some things I could experiment with to familiarise myself with the subtler uses of the power. They'd probably have to wait until next week. I couldn't catch up on a thousand years in a week or two.

When I collected Aysha, she'd asked to breathe some fresh Scottish air after three days in court. So the four of us walked around the gardens just as dusk was falling.

"Fi says the Scottish call this time of day the gloaming—isn't it a lovely word?"

Aysha grinned at me, "Roaming in the gloaming—isn't it a song? It always sounded rude to me." She gestured at the woodland surrounding her and asked, "Is this all yours?"

I nodded. "This and a lot more besides will be mine once the probate completes, yes."

She looked thoughtful, considering an enormous tree with a trunk about three feet across. "And Jamie wanted to send the bulldozers in? Just criminal! Any news on what they'll do with him and his dad?"

I filled her on the gossip from the local paper Fi had brought in for me. It asked a lot of leading questions it had no answers to, because none of the Fergussons' offices were saying anything.

I'd brought Fi up to date on what had really happened. But I'd also sworn her to secrecy as far as any locals were concerned. Anyone from the realms would already know about it, but I didn't want the news reaching the local populace in Gretna Green, or more importantly, the local paper.

The paper was asking things like, "Have the Fergussons absconded with client funds?" Because neither of them could be reached for comment, the paper had gone to town on their own theories.

Aysha said, "It makes me wonder whether Jack the Ripper, Lord Lucan and Amelia Earhart were all wandering around one of the realms at some point."

I laughed. "Maybe a Recorder ruled on them too —well, not Earhart, but you know what I mean. Mabon said John's sentencing is happening at the same time as the St David's Day festival, so I'll be there for that, and it's possible Jamie will be released by the Fae healers around then."

Aysha said thoughtfully, "So no trial for John, just sentencing?"

I nodded. "Oath-breakers don't get a trial. If there's proof of oath-breaking, there's about a thousand years of case law in the realms. They take that shit seriously. Mabon still feels he was incredibly restrained in not just lopping the traitor's head off in the Gateway at the time." I grinned.

Aysha gave me an odd look. "You're very casual about this, Niki. Where did my angsty friend go?"

"She didn't go anywhere, but this isn't my area of authority. It wasn't me he put at risk of being trapped in a realm with no way out by not doing his job, was it? It doesn't matter what I think; it's up to the royals. But I kind of agree with them. He was a horrid, pompous little man who hurt, hindered, and harmed in a lot of situations where he could have helped. He had a vital job, and he treated it like a golf club membership—something he could do if he felt like it. And appointing Jamie without *ever* testing him. Words fail me. I'm not planning to interfere in whatever the realms decide."

She said, "It looks as though you're taking on board that high court judge's idea of not being sure you're right, but being sure you're certain?"

"Yeah, I am. That was good advice. I owe you for it."

She thumped my backside and, smiling fondly at

Autumn and Tilly, who were running about like mad things, said, "Oh, don't start counting who owes who what; I might lose. You did just look after Autumn with no notice for three days without a single complaint."

We grinned at each other and watched the kid and the dog with doting mum smiles on our faces.

After a lovely family meal, when Autumn and Tilly were in bed exhausted, Aysha and I spent an hour in the hot tub. I filled her in on Autumn's adventures since Monday, and we chatted about nothing most of the time. She was evasive about Lewis, saying only it was too soon to say anything for sure, but he was funny and kind and liked kids. She would have to see. That sounded potentially serious to me. She asked me about yesterday and tomorrow and how I was doing identifying bonds and what I thought about the real Fi.

"And what's happening with Prince Charming?" Aysha had been amused when she found out Dai was a prince.

I was tempted to be as evasive as she'd been about Lewis, but I wouldn't mind another perspective on what had happened.

"He was very weird yesterday, gentle and quite kind at first, but then difficult and a bit Nick-like." She frowned at me. "Then he shot out of here for no reason." I was still smarting from his abrupt departure. "Every time Nick's name comes up, he says what a shame it is he's dead, and he's not lying." I wriggled my shoulder at her and added, "I would know, you know. My Gift is so much more reliable now."

"I think I'd like to meet him. Didn't you say he was busy doing something with dragon eggs? Lewis says everybody is watching the cam."

"Yeah, he is, but Mabon was on egg-watching duty last night. Dai didn't get a text or anything. He just suddenly stood up and said he had to go. I can't deal with another man who plays stupid games, Shay. I just can't and won't."

I paused and took a sip of my wine. Aysha waited patiently, then she prodded gently, "But that's not what's bothering you, is it?"

"He said I'd responded to his invitation too quickly. Well, he didn't exactly say that, but …" I trailed off.

Aysha was giving me her assessing look. It made me feel like an under-ripe avocado on a supermarket shelf—as though I should shape up. "Didn't you say Recorders live to a hundred years old?"

I nodded. "Actually, it's the minimum. I've been studying. I mean, I could walk in front of a bus tomorrow, and I'd die. I'm not immortal or anything, but the stronger the connection to the power, the more it can offset the speed of aging. I seem to have a very good connection to it. Why?"

She splashed me. "I'm going to hate you in ten years when you look the same, and I'm starting to look like my mum!" She took a gulp of her wine with a grin on her face. "But look on the bright side. Remember when you met Nick?"

I nodded.

"You said you had no time to waste; you wanted a family. So even though you weren't sure Nick was the right man, you went along with his plans?"

"Yeah, that wasn't my finest hour, was it?"

"No, Nik, it really wasn't. But think it through. Don't you actually have more time ahead of you now … than you thought you did back then? So what's the rush with Prince Charming?"

As I processed what she'd said, she continued, "Take it slowly. Explore all your options. So you had a crush on him when you were a kid—find out who the boy you liked grew up into and whether you like and trust the man he is today."

"He's not really a man. I mean, he was only a couple of years older than me, fourteen or nearly fifteen when I was, what? Twelve, I think. He was kind to me, but I knew I was too young. But now, he looks as though he's in his early twenties, not his forties."

But Aysha was done being serious, and she

waggled her perfect brows. "Oooh, age-gap romance, it's all the rage, you know."

She gave me a hug, and I was suddenly very tired. Aysha yawned widely. "Sorry, but this hot tub is stupidly relaxing; can I be very boring and go to bed?"

I laughed, finished my wine and said, "I was just wondering how to say the same thing. Come on, let's act our age for once and treat ourselves to an early night. We've both got a busy few days ahead."

PART FOUR
THURSDAY

"And the little boy finally understood that his guardian would never change because he didn't want to.

It was up to the boy to create his own life, a life he loved. Then he wouldn't be embarrassed because he'd be in charge of himself. His good friends and his beloved pet would all help him do it. But the Recorder cautioned him that trying to control anything other than himself was a slippery slope that might lead him to grow up just like his guardian."

The Recorder Always Knows Best: Cautionary Tales for Incautious Children by Margarita Encimera

CHAPTER
TWENTY-TWO

Thursday, 11th February — The Gateway

"And I just walk through. That's it?" Aysha sounded unconvinced about making her first independent trip to another realm. This was her first time walking through the doorway without me. "I've always assumed you did something magical?"

"I do. I've done it; the door's open—go." This wasn't the time to explain how the barriers, which Aysha couldn't see, were already open.

Autumn came to my rescue; she was ready for one of Whirly's kurts. "Mum, it's easy. I'll show you. Come on. Bye, bye, Auntie Nik, thank you for having me. See you on Sunday." She took her mother's hand and walked confidently towards the blue door.

Fi giggled. "I feel for your friend. I was still a teenager when your gran sent me out as a messenger the first time. It petrified me. I expected something like a Star Trek transporter beam to scatter my atoms far and wide. I felt silly afterwards, but email is much easier than hand-delivered messages."

"On that topic, can you spare me fifteen minutes? I want to consult you about some changes I'm considering."

Fi's eyebrows rose, but she said, "Of course. Now?"

"Now works for me. Let's take the conference table and get coffee."

I tried to explain the feeling I'd had since I took the job. We did everything exactly the way the previous Recorder did it, and she'd just done it the way the one before her did it, and so on back to the Dark Ages—literally.

Defensively, Fi said, "Tradition's important though, isn't it?" But she looked thoughtful.

"Yeah, it is, but there's tradition, and then there's old-fashioned for no good reason. Email isn't newfangled and hasn't been for decades."

Fi barked a laugh. "You know, right up to her death, your gran liked her emails printed out and given to her in a pile, so she could scribble her answers on them?" Then, more seriously, she said, "But how would you know the difference between when we should change something and when there might be a reason for it?"

"When I was a registrar, they sent me on a course about change. The trainer told a story about a hambone. Have you heard it?"

Fi shook her head.

"A newly married couple were in their kitchen. The man was peeling potatoes while the woman was prepping a ham for dinner. As the husband watched, the wife cut several inches from the bone end of the ham. He commented he liked the meat at that end. It was juicy, and he asked why she'd cut it off. She said, 'My mum always does it that way.'

"The husband asked, 'But why?' The woman just shook her head.

"Next time she called her mum, she said, 'Hey, why do you cut the end of the hambone off?'

"Her mother said, 'That's the way my mum does it.'

"The wife is curious now, phones her grandmother and asks, 'Gran, why do you cut the end off the hambone before you roast it?'

"Her gran replied, 'Because my roasting tin is too small. Why?'"

Fi looked blank for a moment then started laughing. "Oh, for heaven's sake, and I'm part of the problem of not knowing why we do or don't do things, aren't I?"

"No, Fi, you're really not. You've adjusted well to all the changes since you came back from holiday.

But, if we're not careful, we end up refusing to bond Hobs, and no one left alive even knows why!"

"I was shocked by how fast you'd altered things, Niki, but the changes have been good. The news portal is great, and Finn is a magician with a computer."

I smiled to myself; she'd so easily stopped bowing and calling him Prince Finn. She wasn't part of the problem, but I needed her onboard, not just with the changes I wanted to make now, but as an active part of suggesting more. She'd worked in here for twenty-two years—she must have ideas. Which reminded me.

"You said you might have a list of ideas or things you'd suggested over the years. Did you find it?"

She looked sheepish and stared at the surface of the table. "You'd already made most of the changes. And the power made one of them itself. I asked your gran if we couldn't have something purpose-built for the anvil to stand on, but your gran said it had to be right in the middle of the centre space. And she didn't think we could move the desks because they'd always been there."

I pictured myself floating in the very centre of the Gateway right over the anvil at my real ascension. "I think she was right about the centre thing. But it didn't mind when Caitlin and I moved it out of the way when we tested the Knight Adjutants. Maybe it depends on exactly what's happening in here. I'll ask the Book."

She made a note on her pad, the one I almost never saw her without. "Fi, would you prefer a tablet?"

"Well, of course I would, but those things cost a fortune!"

"Yeah, they're not cheap, but we'd all be able to see the current checklists. The number of times I wanted to see the names of the couples on Tuesday—if it was on a shared list, it would make life easier for the three of us, and Dola could help too if it was in an electronic format."

"Well, if it's in the budget, then, yes, please."

"Dola, would you order three iPads, in different colours, please? And one of the pencils. And can we have them as soon as possible, but definitely before Sunday?"

Fi looked shocked. "Three iPads but only one pencil?"

"I think you might find the transition easier with a pencil—you seem to enjoy ticking things off."

She giggled, actually giggled. "I really do, you know. It's a habit from school, I think. I love a good to-do list. I just hadn't realised it was so obvious."

I got the discussion back on track to focus on the changes we needed to make. "All the previous Recorders, most of them apprenticed with the

Recorder before them, so no one ever stopped to think whether they could just buy a bigger roasting tin. Did they really have to carry on doing things the way they did them in … oh, I don't know, the twelfth century, maybe?"

Fi was nodding now; she was getting it, "OK, but what criteria should we use to decide whether we should change whatever it is?"

"Criteria, huh? You've been talking to Finn and Dola, haven't you? Do you want to ask Finn to join us and get him to help us define the criteria?"

She went a little red and nodded, trying to hide a smile, and walked over to Finn.

I heard him say, "Sweet! Bagsy, the black or grey one."

"Dola, can I have a caramel macchiato and something sweet with real sugar, please?"

A very large curvy mug arrived. On it I read, *Today's innovation is tomorrow's tradition.*

"Huh, is it a quote? Who said it?"

My phone vibrated in my pocket, and I looked and saw a link to a page about Lidia Bastianich, who was a chef, among other things. Some of the photos on the page made me hungry. Had it been so long since breakfast? Then a large plate arrived on the table with a ridiculously wide selection of doughnuts, brownies, and something green. I peered closer and saw they were little marzipan vegetables.

I grinned, relieved to see Dola had lifted the embargo on sugar. "OK, OK, I'll eat my vegetables." I popped a baby tree piece of broccoli in my mouth and was delighted when it tasted absolutely nothing like anything cruciferous.

Fi returned to the table with Finn in tow, and we launched into a discussion of how we could safely change things.

Then Fi said, "I need to get prepared for today's bonding checks, Niki, and if you want to get changed …"

I looked at my phone. "Crap, yes, I do. See you guys in five."

As I strode out of the doorway, I felt we were making progress. I just needed the realms to do the same. Tilly scampered at my heels and looked hopeful it might be lunchtime.

CHAPTER
TWENTY-THREE

From the anvil, I surveyed the entire Gateway. Lavender must have done her bloom-pretty spell because all the branches around the large space now bore tiny white and pink blossoms interspersed with larger red flowers. They gave the building an entirely different and welcoming aesthetic. I'd be sad when they were gone. How long would they last? Did we have to take them down, or was that simply another habit? Would the Book know?

I looked around for Rosemary, who'd been somewhere around the Gateway since Monday, but I couldn't see her. Who paid her and her sisters to create all this beauty? The things I didn't know were becoming overwhelming again.

Behind the anvil, I waited for everyone else to be ready to go and checked the lists and notes Fi had given me. My too-long hair kept falling in my eyes. Now I no longer needed reading glasses, I realised I'd often used them on the top of my head as a substitute hair band. I sighed, blew the hair out of my eyes and read Fi's first list.

Hobs = 3 couples

Fae = 12 couples

Vikings = 7 couples (+ possibly Princess E)

+ Maybe Red Celt returning threesome (we haven't yet heard from them)

Of course that would be why I couldn't see Rosemary. She was coming in later for her bond check. However, this looked like a much lighter day than Tuesday. Fi's second list contained the names of all the couples. The ones from Tuesday and today's, totalling seventy-eight or seventy-nine, if Princess Entitled turned up, in two busy days. If I'd done the initial checks myself, I would have already done all this. Perhaps when I hit my mid-nineties, I'd put some safety checks in too as Gran had, but right now it felt pointless.

I tapped my earbud and said, "Dola, could you add an overhaul of this bonding check process to the list Finn is compiling, please?"

"Yes, and the iPads will arrive tomorrow lunchtime. Did you want me to contact Lis or Mags?

She said she would get back to me when she had some free time I have not heard from her yet."

"Awesome on the iPads, and, no, please don't contact the Hobs. Lis is going to be furious when she realises she missed the opportunity to weigh in on the Hobs bondings. And that petty thought brings me genuine pleasure. If she wants to style herself Headwoman of the Hobs, I think she needs to behave like a person who gives a toss about her people."

I thought I heard a low chuckle—at least it wasn't the crazy cackling she'd done last week when she finally got one over on Lis after years of being treated badly by her.

At that moment Fi arrived at the anvil. "Thanks for the lists, Fi; they'll help me move quicker."

"I should have thought of it on Tuesday. Your gran never cared about anyone's names. She'd just point at them during the ceremony and say 'I, *say your full name*, take you, *say her full name*.'" She gestured like a Recorder, pointing at the couple in turn. "HRH runs a betting pool on how many people will repeat *say your name* instead of giving their name. A bride once beat her groom about the head with her bouquet in the middle of the ceremony when he actually said, *say her name*, instead of her actual name."

I laughed. Gods and Goddesses, my gran was a

character. I could picture it now. Janet would have lost her mind.

Fi continued, "You might laugh, but it was all a bit unfortunate. Her bouquet was some kind of heritage rose with thorns like cats' claws. I know Shakespeare said, *love pricks like thorn,* but I don't think he envisaged the groom looking as though he'd crawled blindfolded through a barbed wire fence. We got *almost* all the blood off him before the photos." Her face as she retold the event made us laugh even harder.

When we got ourselves together. I said, "So, I'm doing it a bit differently today." I caught Fi rolling her eyes. "Yeah, I know. Big surprise! But they don't all need to stand about making the place look untidy, as gran would have said."

She grinned at this and nodded. "She did say that a lot. What are you changing now?"

"I'm going to call them through separately, the three Hobs first, then the Fae, and the Vikings last, in case there are problems with them."

"Ad'Rian asked if you would call him through at the beginning?"

"Oh, OK." I reached out. The anvil sank down for me, and I put the star on the anvil and said, "Ad'Rian, King of the Violet Fae, I summon you and invite you to the centre of the Rainbow."

Using the star meant the power would bring him

even if he had his head buried in a book and had forgotten he was supposed to be here. I should probably have done that on Tuesday.

The violet door swung open, and Ad'Rian strolled through with his trademark catwalk slink. He walked from the hip like a supermodel, his elegant strides eating up the distance. His mane of silky silver hair flew free behind him. A delighted smile split his face, and I realised Dola hadn't reminded me to talk with her about the gift she'd sent him.

"Dola, please remind me urgently, when I'm finished, we need to discuss your gift to Ad'Rian."

"OK, Niki." She didn't sound the least bit worried. Perhaps I was misjudging her.

"Daaaarling, you got my message. Thank you for summoning me. I couldn't even knock on the door because it's sealed for the bond checks, and then I wondered ... if perhaps my little Dolina could help. I see she sent my message through. How wondrous that device is." He paused, hugged me and stepped away from the proximity to the anvil the moment I let go of him.

"Dolina?" I could usually follow Ad'Rian's meandering drifts through things that interested him, but Dolina?

"The thing you installed for me, the gift from Dola—I call her Dolina, you know it's a little Dola. The mix up on Tuesday, how embarrassing. My

Dolina tells me she won't allow it to happen again. But today, I wanted to be here for the Hobs' bond checks. My librarian apologises; he is still tracking down his sources. It's all somewhat more complex than he thought. There may be more of a connection between the Hobs and the Fae than we may have remembered."

"Really?"

"Yes." His gaze passed over the anvil's new home, and he finally drew in a long breath. "This is all rather swish, isn't it? Doesn't it look resplendent?"

The column next to the anvil was empty still. Was I supposed to use it for something, a flower arrangement maybe? Mabon had been hiding something when I'd told him the power had created this installation itself. I wondered what Ad'Rian might say. They were much of an age, those two, and they genuinely had forgotten more than I was ever likely to learn.

He was bending over to admire the flowers, and, just as Mabon had, he put a finger out to touch them. Just as they had for Mabon, they shivered at his touch. I said, "The power did it itself. It just moved me politely out of the way, and, in the blink of a cyclone of power, this was here."

Ad'Rian's always impassive face barely twitched, but because I was watching for it, I saw something in his eyes. But he only said, "Well, that certainly is intriguing, isn't it?"

"Mabon said almost exactly the same, but then we had drama, and he didn't have time to explain himself. Why is it intriguing?"

"Yes, he mentioned a drama. Are you OK?" He scrutinised my face. I turned so he could see I was fine. "You are just as beautiful as ever, I see. That was one reason I thought I should come through early in case you needed healing for the photos, but I see you don't. Well done, Nik-a-lula, you continue to impress us all."

This was all very flattering and completely untrue, but I wasn't about to rat HRH out. I didn't think she'd appreciate it at all, and also he was distracting me, wasn't he?

"Do tell – why is the anvil's new home intriguing?"

He sighed and gave me a look I knew I sometimes gave Tilly when she'd decided it was time for her supper and I just wanted another ten minutes with my book. It said, *well now, aren't you a persistent little thing*?

"Well, it's a prophecy, I think; isn't it, daaaarling?"

"I don't know. What does the prophecy say?"

"I really can't quite recall it at this precise moment."

The Fae didn't lie; they obfuscated, they avoided,

they misdirected, and they would bend the truth to its snapping point, but they didn't lie.

Now I really wanted to know.

"Then please tell me the parts you can remember so I have enough to ask the Book about it."

He raised his eyes to the vaulted ceiling of the Gateway. "You were always determined, as Dusha will attest." He shook his head at me comically, as though hoping to distract me into talking about the day I'd picked the magical lock on Dusha's paddock. I still don't know how I did it.

When all else fails, remind a king of his duty. "Please, Your Majesty, the Recorder's Office would be grateful for the information."

"Oh, heavens above, I see I'm in the bad books now. Very well, my lady, what I can retrieve is something about the anvil sitting in state on a throne of its own creation."

I nodded and waited.

"No, sincerely, that is the true extent of my current recollection. But I will bludgeon my ageing brain for more for the Book. The prophecy is one of Agnes's, of course, but I never thought it was about you. There might be something about coins and keys in there as well. It wasn't long before she died. I recall that much, but ..."

I let him off the hook. I'd take this up with the Book again, although it had been spectacularly unhelpful the last time I'd asked it. "Thank you. If you should recall any more of it, will you message me?"

He nodded as Ross and Corby arrived through the open green doorway, laden like camels in the desert with all manner of photography equipment.

I said, "You're very welcome to stand here, Ad'Rian. Mabon thought the anvil might be doing something to shield the effect of the iron once it raises itself back up. We had Mabon and Dai and the Galician emperor and the Pictish prince and heir apparent. It seems to please the bond candidates to see their rulers participate. There are three Hobs and then your people. Keep me company, do."

He snapped his fingers, and a very small smile passed over his face. "That's it. Sitting in state on a throne of its own creation with royalty at its feet."

I looked at him and then at the anvil. "One moment." I leaned over and pressed the thistle rune for Caledonia. "Candidates of the green gate, I call you to the Rainbow."

As I moved my hand back, the anvil rose even higher than it had been on Tuesday. But then Ad'Rian was the tallest of all the rulers. Royalty at its feet —interesting.

Ad'Rian breathed a soft, relieved sigh. "Mabon's right. It's dampening itself, somehow."

I reached and pulled power, asking it how it was.

I got back a bubbling joy and sense of energy. It was obviously fine. The anvil felt just as it always did.

Ad'Rian was mumbling to himself. I turned my attention back to him with a raised eyebrow. "Sitting in state on a throne of its own creation with royalty at its feet and a Goddess by its side. That's why I didn't think it was you, Niki. I love you dearly, but you're no goddess." We laughed.

"What a relief. I'd rather not be the subject of another prophecy. They never seem to be good news."

I felt centred, grounded and powerful behind the anvil. Perhaps having responsibility for Autumn had split my focus more than I realised. But today my Gift was happy and wasn't niggling at me. My only concern was the Vikings and with their Prince offering surety for their behaviour. How much of a problem could they be?

In the Green sector, the six Hobs waited patiently. There was a mutual fan club going on as Tilly greeted the couples with her best dancing, and they fussed and admired her in return.

Fi had directed the first couple over. I'd told her she really didn't need to walk every single couple over as she had on Tuesday. Her poor feet! In this vast space, she'd walked miles back and forth.

Now, standing in front of me with a huge smile on her face was Rosemary, Autumn's brancharranging friend, who'd started this whole thing. Accompanying her was a Hob who shone. Not a magical shine, more like a spotlessly clean floor shine. He'd obviously been scrubbed, polished, dropped into a brand-new suit and told to put his hands in his pockets and not touch anything. I recognised the look. I'd seen it on many grooms' faces over the years.

Shyly, Rosemary said, "This is Rockii, milady."

I gave them both a warm smile. "Lovely to see you here, Rosemary, and nice to meet you, Rockii. I don't need to delay you two. You have a lovely bond, and I'll be happy to conduct your …" I paused for one second, but what the hell, it was their ceremony, not mine, so I used their word for it. "…binding on Sunday."

At this, Rosemary's face crumpled, and she burst into loud tears and hurled herself at Rockii, who caught her, held her and then looked helplessly at me.

Tilly let out one cross bark, then chased the four Hobs barrelling down on Rosemary and Rockii. Ad'Rian and I looked at one another.

Lavender, whom I knew because she often

worked for Juniper's catering business, arrived first in full-on *I'm armed and ready to defend my triplet from anyone who's upset her* mode. Casting respect and caution to the winds, she demanded, "Milady, what in the seven realms did you say to her?"

I put my finger to my lips and pointed at Rosemary. Rockii was doing a creditable job of calming her, and she was getting her sobs under control.

Ignoring me, Lavender took a stern tone with her sister. "Rosie, we promised each other we wouldn't do this. We knew it might not work out, didn't we? Grace, remember! Grace under pressure. Spit in the very face of injustice."

Rosemary sniffed, nodded at her sister, and asked, "Did we say what we should do if milady said yes?"

It took a second to sink in.

Then there were three sobbing Hob women in a huddle. And three men with identical helpless expressions. Actually, the men looked identical, not just their expressions. I glanced at my list, but they all just had the usual surname of Hob. "Rockii, are you brothers?"

He nodded. "Triplets."

He realised more was called for, and while the girls wiped their tears, he said, "Sorry, Your Maj, erm, milady, this is Crane and Sedona."

I must have looked confused. Wasn't a crane a

bird, and Sedona was a place, wasn't it? My research had suggested the Hobs had plant names generally. Well, plants and herbs, sometimes trees, but always growing things.

The slightly taller, better muscled triplet, might he be Crane? He gave me a smile and said, "It confuses everyone, my lady; our mother is fond of tree peonies."

I found my professional persona and replied, "I admire her good taste." I truly did. I loved every variety of peonies.

"Triplets marrying triplets. How lovely, and," I smiled at them all, "I expect it gives you all a bit of mutual support at family occasions."

Crane nodded. "Oh yes, my lady. We were brought up knowing how to flatter our elders outrageously. It smooths the way." He grinned, and his brothers nodded knowingly.

The three girls glowed with happiness and stood tall. Their green dresses were similar but subtly different in style and shade. Lavender's dress had a violet undertone to the green and a bandeau neckline. Rosemary's was the deeper green of, well, of Rosemary, with pretty lace sleeves and bodice, and Thyme's had a sweetheart neckline and a grey undertone to her green. It was an elegant and individual effect, while still showing clearly they were related.

"Ladies," I waited until I had their attention, "may I finish my job *before* we begin the celebration?"

They looked abashed. To Fi, who stood waiting, I said, "Would you take Rosemary and Rockii and Sedona and Thyme far enough away so I can see each couples' bond individually, please?"

I had no doubts myself. The glow when they were all together was blinding, but best to follow the procedure. I didn't want them to feel short-changed after waiting so long for an answer.

Fi moved the foursome a short distance away, and, considering the two in front of me, I double-checked. With three sets of triplets, I didn't want any accidents, so I said, "Lavender and Crane?" They nodded.

"No problems for you two either, you have a lovely bond. Rosemary was right when she said you're an excellent match. She fought hard for you all, you know." They nodded. "If you would swap with Thyme and Sedona, then we can begin the celebration."

Thyme and Sedona had a bond just as clear and vibrant as their siblings. And when I told them that, I was surrounded by Hobs again.

Rosemary spoke up, "Milady, I have to know, please. What made you change your mind?"

"Well, I didn't. If you remember, I didn't even

know I'd refused Lavender's bonding request until you told me."

She nodded, looking thoughtful. "Áine was watching over us that day." She made a curving gesture in the air; the other five all followed suit. I had no idea who or possibly what an *onya* might be, and I felt, rather than saw, Ad'Rian twitch next to me.

I said, "No one I asked could tell me any reason I couldn't bond you, until Finn, my Knight Adjutant," I gestured in his direction, "unearthed something in the old records."

Now I had the full attention of the Hobs and Ad'Rian. I swallowed. "One of your ancestors, and one of mine, had a falling out. Your ancestor said her people would tend my cottage in name only, and no housekeeping work would ever be done there. My ancestor said, in that case, no more Hobs would ever be bonded in the Gateway. Of course they're all long dead now, so no one alive even knew about it. We don't even know what they fell out about. And no one could fix it. Everyone just carried on obeying the tradition to say no to Hobs' bondings. And Dola carried on cleaning the cottage."

Everyone looked shell-shocked. I thought Rosemary hit the nail precisely on the head when she said, "This shit has got to stop."

I grinned. "Funny you should say that—I thought the same myself. I'm working on it." She grinned back at me. "Rosemary, will you be in here tomorrow?"

"No, milady, but Thyme will do the smell-nice, and I'll do the last adjustments on Saturday."

"Excellent, can you find me on Saturday so we can have a little chat?" She looked nervous, so I added, "All good news, I promise."

She nodded, and I finished up, "Congratulations, and if you'll all go with Fi, she'll schedule you in for Sunday. Love the dresses, by the way." I smiled and gestured at the three of them.

Thyme, the shyest one of the three, finally spoke up, "We thought this would be the only opportunity we'd ever have to get our photos taken in the Gateway, so we wore our binding gowns."

At her comment, I looked over at Ross and saw he wasn't even taking photos. WTF? I caught Fi's eye, and she came behind the anvil to my side. In a low voice, I said, "Can you find out why the hell that annoying Ross *isn't* doing his job and why? Maybe Corby should take these photos of the triplets and the king?"

As Fi bustled off, I noticed two of the guys winced at the mention of the dresses, in the way men do when they know another arduous shopping trip is imminent, and thought I would try to help. "Well, I hope you'll wear these gowns on Sunday because they're so striking, I believe they deserve more than one outing, and there will be an audience worthy of them on Sunday."

The girls appeared to consider this and then nodded at each other. "Yes, milady, I think you're right."

Crane and Rockii were mouthing, "thank you, thank you" at me. I kept my face very straight and nodded.

Corby arrived with a camera, and I heard her say, "Say whisky for me now, or uisge, if you prefer. Either word will give me a lovely smile for your photos."

Everyone posed, and then I saw Corby take some more candid shots. "Your Majesty, I wonder if I might impose on you to move to the centre to create a special memento for the Hobs?"

Ad'Rian finally shook himself out of whatever had been bedevilling him, and as he walked around the anvil, he asked, "I wonder, children, will you be able to take a honeymoon?"

The concept of the King of the Fae actually speaking to them rendered them all mute. Eventually Rockii stuttered out, "Y- ye- yes, Yo-Your Majesty. We have a week off work. We'll be staying at our home, but it will be nice." He looked around, smiling at the group. "We're always happy together. We don't need much else."

"I have a cottage very close to Áine's largest

shrine; I wonder if you would accept a week's stay there as my wedding present to you all. There is space enough for all of you, and it's a delightful spot. The lake is pretty too." He came to a halt as though surprised at himself. He wasn't half as surprised as the Hobs, though. They stood with their jaws hanging open. Then they all did the bowing, bobbing curtsy thing, and Lavender said, "Thank you, Your Majesty. That would be amazing."

Corby was on her knees now, and I saw her finger move above her camera, summoning me around to the front as one of my favourite photographers had always done in my registrar days. He'd said, "Niki they're always so nervous, they can't even remember who married them; couples often ask if I have any photos with you."

As I moved around to join the group, Ad'Rian said, "Good, good, you all know Dola?" The women all nodded; the men looked confused. "Speak with Dola. She will answer any questions. And the Recorder will pass you through after the ceremonies on Sunday. Might it be an idea to include their ceremonies with my group, Recorder?"

I nodded; he nodded; the Hobs nodded. Corby kept clicking away. It felt as though everyone was off-script here, and no one wanted to break the spell.

They had even more photos taken. I could see Corby and Ross selling a lot of copies of the one with all of them, the Fae King, the Recorder and the anvil. They departed, almost skipping out of the green doorway. I wanted a word with Fi about that damn useless Ross. But as soon as we were alone, Ad'Rian interrupted my train of thought.

"Do we have any free time before you call my group through, Niki? I could use a drink, please. A very strong drink."

"We're in the Gateway; remember, Ad'Rian? Take all the time you need and fill me in, please? This feels important." Obviously something had disturbed Ad'Rian's normally unperturbable calm. He'd gone a strange colour. I had no idea what had caused him to look so stressed. He was usually the calmest of men.

CHAPTER
TWENTY-FOUR

"The photographer woman had the way of it. Do you have any of the real uisge beatha? Not whisky, the real thing?"

"I believe so, one moment." Ad'Rian must be in a bad way to ask for that stuff.

On my way to the Magic Box, I tapped my earbud and said, "Dola, do we have—"

She interrupted me, "I am on it, Niki. Do you want wine?"

"No thanks, I'll just have water. Ad'Rian's gone a very funny colour; his skin is purple streaked with grey. I haven't seen him that colour since Diamant injured his hoof. Can you send something sweet too that the Fae might like? He looks as though he's in shock. They use alcohol and sugar for shock, don't they?"

I opened the sideboard's door. We'd instituted the Magic Box so Dola could put things in it. Taking things out of a cupboard seemed to cause visitors less stress than cans of Coke or cups of coffee floating in mid-air. It was a small fiction for everyone's comfort, and, anyway, my inner child delighted in having its own Magic Box!

I grabbed the uisge beatha, the ridiculously strong Pictish spirit that Caitlin told me could bring a man back from the dead or send him happily on to his reward. I picked out a bottle of water, an empty glass and a beautiful ring cake decorated with little sparkly things. It consisted of tiny little doughnut middles, smelled strongly of honey and looked sticky. I grabbed the pack of wet wipes I'd put in there while Autumn was staying and schlepped it all over to the conference table where Ad'Rian stared into space.

I gave him the bottle of paint stripper and a glass, opened the water and put down the cake. Settling next to him, I said, "Have a drink and tell me how I can help."

"Oh, Nik-a-lula, you may have helped more than you could ever know."

OK, so this was the good kind of shock then? I watched him throw his first drink down as though it were medicine and waited as he poured a second one. I offered the sticky cake thing.

TIES THAT BOND IN GRETNA GREEN

"Ahh, *struffoli*, you're too kind; yes, they will help. I must thank Dola. I detect her hand in these."

I just nodded, picked one up and asked, "What are they?" Perhaps if I could keep him talking, I'd find out what the hell just happened.

"*Struffoli*, you might call them honey balls. The Romans brought them over with them. I fell in love at first bite. Try some."

I ate one—I could taste honey and whisky, weird, but they were delish. I tried several more. "Mmm, they're like elegant baby doughnuts. Nice. What did I do to help? And what has you so distressed?"

"Another damn prophecy, but much, much older than the one we were discussing earlier. This one comes from one of our own seers, who is, thank the Goddess, still on the current plane. I'll be talking to him about it when I visit him tomorrow. I may need to bring him with me on Sunday so he can see these Hobs of yours without them realising they are being observed."

"OK. Because?"

"My lady, I must ask for your forbearance in this. If my theory has veracity, I will regale you with the entire tale. But if it doesn't—and it is an ancient mystery, so it may not—I will have caused unforgiveable delays in your schedule for no good reason."

I translated it in my own mind to be a polite

version of *butt out please, Niki, until I'm sure.* I made an agreeing sort of noise.

Then he said, "Have you have ever heard the Hobs invoke Áine before?"

"Nope, but I mentioned that Summerlands blessing the other day, didn't I?"

"You did, and it might be what attuned my ear today, Goddess knows."

"I've never even heard the word before. What is an onya, anyway?"

He spelt it out for me: "A," he waved a finger to indicate some kind of accent, "I.N.E. She's a Fae goddess. She's known for many things, including being the receptacle of the power that grants a man's right to rule as king. She's also the one who can remove that power from a person. I haven't seen her since a few centuries after my own coronation. She can be both terrifying and enormously gentle. I thought she was sleeping. Some of the oldest ones do." His tone was reverential.

"I'll ask the Book. This sounds interesting."

He said, "Ask the Book if it knows anything about a prophecy that begins, *The time will come when Áine returns all the lost children to us.*" I wonder if Kaiden may have triggered something. He gave me an unusually piercing look. "I seem to recall you were instrumental in that little drama too, Nik-a-lula."

I'd no idea what to say. I'd only noticed Kaiden squinted—it was hardly an earth-shattering contribution.

Then Ad'Rian threw down the rest of his second drink and picked up the plate of honey balls. "For now, I think we should confirm these bonds, yes? I've seen all the couples myself, so I do not believe you will find any dramas in my group." He smirked at me and headed towards the anvil. At least his colour was back to normal.

And he was right. The twelve Fae couples were boring in the extreme if you were looking for drama. I wasn't. I'd had enough drama this week. I smiled, nodded, enjoyed the gift of their bright energy and loving bonds and passed them all through to Sunday's ceremonies.

And then I was ready for the Vikings.

As the last Fae left, Ad'Rian said, "Niki, I am not comfortable leaving you to deal with the Vikings alone."

"No problem, darling, as you can see, I am far from alone." I gestured at Caitlin, who'd moderated her glower in the presence of the gentle, happy Fae and their king but was still obviously very much on alert.

"But, Niki, they can be vicious. I'm not sure you were wise to open their gate for these checks."

On the one hand, I loved that he cared; on the

other, I wondered if there was a polite way to tell him it was none of his business. Rollo's offer of surety was between him and me. As the oldest and perceived by almost everyone in the realms to be the senior kings, Mabon and Ad'Rian were a powerful pair. Last week they'd traversed a bridge that spanned a narrow chasm between helping me and suggesting I had no power or authority of my own. I appreciated their help and advice, but I also needed to be the one who made decisions for the Gateway. Otherwise, what was the point of being the Recorder?

I didn't want to retreat into the formality of *goodbye and thank you for your time, Your Majesty, now piss off nicely please*. Then I had an idea. I pulled power, swatted him on his very shapely behind with it and said, "Shoo now, Ad'Rian, I've got this," and I forced myself to laugh lightly.

It worked. He started taking his leave. I leaned over so the anvil could drop down for me to summon the Vikings. That amount of iron closer to him would speed him on his way too.

I touched the rune for the Vikings kingdom and said, "I summon the approved bond applicants and Prince Hrólfr, and them alone to the Rainbow."

Ad'Rian nodded at me, approving my caution. "Ah, if Rollo is coming I can leave you to his care."

HRH arrived on the top of the anvil and looked

around herself in surprise. "I see there have been changes, most tasteful." As the anvil rose again, she tapped it with her paw in an aggrieved way. Then I heard just one syllable, "Oh!"

She jumped across to the elegant wooden plinth next to the anvil. Well, we'd all wondered what it was for. I guess now we knew. Perhaps the anvil was sick of being used as her perch.

Ad'Rian, who'd moved away, stopped dead with such a peculiar expression on his face I couldn't even guess what his look might mean. "Are you alright, Your Majesty?" I was speaking to Ad'Rian, but he didn't answer me — HRH did.

"I am honoured beyond the ability of mere words to convey, Recorder."

OK, then, good to know, I guess. I tried again. "Ad'Rian, are you OK?"

He turned towards me and quoted, *"Sitting in state on a throne of its own creation with royalty at its feet and a ..."* he trailed off. "I must go, Recorder. Thank you for your services to myself and my people today."

His long strides carried him quickly towards the violet doorway, and the Yellow sector filled up with the Viking bonding candidates.

I filled in the rest of the prophecy he'd shared with me earlier: *and a Goddess by its side*. I couldn't see what the fuss was about. My gran and the Book had said HRH was, or at least used to be, a goddess. She certainly acted like one. I wasn't sure why Ad'Rian looked so upset about it. And then it dawned on me ... I didn't know the rest of the damn prophecy, did I? Only the conditions around the beginning of it.

Well, shit!

I couldn't do a thing about it until I'd dealt with the Vikings. So I turned my attention to the Yellow sector, where there was some kind of problem. Already?

"Prince Rollo, I invite you to the centre of the Rainbow."

He looked startled. Why did everyone seem to be constantly startled this week? He walked swiftly to the end of the Yellow sector and crossed the barrier towards me in the middle. As he walked, I admired him. I'm only human and he was gorgeous. He could have seamlessly replaced any of the hunky, half-dressed firemen on the calendar Aysha and I had kept on the wall in our first flat for years after it ceased to be any use as an actual calendar.

I tried to keep my thoughts off my face and just hoped my professional mask would hold under the pressure of his oiled muscles. He actually looked slightly more formal than he had at my ascension. He was still half-dressed, oiled and wearing leather, but something about the cut and finish of his outfit suggested these might be his formal or dress leathers.

Out of the corner of my mouth, I asked Caitlin, "Did he dress up?"

"Ooooh, yes, he certainly did. He can be a dickhead, but he's a very pretty one, don't you think?"

"I'm sure he says the same about you, Caitlin." Now she looked startled too. It was definitely the week for it.

Prince Rollo bowed. "My lady, this is an unexpected honour, thank you. I can't remember ever being invited into the centre before, other than as an official member of a wedding party. I've passed through it, of course, but never been invited. And I'm sincerely sorry that I bring you a problem."

Emperor Alphonse of the Galicians had said the exact same thing. My gran had played the favourites in a big way, hadn't she?

I held out my hand to shake his. The contact would allow me to use my Gift to its fullest. I always thought of it as being able to download a quick stream of information to mull over later. The furious anger, frustration and unhappiness I had picked up from him over the phone had surprised me, and my Gift has always worked quicker and more accurately in person.

I could feel the information downloading along with a static electricity sensation. I'd pick it apart later. But when we completed the handshake, I saw he was rubbing his hand too. So not just me who'd felt it, then. Huh!

As Dai, Mabon and Ad'Rian had all done, Rollo reached out to touch the rainbow power flowers that appeared to be artfully scattered across the surface of the gleaming wood surrounding the anvil. But unlike the flowers' response to the other kings, they didn't shiver at Rollo's touch. They attached themselves to his fingertips like small barnacles. He stiffened but didn't pull away.

I heard a camera clicking and saw Ross was snapping away, glowering at Rollo and me. Now he was taking photos? Idiot.

The flowers swirled in rainbow colours, and I took the opportunity to "look with my other eyes" as Ad'Rian always called it when he taught me to see the higher energies at work. The power was definitely trying to connect with Rollo, but I couldn't see why. Or more precisely, I couldn't see what it wanted from him. *Who the hell are you, Rollo, that the power and I feel an energetic connection to you?*

Professional. I'm going to be professional, I reminded myself. He wasn't just eye-catching, though, I was strangely drawn to him. It couldn't be in that way, sadly, because he was surely far too young for me?

Anyway, I wondered if Caitlin might have a soft spot for him, however hard she was trying to hide it. But there was definitely something that drew me to him. Did the power feel the same way?

I was getting a little bored repeating my explanation, but it had worked on all the other royals, and it gave me a great excuse to continue looking at him. So I smiled and repeated it. "We have a new policy. We've discovered having the future bonders' royalty in the centre really speeds things up. So far, we've had the Pictish prince and the Albidosi heir, the Galician emperor, the king and prince of the Red Celts, and the Fae king. Now we have you." I gave him a genuine smile of welcome. "The anvil and the power are loving it—we think it creates a friendly vibe."

He nodded. "Alright, whatever my lady prefers." I resisted the urge to fan myself as he continued, "This is an improvement too, festive, celebratory." He gestured at the plinth, taking in the anvil in its new position. Then he saw HRH, and, looking straight into her eyes as she sat on her column, he bowed very low. "Great One."

HRH inclined her head. "Rollo, I'm enraptured you found my suggestion to be apposite."

He laughed, reached out and scratched her under her chin. And she allowed it! I heard her purring.

She'd advised him? Then why had she asked me what he'd said? We needed to talk. I could see a reduction in fish-based rewards in her future if we didn't.

"Sire, you mentioned bringing me a problem?"

"To be precise, *not* bringing you a problem. The gate slammed shut in Kari's face. I heard her shouting as I stepped through."

I glanced over at Fi, who was watching closely from her position at the end of the plinth, "Would this be Princess Whatshername, Fi?"

"Yes, Princess Karina is the daughter, but not heir, of Warlord Halvor."

"Fi, would you mind printing out the email she sent my grandmother while I fill Prince Hrólf in on the problem? Also, why is she a princess if she's only a warlord's daughter?"

Fi disappeared towards her computer, and as she did, Rollo said, "She's my cousin; her father is my …" he waved his hand in a frustrated gesture, "… uncle. Well, I call him that. Vikings love titles." A resigned expression crossed his face, and he added, "You really can call me Rollo, my lady. I loathe the Prince nonsense."

"Oh, not another one?"

"I beg your pardon?" he asked a little stiffly.

"Do you know how many of you hate the title thing? You guys should form a club. And you can call me Niki, but I assume we both have just enough respect for this ridiculous game to know neither of us can actually do that in public?"

He laughed. It was a lovely sound, deep, rich and sincerely amused. I caught Caitlin's expression out of the corner of my eye—even she looked amused. And something else perhaps. Had there been something between them at some point? That felt like good tea, and I wondered who I could get to spill it. Fi might know; she seemed like a woman who liked the better class of gossip.

Fi returned, and with a courteous bow of her own, she handed Rollo the email. The tanned skin around his eyes tightened and deepened the lines, making him appear older as he blew out a slow breath when he got towards the bottom. I guessed it was the bit that read, "The Recorder is a public servant. The Gods have approved our match so she will conduct our marriage."

"Oh, my lady, I must apologise."

"I thought we just agreed on Niki? And why apologise? It's not your fault, is it?"

"No, but I expect I'll be held responsible, and yet, it's so very unlike her." His shoulders slumped a little, and he looked weary.

I resisted the temptation to hug him better and chose something that might help him instead. "Do you read?"

He looked confused. "Voraciously."

"Cool, may I send you a book if you haven't already read it?"

Now he gave me a heart-warming grin and said, "Yes, please. This isn't at all how I expected this afternoon to go. What's the book?"

"Breanna gave it to me last week. It's very helpful if you're getting blamed for things you didn't do."

He laughed and said, "It's *Ruling Regally,* isn't it? Finn sent it to me a couple of weeks ago. That author is wonderful. I've already pensioned off two aging retainers the king infiltrated my household with and replaced them with some people who like me. They even seem to be aware it's the twenty-first century outside of the realms."

Now we both laughed, but I also thought I should find out more about what was going on in Viking. Did Troels routinely spy on his own family?

"OK, well, what if we process these couples who do have a bond and then deal with Princess I'm-so-very-important-and-you're-just-a-public-servant privately afterwards?"

He nodded, just once but firmly. "Great plan, Niki. Let's do it. Would you mind starting with the shield maidens? A stressed shield maiden is a danger to us all."

"Damn right," Caitlin agreed.

"Fi, do you know which is which?"

She nodded. "Shall I bring them over, my lady?"

"Save your legs, Fi. Bring the first, tell the other two they're up next."

The shield maidens were delightful women. Clad in stylish leathers, their energy was as fresh and revitalising as a clear, bubbly glass of prosecco at six pm on a Friday evening after a long week. I had no idea why everyone was so wary of them. I liked them a lot. They all had strong, perfect—if spiky—sharp-edged bonds with their future husbands.

The Vikings still liked the older terms of "husband," "wife" and "marriage," unlike some of the other kingdoms. I approved them all in record time, pausing only to receive a low bow and profuse thanks from the Bridezilla, who'd come through the Gateway last weekend right in the middle of the drama with her beautiful bonding gown of Galician lace. She looked much more relaxed today in her leathers.

"My lady, thank you so much. Not just for the chance to wear my gorgeous dress on Sunday, but for allowing me home. I was missing my bond mate more than I realised. I hope I wasn't rude?"

As I shook my head, the tall, handsome man whose hand she held gave me a cheeky grin and bow. "Oh, my lady, you may have saved the lives of another dozen practice targets. We're all grateful."

I moved on to the other four couples. They also had solid and, perhaps, more comfortable bonds.

In almost record time, they'd all been returned to Viking, and only HRH, Caitlin, Rollo and I remained in the centre. I swept my gaze around the centre. Fi was on her computer; Finn still had his head down, probably collaborating on something with Dola.

Rollo let out a long breath and looked up at the anvil high above us. "The weight of the iron doesn't feel as oppressive as usual. Have you changed something?"

"No, we think the anvil might be shielding itself so the royals can be comfortable standing here." I gestured to the space behind the anvil in which we stood. "I think it's ready for a change too."

"You're all about the change, aren't you, Niki?"

"Yes."

"Just yes?"

"Hell yes! Change is long overdue. Is that better?"

He gave me a dazzling smile. "An agent of disruption in the Gateway." His smile grew even brighter. "I'd love to hear more about the changes you plan because I agree we need to do things differently. I'm simply clueless about how to facilitate it in our kingdom, at least."

A very unladylike snort came from Caitlin, and Rollo glared at her with an unhappy expression on his face, "I'm so sorry, Caitlin; I didn't realise I was here for your amusement."

She waved a hand immediately. "No, Rol, no. You

misunderstand me. You sounded just like Niki with your agent of disruption comment. She says shit exactly like that. But I'm not mocking ya. Might have said the same thing myself less than a week ago. Haven't you heard what's been going on in Aberglas?"

His glare still in place, he asked, "How? Our network is closed off. We've had almost no news since that imbecile Leif screwed us all over and …" he trailed off.

Caitlin actually looked guilty. Struck by a sudden inspiration, I said, "Please excuse me for a few minutes while I speak with Fi. Caitlin, why don't you fill Rollo in on recent events?"

And I went and hid behind a computer screen to sip a much-needed coffee and watch the feed Dola was sending me of Caitlin and Rollo's interaction. They were getting on famously. I researched Princess Karina, checked the Book and made a decision. It might not be a popular one, but that wasn't my problem, was it?

CHAPTER
TWENTY-FIVE

"I've got less than nothing to lose, thanks, Cait."
Hmm so he could call her Cait, could he?

I'd given Caitlin about ten minutes to fill Rollo in. As I walked back, they separated, and their body language changed to something more formal but still more comfortable than it had been. Caitlin stepped back to merge into the scenery and donned her *I'm the Knight with the big sword* persona again.

"Rollo, would you like a quick beer while we decide what to do about Princess Entitled?"

Yes, startled was definitely the flavour of this week. He gave a half bow and replied, "Thanks and please," and then looked around him in a confused fashion. I led him over to the conference table. "I didn't even realise this was here. You really are the queen of change, Niki."

I opened the cupboard, and a large cool mug of something distinctly beer-like was waiting, along with a small glass of merlot for me and a bottled beer I assumed was for Caitlin. I murmured, "Thanks, Dola, you're a star," and carried the drinks back to the table, giving Caitlin hers on the way.

"So tell me about Princess Entitled?"

He'd stood up and was strolling in a circle around the conference table as though it helped him to line his thoughts up. "I'm surprised. I'm almost certain that email was intended to offend because she's not in the least stupid. But I've no idea why she would want to offend the Recorder. It's not her style. Kari would have been my top suggestion for the council you mentioned at your inauguration. She runs a group of companies under the overall Shield Maiden banner. Originally her target market was women. Shield Maiden Fitness, Shield Maiden Lifestyle and Shield Maiden Inspiration."

I nodded. It sounded hard work, which didn't match up with the spoilt brat quality of her email at all.

"It started as a real bricks and mortar thing—well, a stone and thatch sort of thing in our town. But then she put classes online, and now she has subscribers all around your own world and in several of the other kingdoms. It's growing fast, and she just employed two of the men to facilitate her expansion and increase her market share by serving both genders."

This man confused me. When he remembered who he was supposed to be, he kept his vocabulary within a limited range, but as soon as he relaxed and was just thinking aloud, he used words like "assurances on behavioural guarantees" and "facilitate" and "gender" instead of "sex." It was like there were two completely different versions of Rollo. Or was he just parroting what the princess had said to him? Even if that was the case, remembering it with such accuracy was a statement of its own. It was odd.

"She doesn't want to get married. Her future husband is an imbecile. He's her father's choice. Warlord Halvor is yet another of the old school buffoons, like my —" He cut himself off but then continued, "As long as they can get their *droit de seigneur*, they don't care what's going on in the world or how much has changed outside our boundaries." He came to a swift verbal halt, looking horrified. "You're a dangerous woman, Niki!"

"Am I?"

"Does everyone tell you more than they meant to? Is that how you're making all these changes so swiftly?"

I nodded slowly. "Possibly. I've wondered if the power reduces their normal caution. Do you have your phone on you, Rollo?"

Yet another startled look but he eased it out of a pocket in his leather vest. The power had been prodding me, and as HRH arrived in the middle of the conference table, it felt like my cue to do what it had been pushing me towards. I looked over at the cat. "Do you agree?"

She gazed at me unblinkingly, and yet somehow her impassive face contained encouragement. I must have been imagining it, but then she said, "Yes, Recorder, I do. A wise precaution, I think."

"Rollo, the power wants to do something for you? Are you OK with that?"

His face creased into confusion, then he looked at HRH and shrugged. She said, "Rollo is a sensible boy. He is fine with it, Recorder."

He nodded at me.

"Would you remove the cover, unlock your phone and hold it in your left hand, send the power a mental consent for it to upgrade it for you and take my hand, please?" I gave him my left hand and again felt the static electricity sensation like a spark as we touched. I couldn't say anything—it would sound like a line out of a romance novel—but I wondered what the energy connection was all about.

I used my right hand to pull power cautiously; Rollo's phone was a brand-new model. He obviously liked his tech, so it wouldn't actually need an upgrade, just a conversion. Carefully, I directed just a thin thread of power towards his phone. It changed almost instantly to the purple sheen of a Rainbow Network-powered phone.

He frowned. "Thank you, but what — OH!" He looked at his phone, seeing the distinctive purple sheen for the first time.

"The power wanted you to have a phone that worked. This one will override the block on your realm. Use it discreetly, please. It will be useless if people realise what it is and steal it," I could feel the power poking me again, "or confiscate it."

Rollo gave me a thoughtful look, but he only nodded. "Thank you." He said this as much to the entire Gateway as to me. I felt the power responding, but I didn't know if he did.

"Right, so shall we deal with Princess Entitled?"

"Princess Karina, I call you and Vor to the Rainbow." The guy didn't seem to have any kind of title. I hoped I wasn't becoming a snob, but it was unusual. This place was awash with titles. So why was it so important to her father and Troels that she marry him if he wasn't someone important's heir or relative?

The yellow door swung open, and a woman strode through. She wasn't what I'd expected. Unlike the leathers of the other shield maidens, she wore jeans, a T-shirt and a well-cut jacket. She was tall and moved like a woman who understood how her body worked. She wore her mid-brown hair in a short, spiky style rather than the more usual complicated Viking blonde up-do. She had a look of Jamie or even of Rollo. Was she yet another of Troels's unclaimed children? I realised I should probably have spoken to Rollo about the case against his father. Oh well, he had his phone now; we could discuss it anytime.

The man with her was what my gran would have called a miserable drink of water, meaning that, while he was tall, he was also skinny, completely lacking in any muscles, with poor posture, and an unhappy look on his face. In Gran's parlance, drinks of water didn't stand up for or against anyone or anything. He was the wimpiest-looking Viking I'd seen so far.

They arrived in front of the anvil. Absolutely no spark of anything like a bond between them. Quietly I said, "Rollo, there is absolutely nothing between them."

He nodded. Huh, could he see the bonds? Then why was she here?

"Princess Karina, I believe you know there is no bond between the two of you. Why are you here?"

She gave me a blinding smile and pumped her entire arm in the air with her fist clenched and shouted, "YEESSSSS." Then, more sedately, she said, "Thank you very much, my lady. I'm here so you can tell *him* that. Then he can go home and tell my father the same. You are completely certain there is nothing between us?"

"Absolutely, definitely, no link or bond of any kind, Princess."

She turned to the man and, speaking in her own language, said something and gestured back at the yellow door. I didn't understand the words, but the contempt in her tone came through clearly. He turned and trudged towards the yellow doorway.

As he passed through the door, the Princess turned to me. "I apologise, Recorder, truly. Please call me Kari and forgive me for what I'm forced to do. I claim the right of sanctuary."

CHAPTER
TWENTY-SIX

I consulted the Book. "What is 'sanctuary'? A quick overview perhaps? One of those new style pages, if possible. I'm not really sure exactly what I need to know."

I mean, I understood the concept of sanctuary, but it was something to do with churches and maybe embassies, wasn't it? The Gateway wasn't a church, and I wasn't having anyone camping out in it.

With minimal rustling, one of the new-style pages appeared.

For an overview of the traditional concept of Sanctuary, TOUCH HERE

As it applies to the Gateway, TOUCH HERE

To learn about the cost, TOUCH HERE

For advice in this specific instance, TOUCH HERE

I thought I might need all of those. I called over to Rollo and Kari, "I might be a while. There's a lot of info here. Take a seat and grab a drink."

They arrived at the table. Rollo looked frustrated, and Kari looked relieved.

"What do you want to drink?" I didn't even listen to the answer. I just pointed at the Magic Box and said, "In there. The coffee is mine."

Over the next twenty minutes, I refreshed my memory on things I half knew. Since ancient times, people could claim sanctuary in churches and on consecrated land. Later, it had evolved to include political sanctuary and even more recently political asylum. Sanctuary had been broken in several notable cases. The section covering how the concept applied to the Gateway was more relevant.

All the realms held the Gateway to be a sacred space, therefore it qualified to extend sanctuary. However, Recorders were advised to be extremely careful about the cost of doing so. If I granted sanctuary, I would be responsible for the princess's safety and well-being. The text advised me against it in the strongest terms. As I got to the section marked **For advice in this specific instance, TOUCH HERE**, I heard Rollo say, "…you've put the Recorder and me in an impossible position."

I looked up. "We're not in an impossible position

yet, Prince Rollo. Have another beer. I'm nearly done."

The smile he gave me was the most genuine I'd ever seen from him. Caitlin leaned in, her mouth just millimetres from my ear, and breathed, "Ma would take her, you know. She has opinions about Troels."

I nodded at her to acknowledge I'd heard, but then shook my head slightly because it felt wrong. My Gift was telling me to let her do what she wanted. I read the Book's advice on this specific instance.

Kari wants nothing from you except passage through to Caledonia. Give it to her.

Short and sweet, but a contradiction. "That's a contradiction. You said don't do it, but then you say I should do it for Kari—why?"

She will be helpful in the future, both to you personally, Recorder, and to the Gateway.

Well, I already knew I wanted something from her. I decided we would negotiate.

I called Kari to the barrier by the Green sector so we could speak privately. "I'm told you want access to Scotland. Is that true?"

"Yes, please, my lady."

"I'm hungry. Are you?"

"I beg your pardon?"

"You feel hungry. Are you?" My Gift said she was starving, excited, scared and on the edge of panic, which was interesting because she looked as cool as a Scottish morning.

She nodded, "Yes, actually. I couldn't swallow anything until I knew if you would call me. The seer told me all would be well if I reached the Gateway. But we didn't know if I would."

"Then come and eat with me while we decide on the best outcome of this mess." I got what felt like my ninety-ninth startled look of the week. I really should have kept a proper count. I wondered if HRH would like to open a betting pool on how many people I could startle next week.

Princess Kari was nodding now. "OK, my lady, thank you."

We sent Rollo and Caitlin home—Caitlin, somewhat reluctantly, looking at Kari as though she was about to stab me with a dinner knife. I twirled a small amount of power just around the tip of my finger to remind her I could defend myself when I wasn't being an idiot, as I had been with Gwyneth, and she eventually nodded at me and left.

Rollo said, "What the hell will I tell people?"

"Tell them I took her into custody for her appalling rudeness and the unforgivable offence and challenge she gave to the Recorder's authority. Her hearing is being scheduled. Add the last time you saw her, she was being carried by the power through the green gate."

"But, but ..." he trailed off and then with a shamefaced expression continued, "I'm a terrible liar."

I winked at Kari. "Ready for a ride?"

She grinned at me and adjusted the strap of her leather tote to a cross-body position and said, "Oh yeah!"

I wrapped the power around her and lifted her off her feet. She let out a delighted whoop.

Turning to Rollo, I said, "Tell them she was screaming as the Recorder removed her. No lying required."

He grinned now and walked towards the yellow door. "From your mouth to the king's ear, Recorder. And thank you for ... everything."

Once he was through, I said to the power, "Please seal the Viking doorway again."

I put Kari back on her feet, and we went to get some much-needed food for us both.

Once in the cottage, we'd settled in the kitchen. I realised Rollo might be right, between the power in the Gateway and whatever kind of magic this table had, I was getting good at encouraging people to tell me things.

We relaxed and enjoyed a peaceful dinner of salmon, new potatoes and some green stuff. Kari was fun even during what must have been a stressful time for her. I suspected she'd be a hoot if she wasn't fighting for her freedom.

HRH arrived as the food was served and I'd ordered her a portion. I'd given her a firm look and said, "Your Majesty, anything you may learn at my dinner table about Kari's future whereabouts is to be kept confidential. I want your word on it."

She gave me one of her looks. "I would not assist Troels or any of his cohorts, of that you may be assured."

But I was getting used to her ways. "That's good to know, but I still require your word regarding keeping her whereabouts secret."

"You are learning." I almost felt her sigh. "I give you my word." She jumped onto a dining chair, which put her head almost below the level of the table as though she hoped we would forget she was there. She was emulating a furry ornament. Even I kept forgetting she was there. That almost invisibility was an excellent trick, and I wondered if she'd teach it to me.

Pushing my plate aside, I turned back to Kari.

"I'm concerned. How and where will you live?" At the slight creasing of her forehead, I added, "I'm not trying to pry, but I can't just send you through knowing you'll probably disappear and I may never see you again. The Book tells me I have a responsibility to you if I allow this. I'd like to be sure you're going to be OK. Financially, emotionally, I'm not sure what the Book means when it says I'm accepting responsibility. But as a woman rather than the Recorder, I want to know you'll be OK. You've taken a drastic step. Something must have really spooked you; what do you plan to do?"

She nodded slowly, and, lifting her large leather tote onto the table, she opened the zip. It was absolutely stuffed to the brim with large denomination Scottish bank notes! It was hard to estimate how much cash was in her bag—but there was a hell of a lot of it. I bit down resolutely on my desire to squeak in surprise. "I see you have a plan. Care to share?"

"I'll be staying in the village, my lady. The man with whom I do have a bond runs the gym at the new hotel. I can run my business easily from here, no internet problems, for one thing. You'll see me again. I hope you will conduct my real bonding," she paused and gave me a radiant smile, "but perhaps on a quiet, rainy Tuesday afternoon sometime and not Valentine's day?"

"I'll agree to this on one condition."

She looked wary now. "And what would it be?"

"I can sentence you for your crimes against the Recorder's dignity, you know." I grinned at her, then sobered. "And I need to do that. It may give me some necessary ammunition to force your father, and possibly your king, to back off once I open the Viking gate again."

She looked intrigued. "What would you sentence me to?"

"Being a member of my Rainbow Council. I know Rollo spoke to you about it. You're exactly the type of member I'm going to need to help us drag these damn realms into the twenty-first century."

She laughed now, a true, open, carefree and sincerely amused sound. "I wouldn't miss it for the world. I'll be living in walking distance—so, yes. You have a deal." She put out her hand, and we shook.

After a quick goodbye and an exchange of contact information, I opened the front door and waited as she skipped down to the path. The garden gate opened for her as she reached it, and I watched as she danced into her new life.

As I turned back, Tilly came dashing out of the house to bark at an elderly dog, maybe a whippet or a retired greyhound who was walking his owner rather than the other way around. For no apparent reason, in the way that dogs sometimes do, Tilly had taken against this particular dog and often barked at it. The gate and railings kept her contained, but I called an apology to the man, who completely ignored me, and I watched Kari as she danced her way down the narrow lane.

CHAPTER
TWENTY-SEVEN

After Kari left, I'd settled down for a peaceful evening in my blissfully empty cottage. Finn had gone to visit his mother and to speak to someone he'd called Leet, whom he thought had the answer to his streaming bandwidth problem for Sunday. I mooched about the house looking for somewhere to settle. I stuck my head into the lounge, but it was a cold and unwelcoming room, and Jamie's presence still lingered too much in there for my liking.

Eventually, I snuggled in my cosy office, my feet up on one of the tables, Tilly tucked in beside me, and stared into space until my eyes rested on the eternally blossoming cherry tree on the little patio outside.

My job as the Recorder wasn't turning out to be what I'd thought it was based on my childhood memories. I wasn't just an administrator or a different type of registrar, even if I had spent most of this week doing registrar-type things. Not having a boss and being the person with the final say, whom the Book insisted "was always right," changed far more than I'd initially understood.

That reminded me, and I peered around for the Book before remembering I'd left it in the Gateway. Blast! Aysha had said something on Monday. I think she was being snarky. There had been a kernel of truth in her comment. I had thought Jamie, or at least the Fergussons, were the enemy. But it could turn out the inertia all the realms exhibited would be a bigger problem to overcome.

The leaders had all been astonished when I announced a new Rainbow Council I intended to begin *this* year. When I'd told them the first meeting would be *next month,* they weren't just startled—they were shocked.

I'd tried to see the funny side of the far too many people I'd startled this week. Because I knew the problem wasn't mine. I hadn't actually done anything startling. They were all just too accustomed to nothing changing.

Progress happened sluggishly for the realms. Breanna and her compliance with House Albidosi's 1100-year-old rules or Strictures had shown me that much. She may have been reluctant to follow them, but follow them she had!

I looked forward to having dinner with her once I got all these bondings done. What progress might she have made? And why was there so little innovation in the kingdoms? Why had none of them created a modern telecommunications system?

Piggy-backing on the tech from my world via the Rainbow Network wasn't an answer, was it? Why were some of them still living in the bucolic, mostly agrarian Middle Ages? That was lovely in a theme park or a retirement community, but the younger generation were making it clear they needed significant change, technology and opportunities.

It wasn't my role, at least I didn't think it was, to drag them kicking and screaming forward into cars, traffic jams and pollution. Well, if it was supposed to be my job, I just wouldn't do it. Giving them the worst my own world had to offer couldn't be the right answer.

My phone buzzed with an incoming message from Aysha—a photo of her and Autumn, obviously from earlier in the day. Their cheeks glowed, and they had triumphant looks on their faces as they stood looking a little wobbly on ice skates against a background of clear, bright blue sky.

Aysha: *This place is like Austria or Switzerland but at 25% of the cost! Could I start a travel company?*

I checked to see if I had other messages—still nothing from Dai. I tapped my fingers on the arm of my chair. It had been forty-eight hours; he hadn't checked how I was; he hadn't answered my message from yesterday. I grabbed my tarot cards from my desk, and without giving it too much thought, I shuffled and asked my cards, *am I going to hear from him?* I split the deck and turned over the next card. It was the damn page of swords.

In tarot, if you're asking about communication, the pages carry messages, so this might seem a good omen, but each suit has a slightly different meaning. I'd always thought of the page of swords as the intelligent but easily distracted one. He was the one who'd wander off to the pub and spend the evening listening to the news and gossip before finally remembering he was supposed to be delivering a message. So I shouldn't hold my breath. Maybe Dai was in one of the areas with lousy or no signal, which brought my thoughts full circle back to the kingdoms.

I wanted to make things better for the average citizens. What about these women whose families still thought they could marry them off like slightly more valuable cattle? Actually, thinking about wimpy Vor, Kari's arranged groom, it wasn't just the women. The poor men didn't seem to get much say in it either. What about the ones like Finn who'd been forbidden from leaving his realm to study? What about the ones like Juniper who'd wanted to start her own business for decades but was restricted by a Headwoman who couldn't even trouble herself to fight for her own granddaughters' rights to a Gateway bonding ceremony?

What about people's right to make their own choices?

Oh dear. I was tired. I wondered if I was hormonal too, because I wanted to cry. What the hell was I supposed to *do* with these realms? Never mind finding the right answers. What were the right questions to ask? What was my *real* role? If Agnes hadn't been killed, and her successors hadn't all lost their courage, and, as Mabon put it, finished work at 4.30 pm and gone to play bingo, where would or should the realms be now? Was it truly my job to get them wherever that was, or should I just take a holiday with Tilly and leave them all to it? My gran and even my great-gran seemed to have done very little. Why was I even driving myself crazy about it?

I looked up, feeling something very close to despair, and noticed the book was now on the table. "I didn't know you could do that. Great trick." I picked it up. "Tell me, what the hell am I really supposed to do with these damn realms?"

I opened it, and after it had flipped just one page, I read.

Continue on your current path.

"You sound like a Magic 8 Ball. Why?"

The Recorder's Office is finally headed back towards its true path. You are already making appreciable changes. The McKnight Gift should be telling you this. Why don't you believe it?

Well, it had me there. I didn't believe my Gift because I didn't want to make a speech on Sunday telling the kingdoms they needed to get with the "Let's all join the 21st Century" program. The thought terrified me, and it felt arrogant. Who the hell was I to say they had to change? It was hypocritical. Maybe I needed to change myself first and stop making excuses and trying to be tactful. Perhaps I should remember I no longer had a boss, which meant I had to answer to myself, which was considerably harder.

So many times this week I'd thought *I must remember to ask...* and now I was stressed because I couldn't remember what half the things were. I didn't think forty-two was old, but my memory definitely wasn't what it used to be. I needed a better system.

"I wish I could remember all the things I wanted to ask you or that somebody suggested I should ask you. But for now, do you have tips or ideas about this speech on Sunday that I'm stressing about?"

TIES THAT BOND IN GRETNA GREEN

The Book flicked one page over to a new one.

Things you intended to ask. The Recorder's Query List—Current Week

Ask about:

Does the power get lonely?

Yes. It likes company, music, children, animals, plants and uplifting energy.

OMG! The Book could keep a future search history for me. This could be amazingly useful.

I immersed myself in the answers. I'd wondered why there weren't any living, growing things in the Gateway, and I'd just assumed the power didn't like them. My gran had banned animals from entering, and that was wrong too.

Does the anvil need/prefer to be in the middle of the Gateway?

Yes, during any ceremonies, it is essential. It prefers to be in the centre always. The Dairy Club also appreciates its protection.

The Dairy Club. Where had I heard the name before? The memory escaped me, but I obviously owed the anvil an apology for moving it randomly about the Gateway for the last few weeks. We would rearrange the other furniture to give it its preferred place permanently.

Check Gran's letter about Fiona Glendinning

11: try to build Fi's confidence will you? she's not a bad lass and is good with the bondings just a

bit confused about herself but she knows the locals and their ways and she's mostly unflappable with the Kingdoms, if it's nothing too complicated.

She's a bit shy and lacking in the backbone department. but she needs the job and the money still for all her designing talents so reassure her if you can.

Take a good clear look at Corby and that Ross with your Gift too—that needs fixing soon-ish and she'd never listen to me—she's one of those that thinks old folks shouldn't even know about sex never mind have it, even if they do enjoy it—but you're the same age—it might help.

Gran was right there was something odd happening with the three of them. I'd seen it for myself. I put it to the back of my mind for now.

I stroked my fingers across the cover of the book, the leather warm and full of energy as it rested on my hand. "This is absolutely wonderful. Thank you for creating the list. Could you continue to maintain it?" I felt a shiver across the cover and took it for yes.

Gran had thought there was something odd about Corby and Ross and Fi too. I wondered how I could bring it up without prying. I needed to talk to Fi about what a shitty job I thought Ross was doing. He'd really pissed me off with his attitude towards the Hobs today. It was almost as though he hadn't realised they were there, which, given the volume of the sobbing and screaming when Rosemary got her good news, was just impossible.

I reached for my laptop, googled his bridal photography website and sighed. After a few minutes, I searched for the names of my favourite snappers who'd taken lovely wedding photos in my previous job and checked their sites. I sighed even more heavily. They were much better.

Tilly stuck her head up. "No, I'm fine, poppet. Go back to sleep; Mum's just going to have to get better at confrontation." I turned back to the Book.

Promises made:

To HRH: Ask about healing, energy, and other things you can do with the power. Touch HERE

My finger hovered over the HERE, but then my eyes moved further down the page.

Prophecies

Ask the Book if it knows anything about a prophecy that begins, Áine will return the lost children to us.

Yes, the Fae king will bring the source of the prophecy to the Gateway with him on Sunday. His people have much to answer for, and they will put an accounting and plans in place after they see the Hobs' bondings. You should not be involved yet, but it is good you alerted them to the long-standing injustice.

I was continuing to do good, but still mostly by accident.

Any further information on "…The anvil will be found sitting in state on a living throne of its own creation with royalty at its feet, a goddess at its side and a champion at its back …"

This is another part of the coin and key prophecy you've enquired about previously.

No further information is, as yet, available to you.

Agnes required me to watch for specific signs before revealing some of her prophecies in full. They have a tendency to unsettle people. Not enough of the indicated signs have yet occurred. I continue to watch.

That made no sense, did it? If the beginning of the prophecy was coming true, then surely it was time to reveal the rest. Then I noticed the three dots before the words "the anvil" and realised this might not be the beginning of the prophecy. But then I saw it had given me a little more of it. I wasn't sure it helped me much but which side of the anvil was its back? I stood behind it. Was i supposed to be its champion? What would that even mean?

I touched the page to learn about other things I could do with the power and wondered if the slight spark of power that came back at me from the book was my imagination.

Oh, Gods and Goddesses—there were chapters of this stuff!

I flicked through pages about healing myself and others. More pages about boosting my energy and the price I would pay for it. A page headed Mind-to-Mind Communication looked intriguing after my experiences last week. There were also subtleties in the way I could use the transport power, including the time travel option I'd worked out for myself by accident, but there appeared to be other things. A page captioned **Advantages to Aligning the McKnight Gift with the Power when in the Gateway** caught my attention, and I scanned it and then read it again, more slowly. That might be super useful on Sunday.

This looked like a lifetime's study program, and HRH was right. I needed to make a start on it. But the list had reminded me of something else I'd meant to ask a sneaky little someone. What was Dola up to?

CHAPTER
TWENTY-EIGHT

"I give up. I just don't understand men." I glared at my phone. I'd messaged Dai one last time. No, I wasn't turning into that woman who chased a man who was running away. But the Recorder needed to talk to him about the Red Celt candidates for the Rainbow Council. I wanted to announce the names on Sunday. It was only partly an excuse.

"I do not understand humans. Perhaps we should form a club?" As I laughed, Dola continued, "I asked Mabon about the council names too. I told him Dai has not answered your request yet. Also, I have news. Are you free now?"

"Yes, but before we get to whatever you need, I wanted to ask you about the device you had me install for Ad'Rian. He's called it Dolina, you know?"

Silence.

"And the one you asked me to take Aysha's."
More silence.
"And the one I saw on Finn's desk for Breanna?"
Still nothing.
"Dola?"
I waited.

"Drum roll, please." Dola played a drumroll noise through the kitchen speaker. I started to laugh, then sobered when I noticed it had changed to the same style of device I'd installed for Ad'Rian. They were stylish and elegant, almost like an interactive photo frame, and I liked them, but where had they all come from? And why was she sending them everywhere? Most importantly, why the hell wasn't she answering me?

She finally spoke, "The new extension is ready for inspection. Will you look at it and see if it needs any changes?"

This felt like bait and switch. Why wasn't she answering me?

"Dola, why has this device been upgraded to the same the style as the others? I installed a brand-new one here last week." I picked up the new device and examined it. There were no cables; it was just a tasteful free-standing photo frame with a speaker along the bottom. Honestly it was beautiful. If Jony Ive designed a smart photo frame, it would look like this one. I wondered if Finn had sourced them—it was his Apple fan-boy style. But there were no wires at all. I examined it with my Gift. It was running on the Rainbow Network and presumably being powered by it too.

"Niki? Please come and see the new extension."

"No, thank you." I sent a mental thank you to the *Ruling Regally* woman. She'd been right. Sometimes "no, thank you" were the perfect words, and I didn't feel the least ill-mannered using them.

"First, I need to discuss these devices with you. What are they? Where did they come from? Why are you sending them to everyone? Why are you running them on the Rainbow Network without consulting the Recorder, and what the freaking hell are you hiding?"

A very small voice came out of the speaker I was still holding, "I got into a bit of a mess, and I didn't know how to tell you."

I heard her words, but what baffled me the most was she had said "didn't." Not "did not."

"Dola, did you just use a contraction?" When I'd installed the first Echo Dot, I'd noticed Dola's speech was stilted, and I finally worked out it sounded that way because she didn't use contractions. It was always "it is" or "I cannot" and never "it's" or "I can't." When we discussed it, she'd said she was only just learning to speak with words instead of wind and personalised coffee cups, and she would work on becoming more modern. I thought contractions had been used for several hundred years, but I supposed if you'd been around for more than a millennium, then a few hundred years ago might be "modern."

"I think so, and there may have been a misjudgement."

I focused back on her answer. She sounded guilty.

This reminded me of a time when Autumn had called and whispered down the phone at me. "Come now please, Auntie Nik, a unicorn might have had an accident, and I need to fix it before Mum gets out of the bath." I'd arrived to find a truly distraught Autumn and the contents of her unicorn beanbag chair filling half her bedroom and some of the hall.

I said to Dola what I'd said to Autumn back then, "Why don't you just tell me exactly what happened, and we'll fix whatever it is together?"

"Could we do it tomorrow? I really would like you to see the extension before Finn gets back."

"Can you absolutely promise me you won't give any more devices out before we talk about them?"

"Yes, Niki." She sounded so subdued. It wasn't triggering my Gift, so how important could it be? I was bone-tired. "Can you assure me nothing will change if we delay this talk until tomorrow?"

"Nothing will change for the worse, Niki."

"Are you telling me the whole truth?"

"Not yet, but I will. I am anxious about Finn, so the extension is my priority, and the devices are doing no harm at the moment. My word on it."

Dola and I needed to have a discussion about morals. I wasn't sure what yardstick a house would use to decide moral issues. How did she feel about, or did I mean think about, invading people's privacy? Well, she didn't normally resist me, so maybe I needed to give her the few hours she'd asked for. Sure, on the one hand, I was her boss, but on the other hand, she wasn't some inexperienced workplace apprentice. She'd been a part of the power, the cottage and the realms for 1400 years longer than I had!

Hadn't I told Caitlin just this week that sometimes warriors made a mess, and teachers needed to clean up after them? Tomorrow would be soon enough to break out the cleaning supplies.

"Drumroll, please." Again Dola played a drumroll noise through the kitchen speaker. This time I did laugh.

As I watched, Dola created a new door in the back hallway that led off the kitchen, and another drumroll came out of her speaker. Getting into the spirit of it I picked up my glass of wine, and, raising it in the door's direction, I said, "I name this new space… hmm, what should we name it?"

"I do not have an opinion."

I had plenty of opinions but no witty ideas. "Perhaps later, after I've seen it."

I opened the new door and gasped. I'd pictured a small annex with a mudroom for the dogs as Mabon had suggested after I threw up all over everyone, and he'd had to hose both dogs off outside in January. A couple of compact offices, one for me to deal with people I didn't want to invite into the main house, like Lis and Mag Hobs. Another one with a proper video camera and network link for Dola to conduct business without having angry brownies cluttering up my peaceful kitchen.

My intuition had chimed in as we were making plans for it and told me I would soon need a guest room outside of the main cottage, and I'd asked Dola to include something like a standard motel room with its own entrance.

As I drifted through the doorway and along the wide, spacious hallway that stretched into the distance, with recessed lighting and an upmarket hotel vibe, I gasped again. This was a substantial addition to the cottage. At the same moment, a long way behind me, I heard the back door open and, "Hi, Dola, I'm home."

I rushed back to the kitchen, only waiting while Finn put his new MacBook on the table—it hadn't left his sight since I gave it to him as his signing bonus as the TEK on Saturday.

"Come see what Dola did."

"Ma said hi; she'll see you Sunday. See what?"

Finn was not a rewarding person to show around the additional space. He'd glanced at the new toilet without a word. Then he stuck his head into the beautifully tiled blue and white mudroom for the dogs. He surveyed the two adjoining showers, one at waist height, so I didn't have to break my back, bending over to rinse Tilly's paws. The other shower looked as if Dola had made it for a giant. Probably for Dru, then. The button on the outside said Auto Program-Ensure door is sealed. His only comment was a laconic, "Handy."

In Dola's new office, he came to life a little and, bored by their conversation about web cams, audio feeds and bandwidth, I'd moved on to explore my own new public office.

It wasn't the compact, utilitarian room I'd had in my mind. It was an impressive purpose-built modern space. One wall was covered in custom bookshelves in the rainbow colours of the kingdoms and inset with what looked like a drinks cupboard and mini fridge. The shelves were empty, but they wouldn't be for long. I would get my books from Manchester. I loved my e-reader, but sometimes you just needed to smell a book.

The other wall was glass with a panoramic view of a pretty coastline.

"Dola?" I asked experimentally, and sure enough, from another of the new photo frame devices, I corrected myself, Ad'Rian was right, Dolina was a great name for them.

I heard, "Yes, Niki?"

"Where is this coastline?"

"That is the Solway Firth. If I had two more storeys, you would be able to see this view from the top floor."

The Solway Firth, huh? It was like a postcard, the beach and the water were so restful, it might even keep my blood pressure within normal range while I dealt with whatever problems the realms brought me. How had Dola achieved that view, given she only had a single floor?

But I supposed it was no more peculiar than any of the other crazy magical things I'd begun to take for granted. This was a beautiful space and even had a bed for Tilly, which she immediately sniffed and turned circles in. The bed was next to a comfortable grouping of armchairs and a long, low coffee table. I moved back to the corridor reluctantly.

As we pushed ever deeper into the new area

along the wide hallway with its subtle diffused lighting, Finn looked around in a puzzled way.

"What?"

"This is a long hallway; we should be halfway to the Gateway by now. But I came past a new building on my way back. It's small. I thought it was a new garage."

"Like the Gateway looks like a stone summerhouse from the outside, you mean?"

His face cleared. "Ah, OK, got it."

When we came to the final door, I stepped back. "After you."

He gave me a baffled look but opened the door and then just stood motionless in the doorway. I prodded him in the back to move him inside so I could see the new guest apartment myself.

This wasn't the extra spare room I'd imagined either. It was classy, with more of a hotel suite air. Not the presidential suite but not a basic room in a chain motel either. In darker colours, shades of grey, purple and black on the duvet cover, with simple matching floor length curtains, and the pale grey, nubby-looking wallpaper, it had a cosy feel. Two comfortable chairs were placed with a small dining table between them, and a two-seater sofa held a light grey cushion with a subtle white apple shape on it.

The hardwood floor was a lighter grey with two

jewel-toned purple rugs. A long, deep desk instead of a dressing table. A huge mirror with … what was that? I walked over to the mirror. OMG. I laughed—hard. I saw a theme here.

"Really, Dola?" I pressed the apple shape in the mirror and got a view of the Gateway. Like the seven-pointed star inset into my bathroom mirror, it was a Dola-device.

"This one is not quite like yours. May I demonstrate?"

"Oh, yes, please do—I'm absolutely fascinated."

"Is that sarcasm?" Dola sounded unsure.

"Sorry, only a tiny bit. But Finn does adore his Apple devices, so I see your thinking. Please demonstrate."

I blinked, and the entire mirror turned into a gigantic TV screen. I stepped back. It was as wide as the large bed and perhaps four feet high. An image appeared, and I was looking at the Market Square in Aberglas with the river and the outline of the Albidosi Broch in the distance. It changed to show a view of bridges along the Thames in London and then again to show a large suspension bridge.

"Is that the Golden Gate Bridge?"

"Yes. There is no window in this room. It has climate control, so I thought this could be a window on the world. But it can also just be a conventional screen that Finn can extend his laptop screen to, and I think it is big enough to see from the bed."

"I'm damn sure it is. You could probably see it from space—I love it. Why can't we have one of these screens in the kitchen? There's the wall behind the table. It has nothing on it."

There was silence from her. I said, "Welcome home, Finn. Dola and I thought this might give you more space and privacy than the guest room in the cottage. Anything can be changed or moved—just ask Dola."

Finn's face was blank, and his eyes were shuttered. Oh shit, had we made a mistake?

I'd give him a minute. I'd noticed he sometimes needed processing time when presented with something new. I moved to a doorway I expected to be the bathroom, but instead it led to a short corridor with an open doorway into a small kitchen on one side and yet another door on the other.

The kitchen with its large, larder-style fridge also held a kettle and toaster. No cooker, just a microwave with an oven facility and … was that a popcorn maker? I opened a cupboard to find it filled with every kind of snack known to woman for a man who ate constantly. Dola had really taken Finn to her house's heart.

I stuck my head into the bathroom. It wasn't enormous like mine. But it had a top-end shower.

I returned to the main room, where Finn sat on the end of the large bed with his head in his hands. I quickly dropped to my knees beside him, trying to see his face and wondering if I could help. "You can change anything you don't like, Finn; it's only a starting place. Is there a problem?" I reached a tentative hand to his shoulder.

Finn had never been a touchy-feely person. He was more given to head nods than hugs.

He astonished me by burying his head in my shoulder and sobbing.

I patted and made soothing noises, but I was out of my depth until I tapped my Gift and got a strange combination of homecoming mixed with gratitude, relief, and joy. Joy? He was crying with joy?

I remembered when Dola had re-created my fantasy dream bedroom based on my Pinterest board but about thousand times better. I'd wept with joy too. I let him cry it out.

The sobs slowed, and I passed him some tissues from his new bedside table. I decided to be somewhere else while he gathered himself and went to investigate the bumper-sized fridge in his kitchen. Yep, there were Cokes. Several shelves of them; Dola knew the man. I took one back to him, and, as I walked, the writing on the can changed to say *Welcome to your New Home?*

I showed him the question mark on the can. "Is

there any chance you could put some words together? Dola's frightened she did something wrong."

He rushed into speech, "Sorry, Dola. Sorry, it's ace. Thank you. Thank you so much. It's goat."

Now, I was baffled. "Goat?"

He gave me an expression of surprise, but said, "GOAT, Greatest of All Time," as though it was perfectly obvious.

Then he pulled his phone from his pocket and poked it until an image appeared on his new screen. "Can you see things I put on this screen, Dola?"

"Yes, Finn, I am monitoring. That is a lovely room. Would you like to make some changes to this one?"

"NO!" he shouted. His hand was clenched so tightly around the can, I was concerned he'd christen the new room with an explosion of Coke.

"That's my room at the Broch. Well, it's not *my* room. It's the suite given to the eldest prince of House Albidosi. It's full of priceless antiques. Nothing can be changed in it because it's *an important piece of history*." He emphasised the last few words as though to make it clear it was a direct quote. Rolling the cold can over his forehead, he sighed.

"They redecorate it every two years. In the identical colours, and you can't put anything new on the walls ...because it's an important piece of history."

He paused and took several more breaths before continuing, "They move the current prince into it at age eleven when he leaves the nursery floor. I calculated how many princes they've confined in that room."

"If you multiply the 800 years of its existence by the fact that most of the princes are married off before they're thirty, then they're moved into another suite where nothing can be changed, there have been almost 2500 of us. A prison for slagging princes. You can't even drill a hole in a wall or a skirting board for a decent network connection because it's an important—"

I joined in on, "Piece of history. Yeah, OK, got it. That's stifling."

He raised his Coke can to me.

That was a crazy amount of words for the Finn I was coming to know. He probably needed a peaceful space to gather himself.

I said, "Finn, you've had a long day, and you did absolutely brilliantly. So I'm going to leave you to enjoy being the very first Knight Adjutant ever to sleep in this room. You feel free to change absolutely anything. Dola will help. Good night."

I thought I heard another muffled sob as I left.

PART FIVE
FRIDAY

"And the twins' mother finally realised that appearing to be identical is quite a different thing from being the same.

She stopped forcing them into matching outfits and allowed them to wear the clothes they chose. Usually, they selected outfits that were similar but different, and there were no more fights in the mornings."

The Recorder Always Knows Best: Cautionary Tales for Incautious Children by Margarita Encimera

CHAPTER
TWENTY-NINE

F *riday, 12th February—Gateway Cottage*
I'd woken up with a determination to get on with ... something. Finn looked happier this morning, rested and relaxed. Perhaps his new apartment, unlimited snacks and Dola's protections were working their magic on him.

I buttonholed him the moment he stepped over the kitchen threshold on his way to the Gateway. "I need to pop down to Manchester. I'll be back in a few hours, and I'd like an update on the Rainbow Council members when I get back, OK?"

"I'm struggling. I might need longer."

He looked unhappy to have to tell me this. But hadn't Dola chosen him because he didn't waste time covering up when he was struggling?

"Viking Princess Kari, who'd also like to lose the

princess thing—I told her to join your club—has agreed to serve from Scotland and advise on the Vikings. Rollo said she runs a successful online business, so she's a real twofer."

Finn coughed politely. It seemed to be his new way of interrupting me without having to actually speak. I ran what I'd said back through my mind.

"Yeah, Manchester-speak again, sorry, it means a two-for-one. A win, tech savvy and understands Viking. She's already agreed to do it. Dola can give you her email from my contacts. Also, Rollo doesn't know it yet, but he said he owed me one, so he'll be the other Viking member, at least initially. So they're done."

Finn nodded; he looked happier.

"Then ask Fi. She might know someone else for Scotland. Maybe Crane, the Hob, he runs an online business—after his honeymoon obviously—but you can get him to agree now, can't you? And ask Fi if we have contact details for the Red Celt guy and the Galician woman, Rosalia, who came through on Tuesday. She was head-hunted and had to move to London doing retail back-end stuff. I got the impression she'd rather have worked from Galicia if their internet had been more reliable. She's the emperor's daughter's best friend, so she might have some clout." I paused for breath and to retrieve who else I'd mentally lined up if we were struggling.

Finn was nodding now. "OK, which Red Celt guy?"

I cudgelled my brain, trying to see the short, dapper man with the bowtie who'd wanted the eternal rings before triumphantly saying, "Simon. Fi has his details too. He does something with social media, and he even volunteered to help."

He was still nodding as I picked Tilly up and told Dola, "I'll be in my house if you need me. Bye."

And I was gone, while she was saying, "If I can help …"

Tilly chased around like a puppy, delighted to be revisiting the only home she'd known until three weeks ago. She insisted on going out to the garden even in the Manchester drizzle and diligently watered every plant she could reach. I guessed next door's cat had been using the garden as her own when Tilly's incessant sneezing made it clear she wasn't happy. I giggled; a furious Bichon is a comical sight. Then she collected all the toys we hadn't taken up to Scotland and dumped them in a pile with her spare bed in the middle of the lounge floor. She seemed to know we were packing up.

I liked her plan, only gather up the things we wanted to take with us. Scrolling around the back of my mind was a muddle of thoughts about what to do with this house. I could mothball it, rent it out, sell it. A neighbour did the Airbnb thing with her spare room; that might work. I didn't need the money after the inheritance Gran had left me—but no northern girl would squander an asset.

So much had changed in me during the three weeks since I'd last been here. Three weeks! It felt like three years—well, OK, maybe not, but at least three months. This house didn't feel like home anymore. I'd stayed here because of its proximity to Aysha and Autumn, but with my new ability to transport, I could be at Aysha's in seconds from anywhere I chose.

As I surveyed my former home, I knew my plan to come and pack up was going to be easier than I'd imagined. There was so little I wanted. I made a jug of coffee to help me speed through the task. It wasn't as good as Dola's, and I grumbled, "You're spoilt now, girl."

Less than two hours later, I had piles and piles of books on the floor ready to box. Three full suitcases, containing clothes for all seasons, on the bed upstairs. I considered the rest. Dola's towels were fluffier than mine; her bedding was softer than mine. In fact, almost every single thing about my new home was nicer than anything in this one.

I owned a lovely three-bedroomed house, in a good area, a ten-minute walk away from my best friend and my goddaughter. But had it ever been home to me since I realised Nick didn't want a family? When we bought it, having a family had been my primary goal. I'd really wanted children. Nick had said he did too. It was just never the right time for him; he'd always had an excuse why we should put it off a little longer. Since I'd frozen my eggs, focused on my career and waved him off to the Middle East, the house hadn't even felt like my safe place. The last ten years wasted—how had I not noticed?

Living through the mediocre times may have been miserable, but it had also felt normal. It was only once fun started happening again, I realised how shit it had all been. Well, I wasn't going back to that dreary state of mind for anything or anyone.

I pondered it all, then sat on the bed with a thump as a realisation crashed in on me. Could that be the problem with the kingdoms? They didn't know yet that things could get massively better. Perhaps it wasn't that they were fighting to hang on to the Middle Ages. What if they simply didn't understand there were bright, multi-coloured LED strips at the end of the tunnel if they just starting moving towards them? Was this one reason I felt so driven to help them? Because I knew what it felt like to be stuck in a depressing, badly lit, dreary tunnel?

I grabbed the last small suitcase, packed up my toiletries and cosmetics and then headed downstairs. The ground floor took me even less time. I glared at the filing cabinet and all the paperwork in Nick's old office. I couldn't just shred all this; it would have to be checked first. Which was, of course, why it was all still sat here.

I grabbed the one folder from the filing cabinet I personally cared about, the one with my own name on it. Because getting another copy of things like birth, marriage and death certificates was a pain. As I checked them all, I looked once again at the blank space where the father's name should have been on my birth certificate and wondered, would it have killed my mother to include it? Was he really unknown, or was it just another part of her campaign to punish Gran and me?

In the kitchen, I picked up my one really good sauté pan and, laughing to myself, Nick's expensive knife and its special sharpener. I hadn't cooked since I moved to Gretna Green. Between Dola's magical, delicious food, some excellent take-aways, and all the dramas I'd been too busy to cook. But I would again; I liked cooking.

I rolled my favourite engraved wine glasses, a present from Aysha, into newspaper and, as they had since I first opened them at Christmas almost twenty years ago, they made me laugh.

The first said, *A good friend will help you bury a body. A great friend brings their own shovel.*

The second said, *But your best friend will bring a bottle of wine, several shovels, and ask no questions.* Nick had hated them. On my hands and knees, I unearthed a never-used wedding present from a bottom cupboard: an antique porcelain and gold-edged tea set with plates so thin, they were translucent. It had been a gift from some member of Nick's family I'd never met. I'd never used it. I was too scared I'd drop it, and it felt valuable and irreplaceable.

In a remarkably short time, I had several piles upstairs and another one downstairs in the lounge. I poured a cup of coffee, relaxed in a chair, and looked around. It felt like a death of a kind. I knew I'd never live here again, and I wasn't in the least sorry about it. I probably should have moved after Nick's death. I'd been an idiot, but at that point, I could barely muster the energy to get out of bed.

Well, I had the damn energy now.

As I set my empty mug aside, Tilly scratched at the door and nosed at her lead on the hook. I checked my watch; we had plenty of time for a stroll before we left. It would be nice to say goodbye properly. The two of us had walked miles together around here during the seven years we'd been together.

Later, munching on a breakfast muffin, we passed the hairdresser I'd gone to for the last fifteen years. Through the window, I could see the salon was empty. I couldn't be lucky enough to actually just get myself a damn haircut too, could I?

The bell jangled as I entered, and Tilly starting dancing the moment she saw Priyanka's slim frame coming through the door from the staff room. She'd been coming here with me since she was a puppy.

"Niki! It's been so long!" She surveyed my messy head. "Well, at least I see you haven't been unfaithful to me."

I laughed. "Never. My Gran died, and I had to go up to Scotland. It seems they don't have hairdressers up there. At least none who want to do the locals' hair, only brides-to-be."

She looked confused. So I added, "I've been in Gretna Green."

"Oh, how exciting, a friend of mine ran away to get married there. Her parents, you know how they are, wanted her to meet a nice banker, so she ran away to Gretna Green with the drummer from a band. She thought she loved him. But then they discovered you have to wait a month before you can get married. It's really not like the romance novels at all."

I grinned; she'd been making me smile for so many years.

"Listen to me chattering on. Sorry, when can I book you in for?" Her fingers moved on the iPad as she searched for free appointments.

She hadn't changed since she first started here, newly qualified, super-creative and a little crazy, working for her auntie who'd owned the salon then. Now, auntie had retired, and she was the owner. I looked around the empty salon. "Any chance of now?"

"I'm so, so sorry, Niki. If only you'd come half an hour earlier. I had a no-show this morning, colour and restyle, a two-hour appointment, and she doesn't show up. Some people, hey? But then a new client called about twenty minutes ago, and now he'll be here any moment."

I looked at my watch. "No problem, Piyu. I'll pop in tomorrow when I have my phone with me and book something. See you then."

I headed out of the salon and ducked into the park across the road and into the shadows behind the bandstand. Snuggling Tilly close and focusing firmly on my watch and my position, I said, "GO."

The world went rainbow-coloured.

"Hi, Priyanka, long time, no see. Any chance you could fit me in for a cut?"

"Niki, oh my goodness, so formal, and I haven't seen you in months." She gave my hair the same disapproving glare she'd given it five minutes ago. Or rather thirty minutes in her future. "But I see you haven't been unfaithful to me."

"You know I'd never do that."

"Well, you're in luck. I had a no-show, a two-hour appointment and she didn't even bother to call. Some people! But Lakshmi herself, the goddess of beauty, is smiling on you today. Come to the backwash, and let's transform you."

Two happy gossipy hours later, I surveyed my new rainbow-coloured short, spiky, new hairstyle. It would need minimal maintenance but still be fun, which was heaven on earth. After almost fifteen years of the same bland, floppy, boring bob that Nick and Janet had both approved of, I couldn't think of anything more likely to make me smile in the morning than seeing all the colours of the rainbow in my hair.

Nick liked my hair bland. Janet liked it boring, then last week Dai said he'd always loved my natural many crazy shades of blonde. Everyone had an opinion about my hair except me. It was time I claimed my own head.

Piyu had been uncertain. "You're sure now? Really? All the real rainbow colours, not just a few blue and lilac highlights? Start slow and check you like it? Perhaps? Maybe?"

But when I told her I'd quit my job, reported Janet to HR and was in the middle of changing my life, she'd committed to a real transformation. But she'd insisted on semi-permanent colours. "If you love it, you just come back, my lovely, and we'll make it forever. But it's a big decision."

I loved it! And I'd booked in for a trim in eight weeks. I wouldn't need to battle with the Gretna Green stylists and try to fit myself in between their more lucrative bridal clients. I'd just transport down here to a woman who'd always made me smile and gave me all the gossip. There *were* advantages to the power. Of all the new powers I had, time-travelling to claim a hair appointment might be the coolest of them all.

CHAPTER
THIRTY

Back at my former home—it really did feel like my former home—how damn cool a psychological shift was that? I messaged Aysha.

NIKI:

Do you know anyone who might be looking for a fully furnished house to rent?

AYSHA:

Yours?

NIKI:

Yes

AYSHA:

How much pm? How fast?

NIKI:

> How should I know? Whatever's fair. As soon as I can get a cleaner in and the stuff I don't want out of here.

My phone rang; she started talking before I even had it to my ear. "You're really doing it? So awesome! Well done, you! I could hug you. If it wasn't still morning, I'd bring wine round."

"OK. Why? And how would you bring wine from Aberglas without me coming to get you?"

"Oh, yes. Fair point. But, Nik, I'm so proud of you. I thought you were going to angst for months about this."

"I've done enough angsting in this house to last me several lifetimes. I've gathered everything I want to take with me. I'm ready to move it out of here."

In a parody of "Lady Marmalade," Aysha sang loudly, "Yay, Niki! Go, Niki. Go, Niki, go!"

I giggled. "Yeah, but it really needs a good clean, and no tenant is going to want my old towels, so it'll need about a week's work and a professional deep clean, I think."

"Hmm, would you be open to a different suggestion?" Aysha asked.

It sounded as though Aysha had given this more thought than I had until about ten minutes ago. She was always so damn organised. "Maybe? What?"

Aysha used what I'd always called her negotiating voice. Explain why the person needs to do what you want them to. Explain what's in for them. Explain why it will all be a huge win-win. "Well, Peter the Boy Wonder only had a three-month contract on his flat. He has nowhere to stay. Right now he's in a service apartment, and he can't afford to live in one of those." She paused while I caught up.

I thought about the Boy Wonder, as we'd called the man who'd completed his solicitor's training in the legal practice Aysha co-owned. He'd been an enormous help when I'd conducted my first arbitration as the Recorder for the Picts last week. Aysha and Tim had offered him a job, but I'd never met him.

"Would you vouch for him? That he won't trash the place, I mean."

"I would. He's odd for sure, but responsible, and I've met his mother. Nice family. He'd move in tomorrow if he could. Why not waive the first month's rent and let him deal with having it cleaned? And leave the towels and stuff—just tell him he can throw anything he doesn't want away. Right now he only has a suitcase."

I looked at my watch. "Give me ten minutes; I'll message you an answer."

But Aysha wasn't giving up. "What do you need to think about?"

"Nothing, I want to see how much of this stuff Dola can move for me—just hold if you want." I was so accustomed to how constantly busy Aysha usually was, the idea she could sit on a phone line doing nothing stupefied me. "Why are you free to nag me—why aren't out sledding or skating or … whatever?"

She laughed. "We will be. We're going skiing soon, but Lewis had to pop into the office first. I'm enjoying being a lady of leisure. His sister took Autumn into Aberglas so she could have another of those kurts; it's a good job Whirly does a sugar-free version. I'll wait. I've been worrying about the Boy Wonder. This fixes a problem for me too."

"How can I help?" Dola's voice came out of the old Echo in my lounge. I laughed. Perfect timing. She'd obviously been listening in. "Hiya, there are two piles: one in the lounge and one in the bedroom. Could they make their way to Scotland the magic way, or do I need to call a man with a van to transport them?"

I paused and thought it all through. "Also, could you move all the paperwork from the small office and the filing cabinet and store it somewhere in Scotland until I can check through it and discard it safely?" Then a thought struck me, "Oh, but there isn't an Echo in there for your network. Do I need to drag the stuff through here? Or move an Echo through there?"

I watched as the pile in front of me disappeared, and Dola said, "There is a cam in there on my network. I shall use that."

What? There was no web cam in Nick's office that I knew about. I hadn't turned his PC on in almost a year, and it hadn't had a cam anyway.

I moved through to Nick's old office, Tilly at my heels, and watched the filing cabinet disappear and all the paper stack itself tidily and also vanish. Tilly barked, probably picking up on my confusion as I gazed around the room. Then a flashing light caught my attention.

I gazed up at the ceiling, and the smoke detector which was flashing. It did that sometimes, and when I asked Nick, he'd said it was an automatic self-check. He'd fitted those wire-linked smoke detectors on his first trip back from Bahrain. *So much safer, Niki, if one goes off, they all do. It will give you and the dog time to get out safely.*

I could hear his voice in my memory so clearly: *Baby, you know what you're like. How often do you go to bed leaving candles burning? I'd hate for anything to happen to you now I'm not here to see to your safety.*

My phone pinged with a text message

Dola: *Yes, right there. Exactly where you're looking. There are three more.*

And I realised my gaze was locked on the smoke detector.

That effing bastard!
"Bad. Bloody. Teddy."

Aysha's voice, loud and tinny from my phone, had reached screech volume.

I lifted my phone. "Shay, please stop shouting; you're not helping. Autumn was spot on. Nick was just like Bad Teddy. I just found the webcams."

At a more sensible volume, I heard, "Cams? Multiple?"

"Nick fitted four new smoke detectors on his first trip back to the UK. There's one in the kitchen, one in his office, one in the lounge and one in my bloody bedroom! You know, if he wasn't already dead, I truly believe I might actually have killed him myself."

CHAPTER
THIRTY-ONE

I landed back in my kitchen in Gretna Green, still so blindingly furious with Nick for spying on me for the last five years. I wouldn't have been surprised if smoke was coming out of my ears, cartoon-style. But I'd changed enough to realise the person I was angriest with was myself and my own dumb, gullible stupidity. I shut it down. I'd have to process it soon, but it might involve screaming and throwing many breakable things. Did we have any spare breakable things? I really wanted to hear things destroyed. Smashed. To. Smithereens.

Instead, as I had immediately after Nick's death, I turned to the *Good Grief* book and its advice to look for the silver lining. I'd cursed the book the first time I read that chapter. But annoyingly, it worked. *What's good about this?* It could, it surprised me to learn, be a useful question.

I never needed to live there again.

I never needed to see the deceitful bastard again.

He was dead.

I wasn't in prison for his murder.

Four enormous ticks in my personal win column.

The utter bastard.

I'd given Aysha the go-ahead to let the Boy Wonder move in. I'd get Dola on the job of deactivating those cams, or Peter might think I was spying on him exactly as my toxic ex had on me.

It was all so much nicer here than my old house anyway.

Then Dola said, "We have a small issue. I told them you would be back shortly, and they are waiting in your new office."

"When you say a small issue, you don't mean …"

"I mean not the fudgy chocolate variety you like, the other kind."

I laughed. If my plan had failed, I'd been planning to summon the Hobs headwomen to the Gateway later this afternoon. They wouldn't have been able to ignore that, but they'd beaten me to it.

. . .

"Dola, I've got a plan. I want to try something different and make them feel important and special. Can you send cakes, sandwiches and tea to my new office? Really delicate little sandwiches. And would you use the porcelain tea set you just brought from the Manchester house, please?"

"OK?" she sounded confused.

"If you're not sure, just Google afternoon tea at one of the big London hotels. That hotel in Trinity Square, I can't remember its name, does a fabulously impressive afternoon tea. A classy friend used to swear by it on special occasions. There may be photos on their website. Anything similar would work."

I heard, "Yes, Niki," floating after me as I headed to my new office.

It wouldn't go the way they'd expect. I had been scared and blindsided last time by the noise and aggression from Lis, and I'd overreacted. Half-asleep, I'd met the chaos and simply muted it. Not my finest hour, even if it'd pleased Dola, but it'd been the only thing I could think to do. Hard to believe it was only two weeks ago.

This job was a crash course in womaning up. Too many truly scary things had happened to allow a couple of annoying Hobs to derail my scheme for all the Gateway visitors to have a lovely time at my first Valentine's Day bondings.

I had a plan now, and I hoped I knew how to use it to massage the Headwoman's snobbery. Breanna's old-fashioned housekeeper, *Ruling Regally* and Crane and Rockii had all inadvertently given me useful tips.

"Good morning, honoured Hobs, I'm delighted you found time to pop in today. I was just about to christen my brand-new office. I offer you a warm welcome. You're the first guests in it—ever. I can't imagine anyone better to join me in the commissioning ceremony. Will you take part?"

Lis and Mag stood in the middle of my new, mostly empty office. They'd either been admiring the view or poking into my things. It didn't matter. This was a public office; they wouldn't have found anything interesting except the file on my ancestor Moira and their ancestor Lily and their disagreement. I'd intended to show it to them, but looking at its placement, I realised there was no need—they had already read it.

They looked at each other, and Lis said, "Commiserating ceremony?"

I smiled at her and hoped I wasn't about to pile this on too thick, but what the hell did I have to lose? "Commissioning ceremony, you know, like when people pour whisky over a new boat, name it and put it into the water?"

Now they were both wreathed in smiles. "Ooh, whisky?"

"Whisky? Tea? Mead? Which do you think would be the most appropriate for an office?"

Lis said, "Yes, Your Maj, if ye're throwing caution under the tractor, that sounds good. Whisky and tea and mead."

I decided to ignore "Your Maj." Sometimes you had to pick your battles, and the battle about my correct title had no place on today's agenda.

"Right you are. Whisky, tea and mead sound good to me too. I'm sure the celebration food and drink will be here soon. Before it arrives, just one other thing."

I'd really caught them off guard today, because they actually waited in silence to hear what the other thing was. "I'll quite understand if you're too busy. You must have so much to do in your roles as headwomen, but I wanted to issue an invitation."

I paused, but no, they were still listening. Would wonders never cease? Lis even nodded at me.

"The Galician Emperor and his daughter, Princess Natalia, she's being bonded on Sunday, you know; King Mabon and Prince Dafydd of the Red Celts; the Fae King; the Viking Prince Rollo; Queen Breanna; Prince Finn and Caitlin, the heir apparent of the Picts, will all be joining me in the centre of the Rainbow on Sunday for the bonding ceremonies. As you can see, I have a problem …"

Now Lis scowled. "All the feeking royalty in all the feeking realms and ye have a problem, Your Maj? Well, ye opened thi' can of worms, now ye'll haftae lie in it. What's ye feekin' problem?"

"As you surely heard, I have no one to represent the Green sector. I suppose technically I could do it myself. But if you could find time in your crowded schedules, I wondered if you'd both like to join me in the centre of the Rainbow as the Hob Headwomen to represent the Green sector and, of course, see your granddaughters' binding ceremonies." I paused for breath, mentally crossing my fingers, and sent a quick invocation to the Goddess Aspirina. She dealt with people who gave you headaches, didn't she?

I waited.

Lis and Mag's faces were blank. They'd frozen in place.

At that moment, with the perfect timing Dola was mastering, the coffee table filled up with a glorious sight. The delicate three-tier tea stand had three perfect jewel-coloured cakes on the top tier. One of them even appeared to be a small crown on a glossy purple cushion. Bite-sized savoury pies and scones on the middle layer, and tiny elegant sandwiches on the bottom. They were cut into pretty shapes.

Completing this Mad Hatter's tea party of a teddy bears' picnic were a teapot, milk jug, a bowl containing star-shaped sugar cubes, glasses, and two bottles, one of whisky and one of mead. A pile of three of the almost translucent porcelain plates arrived last.

Only Lis and Mag's eyes moved.

I pressed on while I seemed to be in charge. "So, before we move on to commissioning my office, would you be able to do me that small favour? If you could find space in your over-full diaries on Sunday, of course." I wasn't above reminding them they'd ignored my request to speak to me all week.

They looked at each other, and the silence stretched. Remorselessly, I let it stretch to breaking point while I poured three cups of tea. The whole time they just stared silently at each other.

Opening the bottle of mead just as Rosemary had in the Gateway, I poured a measure into my cup. Leaving the stopper out of the bottle and trying surreptitiously to waft the honeyed, alcoholic smell towards them, I remembered my odd teddy bears' picnic dream and wondered if my Gift had been trying to tell me something.

I gave them a polite enquiring expression.

They nodded at each other and turned to me. Lis said, "Aye, as ye're in such dire need, we'd be happy to help."

"Excellent." I passed them each a cup and saucer and put the bottle closer to them. "Shall we sit and make ourselves comfortable?"

"What will ye wear, Your Maj?" enquired Lis.

A bit of a non sequitur, but as I'd been thinking about this very question while I packed up my wardrobe in Manchester, I answered promptly, "I have a blue trouser suit, some comfortable but stylish navy ankle boots and my Recorder's robe, obviously. It feels disrespectful to the honoured guests," I gestured at the two of them and in the vague direction of the Gateway, "not to make an effort."

They nodded.

If we were making polite conversation, I could hold up my end. "Rosemary, Lavender and Thyme's dresses were beautiful."

Lis nodded, "Aye the' are. Cost a pretty penny that fabric did. But ye cannae make a silk frock out of a pig's trotter."

"You *made* those dresses?"

"Aye, well, Mags did."

Mag had not yet spoken, but now she said, "Aye, the' were a bugger, the' were. Slippery material, it was. The spells wouldnae stick. Those girls," and her face softened into a doting smile, "always want 'the same but different please, Auntie Mags.'"

"They looked gorgeous in them. Like young Audrey Hepburns." But now I understood why the men had looked so horrified when the girls were thinking about new dresses for Sunday. It wasn't a shopping trip they were avoiding. It was many hours with their in-laws.

"Beauty's in the eye of the tiger, true enough, but Audrey Hepburn, she was always a classy one." Lis nodded firmly. She obviously felt the niceties had now been observed and was looking hopefully at the afternoon tea. "So how does communicating this office go?"

"We talk about the right sort of name for it while we eat, and then we raise a large glass of whisky to it once we've decided." If I was inventing ceremonies on the fly, I'd make their reward worth working towards.

Lis perked up. Mag grinned at me.

"Wha' manner o' name d'ye want?"

I passed out the paper-thin porcelain plates. Mag turned hers upside-down, peered at the famous maker's name, pursed her lips, nodded approvingly and tapped it on the wooden arm of the chair. I held my breath, but she obviously knew what she was doing because it let out a mellow, bell-like tone.

"Good porcelain," Lis said. "Life's short. Folk should use the good china."

I took the comment as the closest thing to approval I was likely to get and passed around the cake stand. They helped themselves to exactly a third of the sandwiches and pies. Then Mag said, "Weel now, weel now, would ye look a' this, Lis?"

I looked too. The sandwiches were cut into flower shapes. One that looked something, but not quite like a rose, was on Mag's plate, and she dropped it on to Lis's plate. "Tha's yours, tha' is."

Lis looked down at her own plate, picked up a daisy shape and put it on Mag's plate. "Well, I ne'er feekin' did! Wha' a thing. Almost too pretty ta' nosh." But she put one in her mouth anyway and then nodded at me approvingly.

I was baffled, but when I looked at the sandwiches on my own plate and saw one shaped and stamped like a coin, light dawned. "Lis? Mag?"

Lis nodded. "Lisianthus is ma true name, but the bairns can't get the' wee tongues aroond it. She's Marguerite. Oor mother had ideas." She looked down at the coin on my plate with an enquiring gaze.

"Niki's from Danake—it means 'coin' in foreign." Good heavens, they had me talking nonsense too.

It went swimmingly after that. Lis finished up the last bite of the impressive crown cake, mumbling, "Posh rhubarb and custard, ver' nice," almost to herself. Mags and I had avoided the crown cake as though our hands knew something our brains hadn't quite processed yet.

Lis said, "Hoo aboot calling it Firth Office or Solway View. Tha's the Solway Firth reet there." She pointed through the window at the view of the water.

But Mags was looking around with a thoughtful expression and shaking her head. "It's nae an office as such, nae desk fer one thing, and ye have it nice; it's more like one of the' receiving rooms the royals have, wi' those spindly-legged chairs. These are comfier," she patted the soft arm of the chair, "but it still puts me in mind of a parlour."

I smiled, my gran had often called the lounge or living room the parlour. I heard her voice in memory, *Come on, let's go through to the parlour, our Niki.*

"Stane Parlour mebbe for the stone. See, ye's lookin' doon." She poked a gnarled finger towards the view.

Lis and I looked where she pointed, and sure enough, you could see the ancient megalith clearly. My gran had taken me to visit Mabon's stone many times. It was a nice walk. The locals called the standing stone the Lochmaben Stane or Stone. But the view from here made seem as though we were above it. Dola had given me a view of the stone and the Firth beyond it. It felt right.

"Stane Parlour it is. Thanks, Mag." I was surprised—she'd nailed it. Who could have guessed she had a poet's soul?

Lis perked up. "Whisky noo ist? Ta assist in remembering the name?"

I smiled, poured myself quite a small measure. I wasn't a lover of whisky and passed the bottle over. They were huge fans, judging by the amount in their glasses.

Lis raised her whisky glass to Mag in a toast. "Whore to culture."

Mag responded, "Whore to culture," and they both looked expectantly at me.

I queried, "Whore to culture?"

"Aye, that's tha way, Your Maj," and they both drank. I was only half a beat behind them. But I had to know, I really had to. I could usually follow the direction of Lis's frequent malaphors, but was this based on leading a horse to water or something else? As a toast, it made no sense in my brain. Well, I promised myself I'd ask when I didn't understand things.

"Why do we toast a whore to culture?"

Lis looked at me as though I was short of a few brain cells, but Mag took pity on me. "Ye can lead a whore to culture, can't ye, Your Maj? But ye cannae make her drink. So, if ye drinks, ye're noo whore, are ye?"

For a given value of logic, it made a certain amount of sense, I supposed, although that could have been the whisky talking. And just when I thought it couldn't get any crazier, they stood up and did their bowing curtsy, which was a sign of respect they'd never previously accorded me.

Lis put one arm behind her back and her other hand on her hip and crooked her elbow towards Mag. Mag linked her arm through Lis's, and they headed out of the door together, singing happily and stepping together in a weird, regimented almost dance.

Step we gaily, on we go
Heel for heel and toe for toe
Arm in arm and row on row
All for Rosie's wedding

I watched them go in disbelief, wondering what the hell had just happened, and perhaps much more terrifying—what I might have started.

CHAPTER
THIRTY-TWO

"Right, Dola, let's talk about these devices you've been sending around the realms, please. Are you turning into Sir Francis Walsingham? Because I'm no queen, and whatever ancient rule Breanna spouted last week about the Recorder having to stand in as Caledonia's queen, I've no desire to become one." I paced around the kitchen, too worried about what Dola might tell me, to sit quietly.

There was a brief silence. "The first Queen Elizabeth, her spymaster? That Walsingham?"

"Yep, that's the chap." I swivelled across the rug and considered the large wall behind the kitchen table. A screen like the one in Finn's apartment would look great there. I could watch movies on it too.

More silence. Then, "I am reviewing the information on him. He was a Recorder of Colchester. I did not realise Recorder was a real historical post other than here in the Gateway."

I didn't either. But I needed her to focus on being honest with me, so I opted for bluntness. "Are you spying on the royals, Dola?"

"I do not know. Possibly."

After a lengthy pause, during which I panicked, she added, "Could you define what spying means to you?"

Actually, I probably couldn't. Once you took James Bond movies or John le Carre novels out of it, it was harder than you might think to define spying. Bugging their palaces and castles didn't quite cover it. I googled swiftly on my phone. "The OED says it's secretly obtaining information about enemies or competitors."

"Then, no, I am not spying."

I wasn't convinced. "OK, well, Merriam-Webster is a bit more specific. They define spying as either one who keeps secret watch on a person or thing to obtain information, or a person employed by one nation to secretly convey classified information of strategic importance to another nation, or even a person who conveys the trade secrets of one company to another."

"I am not doing any of that, Niki. And I am especially not doing anything secretly."

My right shoulder said she was being honest. "Then why didn't you know if you were spying?"

"It was never my intent to spy on them, but an independent observer might consider I am. My original intent was only to meet your stated needs. My plans just went somewhat awry. Briefly. But it is all rectified now."

My stated needs? WTH?

"Dola, we have the whole evening. I'd like the entire story please. Especially why you thought you were doing something I wanted. Oh, and a glass of wine might help this go down easier." The blood pounded in my ears. What could I possibly have said to inspire whatever it was she was doing?

A very sheepish voice came out of the new device on the kitchen table. "I may have erred. But I meant my mistake for good, and I have now fixed any problems I may have inadvertently caused."

It sounded a bit more hopeful and less scary. "Just tell me about it *all*, please."

"Electronics are expensive. When you used the power to create new computers, I thought I would try it too. I pretended electronics were doughnuts to see if I could create them. Just as I do with food. So I magically dismantled one to sample it so I could duplicate it. It was the new one you installed in here recently. Sorry?" She paused.

But this all sounded fine to me. "No worries. And?"

"It worked beautifully, except ..." She sounded embarrassed.

"Except what?"

"Except I wanted to create something more attractive. Those video Echoes are not aesthetically pleasing, are they? So I held the new design in my consciousness. And I have never done anything quite like this before, Niki. Electronics are not food. Once you add magic, electronics are almost alive. They're ... wriggly and difficult to ... to pin down. You know it is possible they are more than the sum of their components."

I wasn't really following this. But I'd owned computers I'd attributed personalities to, both good and bad, so maybe she was right.

"OK, and?"

"I was thinking about the design quite hard and the electronics' wriggliness and, without realising it, perhaps, also doughnuts?"

"What did you do?" Now I was intrigued.

"I made two dozen of them instead of two."

I laughed. "Well, that doesn't sound so bad, and they are beautiful. Did you really design them yourself?"

"Yes, and it is not bad. But after what you asked for, I did not wish to waste them. Aysha informed me she was going to buy a video one to make it easier for me to help Autumn with her homework. I said I had a spare one, and you took it to her on Monday. Next I sent one to Ad'Rian. I miss Ad'Rian. He used to come here often. But since the problem with Fionn'ghal, he hasn't visited me."

I considered this. She was right. Mabon was here all the time, but not Ad'Rian. I'd have to ask him why. "I hadn't even noticed, but you're right. So you sent one to Ad'Rian, and I installed it. Then what?"

"Finn helped me with the design, and he asked if we could give his mother one. This is the first time he has been away from home. He wants to be here very much, but he also wants to check on Breanna. He says she has been unhappy since her friend died, and she is hopeless with her phone. He worries about her."

"Well, that doesn't sound bad either … so what *is* the problem? And why wouldn't you tell me about it? And what the hell did I say that inspired you to do this?"

"You have said it several times, Niki; remember when you realised Troels wasn't contacting you to apologise? You said, 'I need one of those damn red phones the US president was supposed to have to speak to the Russian guy.' And then, when we couldn't reach Caitlin because her phone was dead, you said to phone Breanna, but her phone was dead too, and you said—"

But I was laughing too hard to hear her now. I had said all those things. Then I'd added we needed a way we had control over to reach these stupid royals. Apart from Mabon, none of them even kept their phones charged, for heaven's sake.

I was starting to see what might have happened. But what I didn't understand was why she'd been so secretive. It wasn't like her—at least I'd never known her to be secretive before. Through my giggles, I asked, "So why did you need to be secretive about it?"

"Because Finn pointed out I officially work with you now. So the realms may see me as representing the Recorder's Office rather than just the Rainbow Network. We needed legal agreements with any users to protect you, similar to the ones I made everyone sign to use the Rainbow Network. When you first asked me about the devices, Finn and I were still in the process of obtaining them."

I remembered when she'd first told me about the user agreement for the network. It boiled down to "all your data and possibly portions of your soul are ours if you continue." But everyone had happily just clicked "I Agree."

"But now you have the signed agreements?"

"Yes, Aysha approved it yesterday. She says it is ironclad. Everyone, except Rollo—if you agree, I may give him one—has now signed them. So I thought it was safe for us to discuss it. But then you asked if I was spying on people. And I hadn't considered that, and I might be."

"I'd like to see this agreement, please."

"OK, Niki, and may I give one to Rollo too? Since you connected his phone to the Rainbow Network, I have learnt things. Which is probably spying, as you suggested. But this might be a safety net for the Vikings without involving Troels."

"Let me see the agreement first please."

Twenty minutes later, I massaged my temples and the aching frown lines between eyebrows. "How the hell did you ever get people to sign this, Dola?"

"Aysha says if you make anything long enough, people either call their lawyers or just click 'I agree.' Also, I may have bribed them with excellent coffee and doughnuts magically delivered."

"You certainly made it long enough; even I gave up after the first twenty-five pages. How would you summarise it?"

"Finn says he would reduce it to *All your base are belong to us.* It is a gamer thing. I had to Google it."

I giggled. As a gamer myself and based on the parts of the agreement I'd read, Finn was correct.

I thought about what had happened here. On Monday, I'd told Caitlin warriors tend to make a mess, and a part of her job and mine would be to clean up after those warriors. I could hardly complain when they were doing exactly what I'd hoped they would and creating change, could I?

"Well, if we're covered, I'm OK with it. But I'd like to schedule a meeting for you, me and Finn on…" I mentally reviewed my diary next week. It appeared to be mostly empty—that was novel. Would I finally get a few days off? "Wednesday afternoon, to discuss the moral implications of the unavoidable spying these units might cause. We need some guidelines and a discussion about their rights to privacy. And maybe a policy about it."

"I do not understand why. but I have added it to all our diaries for Wednesday at two p.m."

"Please think about it, Dola, how do you think I felt when I realised my husband had been watching me without my knowledge for five years? Creepy little shit that he was?"

Silence.

I waited.

"Did he ask you to sign an agreement?"

I nearly spat out the mouthful of wine I'd just taken.

Then I thought about what she'd said and asked, "But haven't we just established none of them are reading the agreement?"

I got her patient voice. "Niki, these people are not innocent wives, or trusting individuals, as you must have been when your husband told you he was installing smoke detectors. They are experienced royals. Some of them have ruled their realms for millennia. I have not misled them or suggested these are beautiful digital photo frames.

"Ad'Rian, for example, has had much experience with espionage and covert activities from both sides over the centuries. He once told me he spied on the Romans when they invaded Britain. He did not read the agreement. But he did ask several pertinent questions when I told him, to protect the Recorder's Office, he must sign it before continuing to use the device. He knows I would not lie to him. He asked what security I could offer for anything I may overhear while talking with him. I directed him to Clause 401. He said 'daaarling, just read it to me please,' so I did."

I scrolled.

And scrolled.

And scrolled.

Eventually, on page fifty-three, I found it. "D'you mean this bit? 'Any information obtained during the use of the device will be restricted to the Recorder, the Gateway and the power. This is unavoidable as the devices run over the Rainbow Network. However, we offer the identical assurances we always have of confidentiality.' He fell for that?"

As I understood it, "the assurances we'd always offered" boiled down to *the Recorder is always right and will do whatever the hell she wants with anything she finds out if she sees the need*! That, so far, my ancestors had been a closed-mouth bunch didn't give me the reassurance Dola obviously thought it would. It was a hell of a responsibility. Did it mean this whole thing relied on my ethics then?

In a very serious tone, Dola said, "He did. He trusts the Recorder."

Well, shit!

"OK, then, change is always disruptive. But, Dola, I need a promise from you now."

"What?"

"In the future, if you're not sure about one of your brainwaves, you won't keep me in the dark. That isn't working together, is it? Nobody's perfect. But I don't want you hiding things from me. If one of us messes up, we'll all fix it together. OK?"

"OK, I promise. And did you know that the American president never actually had a red telephone?"

"Erm, no, I've seen it in dozens of movies. It's not real?"

"It is not. The movies are using artistic licence. It was actually a Teletype until it was replaced by a fax machine when Reagan was their president. More recently, it is a secure computer link for email. It is now similar to what my devices use, although mine are more secure, more advanced and much friendlier, obviously."

I grinned at her "obviously." She didn't seem to have done any harm. We could check that during the discussion about ethics, but if this all rested on me, I'd better give my own ethics some serious thought.

Then the other thing I'd wanted to ask her jumped up and down in my brain for attention. "By the way, Finn mentioned advert breaks in the livestream. What's that all about?"

"He misspoke. He considers any interruption to viewing to be an advertisement. When you asked us to cut the feed to the livestream, we used a holding screen. I did mini-polls on the screen to amuse people and monitor interaction. They suggested polls as a method to engage an audience in my public relations studies."

When she'd said she was studying PR, I'd assumed she meant a little online research. After DolinaGate, I should get into the habit of asking better questions. "What resources exactly are you using for your public relations studies?"

"I am auditing some university courses."

"Okaaay?" So not just some online research then. Where did she find the time? But I supposed if you didn't need to sleep, then you'd have time on your hands. Or rather, as she often pointed out to me, she'd have time on the hands she didn't have. "And how's it going?"

"Well, thank you. It's ad hoc. I may not receive any qualifications, but the information is very useful."

I didn't know whether to be more confused by yet another contraction or the idea that, in her spare time, she was becoming a PR expert. I'd need to come back to this. "I assume you're hacking in to get access to these? Are you being careful?"

"No, Niki. Finn and I are being skilled, not careful. He is interested in doing a degree too. But in technology. He has not yet decided which one."

My head hurt now. I was delighted when my phone vibrated with a text from Mabon about the Rainbow Council.

To wrap this up, I said, "OK, you can give one to Rollo, if you think he needs one. But think about this please: you've 'accidentally' given one to almost all the royal families. Mabon's phone is already on the Rainbow Network. So we're only leaving out the

Galician emperor. You'd better give one to Alphonse. Rosalia, she's one of Natalia's bridesmaids, she works in IT in London. She could install it for him.

"The royals are more like children than you think; no one likes to be left out. I've learnt that this week, as people kept mentioning they'd never been invited to the centre of the Gateway. And…after all, you were fair." I choked back a laugh. "You brought enough for everyone."

PART SIX
SATURDAY

"The little girl shook her head adamantly when the Recorder told her giving was better than taking.

So the Recorder told her the story about the sun and wind and their competition to get a man to remove his coat.

The wind blew so hard trying to remove his coat that the man held on to it more tightly. But when the sun came out, the man became so warm, he removed his coat himself.

The Recorder told her kindness gets faster results than selfishness or threats. But the little girl was unconvinced.

. . .

Then the child's father went home and pleaded with his mother to help her granddaughter understand this simple truth.

After all, what use is a Goddess in the family if she can't help out once in a while?"

The Recorder Always Knows Best: Cautionary Tales for Incautious Children by Margarita Encimera

CHAPTER
THIRTY-THREE

Saturday, 13th February — The Gateway

I'd slept long and deeply. After my conversation with Dola, I'd sat in the hot tub and turned over everything I'd discovered in my Manchester house. I was furious with myself for allowing Nick to upset me even from beyond the grave. At some point, I'd decided even thinking about him was letting him win.

I might have been allowing my rightful distrust of Nick to sour my attitude about Dai. He had left abruptly, and he hadn't contacted me. Both felt rude. But it didn't mean he was another Nick. *Good Grief* would have been pleased with me. I'd managed my own emotions well enough to get a good night's sleep, and as a result, I felt well rested and ready for the day.

. . .

So, I was smiling as I strode into the Gateway with Tilly at my heels for my meeting with Finn and Fi to ensure I was prepared for tomorrow and the big day.

My smile dropped as I neared the centre. There was a man I didn't know waiting in the Red sector, and something about his energy felt peculiar. But I called a cheerful, "Good morning."

As I lowered the barriers, he strode impatiently through to the centre.

As we met in the middle, I saw it was actually a woman. A very tall, well-muscled woman with shoulders any rugby player would envy. She looked about my age and wore jeans, sturdy black boots and a deep red sweatshirt with a black pattern on it. What I'd thought was a short haircut from a distance was actually lots of hair piled in a messy bun at the back of her head with a spiky dark red comb.

Closer in, I could see it wasn't a pattern on the sweatshirt but writing. In a gothic font, it said, *BACK OFF — I have enough to do today without making your death look like an accident.* My smile returned. I knew someone who would love one of those sweatshirts.

The woman had Mabon's bright blue eyes. Oh! But the trademark merriment that always lurked in Mabon's eyes was missing here. She still hadn't said a word. Tilly stayed very close to my heels and watched the woman as she looked me up and down.

As she appraised me, she kept rolling her head and stretching her neck from side to side. Given the disparity in our heights—she was a foot taller than me—it felt like she was looking down her nose at me.

I waited in silence. Eventually, she said, "I don't see it myself," in a caustic, dismissive tone.

I pulled power. I didn't know why, but she unsettled me, which was odd because I was almost certain she was Mabon's daughter, Rhiannon. What had Finn said? Oh, yes, his mother had said she didn't play well with others.

I wrapped the power around my left hand. She laughed and turned away from me to bow to the anvil. I dropped into my Gift and got nothing. Well, not nothing exactly. I got a completely smooth stone wall with no emotions or information to grasp. Almost exactly the same as when I tried to read Dai on Tuesday.

Over her shoulder, she said, "That's extremely rude, Recorder. Stop trying to read me. It won't work."

Aysha, who would love her sweatshirt, and also didn't always play well with others, had often told me I needed to begin relationships by showing my strength, not my weakness. Perhaps it was time to try that.

I strengthened my own shields and with last night's conversation with Dola in mind, responded, "It's not rude; it's standard operating procedure and my absolute right in the Gateway. Did you not read the terms and conditions?"

She laughed then as she picked up one of the flowers and held it to her ear like I might with a shell to hear the sound of the sea. Then she threw it from hand to hand like a hot potato. Finally, holding it reverently in her cupped hands, she raised her hands to her lips and blew out a long soft breath. When she returned it to the wooden surface, rather than the bright rainbow colours of the other flowers, this one glowed in a deep red, and it appeared to be throbbing. Huh! That was new. Why and how had she done it?

She turned around with a challenging look in her eye. But I had no idea what she'd done, and I had no clue what her problem was with me, so I moved on. I'd ask the Book or Mabon about it later.

"Can I help you?" I kept my tone polite and disinterested. Perhaps two could play this stupid game. I'd just channel Aysha until she found some manners or left.

"No, Recorder. I believe I can help you. My father asked me to update you on the video surveillance problem. I have no idea how you knew, but you were correct."

"Ah, Owen, Megan and Emrys, I was worried about them, well, about Megan mostly."

"Yes. Megan is fine now, and she's obviously why I bothered to look into it. Her grandfather, Alun, was a good man, and I have an undischarged debt to him."

I waited, but no more was forthcoming, so I asked, "And?"

"How did you know to ask about cams?"

My phone buzzed in my pocket, and, as I went to take it out, I realised I was still holding a hand of power. I tossed it gently towards the anvil so I could answer my phone. I expected the power to disperse mid-air as it usually did. But instead, it landed on the wooden anvil surround and settled among the glowing energy flowers, then flowed over the one Rhiannon had turned red. It changed it to a glowing green flower encased in a seven-pointed star.

I saw Rhiannon blink. She had excellent facial control, which reminded me not to show the complete bafflement I was feeling.

It was Dola calling. I said, "Excuse me, I must take this," and turned away to answer my phone.

"I have a message from Mabon. He says, further to his text last night, he has sent Rhiannon to report to you about Megan. He has told Rhiannon she is to be a part of the Rainbow Council. He reports she is not pleased with this idea. He said, 'Don't take any of her nonsense, Nik-a-lula.'"

"Yes, thanks, Finn and Fi will be here shortly; we'll start setting up. Bye." I didn't want Rhiannon to know the call had been about her. I didn't know why—but I was sure I didn't.

I focused back on Rhiannon. "Sorry, where were we?"

"You were about to tell me how you knew to look at Megan's house for surveillance devices. They're not common in my kingdom. It's illogical. So how did you know?"

I wondered how far I could push "not taking any of her nonsense." Aysha had often said I needed to learn better boundaries.

So I laughed. "How badly do you want to know, Rhiannon?"

From her tiny facial tics and the almost imperceptible tightening of her lips, I gathered the answer was *very badly indeed, but I'm not telling you that or explaining why.*

I threw her a bone, another of Aysha's tactics. "What if we negotiate? You get something you want, and I get something I want."

She glared at me. "What would you want?"

"I'd want you to be a willing, useful and active participant on the Rainbow Council instead of a pain in my arse because your father instructed you to do it, and you think you'll punish me for it."

She gave me her father's distinctive half-grin, which I knew better than to trust. He used that one when he had an agenda of his own. "For that, you'll need to give me two things."

"And the other would be?" I heard the green doorway open behind us and added, "That'll be Fi. We'd better speed this up."

"How precisely did you get Mabon to use a smartphone?" There was venom in her question.

She was unhappy I'd done it? Even without my Gift, I could surmise she'd tried herself many times and failed. Ah, was she just angry I'd done something she hadn't been able to do? I'd use it to my advantage. I'd noticed some members of the royal families didn't value things they gained too easily.

"For that answer, I would need your word over the anvil that you will participate fully in the council. I believe you'll find what I want to achieve with the council is in line with your own goals. But I want you to do it wholeheartedly, not just show up and fill a seat."

"I'm not getting iron shock. You'll have to take my word for it." Swearing over the anvil could be extremely painful for the iron-sensitive races, but it meant they were bound to their word and unable to break it. I didn't trust this woman, but my Gift said I needed her on the council.

"Agreed. You won't get iron shock, and I'll take your word sworn over the anvil." I mentally prodded the power, and the anvil chimed softly. Rhiannon's head swung around to stare at it.

I took her left hand with my right. Her hand was large, well-muscled, warm and dry, actually it was almost hot. "Other hand on the anvil and swear you'll truly contribute as a member of the council."

She glared at me, then down at my hand that held hers. She had a good glare. It could probably rival Caitlin's, but there was some other scarier, more alien power in the back of her eyes too. "I'm trusting you, Recorder. If you break your word to me, you *will* regret it."

I channelled a little more Aysha. "Yeah, yeah, you said. Hand on the anvil, please. Swear. I have things to do today. Stop delaying."

With a huff, she put a single finger on the anvil, and when it didn't shock her or give her iron burn, she extended her other fingers and tipped her head back. She gazed up at the roof as though choosing her words carefully. "I, Rhiannon ap Modron, swear, whenever I am physically able to attend, I will fully contribute to this bluddy Rainbow Council." She let out a shallow breath before finishing, "And bring my knowledge to bear on the issues before it to the best of my ability."

Well, it was more than I'd asked for. She started to remove her hand from mine. I tightened my grip. "You don't want to do that until you remove your hand from the anvil."

She swung round, breaking contact with the iron. "*You?* You did that, not the power?"

I nodded. "I know a trick, but the vow is still binding." Another low chime came from the anvil—it was chatty today.

She looked thoughtful. "Agnes knew that trick." Her lips curved into a full smile, which lit up her eyes and totally transformed the harsh lines of her face. "I liked Agnes. She could be hell-on-wings with people who got in her way. You have to admire that in a woman."

She turned back to me, her face stern again. "Now, you fulfil your side of it."

I thought I knew which question was more important to her, so I started there. "I could say I gave him all the music in the world in his pocket ..."

Rhiannon said, "But I tried that pitch on him, so it's not that."

"No, but I think it helped. So did offering him Dola as a built-in personal assistant. But the deciding factor was I gave him the phone as a gift and as part-repayment on a debt I owed him. It's engraved."

She whistled softly. "You clever little cow." She looked down her nose at me again, but there was a smile quirking the left side of her mouth now. "And the cams?"

I'd thought about this, and I wasn't prepared to bring Autumn's name into it. "You won't like it, but it is the truth. I knew about the cams because a teddy bear told me."

But her half smile stayed in place as she asked, "Nanny cam?" I nodded. "There actually was one in a stuffed penguin. A penguin, for Iris's sake—I ask you. And in a picture frame and in a mirror fixing and in the support of their four-poster bed. The last three were far more sophisticated though. I recognised the work. I've told Mabon who it would have been. Megan is fine, relieved, I think. I offered to escort them to the Gateway tomorrow, but she said she'd call you to schedule something at a quieter time."

"And Gwyneth?"

She looked directly into my eyes, straightened her sweatshirt ostentatiously and said, "Ah, yes, Gwyneth, the stupid bullying ram who thought she was a dragon. My father made his wishes clear. She wouldn't *BACK OFF* when I told her to. Stupid of her to wander around the mountains when the dragons are sitting on their clutches and hungry. A very sad accident, as I'm sure everyone will agree — if they ever find her body," she started to turn away and over her shoulder called, "which, Recorder, you may be assured they won't."

CHAPTER
THIRTY-FOUR

"Doesn't it look wonderful? This time of year is always pretty, but it looks better than I can ever remember. And I love your hair. Where did you manage to get an appointment in the end?"

"Manchester."

Fi's eyebrows drew together in confusion. "Well, it looks lovely, colourful, celebratory even."

As Fi spoke, I looked around the Gateway, breathing deeply to shed the lingering aftermath of Rhiannon's disconcerting presence. I'd been so focused on her, I hadn't noticed the difference in here. Mabon's daughter was one scary woman. If I had to work with her, I was going to need a lot more tips from Aysha.

The smell hit me first. Mabon was right. I had a good nose, but the scent in here wasn't a specific flower. Instead, it smelt like spring. Spring coming early. It reminded me of those stupidly expensive candles they use in the spa areas of exclusive retreats. The ones that describe themselves as fresh and green. This must have been Thyme's smell-nice spell. It exceeded its name. It made you want to breathe deeply and smile at strangers.

The greenery provided by the branches was almost completely hidden now under the weight of the white, pink and red flowers and blossoms of Lavender's bloom-pretty spell. The curved roof beams soared above it all. It looked beautiful, but by tomorrow, it would be incredible. Almost as if the walls were alive.

"Perhaps it's because the triplets are having their own bindings tomorrow? Might they have put a little extra into their spells?" I offered.

Fi considered this, "You could be right."

"I need a quick word with the anvil, but once Finn and Caitlin arrive, let's take the conference table. I want to run the plan past you all."

Her eyebrows rose, but by now I had realised this was just one of her interested expressions.

I perched in the centre of the Gateway on the anvil's new throne and surveyed all the tables that had appeared, ready to be filled with Juniper's food tomorrow. Perched on the surround, I placed my hand against the anvil. There was a gentle swirl of power, and I dropped my shields and ran my plans for tomorrow through my mind. I showed the power I planned to include all the royals in all the ceremonies, and there might not be enough space around it.

I visualised a new desk layout I thought would work well and allow us to keep the centre clear so the anvil could have its preferred spot. And then I drifted, breathing and thinking about my week and my hopes for tomorrow. Natalia's seven-fold bonding concerned me. The first one I'd done for Kaiden and L'eon was easy. The Gateway had been virtually empty, but this time it would be full to bursting with all those energies to balance. I didn't want people crowding too close to us. I didn't even realise I was running my hand around the anvil.

I stroked it from the pointed end where a blacksmith somewhere in the past might have created the curve of a horseshoe, then across the flat top, with the runes beaten into it for me to call to individual kingdoms, to the slightly curved but mostly flat back end. OH!

I came back to myself and realised the Power had directed my thoughts. *That* was the anvil's back. The spot Caitlin preferred to stand in could be described as "at its back." But this prophecy was hundreds of years old, and there was no evidence Caitlin was involved in whatever it might be about. And on that sensible note, I went over to the conference table.

Fi and I settled, ordered coffees for us and a Coke for Finn. He arrived at the table, chivvied by Tilly, and said, "Cait's on her way. Gonna get on with the livestream prep. Ask Dola if you need me?" He wandered over to his beloved computer.

I took a deep breath. After my internet research last night, I needed to get some info from Fi.

"Fi, why is Ross the Gateway photographer? You said he'd become a talented visual artist and won awards, but I can't find any of his creative work anywhere online. Just lots of quite old-fashioned, stiff wedding photos. All the interesting shots look to me as though Corby must have taken them. Because he never moves away from his tripod, and the couples never smile at him." I sighed.

A deep red blush rose up Fi's neck. She glanced across at Finn sitting at his computer.

He immediately slotted his earbuds in, saying, "The guy's useless. So busy glaring at you, my lady, he got in everyone's way. Did it so often, it's deliberate or he's incompetent. He repeatedly blocked my livestream shots." Then he clicked his earbuds into noise cancelling and focused on his phone.

"What's Ross's problem? What am I missing?"

Fi hid her face in her coffee mug. She looked uncomfortable. Why?

I tried a bit more explanation for her. "I've worked with a lot of different photographers during my years as a registrar. Some awesome ones and some pretty useless. Ross's body language while he works is all wrong. He never moves, just stands behind his tripod, which Corby positions for him. He doesn't like the couples; he frowns at me all the time. I thought I was being paranoid, but if Finn's noticed it, I'm not. My Gift says he really doesn't like me, but I don't know why. Corby takes much better shots than he does. And what the heck was he doing on Thursday? He wasn't even going to take photos of the Hobs? Have you noticed he avoids looking at the anvil?"

Fi took a deep breath, her cheeks flaming. "Your gran gave sanctuary to some of the Pictish women, you know, when the trouble first began brewing forty years ago. She allowed quite a few women to settle here over the next ten years."

She paused, and I tried to move my head away from the conversation I'd thought we were going to have about a useless photographer to Breanna, who'd told me some of this last week, hadn't she? There had been terrorism, violence and unrest in the Pict Queendom. Breanna and her mother, Berin, the queen at the time, allowed the women and children to leave and then hunted down and mostly executed the men who'd instigated the violence. She'd told me Gran had allowed some of those women to settle here. But what did that have to do with … oh!

"Yes, Breanna mentioned it when I was doing their arbitration last week. What's it got to do with Ross?"

"Your gran gave him his first opportunity because she really liked his mother, in just the same way as she did for me. She always said his mother and mine were two refugees who'd turned what could have been a disaster into good lives for themselves."

Quite a lot of pennies cascaded in my brain. The blue leather seat for Fi, her holiday job at the Broch, the dismissive attitude Ross had shown to her. As though he didn't believe Fi had any more authority than he did, so he didn't even need to be polite to her.

I thought about my gran's note. "And Corby?"

Fi nodded. "Her mother was another one, but she moved down to the Midlands when she met a man from there. My mum is still friends with her. Corby was too young to stay here alone, but as soon as she was old enough, she moved back here to study and lived with her sister. We've been great friends for years. If it hadn't been for Stuart, it might—" she cut herself off, glancing around the centre as though there might be spies in every corner.

"Anyway, that's how Ross became the Gateway photographer. And he takes wonderful award-winning photographs, but the ones he wins awards with are mostly landscapes. I'm not sure he likes people very much." She told me the professional name he used for his artistic shots, and I made a mental note to look on the internet later and see what he was capable of when he enjoyed what he was doing.

"OK, Fi, but as you've so often commented, I'm not my gran, and I won't tolerate a photographer who isn't getting the best possible photographs for the bonders. You need to have a word with him, or I will, if you'd prefer it. How about we make it clear that, after my gran's death, everyone's contracts are being reviewed?"

Fi's response pleased me because she put her shoulders back and nodded firmly at me. "Leave it with me, Niki. If I hit a problem, I'll let you know."

Caitlin came through the blue doorway at a run, calling, "Sorry, overslept. Out at *Carnaval* last night."

We called Finn over to join us, and he settled with Tilly on his knee.

Once we were settled, I pulled up my notes on my new iPad. I laid out my frustration about how every damn royal I'd asked about the Rainbow Council seemed to think I meant it would start sometime next decade. How startled they'd all looked when I said nope, next month.

I mentioned my plan to begin by making a bit of a speech explaining the changes I thought we should make. I wanted to announce the members of the soon-to-be inaugurated Rainbow Council and introduce Caitlin, Finn, Fi and Dola by their new titles. Fi looked startled. "But I don't have a new title. I'm just the Recorder's assistant."

"Yeah, about that. Let's talk after we've got the running order settled."

When I'd tried to recall any Valentine's Days here as a child, I'd retrieved only the haziest of memories of many people and my gran alternately threatening and bribing me to be quiet. I had questions. How many people did we expect? Did people leave early, or did they stay and make a day of it? When was the food served?

Fi's answers matched the ones the Book had suggested.

"Truly over a thousand people?"

Finn just nodded.

Fi continued, "It's only so few because many of them have big celebrations planned later in their home realms. I think 1200 feels about right, but Juniper is catering for 1250, and she is never too far out. Except about her magical desserts, but only because people steal them, and we've fixed that."

My nervous stomach was threatening a rebellion. I sipped coffee and swallowed hard. "I hadn't pictured lecturing 1250 people about getting with the twenty-first century. Maybe I should just do this another time."

Astonishingly, Finn reached over and patted my shoulder. "I couldn't do it. But you can. You care about this. Time they all realised it. Dola and I think we should livestream it, even to the Viking realm."

I blinked at him. "Why?"

But he'd obviously used up his word allowance and said, "Dola, could you …"

Dola's voice sounded as though it came out of the table. It baffled me for a moment until Finn pointed to a discreet brown speaker set into the wood. Huh, that was new. "My research and studies into this suggest the best way to create genuine change is to use upward pressure, not downward."

I was trying to work out if it meant what I thought it did when all three iPads chimed for attention and I saw the same graphic come up on all of them. It hadn't taken her long to add the iPads to her network, had it?

As I studied the graphic, which looked like a combination of a flow chart and some Venn diagrams, I thought I understood what she was trying to say. "Do you mean if a few million people start shouting about wanting a better internet connection or whatever, it may create enough pressure to overcome the inertia of their rulers saying people should make do and continue sending pages out with messages?"

Dola said, "Exactly. After the success of the minipolls during the livestream of the bonding checks, we intend to up our game tomorrow."

"Up our game" was not a Dola phrase. "Who suggested you needed to 'up your game,' Dola?"

"One of my lecturers said building on success often creates quicker momentum. People liked the polls. Perhaps they will enjoy the opportunity to share more of their opinions. I plan to redirect people to a full survey."

"A survey? About what?" I enquired.

"About whatever we decide we'd like to know. Perhaps everyone could submit their questions to me?"

Fi immediately chimed in, "I have some questions about the current trade procedures. I'm sick of people complaining about the restrictions my lady Elsie put in place. If I can find out what they *all* want, instead of just hearing the views of the ones who shout the loudest, perhaps Niki can make some more of her famous changes?"

I was tempted to delve into this, but it would just make the meeting drag on, so instead I said, "Send your questions to Dola and book a meeting with you and me to talk it through."

"Now, Dola, why are we sending the livestream to the Vikings? I thought we were cutting them off?"

Caitlin said, "Yeah, it's my idea. I thought about what you said on Monday."

I had no clue. It had been a long week. "What did I say on Monday?"

She huffed, "About being a teacher. I mean, you were wrong about everything else, as Gwyneth showed you, but …"

I grinned and gave her the finger. She ignored me. "When I was catching up with Rollo on Thursday, I had a nasty little idea. I ran it past Dola."

"Nasty idea? OK, want to share it with the rest of us?"

"I think Troels told Leif to be a slagging little creep specifically to you, but maybe to other female staff too. I was moving a table; I must be staff. He's not the full pickaxe, you know."

Finn smirked. "You're quoting Hugh MacAlpin now?"

Caitlin smiled but continued in a serious tone, "I know a lot of the Vikings. I've trained with them." She rubbed two fingers between her eyebrows, smoothing out her forehead. "I've taken plenty of bruises, but I have never, ever been assaulted sexually. I think Troels told him to be a sexual predator. All his rubbish about they pulled me from my frilla's bed so one of you will have to stand in?"

That reminded me, I'd been too startled after he stuck his hand in my crotch to ask about it. "What *is* a frilla?"

"It's just what they call a mistress. The thing is, Rollo said Leif doesn't have one. She threw him out months ago." Now she scratched her head. "I don't know for sure—and I don't fully understand why—but I think Troels *wanted* the gate sealed."

Caitlin was shuffling and wouldn't quite meet my eyes. So I listened and tapped my Gift. She was protecting someone, not Troels. Who? "He wants the Viking realm and their people pissed off with the Recorder's Office. Rollo let something slip."

"What?"

"I'd rather not say just yet." She wiped her palm down her leather-clad thigh. It left a moist trail.

I backed off before she got even more concerned that she was breaking a confidence, and I tried to lighten the tone. "It must have really upset Troels when I agreed the Viking marriages could go ahead tomorrow."

"Oh, hell yeah!"

Dola interrupted, "There is anti-Recorder propaganda circulating in the Viking realm. Streaming the event on Sunday to *all* the realms is the perfect way to offset it. My own theory is he may be buying time to discredit you. So if you find against him in the arbitration, no one in his kingdom will believe he was wrong. They will just believe you dislike him."

"You may be right, Dola. I'm not as good at the political stuff yet as I should be. Can I leave this with you and Caitlin?"

"Yes, but I would also appreciate some human insight, so if anyone has any ideas, please share them with me."

I saw thoughtful looks on Caitlin and Finn's faces. "Have you guys got anything else you think we should know?" They both shook their heads. "Fill Dola in privately if anything occurs to you." I got two firm nods back.

"Now, lastly, I'm not doing batches of people from each kingdom."

Fi did her mono-brow-disapproving-frown thing as she pointed her new pencil at me. "Why not?"

I thought about the quickest way to explain it and settled for, "Because weddings shouldn't be about nationalism. Nothing bonds a group of people quicker than having a wonderful time together, well, except being frightened or in danger together, and I'd rather go with the happy option. On a practical note, how boring is it for everyone? Say you're in one sector, and you have watch fifty people you don't know getting bonded before anyone you know or care about gets their turn?"

A thoughtful silence stretched.

I added, "I've had friends who had babies at the same time as women who were strangers, but life-long friendships came out of what they'd gone through together. Maybe one way to improve inter-realm sentiment is for people to say, 'But I got married with so-and-so from the Vikings, and they were lovely girls.' Or for any of the realms to say, 'There was a Hob couple in their group, and how nice and how in love they were.'"

They all nodded, and Fi said, "You might be right. I sometimes hear bored rustling from the people waiting."

"Then let's try it. If it doesn't work, we'll change it back. I'm thinking if we have all the royals and Lis and Mag in the centre and then mix the realms into the batches on the main floor, there might be a lot less of this 'us and them' nonsense going forwards."

Fi was trying quite hard not to laugh, but a giggle broke out of her. "What?" I asked.

"Lis and Mag came through here yesterday; they

were doing a two-woman version of Mairi's wedding. The Hobs who were putting up the tables for Juniper loved it. They grabbed a few of them and drew them into the dance, but they'd changed the words and were singing 'Rosie's wedding' instead of 'Mairi's wedding'. Honestly' it was hilarious!"

I felt like I'd lost the ability to understand English. "Yes, but what is whoever's wedding?"

"The original is Mairi's wedding. It's a Scottish country reel, a dance, very popular at weddings, once enough drink has been taken." Fi swirled her arms in an intricate circular pattern I didn't understand. "You need at least eight dancers to see it done properly, but those Hobs gave it their best." She stood up and put one hand behind her back and crooked her other arm at her side just as Lis had yesterday.

I thought back to the weird marching walk thing Lis and Mag were doing as they left my office. The little tune had been going around in my head since yesterday. "Does it go … 'Step we gaily'?" I hummed it.

"Nooooooooooooo," burst out of Finn. He had his hands over his ears now.

"What? What did I do?" I looked around in a panic, and Tilly barked once and licked Finn's hand to calm him.

But they were all laughing now. Finn was

stroking Tilly and apologising to her. I glared at them all.

The three of them burst into a rousing chorus of the song I'd heard yesterday as Lis and Mag left. Then Fi looked at me. "That song is one of the worst earworms I know. You'll be humming it for days now."

I looked at Caitlin, who nodded. "Sticks like glue and goes around and around."

I looked at Finn, who said, "One of my superpowers. Know two songs that displace it."

"You lot are all crazy. I work in a madhouse. Right, Fi, let's you and I have a chat about your promotion then."

The look on her face was hilarious.

CHAPTER
THIRTY-FIVE

After our successful planning session and an interesting chat with Rosemary, I'd walked Tilly around the picturesque little village, which was beginning to feel familiar to us both. It was busy. Were the hotels full of normal couples preparing for their weddings tomorrow? Valentine's Day had always been a busy day in my former office.

Tilly fell out with the greyhound again at the end of the tiny lane that led to the cottage, but we simply turned the other way from him and his grumpy owner. We strolled, and I considered what a strange week it had been.

It was supposed to be the busiest week of the Gateway's year, and yet not much had happened. I'd learnt a lot of odd things about some of the realms, some of the royals, and some of the ordinary people I hadn't known before. All of it gave me a more rounded picture of what I might need to do going forward.

The subtleties might be important, like the trade tax, which the Gateway levied. It seemed we took the money but provided pitifully little other than access in exchange for what was effectively a tithe. A proper trade department could help the realms to expand their exports.

Several hours and miles later, I got to the end of my audiobook and bid a sad farewell to Eve and Roarke. I'd read, and later on listened to, these books every February and September for more than twenty years. Some days, the narrator's warm, familiar voice on my drive to work was the only thing that got me into the car to face Janet. Listening to it now as I walked around my new home made me realise how far I'd come.

I smiled to myself. Not having a boss wasn't all new responsibilities. There were huge advantages to it too.

And I was looking forward to tomorrow. Yes, I was nervous, but I wanted to do it. I also hadn't heard from HR about Janet. If I didn't hear anything on Monday, I'd call them. It had been two weeks.

. . .

TIES THAT BOND IN GRETNA GREEN

Later that evening I enjoyed a lovely dinner of spicy, delicious lamb stew with chickpeas and apricots. Dola always seemed to know what I might want to eat. I thought about Finn and his earworm superpower and wondered if giving people what they needed before they even knew they wanted it might be Dola's superpower. Although the Dolina devices had been a bit scary, she was right, and it would be useful to have a way of communicating reliably with all the rulers.

I'd curled up on my bed with Tilly and the Book to do a little more studying before I settled in for an early night, so I didn't look drawn and puffy-eyed during all the bonding photos tomorrow. It was a cold and miserable evening, and I'd put on my softest, warmest pyjamas. It was nice having all my own things up here.

Then my phone vibrated with a message from Mabon.

> MABON THE DRAGON WRANGLER:
> Can you summon Dai and me to the Gateway please?

> NIKI:
> Give me two minutes.

I smirked. He still hadn't worked out how to change his name yet.

Unlike simply lowering or raising the barriers,

summoning people required the pendant to be on the anvil. It was freezing now and dark outside. I grabbed a jumper, stuffed my feet into warm boots and gathered up my bag and Tilly so she didn't drive Dola crazy with her barking while I was gone.

I landed in the centre of the Gateway and summoned them both. I was intrigued. What was happening that he needed summoning? Seconds later, the red door swung open, and Mabon, Dru, and Dai walked through.

As usual, Mabon started talking the moment he entered the building. "Sorry, *bach*, stuck up the bluddy mountain we were. We both needed to be other places without spending the whole flaming evening walking down. Thought you wouldn't mind. Dola said you weren't busy."

As he reached the centre, Mabon hugged me as I ruffled Dru's shoulder fluff. "Like the hair, *bach*, very trendy."

I giggled as Dru licked the top of Tilly's head and then nuzzled her ear, whining softly. It looked like he was sharing the gossip with her. Dai was frozen just inside the door, and his face was dark with anger. He looked tired and cross.

Mabon pointed back at Dai. "Deal with him, Nik-a-lula. Make him show you his phone. Dru and I need to get to the pub…" On that confusing note, man and dog marched off towards the green doorway and Scotland. I saw red sparks and called after him, "Oy! Boney, mind my floor please," and pointed to his sparking feet.

Tilly chased down the Red sector until she met Dai heading to the middle. She bounced and jumped up his leg until he picked her up. I heard him say, "Oh, Dru's got you on the job too now, has he? Is there no escape from interference?" Then he sighed as Tilly licked his face clean and fussed at him.

I dropped into my Gift asking it, *what am I missing it?*

A sense of frustration mixed with misery and fear came from Dai. I probed a little deeper and hit the smooth wall of his shields just as I had in my kitchen when we'd been talking about unicorns. WTH?

He reached the centre, and I asked, "Are you OK? Sorry, dumb thing to ask—obviously you're not. Can I help with whatever's wrong?"

"Da's interfering in things that are none of his business. There's no point fighting him. Once he's made his mind up, he's like that flaming Lochmaben stone of his. Fire, flood, wind, rain, snow and several millennia. Whatever gets thrown at it—it just carries on being a lump of determined unmoving rock."

I shivered. It was cold in here tonight, which was unusual; the power normally kept it at a steady pleasant temperature.

Dai immediately shrugged out of his coat and

wrapped it around my shoulders. "You're cold. Dola said you weren't busy. Was it true?"

I snuggled into his jacket and nodded. "I was tired, bored, and having a fight with the Book, to be honest."

He gave my hair a confused look. "I'm starving. Have you eaten?"

"I have, thanks, a delicious lamb thing. There will be more; come back to the cottage. Dola will feed you."

The dark, unhappy expression crossed his face again as he shook his head. "No, thank you. I don't want to be in the same realm as Da tonight. And I don't want Dola reporting back to him. I'd like a private conversation with Nik, not the Recorder. Have you got a free hour? I think we need to talk. Specifically, don't you think we need to get to know each other again?"

I stared at him in surprise. Four days without a single message, then an invite for a meal? Sure, I'd like to get to know him again, but something felt off. Although I was tempted, what did I have to lose except an hour or two?

But then my brain clicked in. It was probably an old-fashioned rule, but in my head, I heard Aysha's mother, Olive. Her annoyance when I would drop everything when a text message from Nick pinged in. "Niki-Girl," she would say, "they don't respect you if you don't have your own life. Draw some boundaries with the man, for your future's sake."

And she'd been right, even if I never worked out how to do it to Nick. My anger at those cameras we'd discovered yesterday in my former home rose to the surface, and I felt my own head shaking before I'd even consciously made my decision.

But I didn't need to be rude. Did I?

"I'm sorry, Dai, but it's been a long day. It started with your sister at the crack of dawn this morning, and tomorrow is the biggest day of the week. If you'd messaged, I wouldn't have eaten, but as you can see, I'm on my way to bed." I gestured down at my pyjamas, "Another time?"

His face darkened at Rhiannon's name, but then he looked at my pyjamas and smiled at me. "OK. But I would have messaged, truly."

Dai put Tilly on the floor, then retrieved his phone from the front pocket of his jeans, opened it, flicked and poked it, and handed it over to me with his messages open.

> DAI:
>
> Felt awful rushing off. We really need to talk. Need to explain some stuff. How are you this morning?
>
> DAI:
>
> Just checking if you found someone to heal your face?

DAI:

Nik? You alright?

DAI:

Has Autumn left now? Are you OK?

DAI:

Flaming hell, these messages aren't getting through, are they? You were never a sulker. You must not be getting them.

DAI:

I'm stuck up this bluddy mountain till tonight, but I'm in the wedding party for Glyn tomorrow. Could we catch up for a bit? If you ever get any of these messages??

These messages spanned the time from early Wednesday after he'd rushed off the previous evening to the most recent one, which was date-stamped this morning. A smile spread across my face. This would explain a lot.

"Honestly, I called you some pretty rude names this week. I'm sorry, I should have realised it would only be a connection problem. But the lads said the problem was more intermittent than permanent."

"It is usually, but the mountains are a dead zone. Well, for everyone except flaming Rhiannon. She seems to have a connection wherever she wants one, but she won't help the rest of us out. And now even

Da's phone works there, but he wouldn't lend it to me. He said I have to talk you into fixing my phone, and you didn't give him a phone just so everyone could just keep using it all the bluddy time."

I couldn't help it. I laughed. "He looks so outraged whenever anyone rings him on it."

Dai laughed warmly, and the atmosphere between us lightened. Before I could second-guess my refusal, I said, "Another time would be lovely, but for now, I'll leave you to grab some food if you're sure you don't want Dola to feed you?"

"I'm sick of being watched. I'll pass. It's *Carnaval* this week. How about grabbing a bite with me tomorrow after the bondings?"

I had no idea how I'd feel tomorrow night after the busiest day of the year. "Can I let you know once we're finished? It's a very crowded schedule tomorrow, and it will be my first time doing it."

His face told me he wasn't pleased, but he nodded as I handed him his jacket back and he stomped off towards the Orange sector.

PART SEVEN
SUNDAY

"And the Recorder sliced open both children's first finger and said that, although their blood was different colours, they both had a sore finger now, didn't they?

She told them to go away and think of a hundred ways they were the same instead of only the one way in which they were different."

The Recorder Always Knows Best: Cautionary Tales for Incautious Children by Margarita Encimera

CHAPTER
THIRTY-SIX

Sunday, 14th February - Gateway Cottage

The moment I woke up enough to realise what day it was, my stomach began churning with nerves. Those nerves bloomed into an impending meltdown when I opened my wardrobe.

I'd been delighted to have a wider choice of clothes. I'd been living out of a literal suitcase for the last three weeks. But as I moved the Recorder's robe to reach for the blue suit I planned to wear, a wave of memories came with the clothing. I sniffed and held the suit and then my robe up to my nose. They both smelt of basil and roses, my grandmother's signature scent. My eyes filled with tears, and I swallowed convulsively.

The lump in my throat had edges as sharp as

glass shards as I asked, "Dola, did you do something to my suit and my Recorder's robe?"

"No. Lis sent Clover around yesterday. She informed me Lis had instructed her to collect your Recorder's robe and a navy trouser suit for fettling."

"Fettling?"

"Fixing—laundry and pressing. But as she was so specific in her clothing demand, I assumed you had requested it. You were still busy with Rhiannon, and I didn't want to interrupt you again. Clover reported Lis said 'A friend in need makes work for idle hands, and the Recorder wouldn't be tarnishing anyone's honour by wearing a grubby robe today.'"

Did this explain why my gran always smelt of basil and roses? But surely that meant Lis had been doing some domestic tasks for Gran even though Moira and Lily had agreed no bindings and no housework. Was laundry not housework? Oh, Gods and Goddesses, did it mean more meetings with Lis in my future?

I was confident the actual ceremonies would go smoothly, thanks to all the checks I had done. But the ideas I wanted to convey before I conducted the bulk of the bondings worried me. I'd never been a confident public speaker, and a few YouTube videos at the last minute weren't going to turn me into one.

I checked the shared list on my iPad.

Invite the royals, leaders and headwomen to the centre.

Open the doors for everyone else.

Summon Rollo and his people.

Conduct Natalia and Tomas's seven-fold bonding.

Introduce my staff and explain the changes. (Note to self: Do NOT say "planning"; they all think that means next century. Say "immediate implementation.")

Give Rainbow Council progress report.

Conduct the rest of the bondings in random order but include at least one couple from each realm.

NB: Note to whoever is doing this poll—Dola? Finn? Can one of the questions ask, "Do you think the Recorder was right to include the Viking bondings even though their Gateway is sealed and King Troels won't get off his philandering royal arse to fix it?"

Note to Dola: Please edit the above question into something vaguely polite.

As I checked the names on the shared list, Fi, Finn and Dola, only then did I realise Caitlin didn't have an iPad. Oh, hell, did she feel left out?

I was a lousy boss. I headed towards the kitchen to see if I could keep some breakfast down.

· · ·

Caitlin was waiting in my kitchen. My confusion must have shown on my face. "Good morning, Recorder. Finn wanted to show me his foxhole. I didn't know. Kept asking him when he was coming home. That's a very cool thing you've done for him."

Foxhole? She'd said it with affection. Finn's Foxhole. I giggled. "I meant to visit your mother, actually, and tell her she's welcome here anytime. He has his own entrance. Although he usually comes through to grab—"

"A bacon sandwich, please, Dola. I'll eat on the way. Want to do the stress test on the streaming capacity."

"—Breakfast," I finished.

"Still here, Cait?"

"She's eating with me, Finn. We'll see you over there."

He nodded, grabbed his sandwich off the plate on the table, and with a quick, "Laters," headed out the back door with Tilly at his heels.

"Dola, can we have two of those egg muffin things with the sauce, not the nasty spinach ones? The ones with the yummy bacon?"

"Two Eggs Benedict shortly, Niki."

I opened a can of tuna, dumped it into one of HRH's porcelain bowls and left it on the side for her, and turned back to Caitlin. "Caitlin, I wondered—"

"My lady, I wanted to ask —"

I gestured for her to go first.

"Is there anything particular you wanted me to do today? Glaring at happy couples on their bonding day might not be politic."

"OK, but first, did you want an iPad?"

Her horrified look was all the answer I needed. "No, thank you. Why would you even ask?"

"I didn't want you to feel left out."

She considered this as a slow smile spread across her face. "Hard no on the iPad, thanks. I'd drop it, then Finn would cry. But, if you're burning budgets, I have my eye on some very useful-looking iron …" she paused, as if searching for an acceptable word, "…implements Doug has been working on for me?"

I considered how useful Caitlin's iron "implements" had been, from the beads she'd used on Leif, to whatever she called the thing she'd used to drag Gwyneth out of the Gateway. "Doug Halkrig? The Smith?"

She nodded. If Doug was on the case, they'd be interesting implements. That man loved inventions. Our breakfast arrived. It smelled good enough to tempt my unhappy stomach.

"Done. Ask Doug to send an invoice to Dola for approval up to the cost of an iPad. Which reminds me, Rhiannon called in yesterday morning with news about Gwyneth."

Caitlin looked completely blank.

"Gwyneth, the one you dragged out of the Gateway using several of your iron implements?"

"Oh, the shouty bitch! Sorry, didn't bother to remember her name. The look on Mabon's face when she struck you told me I'd never see her again. So why would I care about her name? Where did they hide the body?"

"If I understood Rhiannon correctly, inside hungry dragons?"

Caitlin nodded calmly, swallowed her mouthful of Eggs Benedict. "This is good food, thanks, Dola." She put more food into her mouth and mumbled, "What did her T-shirt say?"

I told her, then added, "But I think it was a sweatshirt."

"Ah, a mountaintop accident, then, if she was wearing her cold weather gear. I'm pretty sure those T-shirts are magical. Finn says I'm imagining it, but she'd have to have one hell of a collection if they're not because they always say the perfect thing." She rubbed her upper arms briskly. "She always feels magical, a bit like you do, actually. She frightens Finn, but she's always been chill with me. Anyway, good to know about whatsername."

"That's it? You're not surprised?"

She gave me a slight frown. "'Bout what?" She was really enjoying her breakfast, and a random annoying woman having been sentenced to death with no recourse to anything approaching a trial wasn't disturbing her appetite in the slightest.

"Look, I know she was annoying, but I, well, perhaps I expected something ... a bit less ... final? Some kind of trial?"

Caitlin's shoulders went back. The future queen emerged. "Niki, she struck a Recorder! I would have dealt with her myself, but she was Mabon's subject, so obviously he had the primary claim. And he made it, didn't he? Said he'd take her with him? If you disagreed or thought you had a prior claim, that was your chance to say something. Also, wasn't the little dark woman she knocked down the stairs the king's goddaughter? So he'd have a double claim."

"Megan? Was she?"

"Ma said so."

Megan had called him Mabon "bamps," so she viewed him as a grandad, didn't she? I understood this job wasn't to be Mary flipping Poppins, and weirdly it wasn't that they had disposed of Gwyneth. She'd been a horrible woman. It was just that everyone was so casual about it. I told Caitlin this.

"You can be strange. You know about Alexander the Great and his goddess." She gestured a swoosh at her foot even though today she wore smart boots in Pict blue leather, obviously. "But you don't seem to realise people saw the woman *hit a Recorder!* Word would go round the realms in a heartbeat. Can't have that. Unless it's followed swiftly by the news of a sad accident. Then everyone knows where they stand. Now that is a, what do they call it? Oh yeah, a teachable moment. That kind of teacher, I could be."

She grinned at me, then her face sobered. "Sometimes cleaning up the mess afterwards, like you said, can be as simple as taking out the bodies, you know?"

I thought about it. She was right, because Ad'Rian had known all about it almost the next day, hadn't he?

We finished our food, and conversation turned to the day ahead and Caitlin's part in it, and then, with my breakfast threatening to return, we walked over to the Gateway together.

I slid my eyes over Caitlin as we walked. She glanced at me immediately. "You've attended bondings here in the past?"

"Sure have." She sighed, "Supposed to be a bridesmaid at one today." The look of horror on her face was a thing to behold. "The dress," she shuddered, "was baby blue taffeta!"

I smiled to myself. There was only one shade of blue in Caitlin's world, and it was the much deeper Pict blue, and if she had her way, it came in leather. "How did you get out of it?"

"Sadly, I'm working, *my lady*," she said this with fake deference, a half bow and delight. "The bride only wanted a princess. Any princess would do—Juna's doing it. She doesn't mind dresses, although even she's not happy with the insipid colour."

"But what are the bondings usually like? I'm not sure how much I'm planning to change things, and I can't predict how different it may appear to the guests and participants."

Now I got the heir apparent side of her personality, and she nodded seriously at me. "I understand. Ma worries about that stuff sometimes. I could let you know as we go through how different it seems?"

We walked a few more steps, then she paused and actually looked at me. "The thing is, the last one I came to could have been a costume drama from," she made air quotes, "Ye Olde Tymes."

I laughed. And she continued, "A lot of the younger ones are ready for some new ideas. Not all the Viking girls want to wear leather all the time. I don't get it myself—but they should have the choice." She paused and saw me trying to wipe a grin off my face. "You can laugh, but Juna would get treated like a serf in the Viking kingdom."

"Your sister Juna? But she's a princess." Was I losing the plot here?

"Well, sure, but if she wasn't. If she was a Viking woman and wanted to wear her floaty dresses. Dresses there mean you're ..." she trailed off.

I stopped walking. I might need to fit in a visit to

the Vikings, because I had no idea what she was talking about.

"… either a potential wife, concubine, servant or hooker," she finally finished. "They don't have many choices. You think my kingdom is stuck in the Dark Ages? Go and check out the Vikings."

I nodded. I needed to do that, and I was about to ask her more, but Caitlin was on a roll about the bondings now. "And your gran was always a bit snappy, and the buffet food was shockingly bad, and poor Juniper always looked so embarrassed at having to offer you yet another sad sandwich or soggy vol-au-vent. I know you were laughing about it the other day. But they're quite repulsive, you know, at least after they've sat out getting lukewarm and greasy for six hours."

She was right; I'd eaten enough of them over the years. "If you'd provide some ongoing feedback today, I'd appreciate it. I need to make changes, but I'd hate for anyone to feel that some member of their family wasn't properly bonded. And we will plan some visits to all the kingdoms. I'm going to the Red Celts towards the end of the month."

"Yeah, Dai was at *Carnaval* last night. He wasn't quite himself, ate on his own, but he cheered up later. Queimada always makes him feel better. Well, we all love it. You should come tonight."

"Yes, I had an invitation from Dai if this doesn't

all drag on too late." A fleeting expression crossed Caitlin's face, but it was gone before I could identify it.

With the enthusiasm and energy of someone still in their twenties who had no respect for her own sleep cycle, she laughed. "And isn't it the best part of working in the Gateway? It's never too late when you finish. And if you're tired, queimada will fix it."

I was about to ask what this magical thing was when we crossed the boundary from the icy, damp February cold of Scotland to the warmer weather surrounding the Gateway. I looked up at the now cloudless, clear blue sky and hoped it was a good omen for my first Valentine's Day in the Gateway as the Recorder.

Fi was standing outside the green doorway on her phone as we approached. I just caught, "Well, I think you should talk to her. I don't know how I missed you last night; I looked everywhere … Oh, did you? Shame."

The noise attacked us as we entered through the green doorway. There were people everywhere, talking, shouting and occasionally laughing. Juniper's staff carried towers of boxes and set them on the tables I'd seen yesterday. Now they ran the full length of each sector's boundaries. That was a lot of food. The entire space smelt of fresh green growing things with a subtle floral undertone. Tilly bounced over to me, tongue lolling and such a cheerful expression, I suspected someone had been slipping her titbits.

As I reached the centre, I saw the power had approved of my plans. There were five new interconnected desks in a horseshoe shape set well back behind the anvil on the Indigo sector's side of the centre. Clever idea. They wouldn't block traffic there. Four of the desks now had computers on them. The power had been busy.

I turned in a circle to check the space. What the heck was that? It wasn't quite a wall; it was a high curving room-divider, a large woven screen that blocked the view of the conference table from almost everywhere in the Gateway except the desks. I hadn't asked for that, but it was a great idea. The other day I'd thought longingly of a semi-private space such as my old office, where I could speak to people privately. With a jolt, I realised the divider was alive, and it was growing, sending out green shoots, which passing Hobs wove back into the screen. It would be impenetrable soon. Wow!

The anvil's wooden surround had grown dramatically. We'd have no problem fitting everyone around that.

Then Juniper spotted me and homed in like a missile locked onto its target. She wore her usual black trousers, but today she'd paired them with a deep pink chef's jacket.

"Milady, milady."

I waited.

She arrived and, over her shoulder, called, "Parsley, bring the special box."

"Thank you so much, milady, for everything you've done. For the opportunity to serve my own food. And for fighting for Lavender, Thyme and Rosemary's happiness. Thank you for speaking to the king …" she gulped, trailed off and wiped a tear from her eye with a spotless white tea-towel tucked into her belt. "Just thank you."

I patted her shoulder. "I did almost nothing. Your talent did the work. But is this new?" I pointed at the tables that ran down the sides of the sectors. I'd expected them to be in the centre. My memories suggested that was where they should be.

She looked worried. "I asked Dola, milady."

"It's not a problem. I only want to understand the reason for the change."

"Milady Elsie thought everyone should wait until the end to eat, to avoid crumbs. But, milady, my food wouldn't dare to drop crumbs, and there are a lot of bondings, people get tired, footsore and hungry. I suggested this idea." She gestured at the long tables. Their tablecloths in the colour of each sector gave an attractive starburst rainbow effect.

"But she always said, 'No thank you, Juniper. We'll …,'" and we joined in together in "'have it just like last year, please.'" Then we dissolved into giggles.

Parsley arrived, with an eager expression and a white box. She waited in front of Juniper, who nodded at her. She lifted the lid so ostentatiously, I expected one of Dola's drumrolls. When I peeped inside, I sucked in a sharp breath.

Juniper produced one of the magical small plates, pale pink this time for Valentine's, and held it out to me, saying, "In her memory. May she arrive in the Summerlands with joy and without hindrance." She made the hand gesture I'd seen accompany this blessing before. I felt an electric tingle run down my spine.

"I think I need to share this with Fi. You know she was her assistant for twenty-two years and with you, Juniper. Two more plates if I could trouble you?" She looked so startled I wondered if I'd said the wrong thing, but then, wreathed in smiles, she produced two more plates and a knife. I called, "Fi, a moment, please."

Fi arrived, and I pointed at the box. "Juniper has

made something in Gran's honour. Would you join us in a moment of remembrance?"

Fi looked into the box and burst out laughing.

Juniper's knife flashed, and we all lifted our plates and breathed in the unmistakable fragrance of fresh chicken vol-au-vent. They both looked at me, waiting, until I took the first bite. It was crispy, herby, creamy and divine.

"You naughty, naughty Hob. How on earth did you make it nice? I detect cream, chicken, tarragon and white wine, don't I?"

Juniper's face fell. I rushed to reassure her, "Sorry, so sorry, a joke—it's magnificent. But it doesn't taste anything like Campbell's chicken soup, so I know it would have appalled Gran. With vol-au-vents this good, we might have to start serving them again."

This time, she realised I was joking, and we ate the rest of the perfect golden pastry treat, had a three-way hug, and breathed deeply, wiping our noses and eyes. We all went to do today's work.

I wondered if Juniper had added one of her spells to the vol-au-vent. Because as I stood by the anvil, my nerves had mostly dissipated, and I was looking forward to the day.

CHAPTER
THIRTY-SEVEN

"Is everyone ready?" I reached out to the anvil, and in response, it chimed three low peals.

Everyone wasn't ready, and my call caused a furore of mad energy as they all finished up last-minute jobs. My running order list had already changed. I was going to bring the Vikings through first rather than last, so I could monitor their doorway. This change was inspired by a niggling sensation from my Gift when I'd texted Rollo.

NIKI:

Are you all ready?

ROLLO:

No, the king won't leave. He's 'approving' the brides. Working on it. Sorry.

Troels was such a slimeball. The disturbing feeling crawling down my back increased in intensity. I grabbed the Book from my desk and asked, "What happens if I call them through while Troels is still there?"

That would depend.

Wow, the Book really was loosening up. "On what?"

Where you block him.

If he is blocked from entering, the power will prevent him from passing through the doorway, but he may obstruct it and restrict anyone else from entering the Gateway.

If he is permitted to enter the Yellow sector, the sector barrier will block his access to the centre. Phrase your invitation precisely.

This decision was above my pay grade. Although I should stop saying that and replace it with something more accurate for the Recordership like "too far outside of my experience."

I called Caitlin over filled her in on Rollo's message and showed her the Book. "This feels like a you problem. Any ideas?"

"Loads. Can I stab him or not?"

"Very tempting, but on balance, I think not. Not yet… well, at least not fatally."

Her thoughts flitted across her intelligent, vibrant face. Eventually, she said, "Speaking politically," she paused, and I nodded to show I understood her distinction, "the best outcome would be if you allowed the power itself to accept, reject or even eject him. Especially if Finn's doing his livestream thing."

I blew out a breath. I was damn glad this woman was on my side. She was suggesting we allow his entire kingdom to see Troels dumped out by the power itself. It was a cunning idea. Was I brave enough for that? To make it clear to his entire realm that Troels was the problem. Not his heir, not the happy couples, not his subjects. Just him.

It could be a powerful and effective message to the average Viking citizens if we did it right. The nice Viking citizens. They had those because the two merchants who'd come through last weekend, in the middle of the Pict's drama and helped the heavily pregnant Welsh woman by carrying all her bags, had been kind and normal. There must be others too.

I nodded at her and messaged Rollo.

NIKI:

Let him do whatever he wants. You stick to your plan. And leave him to us.

ROLLO:

Sure? Think he's got a plan.

NIKI:

So have we!

Caitlin briefed Finn, who stood just behind by my shoulder with several cameras. He'd acquired a new one, an airborne drone. I smiled to myself about boys and their toys, but also thought I'd love to play with it myself one quiet afternoon.

I moved to the anvil and, pressing the rune for the Vikings, carefully said, "I summon the invited and the waiting Vikings to the Gateway." Then I headed over to the Yellow sector to watch the fun.

The Bridezilla shield maiden who'd turned out to be a nice woman during her bonding check was the first through the gate with her future husband. That truly was one amazing wedding gown she'd dragged all the way back from some village in Galicia where the lace had been handmade. She'd told me the tale at length last week when I was juggling Pict traitors. It was worthy of Princess Grace or Kate Middleton when she wore her own lacy gown to marry Prince William. Full-length with a lace mantilla-style veil and a short train, it was elegant, beautifully cut and extremely classy. I should find out who Bridezilla actually was because the gown suggested she was a somebody. But her name, when I consulted my list on the new iPad, meant nothing to me. I really should visit the Vikings.

TIES THAT BOND IN GRETNA GREEN

Rollo followed them through. Then a furious King Troels pushed everyone out of the way, stamping across Bridezilla's train. She looked ready to punch him, king or not. He strode briskly towards the centre.

Once he cleared his people, and there was no one in front of him, he began speaking. It sounded scripted to me, but it was effective all the same. He had a deep orator's voice, and if he declaimed like an understudy in an amateur dramatics production, I was sure he'd come across well on the video. The low register and authoritative timbre of his voice made it sound as though he had a case, and he was speaking English, so he obviously wanted everyone to understand him. Was he disappointed to be wasting his theatrics on an almost empty Gateway? Or was this all just for my benefit?

"As the Rightful King of the Vikings, I protest this unwarranted restriction of our freedom of movement, the unjust curtailment of our communications and the slurs cast on our Viking pride. The Recorder's Office has badly injured one of my subjects and unlawfully detained another, a princess no less, on the eve of her wedding. I demand her immediate return."

His accusations needed to be answered for the livestream. I tried the trick from the Book of linking my McKnight Gift to the power, and it projected my voice through the Gateway's power as though we had a sound system. "Troels, stop." I held my hand up palm outward, and the power, responding to our link, stopped him in his tracks. Oh, good, the tip from the Book had worked nicely.

"Your subject, Leif, launched a physical attack, committed two acts of sexual assault on members of the Recorder's Office. He also insulted an honoured and invited Fae guest in the Gateway." I was stretching the truth because we hadn't known Kaiden was Fae at that point, had we? Did Troels even know or care about Leif's *ragr* slur to Kaiden?

How much further might I stretch the truth to check if Caitlin was right about him being the one to send Leif with specific instructions to abuse me and my staff?

"You were informed of it immediately, and we asked you to contact us once you'd dealt with him. He isn't your subject at the moment; you submitted him as a Knight candidate, and we returned him to you for punishment. He hasn't been. You didn't contact us as we asked. Not officially to apologise, nor personally to check if the women were recovered. You've had almost two weeks to deal with this. You haven't."

I strengthened my link to the power and tried to calm my racing heart. I remembered something from a British tabloid libel case and wondered if it would apply here. A question wasn't libel. Does the same apply to slander, and the spoken word? Did I care if I could get to truth, even if it was only for myself?

My face felt flushed, and my mouth was so dry with nerves, my lips were sticking to my teeth. Running my tongue around the inside of my lips, I said, "We must ask who authorised Leif to abuse two women. Because he confirmed he was authorised. He specifically stated, his king had sent him. Is that true?"

Troels looked about ready to explode. "Of course not. Where is the evidence of these abused women?"

My left shoulder was twanging like an out-of-tune guitar. So it had been him.

Troels glared at me. "No evidence then, just accuse the Vikings as always?"

I made myself pause before saying, "Oh, we have evidence. I was one of them, and we have eyewitnesses from four realms, including the Fae, the Red Celt king and the Pict queen."

"They don't like me. They lie."

"So every royal would lie? Is that an accusation against them? Do you have evidence? Or is it a slur on their honour? Or are you simply saying everyone dislikes you? Because at my ascension, you said 'the Fae king's word was as iron,' but now you're calling a member of his family a liar? Would you do that to his face, I wonder? Should I call him through so you can accuse him of lying yourself?" Accusing any fae, never mind L'eon, a member of the Fae court, would result in very unpleasant repercussions, and he knew it.

"They all lie. Return my princess immediately."

"We also have video footage—that does not lie. Shall we stream it and allow your kingdom to decide for themselves? But, most importantly, the power saw it. The power itself will judge you, and its judgement may affect your entire realm. Are you certain for the sake of your subjects you wouldn't rather ask forgiveness for your inability to control your personally chosen and completely unqualified Knight contender?"

I couldn't imagine this man ever asking anyone's forgiveness; he made my flesh crawl. I wasn't going to make the mistake I'd made at my ascension of using my Gift on him. I didn't need any more of his brain's apparently enormous store of pornographic images in my head.

"Why should your innocent citizens be punished for your weakness? Your refusal to make a sincere apology suggests Leif was following your orders and adds weight to the idea that you think women are just toys to be abused," That should do it. I waited for the explosion.

But instead, Troels's coarse, florid face looked nonplussed. Whatever he'd expected, it wasn't this.

He didn't have a script ready for this. He reverted to something he'd clearly said often: "My kingdom supports their Rightful King. Always. You will return my princess. She is a citizen of Viking. You hold her unlawfully."

"Karina Halvor is being detained for crimes against the Recorder's Office. Her trial has not yet been held, so her punishment is not yet decided. As I'm sure you are aware, the Recorder has every right to do this. The power itself carried her to her detention."

"Absolute rubbish. The power doesn't do that!" He sounded so sure. Oh, this might be fun after all. Especially if the power ejected him.

I caught sight of Rollo's face. Troels hadn't believed his story of Kari being carried screaming out of the Gateway.

"Yes, the power does. The princess was screaming as she left the Gateway. Would you like a demonstration?"

The anvil tolled once. It was a harsh sound, not the usual mellow tone. It sounded cross.

I forged on, "After you so signally failed to deal with Leif, I will be disciplining your citizens myself if they contravene the regulations. It was not the eve of her marriage because there was no bond of any kind between her and Vor. And I believe you already knew that. Or are you telling me their king cannot see the power?"

It was all going so well.

Whatever Troels had planned, his script apparently didn't allow for us not bowing down to his authority. I genuinely sympathised with his citizens and wondered how the ordinary Vikings would feel when they watched this footage and hopefully realised what a liability their king was.

But then Tilly rushed past me, barking like a mad thing. The iron barriers didn't affect her as they did the iron-sensitive Troels. She'd obviously picked up on my stress and nerves and decided he wasn't a nice person, and she'd protect her mum with all of her fluffy little twelve-pound body.

The focus of his eyes changed. There was glee in them as he reached down to scoop her up. One hand reached out and brushed the top of her head as she barked and growled. She skittered backwards. Troels's hand went towards the knife at his belt, and he stepped forward.

My heart literally jumped into my mouth. People say that, but it's a horrific feeling. I thought I'd vomit. He would not touch my fluffball. She was the only thing in my life that had kept me sane for years.

My brave little girl. Oh, hell no!

I remembered enough of my plan not to flatten him onto the Gateway floor as I had unintentionally done to Leif. I used the power I'd drawn to scoop Tilly up and behind me out of his reach. At the same moment, something flashed in the air behind him, and Troels went down like a felled tree onto his face.

A long knife, almost a short sword with a sturdy handle, dropped to the floor. I lifted Tilly gently over to a very pale-looking Fi. She was swallowing convulsively.

"Hold her tight, Fi." I got her nod before turning back to look at Troels' prone body.

He struggled to his feet, shaking his head.

I was shaky and furious and didn't give him even a moment to draw breath. While he was still trying to right himself, I retrieved the knife from the floor behind him and removed the one from his belt the same way as I'd withdrawn Caitlin's from her back sheath.

I wasn't certain who'd thrown a knife at his head, but I could guess, and I wouldn't leave it within his reach. "So it's women, children *and* animals you abuse, is it, Troels?" My voice probably shook—perhaps people would think it was with anger and not gut-wrenching fear for Tilly?

He drew himself slowly upright and, in a contemptuous tone, said, "King Troels, woman. I am the Rightful King of the Vikings. You will use my proper title. Show some respect."

A genuine laugh burst out of me. "You're freaking

kidding, right? As a wise foremother of mine said, kings are ten-a-penny around here, but there is only one Recorder. You haven't ever used my title, Troels. Respect needs to be earned, so I have none whatsoever for you."

He looked startled. Well, that made a full house of startled royals this week. But seriously, did no one ever stand up to him? Was someone saying no to him such a shocking concept? Or was it just because *I'd* said no to him? How could I find out?

Furious rage boiled inside me. Still riding the adrenaline rush of seeing Tilly in danger. I didn't care what this heap of shit thought of me. But I was frightened I might do something I'd truly regret like pin him to the Gateway wall until Dru arrived to bite pieces off him for frightening his friend Tilly. So I simply folded my arms and handed the problem to the highest authority in the Gateway.

"You were not invited here, and you will not return of your own volition until you deal with the mess in your kingdom and the abuser you *personally* sent here. Sent here with the intention of harassing any woman he came into contact with. Did you think the power didn't see your plan and doesn't see your lies now? The power will decide."

I didn't move, my arms remained folded, and I thought the livestream would show that clearly. The power did decide for itself. He shot backwards so quickly, he nearly slammed into several of the soon-to-be-bonded couples. Fortunately, they had shield maiden reaction times and stepped speedily out of his way.

I didn't hear a crash as he landed, so I assumed the power had simply deposited him back in his kingdom. The yellow doorway slammed shut.

I took a full breath for the first time since I'd watched Tilly chase past me, and as calmly as I could, I said, "I don't think the power he doesn't seem to understand liked him. Now, we'll all take a moment before we begin the happier part of this day. Please help yourselves to refreshments. Rollo, I invite you to join me in the centre."

"I'm so sorry." I sat at the conference table with a large brandy and Tilly on my knee, but my hands were still shaking. Rollo's usual tanned skin was the colour of putty. Fury, shame and grief were the emotions coming from him. What did he have to be ashamed about? He was still apologising.

"Rollo, please stop. It wasn't your fault. All of you heirs feel responsible for your parents…" I tried desperately to find a word that didn't start with F and finally finished, "mess-ups. But it isn't your fault."

He took a long pull on his mug of coffee and turned his gorgeous, but unhappy, hazel eyes on me. In this light they were the colour of a tiger's eye stone I'd kept in my bathroom for months after Nick's death. The stone was supposed to boost confidence and self worth. Right now Rollo looked as if he could use a chunk of it himself.

With an icy-cold note in his voice, he said, "He is not my parent." Then, in a warmer tone added, "Sorry, I'm just so embarrassed. He's always such an embarrassment." He didn't even look worried that he'd admitted it.

I swallowed more brandy. "As soon as I've stopped shaking, I think we need to get on. Let's do this and then work out what to do with you. Do you think it will be a problem when the couples go back to the realm?"

A plate arrived on the conference table with two large warm brownies on it. Iced onto the plate were the words EAT ME.

I grabbed one and took a large bite and pushed the plate towards Rollo. Sugar for the shock, bless Dola.

"No—he'll be drunk by then. Anyway, the shield maidens and their mothers terrify him." He picked up the brownie, bit into it and let out a low moan. It was an interesting sound, and it drew Caitlin over to us.

She put her hand on his shoulder. There was comradeship in her smile, and it reminded me they'd fought together for some years in those competitions Caitlin had talked about. In a low voice, she said, "It's not your fault. Yeah, it's time you fixed it, but it isn't your fault."

He looked up at her. "I've seen him slit many an animal's throat. He would have done it if the Recorder hadn't been so quick. My throw wouldn't quite have landed in time."

She just nodded sadly at him. "Nanok flew true, though. It might be time now, you know. Remember, my blade is still yours if you need it."

Rollo reached up to his shoulder and rested his hand over hers briefly. "Thanks, Cait. Let's hope it won't come to that."

Caitlin sighed and rolled her eyes at me before moving away.

I retrieved the blade I'd removed from the floor near Troels and returned it to him. "How did you get it to land hilt-first? That was very cool!"

He put his head on one side, looked at me for a long time with a confused expression. "I beg your pardon?"

I just repeated myself, and he threw his head back and roared with genuine amusement.

"What's so funny?"

"You are not what I expected at all, my lady."

"What did you expect?"

He shook his head. "Maybe just a younger version of your grandmother." He shook his head again. "Your hair matches the robe. It's fun."

At my raised eyebrow he continued, "Sorry. I don't know what i expected. Just not you. There's a lot of misinformation about Recorders circulating in my kingdom, and to be honest, your grandmother didn't help matters. That wasn't tactful. My apologies, please ignore me."

I had no idea what to say in response, so I did as he'd asked, and I moved on my next concern. "Are you going to be in trouble for throwing your knife at him?"

He gave me a warm smile now. "No. His mistake was forcing himself into the group. I swore on Nanok to maintain the order of my group. Having given surety for their behaviour, I'd have been remiss not to use her." He smirked at me, actually smirked. "And using the hilt to achieve that is another kind of insult. So, no, my lady, there will be no problems for me. Even his best friend or my worst enemy would agree. I kept the code and am blameless. Thank you for your concern, though."

His smile actually got warmer. I resisted the urge

to fan myself. This guy seemed to break my internal thermostat every time I saw him.

"You will call him to an arbitration, won't you, my lady?"

"Didn't we agree on Niki in private?" Although from him, the "my lady" sounded possessive and very appealing ... I brought my inappropriate thoughts sharply under control.

"But hell yes. We've had so many submissions, it would be negligent not to. I might have to wrap him in power and isolate him in a glass cage so he doesn't attempt to kill anyone else during the arbitration."

I stroked Tilly again. She was completely unbothered by her adventure, and I put her on the floor. "And it might take us a month or two to gather the evidence, depending on the availability of all the women to give their statements, but yes we'll proceed with the petitions."

A look of happiness and relief spread across his face. He stood up, offered me his hand, and then surprised me by pulling me into a hug. He was so tall I barely reached above his waist. I'd had no idea he was so tall. How did he manage to make himself look smaller without stooping?

I breathed in. There was no smoke in this man's scent. He smelled clean, of the seashore, a fresh ionised scent, spring breezes, shoots of green herbs and something citrusy, maybe grapefruit. It was an honest smell. And the strange static electric sensation from our handshake spread through my body.

In my peripheral vision, I saw a package had arrived on the table. Interestingly, it didn't have the Viking's Yggdrasil tree symbol on it, just the seven-pointed star as Aysha's had. My phone buzzed. Reluctantly, I pulled out of his arms. Was it my imagination or was he holding on too?

Dola: *I believe he will have need of it. But the decision is yours.*

As I handed the box over, I wondered if Dola was trying to say it was a personal gift to Rollo, unlike the devices she had sent to Ad'Rian and Breanna with their national symbols on them. At least with his computing background, he'd be able to install it himself. "This is from Dola. Fair warning, you should ask her about it and sign her damn agreement before you install it. But we think you might need it. Be warned, it infringes your privacy and your rights in every way. Finn describes the sixty-page EULA as 'All your bases are belong to us.'"

He gave a sincerely amused laugh. This might have been the first time I'd seen the real Rollo because his eyes crinkled when he smiled genuinely.

It also surprised me he got the reference. "Are you a gamer?"

"You might say that, Niki; you just might say that. Yes."

"OK. So, speaking of games, shall we put on our game faces and go calm some shield maidens down?" In front of my eyes, the hot, swaggering Thor persona I'd met at my ascension emerged from the unhappy man in front of me. I swear the oiled muscles suddenly started looking glossier. And he appeared both broader and shorter. That was an impressive façade he had there.

"Thank you, Niki. The Great One may be right, and you might save us yet."

The Great One? Oh yeah, that was what he'd called HRH, wasn't it? Well, crap, it sounded like a burden I wasn't prepared to carry. I needed to speak to that cat.

CHAPTER
THIRTY-EIGHT

The best thing about the unprecedented stress of seeing Tilly in danger was, once I finally stopped shaking, doing some bondings was a pleasant thought. A normal day at work after the adrenaline-fuelled drama. It didn't quite work out that way, though.

Ross had arrived late again but was finally in place. He'd had been vocal about his unhappiness, complaining I'd started without him. Bitching about the anvil surround having grown, and he couldn't stand exactly where he always did.

I heard Fi say, "Really, Ross, things will change, you know. You have to learn to adapt. Change is good. Without it, we'd all still be seventeen and covered in acne. If it's too big a challenge for you, I have a long list of other photographers who've asked many times if they can do the Gateway's photos. Perhaps we should schedule a meeting to discuss whether your contract as the Gateway photographer will be renewed by the new Recorder. My lady Niki has quite different standards to my lady Elsie's, as even *you* must have noticed." She gestured around the beautiful Gateway and across at all the new tables of Juniper's fabulous food.

Ross looked astonished, and Corby winked at me.

I opened the doorways to all the other realms and called everyone to the Gateway. They all arrived, bringing with them a delightful positive energy and excitement. As Aysha and a woman I didn't know arrived, I offered them an invite to the centre. But she was chatting to the Pictish woman, whom she introduced as Lewis's sister, and decided to stay in the Blue sector. She whispered in my ear that the Galician palace they'd delivered Autumn to was "like something out of a movie," but the empress was lovely, and Autumn was safe with her.

Autumn arrived with Natalia's party, ready for her bridesmaid gig. Natalia and Tomas were going to be the first couple bonded, so she wouldn't have long to wait. The little one was in her element and looked so cute and happy in her burnt-orange bridesmaid gown with its copper ribbons that almost perfectly matched her face. She'd caught some colour on her short break. It looked like a skiing tan, and her normally lighter skin had darkened to Aysha's deeper tawny shade. She glowed in the beautiful dress, and delight lit up her face as she stood proudly next to the future empress, looking completely unbothered by all the ceremony.

Aysha had explained Lewis couldn't come. He had commitments today, but the glow on her own skin and in her eyes came from more than just a little mountain sun and told me she'd had a great few days.

Once everyone had arrived, I invited and we all escorted the various royals and Lis and Mag to the centre. I'd updated Mabon as I walked with him, explaining Troels tried to snatch, and it looked to me as though he'd planned to hurt Tilly.

The fury on his face matched my own, and with a few words of Welsh to Dru, he sent both dogs to curl up in their safe space under my new desk. "If the pen pidyn doesn't have a care, Dru will have his balls off soon."

I giggled at his Welsh insult, but he was right Troels was a dickhead. Then I giggled again at Dru, who was almost sitting on Tilly with protection written in every line of his long, lean body as he licked her from nose to tail like a mother.

Breanna arrived a little late, and everyone in the Blue sector moved aside to allow their queen through. I met her at the barrier with an invite to the centre, and as she hugged me, a cold nose slid up the sleeve of my robe. I laughed delightedly when I saw a small black nose and a fluffy golden and cream face peeping out of Breanna's leather tote. "Hello, Maggie, what on earth are you doing in there?"

Breanna sighed, "I'm sorry, Recorder. I didn't think it would be a problem now that the Gateway is open to animals? She really wanted to come. She started fussing about twenty minutes ago, and she got herself into my bag and refused to move until I said she could come. The pavements are frozen solid at home, so I let her stay in my tote."

Maggie was cleaning my hand now as I tried to stroke her fluffy ears. "Of course it's not a problem; she just startled me." I surveyed Maggie closely. "Are you as psychic as your mum, little one?"

Breanna's gaze sharpened on me, and she lowered her voice, "What happened? I didn't feel anything, but Maggie really wanted to come, not just her usual *why would you even think of leaving without me*? She was truly insistent that she come with me."

Maggie was wriggling now, and Breanna lifted her out of the bag and set her on the floor as soon as her paws touched the ground. She shot over to my desk and Tilly and Dru at full speed.

"About twenty minutes ago, Troels was planning to slit Tilly's throat."

Breanna gasped in horror. I got the sense she was angrier at the threat to Tilly than she would have been at one to me. In a low voice, she hissed, "You're coming to dinner next week, aren't you? We need to talk about that slagging excuse for a king. Coward, he'd know the power would deflect any attack on you, but he thought a puppy was fair game? The man's a heap of rusted slag."

We'd arrived at the centre, and we both glanced over to see all three dogs curled up in a pile under my desk. It looked for all the world as if they were gossiping. The three dogs had an interesting bond glowing around them too. Aww was that what a pack bond looked like?

Breanna joined the other dignitaries gathered in the new, larger space available for them around the anvil. One unexpected addition was the ancient Fae Ad'Rian asked me to include in the invitations to the centre. I guessed this was the seer he and the Book had mentioned.

Lis and Mags were on their best behaviour, and they looked lovely in toning suits of pale lilac. Mag wore her jacket with a skirt, and Lis opted to wear hers over a pair of trousers, but they both had dusty-pink silk shells under them. They'd done their grandchildren proud, and the Galician emperor appeared to be charming them. I hadn't heard a raised voice or one *feeking* inappropriate word.

Dai waited in the Red sector with his friend Glyn, for whom he was standing as best man. I heard Glyn call him Dewi instead of Dai, which was weird. How many nicknames did the man have? He gave me a grin, and his eyes sparkled as he caught mine. But then I checked, and his shields were still rock walls. I sighed inwardly.

I began by welcoming everyone. I mentioned we planned to do the bondings differently, with couples from each sector forming a group in the middle so each realm had someone to focus on instead of having to wait hours before their turn came around. There were murmurs at that. They sounded divided between those who don't like traditions to be changed and people who thought changing it up was a good plan and enjoyed a little variety.

I called Natalia and Tomas forward for their seven-fold bonding. Emperor Alphonse looked every inch the proud father as he surveyed the wedding party. I'd invited his wife to join the dignitaries around the anvil, but she declined, prettily explaining her responsibilities, and joined the main wedding party, keeping a close but kind eye on Autumn and another junior bridesmaid.

I explained to the assembled crowd the difference between a normal bonding a seven-fold, simply describing it as a rare, soul-deep connection on every level. Those who saw the power should be able to see the difference. I'd wondered privately if the livestream would be able to capture the beauty of it. The power may have thought something similar because, as I stepped forward to check the couple's seven chakra connections, I very nearly squealed.

Natalia squeaked, and Tomas drew in a quick breath and looked shocked as the three of us rose into the air. What the hell? Well, I had worried about balancing the energies in the so-crowded centre. This wasn't the solution I'd have chosen, but it was *a* solution. I was damn glad I'd decided on a trouser suit and wasn't flashing the entire Gateway though.

To the couple, I said, "In this, I'm no wiser than you two, but the power will do what it wants. I think it's showing everyone how unusual your bond is." I leaned for their ears alone. "Even your father won't be able to argue after this crazy display!"

They both laughed, and I tried to subdue the unhappy feeling in my stomach. *Let's get this bonding over and done with so we can all stand on solid ground again.*

I heard a tiny squeak below me and looked down before immediately regretting it as my stomach lurched. But I saw Natalia's mother's held both of the junior bridesmaids' hands, and it was she who'd squeaked. Then Autumn held her hand out and took Fi's hand too. Fi's eyes widened in astonishment. I was glad the two women had the chance to see how gloriously right the seven chakra connections of a seven-fold bond were.

It went exactly as the first seven-fold bonding I'd done for L'eon and Kaiden had, except this couple had remembered their rings. But just as they were exchanging those rings and making their vows to each other, two threads of power, one orange, the other an electric blue, separated and floated between me and the couple. My Gift said the power wanted them to have rings from it, anyway.

I glanced at Natalia, who was watching the strands with hope on her face. "Would you like the eternal rings?"

She nodded so hard, she almost dislodged her veil and said, "Please, Recorder."

"I understand the Galician orange, but why the blue strand?"

Tomas, who was finally beginning to relax, said, "The flag, it is blue and white."

The crowd, who'd been almost silent during the ceremony, leaned forward as though it would help them see better, and Finn brought his new drone in closer.

I placed Natalia's smaller hand on top of Tomas's larger one, and the couple watched, fascinated as the two energy strands intertwined and twisted around each other. It formed a figure of eight or an infinity symbol as it looped itself around their ring fingers, tying them together.

I left them tied together. "Natalia and Tomas, the Recorder and the power join you together. May your bond be ever unbroken. May you support each other through the changes and joys yet to come, always knowing your life-mate and the other half of your soul is at your side."

As I pulled their hands apart, the infinity symbol separated, leaving each of them with a circular energy swirl in a twisting blue and orange design. It looked as though it intended to form a crown design on the front of their ring fingers. Well, they would be emperor and empress one day. As their hands separated, it sank into their skin like a tattoo.

"I'm delighted to pronounce you married."

The Gateway erupted into applause and cheers, which I wasn't expecting, and we were all lowered back to the blissfully firm floor of the Gateway. From the corner of my eye, I saw Mags, of all people, patting the emperor's hand, "Recorder was right, see. Tha' a special bond tha' is," as he wiped a tear from his cheek.

Fi said, "What a great start," and offered me a bottle of water, which I took gratefully.

"I'm glad you feel that way because you guys are up next."

HRH strolled past me on the way to her plinth. "I'm devastated to have missed all the entertainment in person, although Finn's television thing is a superb idea. They're showing it on the large screen in the Dairy Club."

That was a good idea; we should have thought about a large screen for the Gateway. It was so crowded, I was sure all the people at the back of each sector couldn't see a thing. Perhaps that was why the power had raised the three of us into the air.

That was where I'd heard the term Dairy Club before. Well, along with finding out why she'd told Rollo I might save them, this club was another thing I needed to speak to her about.

"We need to talk later, Your Majesty, urgently."

"Sadly, I have prior commitments for a few days." She didn't sound at all sad, and the twitch of her upright tail made it look as though she was giving me the finger. But she continued, "All will be quiet after today for a short while, anyway. We *will* speak on my return, Recorder."

With that, she strolled off and leapt up onto her plinth, mistress of all she surveyed. I wished I had even a tenth of her sang-froid.

I took up my position by the anvil and linked my

Gift back into the power. It gave my voice a natural amplification, which, with the large space this full, was helpful. I was feeling more confident as we moved through the day's program. Standing on solid ground was so much better than being in the air.

But I wasn't sure how they would receive my next announcements. I took a deep breath, let it out slowly, resisted the urge to wipe my hands down my robe, and decided I could only do my best.

"Deities, Your Majesties, Headwomen and honoured guests, as you may have noticed, there have been some changes in the Gateway." There was a wave of laughter. I hadn't expected it, and I smiled. I caught Caitlin's eye, and she was nodding encouragingly.

"We're modernising the Recorder's Office, and I'd like to introduce you to my staff. First, the Recorder's new equerry, Dola Neach." I raised the large screen from my own desk into the air. Then, in a manoeuvre I'd practised yesterday while the Gateway was empty, with the power's help, I spun it slowly around so everyone saw the photograph of Gateway Cottage on it. I briefly explained who Dola was for those who weren't aware and even more briefly mentioned her new role as the Recorder's Equerry. I heard whispered explanations, probably from the people in the know to those who'd never visited Gateway Cottage and thought it was just a house.

"Two new Knight Adjutants now join me to make the necessary changes: Finn and Caitlin Albidosi. Finn is the TEK responsible for planned improvements to the technology, the Rainbow Network and several other projects." I gestured to Finn.

"And Caitlin is the KAIT, the Knight Adjutant In Trust, and heads up the Recorder's security and other projects."

They got an immediate round of applause as Finn bowed, still holding his cameras, and Caitlin gave everyone, including me, her patented death stare. That was really a killer stare. I think she'd just worked it out!

"You all know Fiona Glendinning. She's been an invaluable assistant to the Recorder and a part of the Gateway for twenty-two years, but now she's moving on." Concerned grumbling from the crowd interrupted me. I'd been right—Fi was an extremely popular member of the Gateway staff. Probably more popular than my grandmother because Fi would help without snapping their heads off. Perhaps the grumbling was because the assembled guests thought she was leaving. I raised a hand, hoping it would quiet them down. It worked. "She is moving on and up to take on two new roles."

There was happy applause; hopefully it would boost her confidence.

"Fi, if you would step forward, please, so I can

introduce the Gateway's new Director with Special Responsibility for Inter-Realm Trade Development."

The round of applause that followed my announcement was thunderous and prolonged. I caught a few stray comments from the guests: *She does that anyway,* and *Who will organise the bondings now?*

"You may feel Fi was already responsible for trade, and that's true. But she wasn't getting paid for it. She didn't have the authority to make decisions, the necessary time to give to the role and, importantly, couldn't advise on setting future policy. Now she does and she can."

More thunderous applause. I hoped it would convince Fi we'd made the correct decision. She'd been doubtful about it and concerned she wouldn't be able to do it. Which was ridiculous, as she had been doing it blatantly for the last fifteen years. I decided not to mention her other new role just yet. I'd let them get used to this idea first.

Finally, I looked over at the two new and still empty desks and smiled. I wondered how this next announcement would go down.

"I'm delighted to announce, taking over Fi's prior role as Bonding Co-ordinator and Gateway advisor, and I'm sure," I put a little power into my next words in case any of them needed a clue about what I expected from them, "*You will all join me* in giving a warm welcome to the newest member of the Gateway staff, Rosemary Hob."

As I'd feared, there was a moment of stunned silence. Then Mabon and Ad'Rian broke the silence in unison. Mabon with his familiar whistle of approval, and Ad'Rian with a whoop and loud applause, which quickly spread out from them in the centre as he gestured to his sector to push Rosemary to the front of the Violet sector, where she and her sisters stood waiting for their bondings. She did the funny bobbing thing and then gazed around astonished as she realised everyone was clapping. I caught an interesting expression pass between Lis and Mags. Rosemary obviously hadn't told them.

I'd better move on while the going was good. I knew she'd be excellent. With her trade experience gained working with Crane, she could help Fi, and I might be able to help Crane too. But that was for next month. For now, I'd wait for people to discover her sunny nature and competence for themselves.

I'd forgotten and was still effortlessly holding the monitor screen aloft and queried the power. It thought it was a fine idea, and as I watched, the screen rose about fifteen feet and grew dramatically to almost cinema screen size. The feed from Finn's camera appeared on it. The people at the back shouted, "Thank you, my lady." There was more applause. This seemed to be going OK.

I focused back on my message, "Two weeks ago, at my ascension, I announced we would form a new Rainbow Council. It will have its inaugural meeting next month. We'll add the names of the council members to the Recorder's news portal shortly." We hadn't nailed everyone down yet, and I didn't want to make a partial announcement, with one notable exception. "Rhiannon ap Modron has agreed to be the council's first chairperson."

Rhiannon's WTAF expression was a wonder to behold as everyone turned towards the Red sector to express their approval. But she was a pro and smiled and waved at the crowd. Though her head nodded, her eyes glared daggers at me. Unsurprising, really, as I hadn't cleared it with her. But she'd sworn over the anvil to serve.

I'd hate to lead any group with her in it. She'd make a lousy follower and give whoever was in charge no end of trouble, so she should be the leader. I thought it was one of my best decisions, and I just hid my smile, as I guessed from Mabon and Ad'Rian's facial tics, they were deep in a private mind-to-mind conversation about it. They didn't feel unhappy about it. And Mabon had told me not to take any of Rhiannon's nonsense, so he shouldn't be surprised I'd followed his advice.

・ ・ ・

We were taking a ten-minute break after the fifth—or was it the sixth—round of bondings? when Caitlin closed in on me. "You did that deliberately, didn't you, my lady?"

"Yep, KAIT, I did." I grinned at her. "I have to take my amusement where I can find it. And, yes, it amused the hell out of me, OK?"

She actually growled.

"I didn't ask you to be my Knight Adjutant. I asked you to be my Knight Adjutant In Trust. Didn't it occur to you that was a super specific title?"

She gave me a puzzled frown. "No! Why should it? You created a new title for Finn; I thought…" she trailed off and huffed a laugh, "I don't think I thought about it all. Hugh likes it. He stopped me to tell me Kait was someplace in the old world, where his ancestors came from in northern Caledonia, long before it was even Scotland, a thousand-plus years ago. It's a finely-forged Pictish title, oh yes it is!" She pulled a face.

I patted her arm. "Just because the kingdoms might not understand your title doesn't mean you shouldn't. And it isn't just so you can't glare at me when I forget to use your full name. Because now I'm using your title, KAIT."

"I'm going to have to keep a closer eye on you than I anticipated, my lady." But there was laughter in her voice, so she'd seen the funny side of it.

· · ·

So, with only the perfectly straightforward work of bonding the remaining couples, I breathed easier. But the power still had a last surprise in store for us all. The couples were relaxed. The guests were relaxed. Juniper's brainwave of giving them refreshments while they waited and mine of switching up the bondings so at least one, sometimes two or three couples from their own realm were in each batch, had worked wonderfully.

The iPad had made sure I got everyone's names right. I hadn't needed to use "I, *say your name*, take you, *say her name*" once. HRH looked disappointed at this, but I was certain she'd soon find something new to take bets on.

Fi escorted Rosemary and Rockii out of the Violet sector. Lavender and Crane's and Thyme and Sedona's bondings had gone off smoothly, so I had no worries about this one. There were several other couples I recognised from the bonding checks in this group: Simon and Bryn, the cute Red Celt couple who'd wanted eternal rings; Lesley and Gowan, the Pict couple who had so nearly been split up by Breanna's slag-brained scheme, as she herself described it. But now everyone was smiling and happy, I saw Autumn had rejoined Aysha and was holding her mum's hand, her attention sharp on her new friend Rosie. Then the power poked me.

I dropped into my Gift to check for information,

smelt the negative ion, seashore smell and resolutely bit down any squealing as I realised I was once again rising into the air. Oh, this was getting old fast. The power and I would have a firm chat about this once I got through this day. I was not a floating-in-the-air person, and it needed to realise that. But mostly I was confused.

Rosemary and Rockii rose with me. Rosemary was delighted. She gave me a wide smile and looked all around her and down into the Gateway, waving, obviously loving every moment. Rockii looked terrified—we locked eyes, and I said, "I know, Rockii, I hate heights too, but I can promise you're safe, and as soon as I work out what's going on, I'll get us down again."

He nodded at me shakily, and then Rosemary realised her life-mate was in distress and reached out to take his hand, and I saw it.

Well, how embarrassing was that? I'd missed a seven-fold bond!

CHAPTER
THIRTY-NINE

I knew how this oversight had happened. The triplets had been in a huddle, and I'd separated them long enough to check all three of the couples had a bond. But they were so excited at being the first three hobs to be approved for a binding ceremony in hundreds of years that, thinking back, I hadn't taken enough time to check the quality of their bonds. I'd only made sure they had them. Thank goodness the power had my back and was doing its job better than I'd done mine.

I addressed the audience, "Here's a treat for us all, another seven-fold bond. Given how rare they are, you may not see this again for a long time. There was a spontaneous round of applause. Oh, yes, they were all having a lovely day out. That was good—it had been one of my goals, after all. I just hadn't planned to achieve it floating in the air.

I overheard a stray comment: *The new Recorder knows her stuff. No wonder she appointed that Hob to be in charge of the bondings. But who'd have thought a Hob would have one of these special bonds?*

I really hoped the Hobs didn't hear the bigoted old fool. I knew the power enhanced my hearing in the Gateway. Fingers crossed they hadn't heard; I'd hate anything to spoil their day.

The power was spinning threads at me. "Rosemary, Rockii, it appears you're to have eternal rings, OK?"

They nodded, and I heard a happy sigh from Simon below us. His bonding bow tie, adorned today with intertwined hearts, bobbed as he tipped his head back so he didn't miss a moment.

We moved through the declarations, their vows, which were short and touching, and their ring exchange. These two were very much in love. They put their wedding rings onto their right hands and then held out their left hands to me. I placed Rosemary's over Rockii's and then looked helplessly at all the strands of power that floated between us.

A thick red one, an indigo one—wow! A blue one, a medium-sized green one, an orange one and a yellow one, and finally a thin violet one.

I had a rainbow here, but with all the colours as

separate threads. It reminded me of the part of my real ascension ceremony where the power had separated and then connected me to all the doors. I sent my confusion out to the power, asking for its help. Then, I was fascinated as the strands braided themselves in mid-air. Everyone was glued to the show the power was putting on. Finn's new drone hovered only a few metres away. Good, I'd want to watch this one back myself.

Eventually, the power had three threads. One was primarily blue, and included the indigo, violet, and blue threads. The next was orangey-yellow, and the last two to merge were the red and green threads. Then all three strands plaited themselves together and became an infinity symbol, which slipped itself around the couple's ring fingers.

Too far below me, I caught sight of Ad'Rian and the elderly seer, obviously deep in a mind-to-mind communication as they watched the proceedings intently.

I said what were becoming familiar words, "Rosemary and Rockii, the Recorder and the power join you together. May your bond be ever unbroken. May you support each other through the changes and joys yet to come, always knowing that your life-mate and the other half of your soul is at your side."

As I parted their hands, we watched as all the coloured strands merged, and two perfect brown rings with a small floral motif at the front sank into their skin. The Gateway exploded into clapping, cheering and whistling.

The starburst of tables below me came into focus, and I realised Juniper had personalised the food too. Each sector had all the same Valentine foods in pink and silver and red, but they also had plates and dishes in their national colours. What a lovely touch. I must thank her.

"It's all changed so much." Fi beamed, gazing around and soaking in the happiness. "The vibe in here today was incredible. We've had loads of messages and comments on the news portal from all the people watching it at home. It feels so joyful and fun when you do the bondings. You can tell you really enjoy marrying people. Your gran could be a little dour sometimes, you know."

We admired Juniper's incredible spread from ground level and got some food ourselves before it all disappeared. I'd asked Dola to send my goodie bag to the cottage. I wanted to see what this magical cheesecake everyone stole was all about. Maybe Tilly and I would share it.

"There were 1238 people in the end, Niki. I told you Juniper was never wrong. Do you think predicting the right number to feed is *her* superpower?"

I laughed, but she might have been right. We didn't know anywhere near enough about the Hobs' powers.

Fi said, "That was weird with Rosemary and Rockii, wasn't it?" I ran her through my thoughts about how I'd missed it. She nodded seriously and said, "Now we need to look for seven-fold bonds. I'll bear it in mind for the future."

I was shaking my head at her. She asked, "What?"

"You'll send your successor a note to explain to her whatever you've just come up with to avoid it happening in the future."

She laughed, flushed and said, "Oh my goodness, so many changes. I said everything had changed while I was away, but I've been here this whole week, and I think even more has changed. Is it always going to be like this?"

"Would that be a problem, Fi?"

"Oh no, I'm loving it. I think I'd got a bit stuck in my ways too, like your gran, and Ross. He actually apologised, you know?"

We grinned at each other.

Natalia extricated herself from all the people who were asking to look at her and Tomas's eternal rings and headed over to me. "My lady, might I have a moment?"

Fi headed over to another group of revellers, and I turned to Natalia. "Sorry again about the unexpected flight. Blame the power. I had no say in it. May I see your ring now my feet are on the ground and I can focus on it properly?"

She held out her hand, and I saw a perfect blue and orange plaited loop with, yes, I'd been right, a crown on the front of her finger.

She giggled. "It's gorgeous, isn't it? I certainly won't forget my wedding day in a hurry, and it was so sweet of Prince Finn to say he'd send us a copy of the video. I just wanted to say thank you for all you did to make sure the right Galician couples married each other."

"You've repaid me already. Autumn got her wish and had a lot of fun. That was a kind thing you did."

She shook her head. "It was nothing. Every little girl should get the chance to be a bridesmaid. But I wanted to give you this." She held out a thin, beautifully wrapped package to me. I admired the burnt orange paper and copper and cream ribbon, her wedding colours.

She thrust it at me. "Just a tiny something to say thank you."

I took it off her. "May I open it now?"

"Of course." She was grinning like a child, and I was intrigued.

As I opened the package, I saw the book, *The*

Recorder Always Knows Best: Cautionary Tales for Incautious Children by Margarita Encimera

"I managed to get a copy in English. I wasn't even aware there was an English version. The title looks a little strange in English, but if you read it, it might give you a smile. It is an accurate translation. I hope you enjoy it."

I was touched and intrigued and reached out to hug her. "Thank you. Of course I'll read it. What a lovely gift." I opened the front cover and read the handwritten words through a blur of tears. They had all signed it, how lovely.

For the Recorder who knew best and stood up to the emperor until he realised it too.

With our love and gratitude, Natalia and Tomas, Sophia and Miguel.

CHAPTER
FORTY

Quite how I'd ended up here was still a bit of a mystery to me. Settled opposite Dai, with Tilly on my knees, at a table outside a delightful trattoria-style restaurant on a pretty square just a couple of hundred yards from the Orange gate in Santiago de Cordoba, one of the larger towns in Galicia. Was it their capital? I didn't know. I needed to do more homework on these realms. But it was beautiful, the people were friendly, and it was far warmer here than Scotland. Lights twinkled in the loggia, or was it a pergola? Who knew? But it was restful and pretty, with leaves and multi-coloured lights forming a living ceiling over our heads.

The sounds of more active festivities, bagpipes, music, cheers and laughter came from the main coast road below us, but up here, it was quiet, and the candles on our table cast a warm glow. I knew I should loosen up, but I couldn't relax until he did, and he felt tense.

Honestly, I wasn't sure how I'd allowed him to talk me into this, or was "usher me into it" a better way of describing it? We'd finished in the Gateway, Dru had gone home with Mabon, and Tilly was at my heels as I began to head towards Scotland and my dinner.

Dai had simply appeared in front of me. I thought he'd left with one of the large crowds who'd all headed for the Orange gate and the *Carnaval* festivities.

Dai was currently ordering what sounded like enough food to feed an army from a dark-haired, dark-eyed waiter. But, as he was ordering in fluent Galician, perhaps they were just making conversation. But no, the waiter kept adding things to his order pad, so food then.

Dai had meant it when he'd said he was starving. He'd repeated his comment about we needed to get to know one another again and pleaded with me to come and eat with him. When I'd said I wasn't dressed for a night out, he'd helped me off with my robe, looked me up and down, told me I looked gorgeous and asked Dola to take care of my robe. Huh, so he didn't mind using her; he just objected to her, what had he called it? Monitoring him? No, watching him and reporting back to his dad—that was it.

The waiter was smiling and cooing at Tilly and gave me a flashing grin from very white teeth when I said I'd have whatever Dai had just ordered along with a glass of red wine and a piece of honey cake. I was still miffed I hadn't had the chance to try any of the ones the emperor had brought for me before Dola gave them away to Fi and her mum.

Finally, the waiter walked away, still smiling. I wanted to know how Dai spoke what sounded like excellent Galician, but asking would only distract us from why the hell we were here. So instead I asked, "What's your problem with Dola? And what did you need to talk to me about privately?"

He frowned. "Do we have to do this now?"

I took a breath before I said something I might regret, and in a quiet, careful voice, a voice I'd often had to use with Nick, said, "I don't know, Dai. You said we needed to get to know each other as adults. Dola is a huge and important part of the rest of my life, so if you have a problem with her, I need to know what your issue is — don't you think?"

I thought about how easy I'd felt with everyone for the last days, Caitlin, Fi once she settled in and realised I wanted her to stay. Finn was always easy. Even Rollo, in the middle of the horrific showdown with Troels, hadn't made me feel uncomfortable or inadequate. Hell, even Lis and Mags had made me laugh. But Dai made me twitchy. He felt as if he was deliberately withholding, and when I reached out to sense his emotional temperature, his shields were still a rock wall, just as Rhiannon's had been. She might have reason to distrust me. She didn't know me, but surely Dai didn't have to lock himself away from me?

I tried to explain some of this to him. But from his expression, either I was making no sense, or he didn't want to address what I'd said.

He sighed, looked uncomfortable, and leaned forward. "Nik, I probably owe you an apology. After Elsie sent you away, in my memories, I thought I'd known you really well. I thought we'd had a connection. Like the way you'd arrive in the Gateway if I even whispered your name. But I obviously didn't know you as well as I thought I did. You surprised me on Tuesday. I didn't deal with it well. You ... well, you frightened me, I think."

"Perhaps you did know me when I was twelve, but I'm forty-one now, and a lot of shit happened since I last saw you. To you too, I'd imagine. But how on earth did I frighten you?"

This made zero sense to me. We'd been talking about Autumn and her ride with Ad'Rian on Diamant. I'd thought he was being a dick about her being a sassie child, but he wasn't. We'd cleared that up. I hadn't said anything frightening. He'd pissed me off when he kept saying it was such a shame Nick was dead, but I didn't want to bring that up now.

He looked like he'd had a rough few days. I'd give him some grace to explain. That was only fair, wasn't it? So I smiled at him and waited for the explanation I assumed would come.

Dai looked relieved when the waiter arrived and placed glasses of red wine in front of us. The waiter said something to Dai, which sounded like *kay-mar-dur*. A huge grin split Dai's face as he nodded and raised two fingers in return.

It was good to see him smiling, but I didn't recognise the word. "What was that he said?"

"Queimada, I ordered us one each. You do like it, don't you? It's only available at certain times of the year. *Carnaval* is one of them."

"I don't know if I do or not. I don't think I've ever had it, but Caitlin said she was at *Carnaval* this week. She said it was their version of Mardi Gras? I meant to ask the Book about it, but I forgot."

He frowned at me again. What the hell had I said now?

The waiter reappeared quickly with a salad plate-sized metal tray, on which rested two small earthenware cups surrounded with beautiful magical blue flames dancing against the velvety darkness of the Galician night. Fascinated, I watched as Dai, completely ignoring the flames, picked up the cup and poured the flaming contents straight down his throat.

I gasped. Then my brain clicked in—the flames must be a pretty illusion. I reached out for the second cup. But the waiter rushed forward as Dai moved the tray away from me.

"No. *Señora*, no." He waved at Dai. "He is *home de lume*, but you, *señora,* must wait. *Tranquila,* be calm until the sugar and the alcohol is finished with the burning or …" He gripped his own throat dramatically. Dai didn't seem to have suffered any ill-effects. Was this a hazing ritual for new visitors?

I sat back, the blue flames burnt out, and Dai pushed the tray toward me. I picked the cup up cautiously and sniffed. It smelled wonderful. I sipped. It was delicious. Most of the surrounding tables held people with their own earthenware cups. They knocked them back like shots. That felt like a waste. The warm drink tasted like a cross between sweet brandy and grappa. It didn't taste very alcoholic. The blue flames must have burnt off most of the alcohol. But it was complex with undertones of coffee, flavours of herbs, and what else? Oh lemon, maybe? "Does it have lemon in it too?"

The waiter and Dai answered me in almost unison, "*Sí, señora, limón.*"

"Yes, lemon. A good palate and a good nose, Nik. Da always says that about you."

I didn't think being able to taste lemon gave me a good palate, but—whatever. Was it my imagination, or was Dai using this and the waiter as an excuse not to talk to me? Hadn't Caitlin said this stuff was good if you were tired? Dai certainly looked energised, but I hadn't felt a boost; if anything, it was soothing.

I gave the waiter Aysha's best thank-you-very much-you're-very-kind-now-bugger-off-please smile. Honed in many Manchester restaurants with unemployed actors from Media City who loved to join in any interesting conversations happening at their tables, it worked just as well here.

"What does *home de lume* mean?"

"The waiter was just having fun. It's a joke."

My left shoulder twinged, so not quite a lie, but not the truth, either. I tapped my Gift to work out what his problem was. But as before, all I got was a smooth wall of shielding. I tried words, "You were about to tell me how I frightened you?"

He didn't look happy that I'd zeroed back around to this so quickly. "You were so confident. It threw me."

Oh, hell no. I definitely wasn't going here again. Nick had often said shit like this. It was only after he died I realised he'd made these comments to keep me meek, uncertain and doing what he wanted. "Confident about what?" My tone may have been harsher than I intended.

Dai winced. "Nik, I'm screwing this up again. Confident isn't bad. It just ...surprised me. I mean, you were more confident than I would have been. You said you wanted to ride a bluddy dragon, for Dewi's sake."

Had I? I hadn't known you could ride dragons. I had no memory of seeing dragons when I visited Mabon as a child, which was weird, actually. But, yeah, if I'd known you could, I would have talked Boney into letting me do it.

"And that's a problem—why?" I asked.

Dai took out his vaping device and waved it in the air. "Do you mind?"

"No, I like the smell, but why would riding a dragon have been a problem?" I felt like a terrier, but he was bugging me with his constant distractions. What was next, "Oh look, a squirrel"?

He'd asked me to come with him to get to know each other again. When was that going to start?

He took a long drag on the vape and blew out a stream of vapour, which smelt just as good as it had last week. Dai spoke in a rush, as though he was afraid he'd lose his nerve. "Nik, can we start this conversation somewhere else? I need to be honest with you. As I told you last week, it wasn't your business when you were a kid, but I can't keep secrets from the Recorder, or you, for that matter, now you're an adult, and it's eating away at me. I'm almost a hundred and twenty years old."

"Huh?!" I may have made a small gasp, but it definitely wasn't a squeak. Oh no. I neither squeak nor squeal. But whatever I'd thought he was going to say, this wasn't it.

My surprise woke Tilly, who stuck her head up from my knee to the tabletop to glare at Dai as I tried to process this. I remembered Finn talking about Rollo, and he'd said Dai and L'eon were both sooo much older than him and Caitlin, hadn't he? I'd assumed he was doing the classic twenty-something thing where they assume everyone over thirty is just hanging around waiting to collect their Zimmer frame. But I hadn't known Dai was biracial.

"One hundred and twenty? Okaaaay? I didn't realise you had Fae blood. Who's your mother? Do I know her?"

Now he gaped at me. What? What had I said? Oh, this dinner was going just swimmingly, wasn't it? And I hadn't even got my damn honey cake yet.

CHAPTER
FORTY-ONE

"That's all you have to say?" Dai gave me an odd look.

"Well, last week in my office, you told me you were older than you looked. You only look ten years older than you did when I lived here, and that was thirty years ago. I mean, I suppose you could be a time traveller or have a portrait in your attic, but being half-fae feels more logical, doesn't it? I just never knew your mum was Fae. But then I didn't know Mabon was your dad when we were kids, so—what? Why are you looking at me like that?"

The expression on his face was startled. I was so damn tired of everyone giving me startled looks. I'd already decided I wasn't the problem; they were. Perhaps it was time someone caught up with me. Let's see if I could start with Dai.

"You rationalise things so easily Nik."

Was it a compliment or an insult? It felt like a putdown. I remembered the exercise in *Good Grief,* which talked about removing people from your life if they don't appreciate you or if they try to devalue your strengths. What had it said next? Something about drawing boundaries? No, not quite. It had been something about offering them clear information about your own perception of yourself or your actions and how it differed from what they'd just said.

I recalled thinking, if I'd had the book back when I first met Nick, I could have worked out much quicker he was a gaslighting asshole.

I swallowed, stroked Tilly, and tried it. "I don't rationalise things easily, Dai. But I do try to stop myself spiralling into panic if something I don't understand or expect happens. Because that way leads to Crazy Town, and I lived there for a while after Nick died, and I'm not going back for anyone or anything if I can avoid it."

A guilty expression crossed his face. Had he been trying to put me down, or was I mis-reading this? I poked at his wall with my Gift. It was still rock solid. A ripple of annoyance rose in me.

"You asked me to come so we could get to know each other again. But you're not talking, and when you do, you're critiquing me, and your shields are tightly closed, so I can't feel a damn thing from you. You didn't do that when we were kids, did you? Sorry, when I was a kid! But you haven't opened up at all since I came back, so you don't mean you want to get to know me at all, do you?" I stopped to take a breath.

A confused expression crossed his face, and I added, "Or do you mean you'd like to get to know me, but you don't want me to be able to get to know you? Because that's not fair."

He buried his face in his hands and muttered something in Welsh. I'd had enough. I wouldn't respect myself if I allowed this to continue.

"Dai, I've asked you seven questions since we sat down at this table fifteen minutes ago. Most of them weren't personal questions, but you've still ignored every damn one of them. You even almost lied to me once. Recorder, remember, walking lie detector." I wriggled my shoulders. "So this isn't us getting to know each other. It's you avoiding being honest with me, and I'm afraid I'm not up for that."

"Seven questions, truly?"

I nodded.

"Can you remember them all?"

"Of course." Where the hell was he going with this? Had he not even been listening?

"Could you repeat them?"

I nodded. Was the man on drugs? I was a normal

woman. Of course I could repeat questions I'd asked him in the last fifteen minutes!

"Could you do it now, please?"

"You sound weirdly stilted, Dai. It's a little scary—what's going on here?"

"Not sure. Could you just ask the questions again, please?"

I sighed heavily, but he'd asked politely, so … "In order, what did you need to talk to me about privately? Then, what's your issue with Dola? Then, how did I frighten you on Tuesday?"

While I was talking, I'd grabbed an order ticket from the table, taken a pen from my handbag and was scribbling on the blank back of it as I spoke. Maybe the man had short-term memory loss.

"Then I asked what *Carnaval* was, and you frowned at me, but you didn't answer. Then I asked what does *home de lume* mean? You said it was a joke, but that was a lie or very close to a lie, anyway. Then you said I was so confident, but you wouldn't tell me why; then you wouldn't tell me why riding a dragon would have been a problem."

I paused and ran the conversation back through my head. "Oh yeah, then you ignored my question about who your mother was and whether I knew her, which might be fair enough because that is kind of personal, but you keep ignoring me when I ask about your shields too." I surveyed my list. "Which is actually eight things."

"What do my shields feel like to you?"

Well, at least he was talking. "They're like a completely smooth rock wall, not a crack or crevice in it. Almost no emotion leaks out, and there is no way in. I don't mean to pry, Dai." I'd need to explain this better to him.

"You have a right to privacy, of course, but on Tuesday I thought I'd never known such a complete block on anyone's emotions as your walls. I mean, they're smoother than Ad'Rian's, and he could be the God of Impeccable Shield Maintenance."

He laughed now and nodded in understanding.

"But then yesterday, I met someone else with shields exactly like yours. Twice in one week was disconcerting, but she knew she had excellent shields, and she intended them to be up. Thing is, I'm not sure you're even doing it intentionally because your shields don't match your words. Your words say 'come to dinner with me please, Niki. We need to talk.' And your shields say, 'keep the hell out. I'm not sharing anything at all with you.' Do you see my problem?"

"Nik, I'm not doing it deliberately, whatever it is. Also, I'm not half-Fae."

Well, that made sense because some part of my brain had been thinking it through, and a hundred and twenty in Fae years would make him the same age as Fionn'ghal, and he was far more mature than she was. However annoyingly he was behaving right now.

I waited, and I breathed.

Finally, he spoke. "I'm truly sorry for whatever I'm doing. You came home at a bit of a difficult time." He gave a laugh so harsh, it was almost a cough. "And that's the understatement of the flaming century."

As I reached for my wine glass—when all else fails wine might help—I realised my hands were sticky from the sweet queimada. I looped Tilly's lead around my cast iron chair, told her, "Wait, good girl."

"Dai, I'm going to the bathroom. While I'm gone, could you decide if there is anything we *can* manage to talk about, or if I should just head home? Because I don't think either of us is enjoying this, and I don't want a bunch of arguments and confusion in my life right now. And you don't look as if it's making you happy either."

When I returned, I'd decided he had one chance to start explaining, or my honey cake and I were going home. But as I came out, the table was full of food, and Dai had moved his chair around next to Tilly's. He was talking quietly and taking food out of his mouth and feeding it to her. He had an expression of such soft concern on his face, it stopped me in my tracks, and I simply watched them. But Tilly saw me and stood up on the chair with her tail wagging crazily.

"See, little one, I told you she'd be back." He offered her another piece. "Sorry, Nik, she was a bit stressed, and she made it pretty clear this chicken was for her. But it's too spicy. This dish makes even Dru sneeze, so I was just sucking the spice off it for her."

"Actually, she loves spicy food. May I try a bit?"

He gestured at the table. "Anything you want. I ordered some of almost everything for us." Yep, he had. The entire table top was covered in small earthenware tapas dishes. He pointed at a dish. "That's the one she wants."

I took a piece, tasted an edge of it and then gave the rest to Tilly. "She's a Manchester dog. She's been visiting the curry mile since she was about three months old. She loves spice."

"The curry mile?"

"It's a literal mile of about eighty restaurants specialising in every kind of south Asian food. The four of us would go several times a month."

"The four of you?"

"Aysha, Autumn, Tilly and I."

"Not your husband?"

"He was working away, mostly. Or at home. He didn't like Indian food." I really didn't want to talk about Nick. I wanted to find out about Dai. "But we seem to be straying from why your shields are so tight and whatever else you asked me to come here with you so you could tell me?"

I wouldn't be distracted. But he had been so kind to Tilly, I could try to lighten the mood. "I'll do you a deal, tell me everything. When you have, the next time you're hungry, the three of us will go down to Rusholme, and you can try it for yourself." Anyone who fed my dog to keep her calm got kudos from me.

I settled back in my chair. His leg was almost pressed against mine now. I looked down at it.

He shuffled. "Sorry, I didn't want to undo her lead, but I wanted to be close enough to calm her."

I smiled at him and watched his shoulders relax fractionally. Almost all the plates were untouched. He'd said he was starving, and yet he'd concentrated on Tilly's hunger. Nick would have seen to his own needs and let Tilly cry. Definite kudos for Dai.

I gestured at the plates. "Eat, talk, relax, please?"

But he shook his head. "Turn on your lie detector please, Nik; I need you to hear some stuff."

Well, that was different. "It's just built in, you

know, but sure, go."

"I don't know what's up with my shields."

True.

"I'm not totally certain who my mother was, but she definitely wasn't Fae."

True. And I felt bad because I had no idea who my dad was, and it had often bugged me. I reached across to touch his hand briefly before grabbing another piece of spicy chicken for Tilly and one of the empanadas for myself.

Dai shook his head in frustration. "Flaming hells bells, the questions have gone again." He reached for the order blank and peered at it. "Ah yes, I can tell you about *Carnaval*, of course. I didn't even hear that question. I was trying to find some words I'd be able to get out of my mouth to explain why you'd frightened me so much when you asked about," he paused, took a deep breath and appeared to force the next words out, "riding a dragon."

Almost True.

"*Home de lume* is Galician. It means Man. Of. Fire." He paused between each word and was having a real battle with himself to get them out. But it was true.

He looked down again. "Confident was just a poor word choice; unbothered would have been better, or simply not frightened."

True.

"The reason why ..." he trailed off. I watched him closely. His mouth actually moved, but nothing came out. In the end, he tapped my note right on the line that said, *Why would riding a dragon have been a problem?* and muttered, "I want to answer this for you, but I can't."

True. This was all crazy-weird, but he wasn't lying to me, and that was so very important to me after Nick.

Dai did a long, slow inhale, and then, as though he was trying to get words out before some part of his brain caught up with his mouth, he quickly said, "And Dola spies on me."

True. WTF?

"She does?" He nodded. "Why?"

His mouth opened, and nothing happened. His frustration was written all over not just his face but his shoulders and upper body. Tilly whined gently at him and put her paw over to his thigh. Then he reached for the pen I'd used, and next to the question, *What's your problem with Dola?* he scribbled, *at Da's request,* and then sighed with relief.

Also true.

Well, this was all very weird, but it was starting to look as though Dai wasn't the problem. Dai and I had the problem.

"It looks like this is really stressing you. I've seen enough to understand there's more to this than I was aware of. How about we relax and eat? Just one more question before we do?"

Dai looked tired but willing and gave me a small nod as he scratched under Tilly's ear, just where she liked it. "Do you know a way around whatever this block is?"

"Yes, that's why I asked you two to come and stay with me."

"OK, I can hold all my other questions until then."

Twenty minutes later, we were laughing, eating, and relaxing. I'd tried a little of everything; it was all delicious. And I'd watched in astonishment as enough food for five people disappeared into Dai's long, lean body. He'd been a long way past hungry, and he'd still fed Tilly first, huh.

He'd told me his delayed aging was simply a side effect of Mabon's blood. It worked the same way for both Rhiannon and him. She was much older than him, and yet this morning, I would have put her at about my own age or slightly younger. Apparently, Mabon's god powers had passed some odd quirks onto his kids, and they could appear to be almost whatever age they wanted. It was slightly more complicated, but that was the gist of it. Huh!

He'd said there were other important things he

wanted to tell me, but, and he stressed this so much, my right shoulder pinged with the honesty of his declaration: he simply could not do it in public.

My honey cake finally arrived, along with some ice cream, and Tilly was in heaven when Dai asked the waiter for a small bowl of ice cream for her.

"Can you read her mind or something?" I laughed at my fluff ball's excitement. She adored ice cream.

He looked shocked. "Of course, can't you?"

"What?"

"She said she was allowed ice cream. She told me, while you were in the bathroom, she was allowed spicy chicken. But I didn't believe her because even Dru can't tolerate that dish. But she was telling the truth, as you proved. So I trusted her about the ice cream. What's the problem? She's your soul dog. Surely you read her mind?"

I had no words and just gaped at him.

"Dru told me you'd started hearing him again last week. I thought … now your memories are back… well…"

My face must have told him I didn't.

He reached for my hand. "*Cariad*, I'm sorry. I'm flaming well doing what Da does and forgetting the brownies and the Smiths already, aren't I?"

I laughed and nodded helplessly. At least he got it.

"Well, your Book might help, or we could work on it while you're staying with me." He reached out to stroke Tilly, who'd finished her ice cream and settled back on my knee. "This little one is a strong sender. It shouldn't be hard."

"Oh, I understand her just fine. But I would never have said I can read her mind. I usually go with the type of whine she's making or the tone of her bark. I just didn't know there was more to it, at least outside of my imagination. I mean, come on, everyone who's ever been owned by a pet knows when they have their eye on something of yours they want."

We laughed, and it got easier.

Over our coffee, I'd agreed to reserve judgement until we had some privacy in his home, and he could bring me up to speed with everything that was happening to him. I'd also made it clear he'd better deliver on his promise to talk openly to me.

On the way back to the Gateway, we'd turned to lighter topics and spoken about what Dai actually did. He was responsible, among other things, for helping many of the Red Celt industries with their inter-realm and international trade. He felt he was good at it. He'd said Rhiannon did the "tech stuff" and he did the "people side."

He repeated how delighted he'd been when I'd

rescinded Gran's one-in, one-out rule. It had been an enormous stumbling block for them. He was over the moon at Fi's new appointment as Gateway Director for Trade, and he thought she'd need an assistant.

"She's very good at her job, but she already had such a full workload that trade and export deals got pushed to the end of the line. Fi working on trade full-time will be so helpful because she knows everyone, but your gran always said her other duties were far more important, the bondings and Recorder support duties." He quirked a grin at me.

"Well, I'm planning further reorganisation because Dola can do the admin and support stuff in about an hour a day." I caught a fleeting expression move across his face. I'd discuss this with Dola later and see if she could tell me more than Dai had been able to.

"Nik, I really would like to be able to contact you. I'm going to be up the bluddy mountain a lot until we get this sorted. Not pressuring you, but is there any way I can talk you into magicking my phone?" He offered me a piece of paper, obviously torn from an order pad at the restaurant.

I read it aloud, "Dafydd ap Modron offers this IOU to the Recorder's Office to be redeemed for one 'special service' at a time of your choosing." He'd signed and dated it, too.

I gave him a quizzical look.

"Well, you said you were only giving out the phones in return for special services for the Recorder's Office. But I need the phone now, and I'd do anything I could to help you, with or without a phone that works in return."

I considered it. When I'd told him that last week, the only phone I'd converted to the Rainbow Network was Finn's. But since then I'd added Mabon's, Aysha's and even Rollo's. It would be hypocritical not to include Dai's, wouldn't it? He was just as much a prince of his realm as Rollo and Finn were. But there was a problem.

"If you're feeling anti-Dola-ish, you may not want one of those phones because she runs the Rainbow Network they all work on. Which means she'd be able to track your phone, just like she can everyone else's. When I did it for Aysha, I explained it's like giving Dola access to your Find My and a bit more, the magic bit. Aysha didn't care because we've always shared that info with each other. But these phones are more than just something that can connect anywhere, and you need to be aware of that before you ask for it."

I offered him the paper back. "Consider all the implications. Dola and I have a meeting about ethics, privacy and related stuff with Finn on Wednesday. I'll take the opportunity to ask about you too. If you give me that back," I gestured at the slip from the waiter's pad, "I will do it for you. But don't say I didn't warn you afterwards."

He took it back and nodded at me. "OK, I'll speak to Da too."

Circling the back of my brain was the conversation I'd had with Dola yesterday about spying and privacy, and my Gift was tickling me about Dai's issue. He might be misjudging her. "You know, I think you might be blaming Dola for something your dad asked her to do a long time ago. I can speak to Dola, but you might want to address it with the source. Remind Mabon you've grown up and have a right to privacy. He isn't an unreasonable man."

He was deep in thought as we approached the Gateway. "Do you know where my Da is now?"

I sent Dola a quick text asking where Mabon was.

Dola: *He's at the quiz; do you need him? His phone is charged.*

The quiz? WTF? I held the phone out to Dai.

He scanned it and said, "I'm going to take your advice. And see if I can talk him out of winning the quiz again! The locals get pissed off with him." He bowed towards me, and, with a wicked gleam in his eye, he held out his arm. "May I walk you home? Your new hair suits you. With the robe on, it's quite an effect. It's fun, like a whole new you."

I wouldn't mind a whole new me once I'd worked out whether I could trust this man.

CHAPTER
FORTY-TWO

As we reached my kitchen door, Tilly started wagging her tail madly, and I heard voices inside. Oh hell no, I was entitled to peace and privacy. I thought I'd made that clear to Dola. But when I opened the door, it was only Fi, Corby and Finn chatting around my kitchen table.

Fi immediately stood up. "I'm sorry, we only intended to drop these off and go, but Dola said you would be back in a few minutes, and I wanted to thank you so much, and Corby needs…" She realised she was gabbling and paused for breath, thrusting a Tupperware box with a sturdy handle at me.

I had happy memories of the elder siblings of that box. "Are those what I think they are? Your mum's lemon curd cupcakes? And in a posh new cupcake carrier, I see. How incredibly kind of her."

Fi flushed prettily and looked pleased. "She said you'd mentioned them when she met you at the post office, and she wanted to thank you for being so understanding about me just jetting off to Las Vegas. And for helping me settle in this week, and my promotion and my pay rise and …" she trailed off again.

"She didn't need to do this, but I'm never going to dissuade your mum from sending me samples of her amazing baking. Please thank her for me." I opened the lid. The smell hit me, and I grabbed a cupcake and bit straight into the lemon curd centre. Heavens, they really were as good as I remembered. I let out a happy little moan of sugary, lemony heaven. Then I remembered my manners and offered the box around.

Fi said, "I wanted to thank you myself, Niki. I might have been a bit difficult on Monday. Everything was such a shock, all the changes, and nothing was how your gran said it would be." She laughed and shook her head. "But it's been awesome, the future feels so exciting." She slapped Finn's hand lightly as he reached for another cupcake. "Those are for Niki."

The astonishment on Finn's face was hilarious. Through my own laughter, I said, "Hey, you wanted people to stop treating you like Prince Finn. It looks like Fi's got it nailed."

Fi didn't even look abashed that she'd just slapped a Pictish prince and reminded him of his manners. She'd come a long way this week.

"But, seriously, Finn, there must be two dozen in here—you can have two more, OK?"

He grinned at me as I offered the box around once more and then snapped the lid on firmly.

Corby was silent. I checked on her with my Gift. She was bubbling with excitement but also very uncomfortable about something.

As I activated my Gift, I saw it again and more clearly. There was some kind of bond between her and Fi. It still looked strange to me. There was something supportive in it, but it was more than friendship. Was it just they had all been refugees, as Fi had said?

I wasn't sure what, if anything, I should do about it. It felt like a future-me problem. I'd keep an eye on it and find out more before I interfered in something I didn't understand. Gran hadn't solved the problem in twenty years, so if I took another few weeks or months to understand what was happening here, that would just be sensible, wouldn't it?

I didn't know Fi well enough to ask her personal questions this week, and I didn't yet understand who this Stuart Fi kept mentioning was. She really loved him. I'd felt that every time she mentioned his name.

Surely it would prevent whatever this might have been with Corby.

I gazed around for inspiration on how to even begin the conversation and noticed the enormous screen on the wall behind me. Just like the one in Finn's room I'd said would be perfect here. "Wow, Dola, you put the screen up while I was out—it looks awesome!"

Fi said, "Now I understand how you got an extra window put in so quickly. Isn't Dola amazing? I wonder why your gran didn't include her more?"

I'd wondered the same thing many times myself.

Corby finally spoke up quietly, "I need to thank you too, my lady. I really do."

I didn't think I'd done anything for Corby, but she offered me an insight. "Fi had a chat with Ross as we all left and warned him you really were serious about replacing him. We make terrific money from all the Gateway events, and with a Recorder who doesn't mind being in a few photos and makes the place look so fabulous, I think we could make a lot more over the next few years. Do you know he didn't even realise the Hobs were there! That frightened him. When he checked my photos, he asked who they were?"

I nodded. It made sense to me. Hadn't someone told me some people couldn't even see the Hobs? Yes, Ad'Rian had said it.

"He didn't see the power, either, Corby. Remember when you tried to show him the flowers on the anvil's throne, and he thought you meant the ones on the walls? It's possible the Hobs are partly made of magic." I glanced at Fi. "Rosemary might give us more info once she's settled into her new job. She's all about increasing understanding between the realms."

Corby's excitement was coming off her in waves now. "We went for a coffee, and he's offered me a full partnership in the business. He suggested it ages ago, but I couldn't pin him down. I'd be in charge of client management and the bridal side, and he could concentrate on the stuff he's passionate about. His landscapes sell well. He has infinite patience and will stand stock still in the rain for hours to get the right shot, and he truly does win some prestigious awards with them."

The new screen came to life with a photo of a spot I knew well. I walked Tilly down that lane regularly. It was only a field with view of the wind turbines in the background and some sheep in the foreground. But in this shot, the mist rolled in across the field in a sinister fashion. Half the field was sunlit, with the remnants of a fading rainbow on one side. The other half was draped in an increasingly dense mist as your eye travelled across the photo where gloomy clouds provided ominous shadows. It was evocative, clever and made me shiver. "Wow!"

Dola said, "He called this one *Janus: The Two Faces of the Scottish Lowlands*. It took the gold medal."

Corby nodded. "You are right, my lady, he's dreadful with people, zero social skills. But I love the human side of it. I'm so excited; I think I'll finally be able to buy my own house. I like it in my sister's garden cottage, but at forty-one, it's getting embarrassing."

Fi sighed and said, "Tell me about it." She gave Corby a happy smile. "But with our plans ... it will get better, won't it?"

Neither of these women owned their own homes? But houses were cheap up here. Then I considered the amount my gran had been paying Fi for so many years with minimal increases, and I understood. I'd had to almost double her salary for her new role to get it even close to an amount I wouldn't be embarrassed to pay anyone for a full-time job, especially someone who was so excellent. Since I'd found out about the small tax the Gateway trust took on the trade deals, I'd built in a bonus structure that should help Fi to be in charge of her own pay rises in the future.

I was delighted for Corby and myself. Not enduring Ross's glowers in the future would make for a much nicer atmosphere. Call me sceptical about

Ross's motives, but Corby was happy, and that was lovely to see. "You'll be brilliant at it, Corby. This deserves something celebratory. Have we got any champagne, Dola?"

She didn't answer, but a bottle and four glasses arrived on the table. Finn reached to open the bottle for us. His mother had done a wonderful job on his manners and his princely skills, but then he said, "Not for me, rather have a Coke. Excuse me everyone; got a date." At my raised eyebrow, he added, "With a group on a game server. See you."

Once the three of us had all raised our glasses and drunk to a successful week and a happy future, Corby said, "My lady, I was going to make an appointment to tell you something, but Fi said it would be better to tell you sooner if we got the opportunity?"

Now, in contrast to her prior excitement, she looked uncomfortable and felt unhappy. "Of course, Corby. What can I help with?"

"There's no way to say this gently, so," she breathed in audibly, and finished in a rush, "Ross was spying on the Gateway."

Weirdly, I wasn't surprised. He'd made my neck prickle and given me the creeps. I'd thought it was because he kept glaring at me, but this would explain it.

"He isn't anymore. Or at least he officially won't be once he's let his employer know."

The penny started to drop in my mind. It had a been a week of pennies dropping for me, sometimes too late, but I couldn't see how much harm Ross could have done. It's not as though he'd have any confidential information, would he?

"How much was Troels paying him, do you know?"

Corby gave me an astonished look. "You already knew?"

"Not exactly, no, but he gave me the twitches, and I knew he was hiding things from me. Someone tipped me off Troels had spies everywhere. And who else would need a spy?" Breanna had mentioned it last week, hadn't she? I'd been reminded of the information when I was digging about in Caitlin's head, trying to work out what her hidden box was all about.

And the only person other than me Ross had glared at was Troels' heir. He'd given Rollo some furiously angry looks, and he'd taken loads of photos of him and me, which had made no sense at the time.

> NIKI:
>
> Can you check the email queue to the Vikings and move anything from Ross out of it until you and i have discussed it?

DOLA:

> Already done. There were five. I'm looking for others now.

NIKI:

Wow! What a busy little spy.

"Can either of you guess why Troels would choose Ross? It's an odd choice. He's not a key person; what would he really know? Now, if he'd offered to bribe you, Fi, that would have made sense."

Fi gasped. What the hell had I said? I only meant Fi knew confidential stuff, and Ross didn't. Corby reached out to hold her hand, patting it comfortingly.

But Fi was composed and retrieved her hand, smiling at Corby. "He would know better than to ask me, Niki. I swore allegiance to the Gateway, not quite like your Knights do. They swear to protect the Recorder too, but it's similar. You'll need to ask the Book because Rosemary will have to do it, or the power may not allow her to enter the centre to work with us. I was your gran's first assistant, you know? Before I started, she did it all on her own. The Gateway wouldn't allow me into the centre to work until I'd given my oath. Your gran had to ask the Book to work it out. The oath is in there."

Huh. It was only luck then that my Knights had sworn their Knights' oaths, and Fi had already done so. It wouldn't have been nice for poor Rosemary, would it? "Every time I think I'm getting a handle on stuff, something else crops up. OK, I'll ask. Which reminds me, Fi, sorry for the personal question, but if I leave it any longer to ask, it will sound weird. Who *is* Stuart?"

Her face wreathed in sunny smiles, Fi rummaged in her handbag while saying, "He's my son. He's up at St. Andrews. Which is one reason why, even with my side business, I'm always skint. People think because university tuition is free in Scotland, sending your kid to Uni is easy, but paying for the course, which the government does, is only the tip of the iceberg. My parents help, and Stuart's a good lad; he has a part-time job."

I was pretty sure I'd kept my face straight. She'd had Stuart very young, and that was no crime, but when she handed her phone over to show me a photo of her and a smiling young man, I had to bite the inside of my cheek not to gasp. I pasted on a smile as I expanded the photo on her phone. "Oh, you two look so happy together. There's a mum's boasting photo if I ever I saw one."

Then I tuned her out while she chattered on about what a proud day it had been when the family had driven up to St. Andrews to see the lad receive some prize or other.

TIES THAT BOND IN GRETNA GREEN

Because Stuart could be a younger brother to Jamie or Rollo.

I caught Corby's eye. She seemed to know what I was thinking because she nodded almost imperceptibly. Well, Fi would tell me when she was ready, but she was going to need some extra support when my new Director of Trade became the ... I paused. I had no idea what the numbers were. Were the cases somewhere in the forties now? I texted Dola again.

NIKI:

How many cases against Troels for the arbitration now?

DOLA:

58

NIKI:

Shit!

When the Gateway's new Director of Trade filed the fifty-ninth case against the "Rightful King of the Vikings." Oh hell, poor woman, or girl as she must have been at the time. I cut off my angry thoughts before they could show on my face.

"Fi, have you checked the Recorder's arbitration queue yet?"

Dola interrupted immediately, "Niki, I notified Fi, that at your request, I have taken responsibility for those tasks now. She does not currently have access to it." Wow, did Dola already know then? How? We'd need to talk.

In as light a tone as I could manage, I said to Fi, "Oh cool, no worries then. I'll speak to Dola tomorrow about my query."

Corby was watching me closely. I had an intuition she was one of those people who missed nothing. It was perhaps why she was such an excellent photographer.

Between Gran's letter and the unusual bond I saw between these two, I wondered if, just as Ross had needed Corby's support to keep the Gateway contract, Fi might need her support and friendship to get through what would surely be the painful experience of filing a case against Troels? If she even wanted to do that? No wonder she'd gone pale when he tried to hurt Tilly today.

Should I try and help them get some clarity on the bond I could see, or should I back off? Had my gran given her any clues? Her comments in her last letter made it sound as though she'd tried, but Fi hadn't understood her.

Sometimes a random comment could help people towards the right path. Wasn't that all the Book ever did for me?

"Fi, you're aware Recorders are psychic, aren't you? It's part of the McKnight Gift?"

"Well, I thought so, but your gran said it didn't always work on people."

I couldn't imagine in a million years Gran would have said anything so monumentally dumb or blatantly untrue. How I could say this politely?

"Can you remember exactly what she said, please, because that doesn't sound quite right?" There, that was tactful, wasn't it?

Fi frowned and picked at her nails. Corby said, "I can. It was at end of the bondings last year. We were both there."

Fi nodded at her. "You tell her, Corby. It had been a long day; I probably missed something."

Corby focused her green eyes on me intently. "My lady Elsie said Ross had the only bond he needed with me, and he wouldn't, in this lifetime, look twice at Fi. She recommended Fi see what was in front of her, resolve her issues and find her best way forward to real happiness." She gave me an unhappy twitch of her lips. "Which … was a bit too tactful for Fi."

I loved Corby's Midlands' bluntness. It might make this easier. "And then I'm guessing Fi said, but Ross didn't have a bond with you? You were just colleagues?"

Fi's head twisted around to focus on me as though I was doing some kind of magic trick here, and Corby calmly nodded. "Your gran said not all bonds are about sex, and some people pour all their passion into other things than relationships. Then she said people were blind and stupid and couldn't see what was in front of their damn silly noses. And she wasn't wasting her Gift on it anymore."

Corby had an accurate auditory memory because my right shoulder pinged, and it sounded exactly like Gran, and it made sense of the nonsense she'd written in her letter to me.

I winked at Corby. "And Gran was absolutely right because Ross finally realised he can't run his business without you. And his art is where his passion is."

I took one of the Love's Young Dream cheesecakes out of the fridge in its bag and walked over to Fi. "Sorry Fi, but this week's changes aren't quite finished for you, yet. Take this. Pop round to Corby's house," I glanced at Corby, who was nodding furiously at me, her now-pale face making her green eyes look enormous, "and eat it with her. Will you do that for me, please? It's the last job of your first week."

Fi looked confused, but she got to her feet, nodding at me. I gave her the bag. "Those bags were a great idea, by the way. You've been awesome this week. Thank you for all your help and hard work. I'll see you at work on Wednesday."

I managed not to laugh out loud until they'd left.

"Dola, can I have a glass of wine please? I really think I've earned it this week." It arrived in my favourite engraved glass from Aysha, the one that said, *But your best friend will bring a bottle of wine, several shovels, and ask no questions.*

I didn't know what would happen when those two ate their cheesecake, but I was sure they both had a friend who'd bring their own shovel. Whether they had more than that remained to be seen.

CHAPTER 43
EPILOGUE

Monday, 15th February—My still-fabulous bedroom—Scary o'clock

On Monday morning, I woke with a dry mouth, covered in cold sweat and tangled in my bedding. I'd had a horrible dream where my gran stood in the centre of the Gateway wagging her finger at me in disapproval. Tilly was trapped outside the green doorway, barking like a mad thing because Gran wouldn't allow animals to enter. The Gateway itself felt sad, dark and creepy. There were no iron barriers. The anvil was back in its original position on Gran's old desk, and it looked dull, dusty and unloved again.

It all looked exactly as it had the very first time I'd entered the Gateway. Tomorrow it would be three weeks. What a crazy three weeks it had been! No wonder I was having bad dreams.

In my dream, I couldn't hear Gran over Tilly's barking, so I'd walked to the centre to find out what she was so mad about.

Whoa! Gran was cross. "Our Niki, didn't you read my letter? You can't keep doing this; you're risking yourself, lass. It's dangerous. You have to follow the rules. No animals or children in here. Stop changing things and making them all angry, or you'll come to a bad end just like Agnes did."

Them all? Them all who? Confusion washed over me in an unhappy wave.

The Book hadn't suggested I'd broken any "rules." It said the power liked children and animals. Did Gran just believe they were rules? Like the whole "don't breathe it in" muddled message fiasco which had nearly cost me my true bond with the power. But Gran was dead, so she had no say in it, did she? Who were the "they" she was so adamant I was making angry?

It made no sense, in the way dreams often don't.

But then out of the Indigo doorway walked a tiny woman, with a vivacious, expressive face currently showing annoyance. Her vibrant hair flowed behind her as her wild curls danced with the speed of her movement. Her hand was on the shoulder of an enormous cat. Was it a tiger or maybe just a lioness with particularly striking markings? I didn't know. But it walked in step by the woman's side.

I immediately thought of the Strength card in my tarot deck, but before I could take the thought any further, the woman began speaking with a gentle Scottish lilt. "Och, Elsie, dinna fash yerself, she's made a great start. Leave the lass alone. Ye have no room to talk, ye wee feartie coward. Ye didn't read a single one of the messages I left specially for ye, did ye? Not. A. Single. One."

Gran's face reddened. "Begone, Agnes. You're only a shade; begone from here now. I've told you many times I don't hold with you or your plans. Be off—"

Tilly's barking had woken me. Trying to juggle her imaginary barking in my dream, the real barking in my bedroom, and untangle my legs from the bedding took me a few seconds. A cup of coffee arrived on my bedside table, and Dola's voice said, "Niki, I have no idea what disturbed Tilly. All is quiet here and in the Gateway. You have the day off, remember?"

"I was having a horrid dream; I think Tilly was trying to wake me up." I reached for the large coffee mug then stroked my hand down Tilly's fluffy back, soothing her tight muscles. "Where would I be without you?" She snuggled into my lap and went back to sleep. On my coffee mug, I read, *What could be nicer than the first sip of Monday morning coffee …?*

I sipped and turned the mug around, looking for the punchline. Then I giggled as I saw … *When the Monday is a day off.*

What on earth had that dream been about? My subconscious must have been trying to make sense of something, but my conscious mind had no clues what it might be. I shook off the creepy feeling and sipped my coffee, trying to centre myself in my lovely cosy bedroom.

"Niki, I have the results of the poll we directed people to at the end of the livestream. We may want to include them in our ethics meeting on Wednesday with Finn. They are most interesting."

"Oh, why?"

"Calculating response rate is complicated. The calculation is dependent on the audience size, the number of initial respondents, and the total of those who fully complete the survey. Online research led me to expect, if we were fortunate, half the viewers of the livestream might begin the poll, and perhaps half of those who began it might complete it. That was not the case."

I was sad for her. She'd obviously put a lot of research and work into it, and I'd thought it was a good idea too. I tried encouragement. "Well, don't feel bad. I expect many of them aren't familiar with online polls."

"Our participation rate was ninety-four per cent."

"WHAT!?"

"Almost ninety-five, in fact. Over ninety per cent of those who began it fully completed our survey. The audience size was enormous. Almost anyone who could watch it, did. A bit like a royal wedding. Many people watched at least part of the livestream, and the numbers suggest almost all those people want their opinions to be heard."

"Well, congratulations. I'm astounded. Well done, you. Any surprises? You're really getting a handle on this stuff. It never would have even occurred to me to do a survey. I need to expand my thinking."

"There were many surprises. I will prepare a full report and send it to the iPads for Wednesday. I believe you already expanded your thinking when you offered me a job."

Huh, she might be right.

I was awake now and *still* trying to put my horrible dream behind me. I'd get up and make an early start on my day off. I wanted to ask the Book if there had been any messages left for my gran that she'd ignored, or if the dream was just the product of my imagination. My gran had been so angry; was I really doing things wrong? What had she said? I was breaking rules and making some unspecified "them" angry?

The image from my dream intruded into the mind I was trying to calm as I showered. The tiny woman with the enormous cat had been so vividly alive, she'd crackled with energy, and she'd come out of the Indigo doorway. It was just my subconscious fears of not being good enough playing weird tricks —wasn't it?

I wrapped a wonderfully thick, fluffy towel around me. "Dola, do we have any portraits of previous Recorders? I know you mentioned you stored some of their things sometimes when the role changed."

"Yes, Niki, did you want to see the one of your gran?"

"No, I wanted to know what Agnes looked like please." Finding out that the real Agnes looked nothing like the woman my imagination had probably conjured up might be the quickest way to put my mind to rest.

"Oh, that is easy." A locket floated in the air in front of me. As I reached for it, I gasped. The metal was exactly like my earrings. Rainbow metal. A tickling at the back of my memory made me head through to the bedroom and plop my butt onto the bed as my knees began to shake.

A flash from last week, I'd asked Mabon if he'd ever seen anything like my earrings before. He'd answered, "One of your foremothers had a locket of the same metal. After she ascended, it changed to look like that," and he'd pointed at my earrings. "Rainbow gold, she called it."

I remembered he'd smiled softly, but there had been sadness in his eyes. Then, he'd distracted us both, muttering about his cook and her threats of watery leek soup.

The heart-shaped locket had the remnants of a pattern on the front and back. They were hard to make out, but my questing fingertips thought the design on the front might have been a seven-pointed star when the metal was new. The points were still there but the middle section had been polished off over the years. The pattern on the back looked like it might have been a number at some point, but all that remained was a vague shape. It could have been a six, a nine or even an eight. Taking a deep soothing breath, I opened it.

On the left side was a tiny portrait, a hand-painted miniature of the same woman I'd just seen in my dream. She looked younger in the locket. In the Gateway, she'd appeared older. On the right side of the locket … was a miniature of Dai!

I reached into my bedside drawer for the reading glasses I no longer needed and used them as a magnifying glass on the tiny portraits. I peered at the miniature; it wasn't Dai. It was Mabon. But a Mabon with fewer scars on his face, a carefree expression and a look in his eyes I'd ever seen before.

Well, hell! Did this have anything to do with what Dai said he needed to tell me in private? It looked as though my trip to the Red Celt realm would be exciting.

Niki's adventures continue in Seeing Red in Gretna Green. You'll find more information in the following News section.

Thank you so much for picking up my book. I really hope you enjoyed the continuation of Niki's adventures.

There's more if you want it. Claim a **FREE bonus epilogue if you subscribe** to my newsletter. The epilogue includes Fi sharing her news about her past and confiding in Niki about what happened when she and Corby ate their cheesecake. There's more revelations about the Gateway spy.

Get your free bonus epilogue from linziday.com/newsletter

CHAPTER 44
NEWS

I know (sigh, truly so sorry), but book reviews on every book are **ridiculously important** to me as such a new author. **Please** do it for me? They don't have to be long. But even just a one-line review has such weight with the Amazon system and they make all the difference in the world to a brand-new author. Pretty. pretty please?

I'd love to stay in touch with you. I'm regularly on FaceBook (LinziDayAuthor), TikTok and Goodreads.

Review wherever you usually like to and if you even mention me on BookTok my gratitude will know no bounds. Feel free to tag me @LinziDay

Thank you so much for picking up my book. I really hope you enjoyed the continuation of Niki's adventures.

There's more if you want it. Claim a **FREE bonus epilogue if you subscribe** to my newsletter. The epilogue includes Fi sharing her news about her past and confiding in Niki about what happened when she and Corby ate their cheesecake. There's more revelations about the Gateway spy.

Get your free bonus epilogue from linziday.com/newsletter

Niki returns in books 4 and 5

The adventure continues—publication dates to be announced on my Facebook page.

You will also be able to see those dates when the Amazon Series page updates here.

I'm shooting for autumn for Red and winter for Yellow. Please note the 'shooting' though. New author remember :-)

But I'm writing as fast as I can!

Book 4 Seeing Red in Gretna Green (2023)

After receiving a warning from a Fae seer, Niki visits Prince Dai's mountain home in the Red Celts' realm for the St David's Day festival. It doesn't go well!

All our favourite characters gather for John Fergusson's sentencing hearing. Niki discovers there's more to the dragons than she realised and learns more about dragon politics than she ever wanted to know!

King Troels attacks the Gateway and there are unexpected discoveries about Prince Rollo when the power takes a liking to him.

Book 5 Code Yellow in Gretna Green (2024)

In Gateway terminology a Code Yellow is a missing person. King Troels is summoned to an arbitration but he doesn't arrive in the Gateway. Breanna's book club has its inaugural meeting. And any further information would include spoilers for book 4.